THE
SHADOW
OF ALBION

Carolus Rex: Book I

ANDRE NORTON

ROSEMARY EDGHILL

TOR°
fantasy

A TOM DOHERTY ASSOCIATES BOOK
NEW YORK

This is a work of fiction. All the characters and events portrayed in this book are either products of the author's imagination or are used fictitiously.

THE SHADOW OF ALBION: Carolus Rex: Book I

Edited by James Frenkel

A Tor Book
Published by Tom Doherty Associates, LLC
175 Fifth Avenue
New York, NY 10010

www.tor.com

Tor® is a registered trademark of Tom Doherty Associates, LLC.

ISBN: 0-812-54539-7
Library of Congress Catalog Card Number: 98-43790

First edition: April 1999
First mass market edition: February 2000

Printed in the United States of America

0 9 8 7 6 5 4 3 2 1

ACKNOWLEDGMENTS

I'd like to thank Sherwood Smith for help and quick answers to tough research questions involving the France of 1805; Andrew Sigel for settling thorny questions of proper address; the rest of the SFRT1 gang (of fond memory, alas) for the usual hijinks (hi, Esther! hi, Lois!); Jennara, for putting up with the usual fuss; Jane Emerson, for Lt. Stephen Price of the Royal Engineers; and (of course) The Lady herself, Andre Norton, for her endless patience and graciousness during the long, drawn-out, and sometimes downright baffling process of writing a collaboration. It's been a privilege to work with her and learn from her.

—Rosemary Edghill

Hence, horrible shadow!
Unreal mockery, hence!

—Macbeth

A Regency That Never Was

The "If Theory" of history is that oftentimes in world history distinct and radical changes rest upon a single event or person. From that particular point two worlds then come into existence, one in which the matter goes one way and one wherein it goes the other.

The point of divergence here is the affair of the Duke of Monmouth in the days of Charles II. The majority of the English people at that time were bitterly opposed to the return of a Catholic ruler. Unfortunately, Charles II had not been able to produce a living heir by his Portuguese wife, though he had a number of illegitimate children by various mistresses, upon whom he settled dukedoms and other major honors.

Charles's brother and heir presumptive, James, was a Catholic and was narrow-mindedly determined to return England to the Catholic fold. James was a severe, arrogant man, unlike Charles, who had all the Stuart charm in rare abundance.

There has always been a rumor that the Duke of Monmouth, the eldest known of Charles's by-blows, was actually legitimate—that Charles, while in exile, did marry Mistress Waters, the Duke's mother.

Monmouth had much of his father's charm and was strongly Protestant in his religious views. In the real world, following Charles's death Monmouth led an uprising against his uncle, King James II, failed, and was beheaded.

In this "If-World," Charles II, during his protracted dying, realizes that James's inheritance of the throne would mean trouble for all, and finally admits to a selected body of his strongest council that the rumor was true, that he had in fact made a marriage (there was no Royal Marriage Act in those days!) with Mistress Waters and thus the Duke of Monmouth was the legitimate heir of his body. Thus, upon Charles II's death, the Duke of Monmouth is crowned Charles III.

The new king has difficulties with a diehard group of strong Catholic lords, and with James, his uncle, who believes the throne of England should be his. This will have a bearing on the events of later years—even centuries—but immediate events are similar to those in the real world. The strongly Whig-Protestant English fight against France. The Duke of Marlborough comes to center stage as a military leader—he is also a bosom friend of the Duke of Clarence, the late king's illegitimate second son and Charles III's half-brother. (The Stuarts continue their merry custom of producing bastards and granting them titles so the highest grades of the English peerage are frequently expanded.)

After the reign of three more Stuart kings (Charles IV, James II, and Charles V) we reach the 1800s, and a world like—and unlike—our own. The English government is strongly Whig and the King depends on that party for backing. Without the weak and unpopular Hanovers on the throne, political relations with the American colonies have never degenerated into warfare; in 1805 America is simply the westernmost of England's possessions. Its citizens are English citizens with full representation in Parliament. It is governed (similarly to Ireland) by a Lord Protector; in 1805 the Lord Protector of America is Thomas Jefferson, the Earl of Monticello. Like Irish titles, American titles are considered "second-class" titles, but many of the nobility holds both English and American titles, and America is a popular destination for land-hungry younger sons. The ties between the mother country and her vast colony are becoming thinner with time, and political theorists predict that someday America will govern itself practically free of any strong supervision from the motherland.

One major divergence from history as we know it in this alternate 1805 is that the Louisiana Purchase does not take place, and the thirteen colonies' western expansion is halted in the vicinity of Kentucky (or, as it is known in this world, Transylvania).

The French Revolution of 1789—which occurs in both worlds—is a shock to both England and her New World colony. There were suggestions in our world at the time that England intervene, which she does not do in either world. In 1795 Napoleon Bonaparte begins his climb to power and France's ambitions become imperial. England goes to war once more. Though plagued by civil and religious unrest at home, it is Britain's funding that keeps the Triple Alliance—England, Prussia, and Russia—in the field against Napoleon. The simmering discontent at home might break out into full-fledged civil war, however, were England suddenly left without an heir.

Just as in the Real World, many European nations considered making a "separate peace" with Napoleon. A key player in this political arena is Denmark, which, as a member of the Baltic League, vacillates between neutrality and a pro-French position. A French-allied Denmark would cause Russia to withdraw from the Triple Alliance.

In the Real World, England sent fleets to Denmark in 1801 and 1806 to keep French sympathies at bay. In our world, the widowed King Henry IX of England hopes to accomplish the same thing by betrothing his only son, James Charles Henry David Robert Stuart, Prince of

Wales and Duke of Gloucester, to Princess Stephanie Julianna, granddaughter of the weak and vicious King Christian VII, whose eldest son, Prince Frederick, is currently his Regent. This marriage, to one of the few Protestant royal houses in Europe, will link Denmark firmly with the Allied cause.

And our story begins. . . .

—Andre Norton

1

A Lady Bought with Magic
(Wiltshire, April 1805)

❋ The house had always been called Mooncoign, though it had passed through several families before becoming King Charles III's gift to the first Marchioness of Roxbury over a century ago. The Roxburys had reigned at Mooncoign for longer than living memory ran, and to those within their domain, it seemed they always would.

Even in that bygone generation there had been no one left who could say how the house had come to be so named—or if there were, they deemed it wiser, in a climate of uncertain political and theological tolerance, to keep the knowledge to themselves. For while Charles II, that merry monarch, had often said that the witches of England should be left in peace, the temper of his son, the once-Earl of Monmouth, was a chancier—and far more Protestant—thing.

But the time of both merry father and ambitious son was long past now. It was early in April, on a morning of no particular note in the calendars of alchemists and philosophers: a day much like any other day on the Wiltshire downs for every inhabitant of the great house save one.

The room's furnishings were opulent and old; heavy walnut pieces that might have occupied this very chamber when Charles Stuart had used it to shelter from his Roundhead persecutors some one hundred fifty years before. The oak wainscoting glowed golden with long and loving application of beeswax and turpentine even in this pallid early spring sunlight, while higher upon those same walls fanciful plasterwork ornamentation spread its delicate lacelike tracery against the darker cream of the limewashed background. The room was oven hot, heated by the blazing fire of sea-coals upon the hearth and by the tall bronze braziers the doctor had prescribed.

Now that same physician regarded the luxurious scene with disapproval, although it was not the elegant Jacobean room itself which had earned his censure. He turned to the waiting servant and, reluctantly, said what he must say.

"You ought to have called me earlier. Her Ladyship's condition is very grave. In fact—" He hesitated, choosing how best to break the hateful news.

"Speak louder, Dr. Falconer; I cannot quite hear you." The mocking young voice was hoarse with coughing and breathless with its owner's affliction, but it still held arresting power.

Dr. Falconer straightened from his colloquy with Lady Roxbury's formidably-correct dresser and returned to the ornately-caparisoned bed of state. Pulling back the bedcurtains with one well-manicured hand, he gazed down at the bed's occupant. His patient stared back with brilliant unflinching eyes.

Sarah, Marchioness of Roxbury, had never been a

beauty—her eyes (quite her best feature) were grey, her hair was silk-straight rather than fashionably curled (and light brown rather than guinea-gold or raven-black or any of the other unlikely hues so beloved of the *romancers*), and she was tall and slender—but she had always carried herself with the arrogance and style of the Conynghams. Now, however, even the animal vitality that had lent her passable plainness an aura of glamour was gone: the Marchioness of Roxbury looked exactly like what she was. A plain woman, and a dying one.

"As bad as that, is it?" she whispered. "You had best tell me, you know; Knoyle is a treasure with hair, but she will only cry."

The Marchioness's mother, the second Marchioness of Roxbury and illegitimate daughter of James the Second, the present king's grandfather, had died in childbed along with the babe who would, had he lived, have been the two-year-old Sarah's younger brother and heir to the Marchionate. Now mother and son slept in the small family burial ground at Mooncoign, and from the moment of their deaths, Sarah Marie Eloise Aradia Dowsabelle Conyngham had become Lady Roxbury, Marchioness of Roxbury in her own right. And each year, since her presentation to the Polite World at the early age of sixteen, the young Marchioness of Roxbury had anticipated the Season with a houseparty at Mooncoign. The entertainment was lavish and theatrical, and in this year of Our Lord 1805, ten days since, during an enactment of the Battle of the Nile upon Mooncoign's ornamental water, her ladyship's craft had accidentally been sunk, even though it was meant to represent Admiral Nelson's flagship, the *Victory*.

She had been rescued by the Vicomte Saint-Lazarre

and, though her crew had deserted to the house to repair their soaked toilettes, Lady Roxbury had remained to fight the engagement to an English triumph. She had ignored a steadily-worsening cough to mastermind the entertainment of her guests all the following week; the cost of that mock sea-battle was something she had not counted until today.

Outside the windows, pale April daffodils pushed up through the rich loam of the downs. Dr. Falconer studied Lady Roxbury for some moments before he spoke. "It is a galloping consumption, Your Ladyship. You will not see out the month."

Lady Roxbury's mouth tightened and the teasing light vanished from her eyes. She had suspected as much; only a fool would not, once the blood began to appear on her lawn kerchiefs.

There was a strangled sob from Knoyle.

"Hush your howling," Lady Roxbury rasped hoarsely. "Anyone would think you were to be turned out without a character! It was only a chill," she said to Dr. Falconer, hating the note of pleading she heard in her voice.

"It has settled on the lungs." His voice was gentle, but her ladyship heard the death sentence in it. Dr. Falconer was no country horse-leech after all, but King Henry's own physician. His skill was preeminent; there were few he would have left Town for, but the Marchioness of Roxbury was one.

"I . . . see," she said. Each breath was a struggle. A greater struggle was to resist the feathery unsoundness in her throat and chest that brought the wracking spasms of bloody coughing. "Thank you for coming, Doctor," Lady Roxbury said. She held out one slender jeweled hand, and Dr. Falconer bent over it with courtly punctilio.

"Please consider yourself my guest for as long as you care to—and assure my other guests I will be joining them soon," she said.

Dr. Falconer hesitated a moment before replying. "Of course, Your Ladyship. I shall carry out your wishes to the letter." He hesitated over her hand a moment longer, as if there were something he would say, then turned and left.

Lady Roxbury turned to her abigail.

"Knoyle." The one word was all she could manage; the tainted brittleness in her chest was rising into her throat, choking her. She reached out blindly, grabbing the abigail's broad warm hand with chill fingers of surprising strength.

"No one! Tell—no one!" she gasped. Then the treacherous creature in her chest woke to willful life and spasm after spasm shook her slender body, until she lay weak and trembling beneath a coverlet starred with her life's blood.

It is not fair, she thought to herself some hours later. The pop and hiss of the burning coals and the measured ticking of the long-case clock in the dressing room were the loudest sounds in Lady Roxbury's world. She did not doubt that all was being done within Mooncoign's walls just as she would have it done, but she realized unwillingly that the time was coming when she would no longer be able to enforce her wishes—when, in fact, she would have no wishes at all.

And then Mooncoign and the Marchionate, which was entailed upon the heirs of her body, male or female, would revert to the Crown, and someone not of her blood would walk Mooncoign's galleries of age-mellowed stone.

It is not fair! Though the side-curtains of the bed were

closed, Lady Roxbury had ordered the curtains at the foot drawn back so that she could see the portrait over the fire. Within its frame of gilded plaster, the painted visage of Lady Roxbury's grandmother Panthea, the first Marchioness, gazed mischievously down at her descendent, magnificent in satin and lace. Panthea's bejeweled hands toyed with a key, a dagger, and a rose, in sly allusion to the Roxbury arms and their motto: "I open every door."

Oh, if there were only a door for this, away from the cruel weakness of her body and the knowledge of duties unfulfilled—!

"A visitor for you, my lady." Knoyle's voice trembled—as well it might, since she was acting against her mistress's express orders to admit no one.

Lady Roxbury struggled upright against her pillows, anger deepening the hectic color in her cheeks. "Who—" she began, before the inevitable spasm of coughing took her. As she clutched her handkerchief to her lips, she felt strong cool hands against her back, supporting her and pressing the worst of the pain away.

"Who dares?" she demanded at last, when the paroxysm passed.

"I dare," a voice said calmly. "As Your Ladyship knows, there is little I do not."

Lady Roxbury's eyes widened fractionally as she caught sight of her visitor for the first time.

Dame Alecto Kennet had been a great beauty in her day, and was still a woman of commanding and formidable presence. In her time she had been actress and confidential agent, mistress to two Kings, and more. In later life she had chosen obscurity as the companion of the Dowager Duchess of Wessex, herself a woman who shunned the limelight. Even so, only the veriest of greenheads would hold Dame Alecto at naught.

"I had thought you in Bath with Her Grace of Wessex,"

Lady Roxbury managed to say. She lay back against the mounded lace-trimmed pillows, trembling with the effort of showing an untroubled countenance to her visitor.

"And so I might yet be, did you not need me more," Dame Alecto replied. She unpinned her wide, plume-trimmed scarlet bonnet and set it upon the bench at the foot of the bed next to a slightly-battered hatbox done up in coarse string. Her hair, titian in her youth, had faded almost to pink with age, but was still elaborately dressed beneath its rich lace cap. She studied Lady Roxbury intently through eyes that Time had washed to silver as she unclasped her wool traveling cape and laid it beside the bonnet.

Lady Roxbury managed a bleak smile. "I shall soon need nothing at all," she said wryly, "or so my physicians tell me. I wonder who shall have Mooncoign when I am gone?"

"You would be better employed in wondering who will do that which you ought to have done, when you are not here to do it," Dame Alecto snapped. "Who will take your place, Lady Roxbury?"

Such plain speaking was not something her ladyship cared for at any time, and still less at a time like this. Ignoring the effort it cost her, she forced arch indifference into her voice as she replied.

"I dare say Wessex will find someone. But you have not come to tease me because my dying releases your mistress's grandson from his betrothal?"

It suddenly occurred to Lady Roxbury that, though Bath was a day's journey away, she had received her death-sentence from Dr. Falconer only hours before. Even if the doctor had talked, there was no way that the Dowager Duchess could have known of it and dispatched her henchwoman hither. Lady Roxbury struggled upright against her pillows, groping for the tasseled cord that would summon Knoyle to her.

"Your betrothal is a minor matter, beside the Great Work that you have left undone. Or do you forget who you truly hold these lands of, Lady Roxbury?" Dame Alecto's gaze was silver and ice; a formidable thing to face. But it was a formidable woman who faced it.

"I hold them of the King. I am Roxbury," the bed's occupant replied. But the bellpull slipped unrung from her pale jeweled fingers. Whatever was afoot, she would face it herself, and not spread gossip to the servants' hall.

"And have you sworn no other oath?" Dame Alecto demanded, still standing at the foot of the great bed as if she would summon Lady Roxbury from it.

It was on the tip of her ladyship's tongue to end this wearisome interview when sudden images rose up unbidden behind her eyes: Midsummer's Eve four years ago. She had been one-and-twenty, and Mooncoign's steward had summoned her from Town—had brought her, over her protests, to the Sarcen Stones that lay at the edge of her land, to show her to the Oldest People, and to take her promise that Roxbury and Mooncoign would always do what must be done for the People and the Land.

She came back to herself to meet Dame Alecto's gaze. There in the moonlight she had promised, but who would take care of her people and her land once she had gone? For the first time Lady Roxbury regretted her death as more than her own loss. It was a mystery no longer as to why Dame Alecto was here or how she had known to come. The Oldest People had avenues of information unknown to the human world—but even they could not change the appointed time of one's dying.

"If you can tell me how I may fulfill that oath, I shall be indebted to you," Lady Roxbury said dryly.

"You must summon another to take your place," Dame Alecto answered.

She moved from the foot of the bed to its side, to fling back the heavy velvet coverlet and draw Lady Roxbury from her deathbed. She tottered and would have fallen without Dame Alecto's strong support. The room spun and reeled about Mooncoign's mistress, and the young Marchioness trembled as if in the grip of an arctic chill. The edges of her vision darkened and curled like the edges of a painting thrown upon a fire to burn. She barely noticed as Dame Alecto half-led, half-carried her to a chair before the fire and seated her in it, wrapping her in her heavy winter chamber-robe, its silk velvet folds still smelling faintly of cedar and lavender from its months in the clothes press.

"Mooncoign is not in my gift," Lady Roxbury protested. Dame Alecto had poured out a cup of the cordial that Dr. Falconer had left her; now Lady Roxbury held it to her lips and breathed in the strong scents of brandy and laudanum. She sipped at it and felt the pain in her chest recede.

"Nevertheless, you may choose your successor—if you dare. Look into the fire," Dame Alecto commanded, "and tell me what you see."

Gypsy foolishness, Lady Roxbury thought scornfully, but spellbound by the force of the older woman's personality, made no overt demurral. She stared obediently into the pale translucent flames on the hearth. At last she was warm, no, more than warm, hot, burning, a creature of fire—

"Creature of fire, this charge I lay—" There were others in the room, standing about them in a circle, chanting, their voices blending into the thin music of the flames—

"Tell me what you see," Dame Alecto repeated.

The fire shimmered before Lady Roxbury's eyes, and

to her feverish mind the flames became a portal, a window, the curtains a stage upon which fire-phantoms capered—

The tumbrel lurched and swayed, moving slowly through the streets of Paris. All about the cart the mobile *surged, jeering and catcalling, come to see the Marquise de Rochberré brought low at last. Sarah gazed out at them icily, as if she wore silks and jewels instead of a filthy calico shift; as if her head were elegantly dressed with feathers and lace instead of shorn nakedly bare—*

"We can do nothing for her, whose pride was greater even than yours. Look again," Dame Alecto commanded.

White Bird Dancing, a warrior of the Cree, gazed down at the paleskin village from which her father had stolen her as a babe. Around her a dozen of her brother warriors lay concealed, awaiting the signal that would commence the raid—

"That one has the spirit that we need, but we cannot reach her—nor do I think she would help us if we could. Again."

The deck of a ship, the wooden railing salt-harsh and slick beneath her hands. She was Sarah Cunningham of Maryland, and in a few moments the ship that bore her would dock in Bristol Harbor. There was no one she could turn to, no one who could help her—

"That one," said Dame Alecto decisively, and the fire-pictures dissolved, leaving Lady Roxbury blinking dizzily, the jumbled memories of half-a-hundred Sarahs inhabiting all the worlds of What Might Be capering through her brain.

"What have you done to me?" she demanded at last. "You have *bewitched* me! Pictures in the fire—I do not have *time* for such shabby hoaxes!" That other Sarah's life lay like a shadow in her brain; the unimaginable childhood in an independent America that was not a Protectorate of the Crown; the self so like Sarah's own and the temperament so different.

"As much a hoax as the oath you swore among the

stones," Dame Alecto said imperturbably. "You must summon this other Sarah to you, Lady Roxbury. She rides not to fortune, but to Death, do we not interfere—and so we may take her without breaking the Great Law. You, child, will take her death, and she—"

"Will have my life? Her? That Puritan churchmouse?" Lady Roxbury demanded indignantly. She gasped for air, choking on the struggle and then surrendering to another spasm of coughing. It seemed to her that she could feel her life ebbing with every wracking spasm—and with her life, all the things that she might have done, ought to have done; the things that needed desperately to be done. . . .

"That *child?* She will never do what I might have done!" Lady Roxbury cried breathlessly.

"She will do all that you could have—and more. She will save England—if you have the courage to bring her to us," Dame Alecto said.

Lady Roxbury lay back against the ornate brocade of the chair. Behind her closed eyes the room seemed to spin; she could feel *Grandmere* Panthea's painted gaze upon her, and felt the weakness pulling her on a blood-dimmed tide toward an eternal starlit ocean. Eternal peace, eternal rest, but not yet, not yet . . .

She raised her head proudly.

"Say what you want of my life, madame, but never say I lacked courage!" It was madness to follow this madwoman, but fate had left her no choice. She was Roxbury; her death would leave no promises unkept.

Dame Alecto nodded approvingly. "You must go at once, and alone. Take your fastest chaise and drive like Jehu to that place where you swore your oath. You must reach it by sunset. Can you find it again?"

Lady Roxbury was a notable whipster, audacious to the point of suicide. Her cattle were prime blood-and-bone, the best to be had—by money or favor—in all of Europe.

Yet such a race with the sun as Dame Alecto proposed was a wager even she would have hesitated to accept. Miles of narrow country lanes separated her from the Sarcen Stones, and the day was far advanced.

"I could—did I have the strength to hold the ribbons." The admission of weakness was made with bitter reluctance. "If that is what you wish, madame, then you have come too late."

"Would you have listened had I come earlier?" Dame Alecto said.

Lady Roxbury did not answer, but she knew Dame Alecto's accusation was just; until Dr. Falconer's visit this morning she had still believed, deep in her heart, that some special providence would allow her to escape her death sentence. She watched as Dame Alecto turned away and undid the strings of the hatbox she had brought with her. From among its contents Dame Alecto selected a small silver flask. It glittered in the pale afternoon sunlight.

"This will give you your health again for sufficient time to do what must be done. There is a price, as for all such tampering; the drink will consume all the hours left to you and distill them into this brief span. When it is over, there will be nothing left. Do you understand?"

"Give it to me." Lady Roxbury's voice was steady as she held out her hand. She closed her fingers about the flask's fluted body, and seemed to feel the power of what it contained burning against her palm. She closed her eyes again, fighting the veils of darkness that danced across her sight.

"I will leave you now. And I trust Your Ladyship will pass a pleasant afternoon." Alecto Kennet's voice was neutral.

Lady Roxbury did not answer. From behind closed eyes she listened to the sounds of fabric upon fabric as Dame Alecto donned cloak and cape. After a moment Lady

Roxbury heard the door to her room open, then close, as the woman took her leave. Whatever came next, Dame Alecto had no part in it.

She does not care for me at all. The unexpected revelation gave Lady Roxbury momentary pause. The Marchioness of Roxbury was not one used to considering the feelings of others, and never had been in all the brief quarter-century of her life. But soon she would be Roxbury no longer, and the title would pass, not to her child, nor even to the Crown, but to a stranger snatched from Might-Have-Been—or so Dame Alecto said.

And I am fool enough to believe her.

To believe—or simply to snatch at anything that offered escape.

Lady Roxbury lifted the brandy decanter from the side table and splashed a half-inch of dark amber liquid into the glass in her hand. Before she could change her mind, she uncapped the flask and upended it, discharging its contents into her glass.

The fluid was dark and syrupy. It swirled slowly through the brandy, turning the liquor blood-red and faintly iridescent. With only a moment's hesitation, Lady Roxbury raised the glass and gulped its contents down.

It was as though she had drunk the flames of the hearth. A hot bright fire beat through her blood, driving out the heavy giddiness and fever-chill of her illness. She gasped at the strangeness of it, and then drew a deep breath for the first time in a fortnight. Her chest was clear. Her lungs were whole.

"The drink will consume all the hours left to you and distill them into this brief span. When it is over, there will be nothing left."

Lady Roxbury got to her feet, and the half-expected dizziness did not come. So this much, at least, of Dame Alecto's promise was true. She wondered if all the rest was. She glanced out the window and measured the progress of the sun.

If it is true, you will never know.

Lady Roxbury's lips curved in a reckless smile. To bring that other Sarah to Mooncoign, she must reach the Sarcen Stones by sunset. If this was her fate, so be it—and she wished Dame Alecto much joy of her successor.

"Knoyle!" she shouted, jerking vigorously at the bellpull.

In an instant the abigail appeared, fear and astonishment vying for pride of place upon her face.

"I wish to go out," the Marchioness of Roxbury said to her maid. "Lay out my driving dress—and tell Risolm to harness the match bays to my phaeton and bring it around. Well?" she added, as Knoyle stood there goggling.

The abigail dropped a stupefied curtsy and fled. Lady Roxbury shrugged off the now-too-warm chamber robe and let it fall to the floor in a puddle of fur and velvet. She turned back to the fire, and for a moment she seemed to see that other Sarah's face within the flames: plain and young, unadorned by paint and jewel. . . .

"Milk-toast-miss!" Lady Roxbury jeered, turning away.

2

Between the Salt Water and the Sea Sand
(The Frigate *Lady Bright*,
Bristol Channel, April 1805)

❄ Miss Sarah Cunningham, late of Baltimore, Maryland, in the United States of America, stood at the rail on the foredeck of the good ship *Lady Bright*, gazing miserably out to sea. The dawn wind coming over the ocean was a biting coldness on her face, its constant pressure threatening to unseat the demure dark grey bombazine narrow-poke bonnet whose strings were knotted firmly beneath her chin. Tomorrow or the next day, depending on the luck of wind and tide, the ship would arrive at Bristol Harbor.

Mrs. Kennet had told her that Bristol was a great city, second only to London; from there Sarah could surely find transport to the metropolis. What reception awaited her in London—even assuming she could manage to gain an interview with the Duke of Wessex—Sarah did not know. Why should such a grand man as he listen to an American interloper with the wildest of tales and the flimsiest of proof? If only Mrs. Kennet . . .

The tears dried on her cheeks as fast as they were shed, and her gloved hands worried a fine cambric handkerchief into a crumpled ball. She looked around blindly, hoping to distract herself from her bleak thoughts.

Behind and to her left lay the great green bulk of Ireland, and ahead, an indefinite blur in the early morning light, lay what Captain Challoner assured her was the Welsh headland: St. David's, and the *Lady Bright*'s first sight of home.

But if England was Captain Challoner's home, it was not Sarah Cunningham's. In the short space of six months her fortunes had tumbled end over end so many times that she had become quite philosophical about disaster, but this latest bereavement left Sarah even more forsaken than had the deaths of her parents only a few months before. Now Sarah Cunningham stood entirely alone in the uncaring world.

In a way, the shattering tragedy of her parents' deaths had been a dark blessing, as it left Sarah too numb to care about the blows that followed. The sale of the house and its furnishings had barely served to pay the bills left by nursing and burial, and shortly Sarah had found herself resident in the home of a distant cousin of her mother's, coming slowly to realize that she served there as the most menial of unpaid laborers. Not that any brighter prospect had presented itself—not to Alisdair Cunningham's daughter. . . .

Sarah Cunningham had been born twenty-five years before, almost simultaneously with the new Republic, to parents who'd had the best of all reasons to wish an end to kings and crowns in this new land. She had grown up between two worlds: bustling, forward-looking, Republican Baltimore, and the timeless woodland peace of the Maryland hills and forests, where Sarah had learned to hunt and fish, shoot and track, as well as any of her Indian playfellows. Even as a child she had always known that someday she would have to give up that Arcadian freedom, but as she grew older, Sarah saw what the eyes of childhood had not: that two wars had taken their toll on her father's health, so that she, not he, must work to keep their family fed.

And so, at a time when other girls dressed their hair high and lengthened their skirts, and cast their eyes upon the masculine companions of their childhood with a new interest, Sarah Cunningham wore beaded buckskin and carried not a delicate fan but her father's hunting rifle. The skins and meat she brought home bought other necessities, and if anyone knew that it was not Alasdair Cunningham, but his daughter, who provided the furs and skins her father brought for trade, they had kept that knowledge to themselves.

A husband for Sarah would have solved much, but such luck was hardly to be expected. Sarah, after all, was plain, and well she knew it. Though her eyes (quite her best feature) were speaking and grey, her mother's young students assured her the fashion was all for eyes of pansy-brown. Worse, her hair was straight rather than fashionably curled, and light brown rather than guinea-gold or raven-black or any of the other unlikely hues so beloved of the *romancers*. Dowry would have compensated for lack of beauty, but there was no dowry.

Even so, an outgoing charm of manner might have taken its place in this new young land—but Sarah was quiet and shy, and rather better acquainted with powder and shot and the best way of dressing a hare for the pot than with dancing-school graces. There was very little likelihood that the matrimonial offers Sarah Cunningham would receive were the sort that Alasdair Cunningham would allow her to accept.

And so the years passed. Sixteen became twenty-one, then twenty-five.

Then disaster. Cholera, and death. And, just when she thought her fortunes had changed, death again.

A change in the wind lashed her with chilly brine, and Sarah was jerked rudely back to reality. The pain of past and present tragedy blended into one miserable ache, and she scrubbed ruthlessly at her eyes with the mangled handkerchief.

"Miss Cunningham?" The voice at her elbow was low, in deference to her loss. "The Captain sends his respects, and says they are ready to read out the service now."

"The Lord have mercy on this His servant, Missus Alecto Kennet of London, who sleeps now in expectation of the Glorious Resurrection to come—" Captain Challoner's deep voice intoned the rote words of comfort and promise.

Sarah Cunningham stood in the forefront of the small company of mourners gathered around the slender, sailcloth-wrapped bundle awaiting its final disposition and tried not to feel terror at the thought of her future. At last the brief service was over and the chain-weighted bundle was tipped over the side, to vanish in the *Lady Bright*'s wake. Mrs. Kennet had been the agency by whose aid Sarah had come this far; to lose her to a sudden fatal fever only days before reaching her goal was a cruel blow. Now Sarah was alone once more, this time thousands of miles from the only home she had ever known.

"Miss Cunningham? Are you all right?" Once again Sarah was summoned back to the present, this time by Captain Challoner.

She smiled sadly, hoping her face showed the appropriate emotion for the occasion. Among the Cree, it was considered the height of rudeness to wear your feelings plainly upon your face, forcing everyone you passed to share them. Joy and sorrow alike were private things.

But the Cree and her freedom were both long-lost to her, and she must make the best of her fate.

"The loss of your companion grieves us all deeply," Captain Challoner told Sarah dutifully. "Mrs. Kennet was a gallant lady and her passing is a sad thing."

"You have been very kind, Captain Challoner," Sarah said, wondering where this conversation might be leading.

"I should not like to think you any more bereft than you must now be, and so I hope you will forgive my inquisitiveness, Miss Cunningham, if I ask you what provision has been made for you once we dock?"

"Provision?" Sarah echoed blankly, while a carefully tutored part of her reminded her that she sailed to England, the Old World, where even what circumspect mobility she had been permitted in the last few months of her residence in Baltimore was considered wanton freedom. In England no young lady of gentle breeding went anywhere alone; constantly accompanied by maid, chaperone, or family member, she was watched every moment until the time came to award her in marriage to some privileged scion of entitlement and perquisite, when matronhood would confer upon her very little more freedom than she had enjoyed as an unmarried girl.

"You were traveling with Mrs. Kennet, were you not? Who will accompany you now?" the Captain pursued, a note of worried concern in his voice.

"I shall—I am being met; pray excuse me," Sarah said quickly. Before Captain Challoner could stop her, she pulled her cloak tightly around her and fled to the solitude of her tiny cabin.

*   *   *

*Fool—lackwit—cloudhead—*Sarah berated herself in the strongest language she knew, standing trembling in the center of the tiny accommodation she had shared with her benefactress. Captain Challoner was honestly concerned for her welfare—there was no cause to flee him as if he were an entire English press-gang in himself!

Only his concern would mew her up with companions and chaperones, and in providing so much help he would certainly be entitled to the whole of her story—and Sarah, who now faced the sickening certainty that she had crossed the ocean with no more incentive than a bag of moonshine, could not bear the thought of making the Captain a present of her foolishness.

Calming herself by degrees, Sarah sat down on the hard narrow bunk and pulled her traveling-case to her. Lifting out the topmost tray, she withdrew the stiff packet of folded vellum sheets and opened them to read them again. As she did so, the faint sunny odor of orange blossom that still clung to the pages wafted up from them, and Sarah was borne back through the weeks to the first time she had smelled that particular fragrance.

The early-morning sun warmed Sarah's back through the thin calico muslin of her dress as she stepped carefully across the cobbled Baltimore street, avoiding the inevitable refuse. The large willow marketing-basket she carried was empty save for a lengthy list in Cousin Masham's spidery scrawl of items Sarah was to procure in the shops.

Tedious as the task was, Sarah welcomed it, as the alternative was more of the endless round of drudgery that had fallen to her lot since she had become—as she was frequently told—a pensioner upon her cousin Masham's charity. She had come to realize that the Mashams held their blood relationship at naught and looked upon her as just another servant—one whom, due to that same blood tie of kinship, they fortunately did not have to pay. Sarah was quite without talent for sewing or spinning, and thus her days were an endless round of kitchen and laundry. There was little prospect of anything better; the only possible alternative was to hire herself out as servant in truth. And marriage was even less of a possible escape than it had been eight years before, for now that her parents' estate had been settled Sarah's entire fortune consisted of a single small trunk of clothes and the few dollars she had been able to save from the sale of her father's property.

And the ring.

The ring had belonged to her father, but even when it had come to him it was not new. Stopping in the doorway of a not-yet-open shop, Sarah had pulled upon the blue ribbon that held the ring concealed safely beneath her bodice and inspected her dearest treasure.

It was of massy gold, set with a smooth rectangular black stone, but it was more as well. With practiced fingers, Sarah rotated the stone with the ball of her thumb. The black stone rose up and out on an armature that had seemed, moments before, to be the rim of the bezel, and, under Sarah's control, spun to reveal its obverse. In precise, exquisite enamelwork, an oak tree in summer foliage glowed against a silvery field. At the oak's foot a unicorn slept with head upon the ground, and in the tree's branches, a crown in glory burned. Boscobel—the King's Oak. Sarah did not know what this ring had meant to her father, only that it had been his greatest treasure, and so now it was hers.

The clatter of an arriving coach roused Sarah from her contemplation. Hastily dropping the jewel back into concealment beneath her bodice, she crossed the street to see who might be arriving.

She reached the post-house in time to see a woman dressed in the first stare of London elegance descend from the carriage. Though quite as old as Cousin Masham, there was an air of vitality about the newcomer—with her silvered once-red hair tucked demurely beneath both elegant traveling cap and a dashing bonnet of deep green lutestring trimmed with egret plumes—that marked her to be as different from Sarah's pallid cousin Masham as night from day.

The newcomer found her footing with the aid of an elegant ebony walking stick and gazed about herself, though if the stylish stranger held any opinion whatsoever on the street upon which she found herself, she presented only the blandest of countenances to the world. Behind her, the coachman scurried to unload her trunks, and the proprietor of the post-house, sensing custom, came out into the street to welcome this new guest.

"I am Madame Alecto Kennet of London," the woman announced, much as if this intelligence must have some meaning to the gathering watchers.

"Yes, Your Ladyship; we received your letter," the man said.

Sarah saw a faint shadow of distaste cross the woman's features, as if she disliked the form of address—which had, if anything, been too formal rather than too familiar. Sarah's eyes widened at the size and number of the trunks disgorged by the traveling carriage, but with all their variety they still seemed to lack a maid or personal servant to tend them.

"Then perhaps you would be so good as to oblige me with the information I requested of you, and provide me with the direction of Miss Charlotte Masham of this city. Of course, it is possible that she has married, and is no longer known by that name," Mrs. Kennet added with grudging reasonableness.

The innkeeper drew breath for a lengthy disquisition when Sarah, quite surprising even herself, stepped forward.

"I am afraid you have come too late if you wish to speak to my mother, ma'am, but I am Charlotte Masham's daughter. I am Sarah Cunningham."

Mrs. Kennet turned a brilliant silvery gaze upon her, and Sarah felt her own face go still and watchful. She met the inspection unflinchingly.

"You do have some look of the Mashams about you girl—and if you are indeed Charlotte Masham's daughter, then I have a letter for you."

Soon Sarah had been installed in the Bell and Candle's best—and only—coffee parlor, awaiting her hostess, who had retired to repair the ravages of travel. Sarah had no doubt that every word spoken on the curbstone before the post-house had already made its way to Cousin Masham's ears, nor that she herself would be called upon to render up a fuller accounting when she returned home.

Best to have something to account for, in that case. Sarah frowned faintly. She could not remember any English correspondents among her mother's infrequent letters, and Charlotte Masham was the third generation of her family to have been born in America, so it was hard to believe that any familial ties to the Old World remained. Sarah sipped at the boiling black coffee before her, and bit into one of the warm sugary doughnuts from the plate piled high at her elbow. The innkeeper had been extremely eager to please. Whoever Madame Alecto Kennet might be, she certainly had the knack of getting things done in her own way.

As if summoned by thought of her, Mrs. Kennet chose that moment to reappear.

Bonnet and cap had been exchanged for a finer cap of nearly transparent lace which neatly confined, while doing nothing to conceal, the cinnamon-sugar hair. Pearl-and-garnet earbobs dangled from the lady's ears, and a cameo brooch set with matching stones glowed upon a black velvet ribbon at her throat. The dull green traveling pelisse was gone, and in its place Mrs. Kennet wore a deep blue dress of twilled *gros de Naples* with long narrow sleeves trimmed and edged in blonde lace. The square neck of the dress was made up high and trimmed in blonde lace as well, and the long straight skirt was relieved by two courses of black velvet vandyking appliqued six inches above the hem. A cashmire shawl of deep jewel colors and fantastical design hung carelessly over one arm, and tiny fanciful slippers of blue-dyed Turkish leather, which would not have survived an hour's use on the cobbled streets outside, completed a costume of quite stupefying elegance.

Mrs. Kennet drew a quizzing-glass from her sleeve and regarded Sarah, and suddenly Sarah was bitterly aware of the picture she herself must present: the sturdy muslin cap concealing her light brown hair, the plain calico *fichu* pinned close at the throat of an unadorned blue woolen round gown that had already seen its best days. Her white cotton apron and plain red wool shawl only served to complete the picture of Colonial dowdiness, and Sarah tucked her feet behind the rungs of her chair, knowing that nothing would serve to conceal the sturdy, sensible, and unfashionable boots upon her feet.

But Mrs. Kennet apparently saw nothing to dislike in the picture before her. She seated herself carefully in the chair opposite Sarah, a momentary look of unease crossing her mobile patrician features, as if she suffered some inward pang.

"Is something wrong?" Sarah asked.

"A touch of indigestion, perhaps—I will not say that travel disagrees with me, but the victualing that one finds in one's travels certainly does. But you will wonder, and rightly so, what business an entire stranger may have with you," Mrs. Kennet said briskly.

Sarah had schooled her features to polite interest, and Mrs. Kennet smiled. "How rarely one finds such mannerliness in the young!" she commented. From her sleeve she withdrew a billet of ivory vellum sealed with a red blotch of wax, and extended it toward Sarah.

Sarah took it and gazed down at the picture in the wax: a crowned Salamander in flames, surrounded by a ribbon of Latin motto too blurred to make out.

"It is the seal of the Dukes of Wessex—a not inconsiderable power in England," her mentor commented.

"This cannot be for me," Sarah said in bewilderment.

"It is, if you are Cordelia Herriard's great-granddaughter. She married a Richard Masham, did she not?"

"Her son was my mother's grandfather, so I suppose I am. But—"

"Read your letter—and then, if you please, you may tell me what it contains, for that is one consideration Her Grace never rendered me."

Sarah broke the seal and scanned the pages of precise elegant script, her confusion deepening by the moment. The writer spoke of an ancient wrong done to the Herriards by her own family, of betrayal and unlawful attainder, and of a suit before the Chancery Court that had taken more than a century and the reigns of half-a-dozen kings to wend its way to completion.

"But this is foolishness!" Sarah burst out, passing the pages to her companion half-read. "What can any of this have to do with me?"

Mrs. Kennet glanced over the pages briefly before she replied.

"It is best you know from the first that my patron is the Dowager Duchess of Wessex, and I have some cause to know that noble family well, for mine has served theirs since before your unhappy ancestress was exiled to this bitter place. If the St. Iveses and the Dyers feel that some redress is owed you, then be sure they will find some way to pay their debt down to the last ha'penny."

"But what can they owe to me?" Sarah asked again.

Mrs. Kennet smiled. "Child, that matters not in the face of their determination that they *shall* pay. I see from this letter that the Dowager wishes you to come to England—is there any reason that you may not accompany me when I take ship next week?"

Sarah had hesitated only momentarily, the certain future here at home weighing very lightly against a future that held, at least, the allure of *difference*.

"There is no reason at all, Mrs. Kennet. I shall be delighted to accompany you," Sarah said firmly.

In her tiny cabin on the *Lady Bright*, Sarah refolded the Dowager Duchess of Wessex's letter once more. She had withdrawn her promise a thousand times in the week that had followed, for Cousin Masham was not shy in awarding the rough side of her tongue to both Sarah Cunningham and the "English adventuress" who had beguiled her, but Mrs. Kennet was one who delighted in pitched battle, as well as one who listened to one's first words and conveniently ignored the last. Sarah had said she would accompany her when the *Lady Bright* sailed from Baltimore to England, and nothing Sarah might say afterward would be allowed to alter that impulsive decision in the slightest. Borne upon the spring tide of Mrs. Kennet's formidable will, Sarah had never looked back; Cousin Masham was read such a jeremiad as must have caused her ears to ring for weeks afterward, and at the end of that confrontation Sarah and the single trunk containing all her worldly possessions reposed within Mrs. Kennet's well-sprung traveling coach and were wheeling smartly along the road to the harbor.

But what had begun as seeming indigestion had in the end been death for Sarah's fiery mentor only a few weeks later, and now Sarah was more alone than ever before. She was not so certain as she had been in Baltimore that the words written in the missive Mrs. Kennet had given her constituted a legitimate claim upon the Duke or Duchess of Wessex—and even less certain, now that Mrs. Kennet was gone, that the form of payment would be anything that plain Sarah Cunningham of Baltimore, Maryland, and the United States of America could like.

It is your own fault. You made this choice; you must make the best of it, Sarah told herself firmly, and began to determine, with utmost practicality, what she might best do in Bristol to engage transport to London so that she might do what Mrs. Kennet had so wished her to do.

3

Ten Leagues Beyond the Wide World's End
(April 1805)

❊ It was good to be out in the open again, even if her life could now be measured only in scant hours. The sharp April air cut at her lungs and the whipping wind brought roses not of fever, but of frost, to her cheeks, but Lady Roxbury did not care. Her sleek brown hair was covered by an ermine shako tied with wide grosgrain ribbons dyed to match the coquelicot velvet of her ermine-lined driving pelisse. Wrapped in the garment's elaborately frogged and gold-laced folds, Lady Roxbury did not feel the bite of the evening chill as the gentle Wiltshire countryside unreeled behind her.

The high-perch phaeton shivered and trembled beneath her as she urged the four match bays to speed and more speed, racing against the Sun itself. It slid inexorably westward as Lady Roxbury flicked her whipstring out over the ears of her leader, being rewarded with a marginal increase in speed. She must reach the Stones in time, or all this would be for naught.

In the distance, the broken outline of the Giant's Dance appeared on the horizon of the rolling Wiltshire downs. At the same moment, Lady Roxbury became aware of her own heartbeat as a thundering in her blood. Suddenly the westering sun flared dazzlingly bright, burning like the jewel in the skull of the salamander, creature of fire.

And then the world changed, and the sun that Lady Roxbury raced toward was rising, not setting. The air was chill and damp with morning and blue mist hung upon the ground. In the distance the Sarcen Stones were still veiled in night as the rising sun kindled an azure world into color.

And then the picture changed again, blue to fire-scarlet, as the sun hung spellbound above the evening horizon and all the world was gold. Gold—

Blue. And only Lady Roxbury's determination pressed her forward, as night flickered into day until the interlocking worlds danced in time with her heartbeat, fire to ice to fire. A heaviness, neither cold nor hot but slow as earth, was creeping through her limbs, stealing toward her heart. Mercilessly Lady Roxbury plied her whip now, cracking it over the heads of her team until their bay coats were dark with foam and they were running flat out. She had passed the kingstone of the Dance and barely noticed, so caught up was she in the desperate determination to reach her appointed place. The world was mist-grey and now, at last, Lady Roxbury heard what she ought to have heard earlier—the earthshaking rumble of an eight-horse coach on the road ahead.

And suddenly the coach was there, filling all the road, and she was desperately dragging back on the ribbons to save her team, but the reins slipped through her nerveless fingers and she felt the phaeton lurch wildly, uncontrolled, before she felt nothing at all.

* * *

Only a stubborn determination to have her own way, and the ability to pass unobserved that she had gained in the forests of her New World childhood enabled Sarah to reach her goal in safety.

The conversation of the other passengers, overheard as the *Lady Bright* sailed into Bristol harbor, informed her that a coach carrying mail and passengers left the port city each day at noon, reaching London the following morning. With that information to guide her, it was a simple matter for Sarah to pack an inconspicuous bandbox with the most necessary items for her journey, muffle herself to anonymity in a hooded grey cloak, and slip down the *Lady Bright*'s gangway in the bustle of departing passengers before Captain Challoner or any other well-meaning good Samaritan could stop her. Unfamiliar sounds and smells assailed her on every side, and at any moment Sarah expected to hear Captain Challoner's voice raised behind her. She hated to deceive him—even if only by misdirection—but Sarah was quite certain that if the *Lady Bright*'s captain had known of her plan to travel to London by the Mail he would not have allowed it.

Fortunately, through the late Mrs. Kennet's good offices Sarah was provided not only with a bank-draft which, Mrs. Kennet had assured her, any English bank would be pleased to honor, but with a small budget of English coin as well, which contained enough to pay the eleven-shilling coach fare with something left over.

As wary as any wild creature, Sarah walked onward, and soon found that she had left the Bristol docks behind for a world of imposing brick warehouses whose construction made even the vast Baltimore wharf from which Sarah had embarked scant weeks before seem small and shabby. Then the warehouses gave way to a street of buildings jammed cheek by jowl—a street filled with vehicles of every kind and people of every description. Sarah pressed her hands to her cheeks in utter confusion. Though Mrs. Kennet had spoken of Bristol as a great city, never in her wildest nightmare had Colonial-bred Sarah imagined that a city could be so large, so noisy, and so filthy. And London, so she understood, was even larger.

For a moment her resolve failed her, and Sarah wished nothing more than to flee back to the familiarity of the *Lady Bright* and let Captain Challoner determine her fate. But that stubborn streak of independence which, more than any other characteristic, had shaped Sarah Cunningham's life so far, forbade so craven an action. Only boldness would serve her purpose now, so bold she would be. Sarah took her courage firmly in hand and approached one of the street's inhabitants for directions.

"If you please, sir, which way is it to the Goat and Compasses?" she asked.

The man thus hailed possessed a certain air of respectability which, on closer examination, had a marked taint of illusion to it. He wore a suit of plain brown cloth elaborately faced with purple velvet, and his sleeves were trimmed with buttons that resembled nothing so much as a row of large brass sovereigns.

"Well, now, and what would a pretty country miss such as yourself be wanting with the Goat? I know a place quite near here that can answer all your wants, and a sweeter snuggery you'll not find, or my name isn't Reverend Richard Blaine!" The man smiled ingratiatingly and stepped forward to take Sarah's arm.

"And no more it is!" rumbled a deep voice from behind Sarah. She spun about to confront the most enormous coal-black man she had ever seen.

He was at least a handspan over six feet tall, and nearly as wide. He wore no coat, and his workshirt bulged over a massive barrel chest. On one shoulder he carried an iron-bound wooden keg of the sort that usually contained spirits.

"You're no more a Reverend than I am, Dickie Blaine, and your kind isn't wanted here," the newcomer said meaningfully.

If Sarah had possessed any doubts about the "Reverend's" bona fides, they were substantiated by the speed with which the man took to his heels.

"I suppose I must thank you, sir," she said to her rescuer.

He shifted the keg upon one work-shirted shoulder and grinned down at her from his formidable height, a brilliant white smile upon his smooth ebony face.

"The docks is no place for a mite of a girl like you. Run along back to your nurse before worse happens to you, little miss," he said, not unkindly.

"But I must reach the Goat and Compasses! They said on the—I have heard that the London Mail leaves from there, but I don't know where it is," Sarah finished in a rush.

"The Mail, eh? Skipping out on your articles to become an Abbess, eh?" The man's easy smile was gone, and he regarded her critically.

Sarah gathered her dignity as best she could, though she had understood not one word of what seemed to be a condemnation of her plan.

"I do not perfectly collect your meaning, sir. I am from Baltimore—and I have an appointment in London."

He inspected her for one more critical moment, and then the easy smile returned. "American, eh? Well, then, best you come along of me. I knows the Goat. Just you come along of old Cerberus, Missus, and he'll have you there quick as cat can lick her ear—aye, and safe aboard the Mail as well."

With the aid of her Brobdingnagian companion, Sarah reached the Goat and Compasses without further incident. There Cerberus delivered his keg and Sarah purchased her ticket. At his advice, she purchased a dish of coffee as well, which allowed her the use of the common parlor in which to await the coach's arrival. The last she saw of her savior was his head and massive shoulders towering over the press of humanity in the street as he strode in the direction of the docks once more.

Several hours later, Sarah looked back upon that moment as the last one in which she had enjoyed any degree of physical comfort whatever. Upon the coach's summons, she had left the coffee room of the Goat and Compasses to be packed, with ten other fortunate passengers who had paid the extra shilling to ride "inside," into the Mail's cramped, stuffy, ill-sprung, unpadded interior.

Over the thunder of the horses' hooves, Sarah could hear the crack of the whip and the hoarse cries of the driver. Though the horses would receive frequent changes, the driver would not, and Sarah wondered with some small part of her mind how he would endeavor to maintain such a performance until they reached London with tomorrow's noon.

The vehicle had rattled quite fearfully at first—its entire exterior was covered with bags and bundles, the possessions of the passengers, and those persons who had chosen for reasons of economy to ride on the roof—but now everything capable of making noise had either fallen off or been jammed immobile into some corner of the coach. Everything, Sarah reflected unhappily, except the passengers, who continued to be flung back and forth at the whim of rut and road.

The pauses the coach made to take up mail and discharge passengers were the only respite from the eternal battering of the journey, and none of them, even those including a change of team, lasted more than a few minutes. Day fell into night and Sarah dozed fitfully, body numbed at last by the relentless jarring of the coach's headlong progress.

She roused to see the faint light of dawn leaking in through the coach's leather curtains, and pushed one aside to see where they were.

Beyond the coach window lay a landscape unlike any she had ever known: treeless and flat, strangely colorless in the grey morning light. To her left she could see what she thought at first were the stumps of mighty trees, but as the coach passed closer she saw that the figures were not trees, but vast, rough-hewn pillars of stone, placed in the middle of this plain by some unknown people for some unfathomable purpose.

The sudden awareness of danger was a cold thrill along her limbs, and at the very moment Sarah recognized it and searched for its source, the music of the mail coach's thundering progress changed. She heard the driver cry out, the crack of his whip, the faltering of the horses' headlong pace. The other passengers began to rouse, and then the coach slewed violently.

Sarah was half flung through the window with the jolt, and in the split-instant before disaster she saw the cause—a woman, standing upon the high perch of some strange spidery chariot, her arm flung back to wield the whip upon her wildly plunging four-horse team. The woman's face was pale, intent—

—and suddenly Sarah realized she was staring at her own face, as if she gazed into an eerie mirror. In the next moment, the coach was struck by some heavy unseen hand, and Sarah felt herself falling, the image of her own face seen from without frozen in memory.

*   *   *

She opened her eyes in a room she had never seen before. Through long windows to her right, sunlight shone at the slanting angle of late afternoon, and when she turned toward that light Sarah could see pale blue sky and a line of trees. The movement of her head was rewarded with the commencement of a dull throbbing ache in every limb. Now she remembered: there had been a coaching accident—a hideous crash. She had been there. And now she was here.

Sarah opened her mouth to summon help, and a wave of giddiness threatened to whirl her back into unconsciousness. She bit her lip, willing the darkness to recede, and concentrated on her surroundings to distract herself from swooning.

The bed upon which she lay was very fine, with elaborate carven posts and fringed canopy. Blue velvet curtains, lined in white silk and embroidered in silver, were drawn back from the sides and looped to each bedpost with a tasseled bullion cord. A merry fire crackled in the carved stone fireplace at the foot of the room, and such of the furnishings as Sarah could see from her supine position rivaled for elegance any of the engravings in Cousin Masham's pattern books. Some private house in the neighborhood of the accident, no doubt—but why was she here?

Sarah clutched at a strap dangling near the head of the bed, and by its aid managed to pull herself upright, realizing only then that her traveling clothes had been removed and a nightdress substituted. In a sudden pang of fear Sarah clutched for her father's ring, and relaxed as she felt the hard shape of it, still laced on its ribbon beneath the bosom of the nightdress. She leaned back against the carved maple headboard, weak with the effort of moving.

"Oh—!" A gasp of dismay made Sarah turn her head. A maid stood in the doorway to the right of the bed, regarding Sarah woefully.

"I'd only stepped out for a moment when I heard you ring—Mistress did not think you'd wake before sundown, my lady."

Sarah smiled reassuringly, though the effort made her entire face hurt. "There is no harm done. But tell me— where am I?"

The maid bobbed a nervous curtsy. "Bulford Hall, my lady. Mistress Bulford said I was to sit with you until you woke. Shall I—"

"Please help me up," Sarah said, not meaning to interrupt, but unable to bear lying helpless a moment longer. The maid came to the side of the bed and helped to turn back the heavy brocaded coverlet. "What is your name?" Sarah asked kindly, hoping to dispel some of the girl's nervousness.

"Rose, my lady."

It was the third time since her awakening in this strange place that Sarah had been addressed by a title that was not hers. Before she could correct Rose, the girl had turned away, collecting a voluminous woolen shawl from a nearby table and returning to wrap it about Sarah's shoulders.

"Mistress says—or she would say if she was here, my lady, how very sorry she is that you hasn't your own things to hand, but never you fret, 'coz Jem has ridden for Mooncoign and t'will not take him long at all, with the Squire putting him up on the fastest in all the stables—"

Sarah leaned upon Rose's arm and stood shakily upon limbs that quivered with more than the aftermath of the accident. The girl chattered on nervously, to Sarah's growing unease. The nightdress that had replaced her plain traveling costume was of fine Indian lawn, lavished with ribbons and lace and far too fine for the succor of some nameless accident victim. And surely all the coach's injured passengers could not be lodged in this splendor?

Rose settled Sarah in a chair before the fire before running to the clothespress to return with another shawl to wrap Sarah's legs. "Is there aught else I can fetch you, my lady?"

"I'm afraid there must be some mistake," Sarah began weakly, wondering how best to explain that she was not whatever highborn lady Rose mistook her for.

"*There* you are, Rose. I must say—" What the speaker must say would remain forever a mystery. Catching sight of Sarah, she swept a deep curtsy.

"Your Ladyship! How sad that this dreadful accident should be the cause of your visit to my humble establishment—which is, nevertheless, honored by your presence," Mistress Bulford amended firmly.

"Where are the coach and the other passengers?" Sarah asked, but apparently her hostess misunderstood, for she replied:

"Jem has just ridden back from Mooncoign, my lady. Dr. Falconer is coming, with your coach to bear you safe away as soon as you are well enough to travel."

"What is—where is Mooncoign? I am Sarah Cunningham. I am afraid there has been some sort of mistake."

To Sarah's utter bewilderment, mistress and maid exchanged wide-eyed fearful glances. Mistress Bulford moistened dry lips before responding.

"You must still be sadly shaken by your ordeal. Perhaps you would like some tea, Your Ladyship?"

At her mistress's gesture, Rose dipped another hasty curtsy and fled. With Rose's departure, Mistress Bulford seemed to lose all sense of what to do. She seated herself upon a low stool at Sarah's side and gazed up at her imploringly—almost as if Sarah were some sort of public performance, Sarah thought uncharitably. Her head pounded abominably, and every bruise she had collected on the so-rudely-interrupted coach ride burned and throbbed.

But even so, the sense that had warned her of danger in the forests of the New World warned of danger here. This was more than a simple case of mistaken identity, and—alone and friendless in an alien land—Sarah must walk as softly as ever she had in the wilderness.

"Tea will be delightful," Sarah said cautiously, and was rewarded by a faint lessening of the inexplicable tension which gripped her hostess.

"So this is Bulford Hall," Sarah hazarded next, gripped by a strong sense of the absurd unreality of her situation. She, who had always been tongue-tied even in the presence of those she knew, was now compelled to make small-talk with this strange Englishwoman who stared at her as if she were mad.

"Yes, Your Ladyship."

"And you, I collect, must be Mistress Bulford?" Sarah pursued doggedly. She smiled, to turn the remark into a jest in the all-too-likely possibility that the woman was someone else entirely.

"That's right, Your Ladyship," the woman said in tones of relief. "Don't you remember? When Bulford and I came to wed it was you as sent as handsome a pair of silver tankards as ever anyone did see, and said as how the Bulfords might always look to Roxbury."

Roxbury. Worse and worse. For a moment Sarah entertained the distempered freak that she might in fact be whoever Mistress Bulford thought she was—and had simply run mad—but the vision of that other Sarah, glimpsed in an instant before the crash, robbed the notion of much of its humor. Sarah's heart beat faster as she phrased her next question.

"And so of course you know who I am?"

Innocuously as the question had been put, it had still been the wrong thing to say. Renewed fear showed in Mistress Bulford's eyes as she replied, "Why, you are Lady Roxbury—the Marchioness of Roxbury—Your Ladyship."

4

A Knight of Ghosts and Shadows (Paris, Germinal, 1805)

The tall man with the dangerous eyes knew that someone was going to die tonight.

Rupert St. Ives Dyer, Captain His Grace the Duke of Wessex, coolly surveyed the salon from the privileged vantage-coign of the entry-hall. When he had arranged with the Underground three days ago to meet Avery deMorrissey somewhere here among these privileged New Men and successful turncoats of the *Ancien Regime*, Wessex had been reasonably certain of retaining both his liberty, and his life.

Now he was less so.

A note smuggled up the backstairs of the Hotel des Spheres, Wessex's residence on this trip to the City of Light, had tipped him that the Jacquerie—the Red Jacks—Talleyrand's secret police—wished very much to have speech of the Chevalier de Reynard, which *nom de guerre* was Wessex's own for the moment. He did not know if it was the foolish loyalist Reynard, or Rupert, Duke of

Wessex, King Henry's political agent, who had earned M. Talleyrand's enmity, and at this moment it did not matter: the Jacks were only a few minutes behind him.

Wessex had left the Chevalier's lodgings in the Hotel des Spheres by way of the roof, but it was only a matter of time before the Jacks took his scent and ran him to ground. The *carte de invitation* for this evening's party had still been on his dressing-table, after all.

It was foolish to have come—but without him de-Morrissey had no chance of reaching England. De-Morrissey was English, a naval officer who had been interned at Verdun where he had learned something of interest. Holding this information to be of more importance than his life, deMorrissey had managed to escape the walled city and blunder into some members of the Royalist Underground who'd covered his tracks, at least as far as Paris. But the man hadn't a word of French, and if the Royalist Underground had not managed to put him in touch with "Reynard," deMorrissey would have been dead long since. And if the Red Jacks had anything to say about it, he might yet be.

Reynard/Wessex lifted his quizzing-glass and surveyed the room with maddeningly languid affectation. *La Belle Paris* was not what she had been in the days of Wessex's boyhood, but to the casual observer she had made a phoenix-like recovery from the bloody events of the "glorious" '93—at least assuming one had no memory of her original splendor. In this modern incarnation the appointments were a little too opulent, the talk a little too loud, and dress and manners veered self-consciously between Republican and Imperial.

Wessex allowed his quizzing-glass to drop and flicked imaginary grains of snuff from the lapel of his wasp-waisted celadon silk evening coat as he shook out his ruffles. He was dressed slightly beyond the cutting edge of fashion, and on a lesser man the mode might have appeared ridiculous, but not upon my lord Wessex. He had the height, the carriage, the killdevil black eyes to support any freak of fashion, and enough cold swords-edge charm to beguile any lady save *Madame la Guillotine* herself.

Wessex descended the three shallow steps to the black-and-white tiled floor of *Princesse* Eugenie's drawing room. The Red Jacks were only moments behind him—and deMorrissey was in the miniature summer house in the *Princesse* Eugenie's garden. Wessex might, just, have enough of a lead to winkle deMorrissey out of the garden and along the route prepared for him. Just.

A hand fell heavily upon the immaculate brocade of Wessex's coat. "My dear Chevalier, how fortunate indeed that I should find you here."

Wessex turned, and raised his glass to regard the smaller man. *So now I know who it was that gave Talleyrand my scent.*

M. Grillot was round, red-faced, and ambitious. He was a frequent visitor to the shadowy half-world in which Wessex lived his real life, and this time had managed, it seemed, to lay his gaff upon quarry of note.

"Fortunate, my dear Grillot? Fortune favors the brave, it is said," Wessex answered idly, in the person of the Chevalier de Reynard.

"And my very dear Chevalier—it was brave of you indeed to venture among us!" Grillot could not quite repress a smirk at the cleverness of his own double meaning.

Wessex-as-Reynard made an elegant leg, slowly. Almost he reached for his quizzing-glass again, but not quite.

"No, Monsieur Grillot," he said cordially to his betrayer, "it was you who were the brave, to venture to attend a party with such a potential for dullness. And your bravery is my good fortune—do let us celebrate it in a glass of wine."

Wessex's French was flawless, but then, French had been one of the civilized accomplishments only a generation ago . . . in the world that had preceded the Revolution, before the self-anointed Emperor of France's bloody conquest of half the world.

"But of course, my dear Chevalier." Grillot was minded to relish his triumph. "The *Princesse* keeps an excellent cellar and a dull guest-list, eh?" He linked arms with Wessex and the two men strolled away. No one would expect "Reynard" to make the bow to his hostess. The license of Eugenie's gatherings was nearly as proverbial as their dullness.

Wessex smiled. Certainly *Madame la Princesse* should thank him—after tonight no one would ever again call one of her soirees dull.

Grillot and Wessex passed a number of small knots of conversants debating everything under the sun in fervent obsessed voices. Only a few of them glanced up from their talk to mark "Reynard" and Grillot's passing. The attraction of Eugenie's salons—aside from the excellent table she kept—was that one might meet anyone and talk of anything here. From crop-headed *Incroyables* and their slovenly damsels to the properly corseted and bewigged *haute bourgeoisie*, eyes and tongues burned with the light of the Idea—the Idea that France had the moral obligation to enslave half the world.

The two men reached the buffet. Wessex shook back his lace and poured wine for them both. Grillot gazed with affected distaste at "Reynard's" fantastical mode of dress.

"But my dear sir, what would you have me do?" Wessex protested blandly, catching the direction of Grillot's glance. "All the world knows that Man's natural state is to be at war, and yet some of us are not meant for rude martial exercise. We must each choose our battlefield where we may."

Grillot snorted and tossed off his wine. Wessex poured him another glass. Above the buffet the wax candles in their gilded wooden garlands burned with a steady white light multiplied in the mirrors that hung upon the walls.

"Ah, the battlefield. . . ." For some reason, Wessex's choice of words was a source of particular amusement to M. Grillot. "But there are battlefields and battlefields, are there not, my dear Chevalier?"

Grillot was not a subtle man. Any person not already awake to his treachery would surely be alerted by the gloating in his voice now.

"It is entirely as you say." Wessex obstinately continued to act the part of the foolish and oblivious Reynard.

"But you doubt me, my dear Reynard." Grillot's smile grew more feral as he spoke. "Perhaps you will find a walk in the garden a spur to the intellect?"

If Grillot had expected Wessex to deviate from Reynard's persona by one iota, he was to be sadly disappointed.

"Certainly my good Grillot, if such is your desire," Wessex said urbanely. But in his pocket, where no one could see, his fingers tightened upon the butt of a very small pistol.

The *Princesse* Eugenie's little garden was meant to be seen at night. Narrow paths surfaced in white stone and crushed seashell curved around ornamental plantings designed to encourage assignations. A high wall concealed the garden from the street and from the prying eyes of neighboring houses. Grillot stopped just short of the tiny ornamental gazebo.

"But you will wonder, my dear Chevalier, that *Madame la Princesse*'s garden is so quiet?"

"Will I?" asked Wessex politely. He glanced behind him. They were out of sight of the house. Good.

"The English boy who was here now awaits the Jacquerie in the kitchen—but he will not be lonely long. *Madame la Guillotine*'s kiss is one that he will remember for eternity—thus perish *all* such enemies of France!"

There was a sudden shout from the house. Grillot fumbled a bulky and obvious pistol from his pocket, undoubtedly already primed and loaded and carried on the cock for just this moment. Wessex waited patiently while he did so. The Duke had no intention of grappling with him for the firearm—not while he was trying to avoid the attention that pistol-fire would surely draw.

"My dear Grillot, now that you have discovered all, there is one question I should like to have answered," Wessex said—in English and a voice quite unlike "Citoyen Reynard's."

He spoke to cover the soft clicking sound as he pressed down on a hidden button on the shaft of the quizzing-glass held between his fingers. A snap of the wrist, and the lens hung free, connected to the ornate golden handle only by a thin cord of braided silk. It was not meant for the work he was about to put it to, but it would have to serve.

"Soon you will answer questions, English *cochon*—not ask them," Grillot snarled theatrically.

There was a crash from the house and the man turned toward it, forgetting, in that fatal moment, to beware of his companion. As Grillot turned, Wessex flung the invisible coil of silk about his neck and jerked it tight, pulling the smaller man back against him and muffling Grillot's death-struggles with his own long limbs.

"Nevertheless, I shall ask," he breathed softly in Grillot's ear as the Frenchman died. "Did you actually believe that you might sentence an Englishman to death with impunity? It is not done, my dear Grillot; you must hold me your preceptor in this."

Wessex spoke to cover the bitterness in his own soul—clean death on deck or battlefield might be any man's fate, but this sneaking soft-handed game of shadows, fought with weapons that were not even honest steel—!

Grillot went limp, and Wessex lowered Grillot's dead body to the ground. He drew the silk cord back into the shaft of his quizzing-glass once more, then dragged the body into the cover of some of the *Princesse*'s ornamental shrubbery, stripping off the gaudy coat and waistcoat of the Chevalier de Reynard once he'd done so. With a few deft motions he turned the waistcoat inside out, concealing the lurid vermilion of the embroidered Chinese silk behind a veil of dully respectable ecru satin.

The outcry from the house was louder now. There was a sound of breaking glass and a woman's squeal. The Jacks were quite as crude in their methods as their predecessors at the height of the Terror had been; their motto one that all the world knew: *Extremism in the defense of Liberty is no vice.* Wessex wished their countrymen much joy of them.

As he listened, Wessex pulled out the whalebone stays that had given his coat its fantastic shape, tossed them into the bushes, and shrugged himself back into a coat of dull brown velvet that had only a faint acquaintance with fashion. The five gold *napoleons* that were concealed in the heel of each slipper should be enough to see him through to the inn on the Calais road where new clothes, identification papers, and a fast horse awaited him—if the Jacks had not discovered the hideout already. But deMorrissey—if the late M. Grillot could be believed—lay a prisoner in the house beyond. It might be possible—just—to go in and extract him while the Red Jacks were smashing the teacups in the parlor.

Without any pause for thought Wessex was running lightly toward the house. He avoided the pools of light spilling from the open doors and windows of the function rooms, and skirted the edge of the house until he reached the side door that led down into the servant's quarters beneath. One flat-footed thrust at the door gained him entrance—along with Wessex's fervent wish that he had been able to wear his hunting boots upon this expedition, instead of dancing slippers—and then he was within.

In the midst of such an entertainment as was taking place elsewhere, one would expect the servants' quarters to be filled with activity, but the kitchen in which Wessex found himself was entirely deserted. An overturned bottle of wine, its lees still dripping slowly into a scarlet puddle spreading on the wooden floor, gave mute testimony to the abruptness of the evacuation. It seemed that what the Underground had surmised was true: that if the Red Jacks had spies in every kitchen in France, every kitchen in France also had advance word of the Jacquerie's movements.

There was the thunder of proletarian boots upon the stairs. Swiftly Wessex identified the green baize door that separated the world of service from the elegant damask of Madame *la Princesse*'s drawing rooms. An immense oak dresser was the nearest article of furniture; Wessex ran to it and shoved, the long muscles of his elegant lean frame bunching with the sudden exertion.

There was a rattle of dishes as the massive piece began slowly to shift away from the wall. The oak dresser slid slowly forward, and just as it did so the door to the kitchen began to swing inward. With one last desperate heave Wessex thrust with all his might, and the dresser teetered, tipped . . . and toppled gracefully backward into the door with a musical breaking of glass. There was a roar of thwarted anger from the other side of the door—to which Wessex responded, genially, in an even fouler gutter argot.

Wessex smiled faintly as the faint sound of determined battery came distantly to him through the barricaded door. Best to hope that the late M. Grillot was to be believed regarding deMorrissey's whereabouts, as Wessex had just sealed the kitchen off from direct communication with the house above.

It seemed, however, that at least in that much Grillot had been truthful. His Majesty's Captain Avery Richard Harriman deMorrissey, most recently of Verdun, lay face-down upon a pallet in the butler's pantry, trussed like a prize Christmas fowl. The disheveled state of the Captain's borrowed clothes gave eloquent witness to the difficulty of his capture, and when his eye fell upon Wessex his color deepened alarmingly.

"I pray you, my good man," drawled Wessex in the most well-bred of Pall Mall accents, "that when I release you, you will confine your martial ardor to our mutual enemies. I am Wessex, and we were to meet this evening under slightly different circumstances."

"The King must be told!" gasped deMorrissey as soon as the gag was removed from his mouth. "There is a plot!"

"There is always a plot," Wessex murmured absently. His fingers were busy on the knotted cords that bound deMorrissey's hands and feet. They were bound so tightly together that he did not dare to use the tiny knife he carried, and the knots were difficult. And surely it could not be so very long until the Jacks realized that the kitchen had *two* entrances.

"Saint-Lazarre is to be killed!" deMorrissey gasped. "In England—an assassin is on his way."

"Who?" Wessex demanded sharply. Victor Saint-Lazarre, that loyal French expatriate and able courtier, seemed to be the only man who could hold the squabbling French Royalist factions together. Without Saint-Lazarre to unite the various Royalist cabals in support of the English war effort, King Henry's hopes of sparking a Continental counterrevolution to restore a member of the legitimate Bourbon line to the throne of France would suffer a fearful blow. The man's assassination would be a magnificent coup for the Republicans, as well as touching off a wildfire of terror throughout the country once it was learned that the Corsican Beast's reach stretched to murder in England itself.

"Don't know. The courier we retrieved knew only that Saint-Lazarre was to be killed on sixteen *Germinal.*"

"The *Gazette* places Saint-Lazarre at the Marchioness of Roxbury's country seat until Parliament resumes. That is where the assassin will strike. If we are separated, you must do your utmost to reach England with the news," Wessex said quickly. Sixteen *Germinal* in the Revolutionary Calendar translated to the twentieth of April by civilized reckoning. Eight days from now. To reach London in time to warn those in power would take superhuman luck and inhuman speed.

The last knot came free beneath Wessex's expert fingers just as the door leading to the kitchen garden burst inward with a crash. DeMorrissey rolled from the pallet and stretched cramped limbs; a young John Bull in the flower of his manly strength. His white teeth gleamed in the half-light as he smiled.

"You may depend upon me, sir."

And then there was no more time for talk. The first Red Jack through the doorway took a bullet in the throat from Wessex's tiny pistol and fell to the floor in a bloody thrashing of limbs. DeMorrissey seized the Red Jack's truncheon of office from the dead man's hand and used it to great effect upon the jaw of the next, gaining Wessex not only a truncheon of his own but a matchlock pistol primed and cocked.

"Who wishes next to die?" Wessex's tone seemed to hold genuine curiosity as he regarded the three men he faced. None of them, it seemed, was willing to give him his answer.

From the corner of his eye Wessex saw deMorrissey edge around him and out through the kitchen door. And that was well enough, save that in his disheveled condition and lacking identity papers, deMorrissey would soon enough be seized by any of the Citizen's Safety Committees that roamed the city with vigilante watchfulness. And deMorrissey, still, did not have a single word of French.

The Jacks' scarlet caps were dyed even bloodier by the light from the stove, and with admonitory gestures from his borrowed weapon Wessex herded them backward until they stood in an untidy clump before it. They shuffled uncertainly, mesmerized by the darkness at the end of his pistol, but in truth the advantage was theirs and soon enough they would realize it.

"Come on!" deMorrissey urged from the doorway in a strangled whisper.

Wessex raised the pistol and fired.

The ball struck none of the three men, but the Red Jacks had not been Wessex's target. He had been aiming at an object upon the shelf above the stove, and his ball had flown true. Oil from the shattered jar his bullet had struck dripped down onto the hot iron surface of the stove.

Dripped—

Smoked—

Ignited.

With a sizzling flare, the iron surface of the stove burst into bright hot light. In their scramble to evade the flames one of the Jacks was flung into the midst of the fire by his companions, and another fell to a blow from Wessex's cudgel. His Grace did not remain to see the end of the play; he was out the door upon the instant, grabbing deMorrissey by the shoulder as he passed and running fleet as any fox before the hounds. Together the two men fled through the moonlight garden and into the street of what until quite recently had been a quiet respectable Paris neighborhood.

Wessex knew the city of Paris well; it was his business to know such things. Soon he and his charge were several streets away, and had, temporarily at least, lost their pursuers.

"What now?" deMorrissey panted.

"A fast horse and the Calais road," Wessex replied. "It seems I have an engagement at the Marchioness of Roxbury's—and I should so hate to disappoint a lady."

5

La Belle Dame Sans Merci (April 20th, 1805)

It was April 20th—four days since the crash of the mail coach on its way to London.

The young woman in the massive four-poster bed tossed fretfully, trying to throw off the heavy embroidered velvet coverlet that insulated her from the April chill. But each time she managed to do so, the quiet woman who sat in the chair by the fire would get to her feet and replace the coverlet over the young woman's restless body. Her name was Gardner, and not so many years ago she had been the young Marchioness of Roxbury's nurse, just as she had nursed Roxbury's mother, and her mother before her.

Gardner's skin had the frail porcelain color of extreme old age, but her spine was still poker-straight and her mismatched eyes—one blue, one brown—were bright and intelligent.

"How does she?"

Dame Alecto's entry into the room had been as silent

as that of any of Sarah Cunninghams's Cree companions. The Dowager Duchess of Wessex's trusted emissary glanced toward the bed where the woman the world knew as the Marchioness of Roxbury—a Roxbury mysteriously restored to vibrant health—lay in laudanum-induced dreams. In her hands, Dame Alecto—this world's Alecto Kennet—held a small carved wooden box inlaid with silver long since darkened to soft black by the passage of uncounted years.

"Well as might any whose soul still wanders Between the Worlds," Gardner said, the Scots burr of her girlhood still evident in her soft voice. "I pray me that the Luck is with us, and we may lead her back to us again."

"It wants more than luck," Dame Alecto said, as if to herself. Strong magic had opened the Veil Between the Worlds, allowing one Sarah to pass away through it and another to arrive. The woman who had been born in this house and this bed was dead in a world now sealed to them, but her world-double was here, and in their power.

Dame Alecto regarded the figure in the bed with a gaze more critical than any the false Roxbury's servants had employed. If one knew what one was looking for, it was easy to tell this was not the trueborn Marchioness. The weathered skin, the work-roughened hands, small scars from wounds that Sarah Conyngham, Lady Roxbury, had never suffered . . . the differences were patent, if subtle. Even Dr. Falconer, her ladyship's personal physician, when called to her side in haste for the second time in one day, had only taken Sarah for the Marchioness in the heat of the moment—and in the heat of his fury at finding her breathing strong, the raging consumption vanished. Falconer had ascribed the Marchioness's improvement in health to some other device than the one that Dame Alecto had employed. . . .

"I might have expected this of you," he said in a fury to the

baffled Sarah. "Doesn't Your Ladyship know that such bargains only come to ill ends?"

Dame Alecto smiled her small cat-smile at the memory of the moment opened to her in the scrying glass. Let young Falconer think that Roxbury had forged a forbidden bargain with the Oldest People—it was better he suspect that than guess the truth. And Dame Alecto would take care to keep him from returning to the chit's side until there was nothing about his patient to distinguish her from the woman he had known from her cradle. The marks of work and weather would fade with time and soothing lotions, scars could be covered with paint and patch and long satin skirts.

There was only one difference that the Lotion of the Ladies of Denmark could not erase, and that was an inward one. This Sarah knew nothing of her double's life and obligations, and they dared not count upon her assuming them willingly. To shape this new Sarah to their plans would require an even more cunning trick than any Dame Alecto had yet worked, and a ruthless one at that, and Dame Alecto was more than willing to supply it.

"Do you go on reading to Her ladyship, Gardner," Dame Alecto said. "And I will prepare her cordial."

Gardner's voice took up her reading once more. " 'April 14th, 1798: Mama's funeral was held today, a most extraordinary fine turn out. The death-coach was drawn by six black horses, all in plumes, and King Henry himself sent his warmest condolences; all the County was there, and I do not know how many Pairs of Gloves Buckland distributed to them all. Now Mooncoign is mine, and I am the Marchioness! How strange it all seems: they tell me I must make my bow to Society this Season instead of waiting until next year, even though of course since I am in Mourning for Mama everything must be Very Quiet. And there is to be a Court Presentation as well and

I must have a Whole Wardrobe in the First Stare of Fashion—although it must all be Black; how dull! But perhaps I shall set a new mode, for I am *Roxbury* now, after all—' "

Gardner's quiet voice droned on in the background, reading aloud from Lady Roxbury's diary, as Dame Alecto set the small ebony box down on the table beside the bed. Opening the casket, Dame Alecto lifted out the small crystal flask of Cordial of Lethe. The liquid gleamed a baleful violet in the dim light of the bedside candle.

A full draught of the cordial—crafted from La Montespan's own recipe, faithfully handed down through the centuries—would destroy all memory, leaving its victim as mindless and unknowing as a newborn babe. But that was not what they wanted for this new Sarah. This hard-won substitute must take up Lady Roxbury's place in Society. She must do their work in Mooncoign's name against the oppression of the Corsican tyrant who so ravaged the Continent, and take the place of her world-twin whose life had been cut so untimely short by her own recklessness and folly.

Carefully, Dame Alecto measured a few drops of thick liquid into a silver spoon. After tipping the cordial into a brilliant cut crystal wineglass, Alecto poured in enough wine to cover the bowl of the spoon, then stirred until the two liquids were well mixed.

"Come, Your Ladyship," she said to the drowsy girl. "It is time to take your medicine."

For the past week Wessex had been on the road, the warning he carried too sensitive to trust even to the heliograph that could communicate between men ashore and the English ships that patrolled the Channel. It had taken three precious days to get himself and deMorrissey from Paris to Calais, and another endless day waiting until a longboat could safely beach to take them off. Once they reached Dover their ways would part, Wessex to London a-horseback, leaving deMorrissey to follow a little more sedately in what ever transport he could commandeer or hire.

All during the turbulent day-long Channel crossing Wessex had paced and fretted, thinking only of delivering deMorrisey's information and saving Saint-Lazarre.

Saint-Lazarre was at Mooncoign. Wessex cudgelled his brains. He had to admit he did not know Roxbury at all well, even though his grandmama had stood her godmother and Wessex himself had been formally betrothed to her when she was sixteen and he was twenty-four. His work for King and Country meant he had not seen much of the girl in the intervening years—it was, however, impossible not to have *heard* of her: the dashing parties, her autocratic behavior, her outrageous friendships. These scandals had been among the hottest *on-dits* of the Ton since the Marchioness had made her bow to Society—but her betrothed had taken little notice of them. A man playing the Shadow Game possessed little time for the claustrophobic world of the Upper Ten Thousand. And in fact, no matter how hideous Roxbury's behavior, his own was worse.

Rupert St. Ives Dyer, Duke of Wessex, was the third of that noble line—although his grandfather, before being so exalted, had been heir to the Earldom of Scathach, a dignity that had been old when William the Conqueror first beached his boats on Saxon shores. The Dukedom of Wessex, like so many English peerages, was the whimsical creation of a Stuart King—in this particular case, of King Charles the Fourth, upon the memorable occasion of Wessex's grandfather's birth. As might be expected from the nature of the creation of the title, the mark of Stuart kinship was writ plainly upon Wessex's long-jawed countenance. Though the pale wheat-gold hair worn Continentally long marked the Plantagenet strain in the line, the hot black eyes were purely Stuart, and Wessex was as stubborn and inflexible of purpose, as feared an enemy and as loyal a friend as were all the descendants of that kingly lineage.

Though in the eyes of the world, Wessex was merely Captain His Grace the Duke of Wessex of the Eleventh Hussars—the Cherubims—a regiment currently with General Wellesley doing what they might to render Napoleon's possession of Europe a matter of doubt—his captaincy was almost a formality; a liveried *carte blanche* that provided him the *congé* to some of the circles in which he must move. Wessex's war was fought, not on battlefields, but in shadows and in country houses, in foreign courts and behind enemy lines.

For the organization for which Wessex truly worked was not even remotely military in nature. Half a club of the most exclusive, half an order of chivalry sprung full-flowered from a most unlikely century, it was the Order of the White Tower.

The White Tower was named for the earliest stronghold of English Kings. It had been founded by Charles the Third, and was the descendant of the espionage network that Lord Walsingham had run in Gloriana's time. Its badge was gules, a tower argent, and a brooch with such a device resided somewhere in the back of a drawer in Wessex's Albany rooms, unearthed only on those occasions when full Court dress was required of him.

The White Tower was the English Crown's official covert organization, and membership was an honor conferred by the King alone—quietly, without public display. The White Tower acted under conditions of strictest secrecy, its true function known only to King Henry and a handful of his most trusted ministers. Ever since its founding, the

White Tower had served to defend the interests of the British Crown in any corner of the earth where those interests were threatened . . . and to gather the information to keep England free of Continental entanglements. For over a dozen years now, the eyes of the White Tower had been turned to France, and France's regicidal and imperial ambitions.

Wessex had been formally granted the Order of the White Tower at a levee held on his twenty-first birthday, just after he had come down from Oxford. The White Tower's members met once a year for a dinner held in the White Tower itself, and so far as the world knew, that was all there was to the White Tower and its membership. It would never do to let the truth become common knowledge. In an age which venerated the Miles Gloriosus and thought of the Exploring Officer and his even more shadowy kindred as jackals and cowards, the news that the King himself employed such creatures might be enough to trigger a second English Civil War. It would surely topple the government.

From the moment his loyalty had been given, Wessex had dreaded the thought of his family discovering just *how* he served the Crown. The knowledge that her adored grandson was a wretched sneaking spy would, Wessex was certain, quite kill his grandmother—or if it did not, public knowledge of his shameful trade would force her complete sequestration from Society, a fate nearly as dire. It was out of shame as much as for any other reason that Wessex had shrunk from taking his fitting place in Society, but now he regretted his indifference to the traditional amusements of his class. Was it mere chance that Saint-Lazarre had gone to Roxbury's house in anticipation of the Season, and that it was to Mooncoign that a French assassin sped even now? Did Roxbury play a double game, just as he did?

For a moment the very thought made Wessex close his eyes in utter weariness. Englishwoman or no, betrothed or no, if Roxbury served the enemy, Wessex would show her no mercy. His masters had set him on; let the hunt fulfil itself without mercy or weakness.

Less than an hour after the ship had reached Dover, Wessex had claimed the horse he had left stabled there and was galloping along the post road to London. The Frisian asked only to run; as soon as his master was in the saddle, Hirondel laid back his ears and lunged across the stableyard cobbles, clearing the gate at a flat gallop.

A coach-and-six took nearly a full day to drive from Dover to London; a specially-built racing phaeton with a pair of twelve-mile-an-hour tits between the poles could go the distance in six hours.

Wessex and Hirondel did the journey in four.

It had still been dark when they'd left Dover; it was broad day now—the morning of April 19th—and Hirondel was covered in foam and staggering by the time the spires of London were in view. Wessex slowed to a walk to spare the exhausted animal as much as he could, but he could not afford to pause long enough to leave Hirondel in his home stable under a groom's expert care. The intelligence Wessex carried was too urgent to brook even that little delay.

But no one who saw the dark-eyed man as he rode up Bond Street and tossed Hirondel's reins to the one-legged man in tattered regimentals who lingered outside the select tailor's shop for just that purpose would have thought that Wessex was on an errand any more urgent than deciding upon the fabric for a new coat. Nothing in his carriage or demeanor gave any hint that it had been many days since Wessex had seen a bed of any sort. His mud-spattered boots and dusty coat hinted at a night of hard riding, but the Bloods of the Ton were noted for amusements that were nearly as dangerous as war.

"Walk him," Wessex said, tossing a yellow-boy to the veteran. "I will be some time."

He crossed the pavement that separated him from his destination, pushed the door open, and entered.

"My Lord Wessex."

The man called Flowers—though Wessex had no notion whether Flowers was his real name, or whether he actually had any hand in the coats Wessex occasionally ordered from his shop—came forward to greet his noble patron, his mien perfectly that of a most superior tailor who might pick and choose his customers from among the Pinks of the Ton. "We had heard you were to rusticate upon the country for some weeks yet."

Wessex smiled grimly to himself. The man could hardly say that he thought Wessex was still in France, now, could he?

"I am afraid I have come upon a most urgent commission, Flowers. The French-cut velvet turns out to have some unique difficulties."

"If Your Grace would be so good as to step into the fitting room?" Flowers said smoothly. He led Wessex past the cutting room, with its mannequins and half-finished coats, into a small cubicle at the back of the shop and left him there, closing the open side of the booth with a brass-ringed curtain of faintly dusty green velvet.

Wessex pushed down upon a certain section of the paneling of the back of the booth and waited a moment until he heard the click of the inside lock being released. The panel slid back, and Wessex walked through into a foyer that would not have been out of place in any Piccadilly townhouse.

The impeccably-liveried butler Charteris was standing

ready to greet him, and flanking the entrance Wessex had used were two strapping footmen, whose slightly archaic staves of office could be turned to formidable weapons at need.

"I need to see Misbourne," Wessex said curtly, his weariness breaking through his speech at last.

"I shall enquire if my lord is at home," Charteris said austerely, just as if this secret sanctuary were the town-house it so thoroughly resembled. Wessex repressed once again the irreverent impulse to send his card up with the perfect butler. "If Your Grace would care to wait in the Blue Parlor?"

There were four small rooms on the ground floor of the premises; in his years with the White Tower, Wessex had waited in all of them at one time or another. Except for the colors for which they were named—Red, Yellow, Violet, Blue—and which were carried out in their decoration and appointments, the four rooms were virtually identical. Wessex had never discovered any rhyme or reason for his assignment to one room or another. However, the color of the room was a small matter compared to the selection of well-filled decanters on each room's sideboard.

After so long without sleep, Wessex bypassed the claret and filled a cut-crystal tumbler halfway to the brim with smuggled French brandy. The heady kick of the neat spirit revived his flagging energy, and he made what repairs to his bedraggled appearance he could in the moments before Charteris returned.

"If you will accompany me, Your Grace," the butler said impassively.

Wessex followed Charteris up the curving staircase to the first floor. The door at the end of the corridor was covered in padded red leather, and Charteris did not scratch at the door before pushing it open and allowing Wessex to pass through.

From long habit, Wessex stopped just inside the door to give his eyes a chance to adjust to the dimness. The room was lit by several cobbler's lanterns; the candle flames reflected through flasks of spirits, filling the room with a warm, diffuse, brandy-scented glow. There were no windows in this room, which was otherwise lined with books and curiosities much as any gentleman's library might be. The drawn curtains to his left gave the apartment the look of an ordinary room, but their folds concealed only a plain brick wall.

Lord Misbourne had been sitting at his desk; he stood when Wessex entered, a pale and patient spider, waiting for information to drift into his nets.

Jonathan Milon Arioch de la Forthe, third Baron Misbourne, had begun his life in the shadow of three great disadvantages: he had been born a Catholic, he had been born an albino, and he had been born a brilliant mathematician. It was this third defect that was perhaps the greatest of all, for his preoccupation with pure numbers in the days of his youth had kept him from working to erase the twin stigma of a suspect foreign faith and a freakish appearance. Instead, he had allowed his ostracism to push him deeper into his studies, and he used his studies to blot out the whole of the world beyond.

It was time that had played Lord Misbourne the cruellest trick of all, for Mathematics, Queen of the Pure Sciences, is a fickle mistress, taking up her lovers early and leaving them while they are still young. The Baron awoke one day in his early thirties to discover himself master of an ancient name and a dilapidated estate, and very little more.

But his time had not been entirely wasted, at least in the eyes of the world. A byproduct of his interest in numbers had been an interest in codes, a freakish puzzle-solving ability that had always brought him admirers from

among a certain segment of society. Barred by his albi-
nism from outdoor pursuits—for even the gentle winter
sun of England could dazzle his pale eyes to blindness—
and by his religion from any public office, he could not
easily find a new outlet for the energy that had once been
funneled into the fervid pursuit of pure knowledge. But as
his precocious brilliance had faded, an interest in more
temporal puzzles had risen in its place, and guided by the
friends he had made in a youth now half-a-century gone,
Misbourne had come to test his theories with men instead
of numbers, and play out his gambits upon the chessboard
of Europe. It was to Misbourne that Wessex reported, and
from Misbourne that Wessex took his orders.

Wessex had never been able to formulate the least idea
of the man's age. Misbourne had looked much as he did
now for as long as Wessex had known him: his gaunt
scarecrow form the despair of his tailor; his brilliant colorless eyes taking up the color from the cobbler's lamps
and glowing almost coal-crimson in the dimness.

"Wessex." Misbourne's greeting was understated as always. "We had feared you lost; our politics in Paris suspected a trap was being laid for one of our agents there."

He gestured toward the deep armchair before his desk;
Wessex shook his head regretfully. "I am too many hours
on the road," he explained. It would not do to find himself
asleep in his master's presence. Misbourne reseated himself and gazed at Wessex expectantly.

"A trap of sorts; I fear that the Chevalier de Reynard
is dead," Wessex said with faint regret at abandoning so
useful a persona, "and Monsieur Grillot most certainly is
dead. But it was no trap—or if it was, the bait was genuine. DeMorrissey's information seems sound enough—
and whether it is or no, we dare not refrain from acting
upon it."

Omitting information Misbourne knew as well as he—

the problem of the internally divided and quarrelsome Royalist factions—Wessex explained that Victor Saint-Lazarre—who had renounced his aristocratic titles when King Louis XVI had been executed in 1793, vowing to resume them only at the coronation of the next Bourbon King—was attending a pre-Season houseparty at the house of the Marchioness of Roxbury, where an assassin would seek him out in not quite two days' time.

"And did our good Captain deMorrissey explain how he had come by this information?" Misbourne asked, with pardonable skepticism.

"The assassin boasted of his coup-to-be at a party deMorrissey attended while interned. They do have a certain amount of society in Verdun." Wessex sighed—as much in exasperation as from weariness. It was not impossible. Who would believe that a prisoner interned in the heart of Republican France had any hope of communicating anything he might learn to France's enemies? Under various names, Wessex had made a number of clandestine pilgrimages to the walled city where the French interned foreign nationals, and he knew its ways from personal experience.

"At least," Wessex amended, "it passes for society."

"I see. And was Captain deMorrissey able to provide any sort of description of this putative assassin?" Misbourne's tone was professionally resigned.

Wessex's mouth quirked in mocking sympathy. "He said the man was short, my lord. With brown hair—or, as it may have been, a wig. Rather ordinary, in fact."

"Thus describing half of France and three-fifths of England." Misbourne sighed. "I take it we may not pursue the simpler course of simply whisking Saint-Lazarre to safety?"

Misbourne was baiting him and at the moment, Wessex's temper could not support such stress. "And lose the chance to question one of Talleyrand's confidential agents?" he snapped. "Or to find out who else may be implicated in such a plot?"

Charles-Maurice de Talleyrand-Périgord—the butcher with the face of an angel and the manners of Satan himself—was the head of Bonaparte's secret police. Even General Savary reported to him. Talleyrand had been born into the French nobility half a century before and had been nearly as oppressed by it as any impoverished peasant. Lamed by a careless wet-nurse, disinherited by callous parents in favor of a younger brother, and forced into the Church that he loathed, Tallyrand had championed the Revolution that had freed him from spiritual vows. He had risen high in the Revolution's bloody councils, and had managed to persuade the then-First Consul— Napoleon Bonaparte—to give him even greater power. Now Talleyrand was the poisoned thorn in the English lion's paw . . . his reach was as long as his ambition was vast.

"Peace, Your Grace." Misbourne raised his delicate white hands in capitulation. "You are quite right: the assassin must be taken, and alive if such a feat can be managed. The only question remaining is who I may send who will have the *congé* in such circles. It would not do to twist Roxbury's tail without need—she is a connection of yours, if I recall correctly?"

"The Marchioness is my grandmother's goddaughter, and my betrothed. I suppose I shall marry her someday, if both of us live long enough," Wessex said briefly. He shrugged. Futile to think that Misbourne would not remember that small fact; the man had the encyclopedic grasp of minutia that had spelled the difference between defeat and victory in a thousand shadow tourneys. "Let me go to her. I suppose I must have the right to call upon Roxbury if anyone does."

"You must·be at Roxbury's by tomorrow night—and today would be better," Misbourne pointed out. And Mooncoign was in County Wiltshire, almost a day's journey by coach from London.

But the thought that his family name might be compromised—however obliquely—made Wessex, exhausted as he was, unwilling to leave the completion of this hunt to others.

"Give me a coach and driver and I can be there by sundown," Wessex said. "I would back myself to be there sooner, but I rode Hirondel from Dover and there is nothing left in him, poor lad."

"Someday you will kill yourself, and not just your horses," Misbourne said. "Very well—go to Wiltshire and catch me a Frenchman. And then let us see what other game we may flush."

Misfortune had plagued every stage of Wessex's journey, beginning with a lame wheeler a dozen miles outside London and ending in a broken axle, and so it was the morning after and not the night before that saw Wessex's arrival at Mooncoign—on a hired horse, and far in advance of his luggage.

He had stopped at the Green Maiden in the village of Moonfleet long enough to ask directions that he did not really need and collect gossip that he did. There he had discovered that the Marchioness's usual spring entertainment went on as usual, with lavish displays of fireworks and other entertainments of a havey-cavey nature. Though Lady Roxbury had suffered an illness that had seemed serious for a time, and not a week past had been involved in a smash-up with the Bristol Mail that had killed her famous team of match bays, her ladyship was now reported to be in excellent health. This very night, in fact, her ladyship was hosting a masked ball—an intelligence that did nothing to relieve his grace's feelings. Anyone might choose to appear at a masked ball, and with nearly all the County invited and many guests arriving from Town, one more interloper would scarcely be remarked, even if he happened to be a French assassin.

Had this been Roxbury's plan?

Loyalty to his class rather than any particular feeling for his betrothed kindled Wessex's anger. As much as he wished to take the killer in hand, he wished even more to settle, at least in his own mind, all question of the Marchioness's guilt or innocence. He was brooding over that matter as he rode up Mooncoign's long drive an hour later.

In the light of early afternoon, Mooncoign's northern facade, faced all in white stone, shone with a brilliant light. Mooncoign's roof was edged in crouching stone figures that—to Wessex's jaundiced eye—looked ready to take wing and fly. Three generations of Roxburys had so enlarged the house that its consequence rivaled that of Blenheim Palace.

He was not, upon his admission to the house, much in a mood to be told that Lady Roxbury was not receiving visitors.

Sarah tossed fretfully in her half-sleep, a bitter taste lingering on her tongue. Bizarre images capered through her dreaming mind: fantastic horses dressed in plumes; a black-lacquered coach with its dead-lights burning. She was . . . She was . . .

She was Sarah.

But disparate images accompanied the naming: a quiet young woman, dressed in beaded buckskins—a painted lady, dressed in satins and jewels.

Which was she? Which was Sarah?

Sarah groaned and opened her eyes. Above her head stretched an unfamiliar canopy of embroidered silk with bullion fringe. Memories of the recent past crashed and collided in her brain, making her whimper aloud with vertigo.

She remembered the crash—yes, the aftermath of it was clear enough now—the screams of mangled horses and the wails of injured passengers—the sickening pain in her head. Everything before that was grotesquely clouded, but the aftermath was relatively clear: Mrs. Bulford, in whose house she'd awakened; a man named Falconer—whose words had been utterly baffling but whose tone had conveyed both anger and disappointment; the ride in the coach back to her—*her?*—home.

This isn't my home, Sarah thought with chill fear. *I don't belong here.* But of course she did. Of course it was. Everyone had told her so . . . at least she thought they had.

Sarah sat up, stretching muscles that protested days of disuse. She rubbed at her eyes; the voluminous sleeves of sheer muslin that trailed from her arms made her look down at her gown; the night-dress, of a muslin so fine it was called nun's veiling, was elaborately tucked and embroidered, dozens of yards of material going to make up the costly and etherial gown she wore. Numbly, Sarah stared at the sleeve as one transfixed. It seemed wrong, somehow: not evil, but out of place, like a frog in a butterchurn—

Galvanized by her own disquiet, Sarah swung her legs over the side of the bed and stood, a renewed bout of dizziness making her clutch at the heavy bed curtains to steady herself. Breathing deeply and carefully, Sarah looked around the deserted room.

Her gaze was drawn inexorably to the portrait above the mantlepiece, where a woman in a most indecent gown and a face painted until it was only a white mask looked down at Sarah with a challenging gaze that Sarah could see in the looking glass any time she chose. Were they related? The painted woman's jewel-covered fingers held a key, a dagger, and a rose, items that held no familiarity for Sarah.

As if of their own volition, her hands flew to her bosom, but the comforting lump of her father's ring was not there.

The ring!

Casting aside all other worries, Sarah tore the room apart until she found the ring, set aside in a drawer by her bedside. Quickly she worked the catch, rotating the black stone until the enamelled unicorn and the King's Oak were revealed on its silvery obverse, and gazed on the image with relief. No matter what else was hidden from her, this memory was real and true.

The blue ribbon she had worn the ring on was gone; hesitantly Sarah tried the ring on all her fingers, until she settled it upon the forefinger of her left hand. At least this treasure was still with her.

But why should she think that? All she owned was with her: this was Mooncoign, her home.

Sarah raised her hands to rub her throbbing temples. Alien luxury beguiled her upon every side, but her gaze was drawn longingly to the window, beyond which Mooncoign's lavish mock-wilderness was visible, bright emerald in the midday English sun.

It is not the true woodland. It is false, just as everything else about this . . . mummery, Sarah thought sulkily.

Yes, that was it! All this was false, unreal, a playlet all enacted for her benefit in which none of its actors believed. All these people treating her with outlandish deference, granting her impossible titles . . . it was a *game.*

But who played this game, and why? Sarah stared through the enormous windows and saw no answer waiting beyond the lavish expanse of glass. Her certainty began to fade back into troubled confusion, and she became slowly aware that for the last several minutes she had been hearing a gradually increasing commotion through the great oak door that led to the world outside.

"To the devil with her headache—I will see the woman!" a strange male voice shouted, just as the door flew open.

Sarah stared.

The stranger had the night-black eyes of a fallen angel, and his moon-cream hair was brushed straight back and held at the nape of his neck with a black ribbon. He was dressed in a neat coat of blue superfine, white buckskin inexpressibles, and gleaming tasselled Hessians—riding clothes. He still wore a pair of Cork tan gloves and carried a silver-headed crop, and as he moved, light flashed from the gemmed pin in his cravat. Sarah stared at him, enchanted in the oldest sense of the word.

Incredibly, the stranger blushed, staring at her billowing and all-concealing muslin nightgown and averting his eyes hastily.

"I—Your pardon, Lady Roxbury. I did not—I shall await you—Pray excuse me."

While Sarah was still belatedly registering the fact of his arrival, the Duke of Wessex removed himself to her sitting-room, closing the door swiftly behind him.

Wessex stood in Lady Roxbury's withdrawing chamber, striving to master the flush of sheer mortification that stained his cheeks. The manner of the aristocracy was quite free-and-easy, but there were still well-defined limits. Wessex was aware he had passed one of those limits by bursting in upon an unmarried female who was *en desha-*

bille, and he did not care for the sense of humiliation it gave him.

And Lady Roxbury's astonishment had only added to his sense of culpability. When he had stormed into her chamber, the Marchioness of Roxbury had been standing clinging to one of the velvet bed curtains, her muslin nightgown sliding down her narrow shoulders. Her light brown hair spilled about her arms, and her pale skin was bare of paint. She looked much smaller than he had remembered her as being, and far more vulnerable.

As he waited impatiently for the Marchioness to emerge—for what else could he do, after all, having burst in to her private chambers like a man demented?—Wessex heard the outer door to the withdrawing room open. A fragile old woman—who nevertheless conveyed the indefinable imperious air of a very superior servant indeed—appeared.

"What is your business here, sir?" the woman asked with the fierceness of a mother hen protecting her only chick. Through the open door behind her, Wessex could see a brace of stout footmen hovering, obviously hoping their assistance would be required.

"I have come to pay my respects to your mistress," Wessex said. "Pray enquire if she will receive me," he added, as blandly as if he had not just rudely accosted Lady Roxbury minutes before. "Tell her that her bridegroom has come to pay her a call."

Wessex disliked trading upon that future affiliation, particularly as he was not entirely certain he intended to honor the betrothal, but it was imperative that he speak to the Marchioness. He only hoped that after a singularly inauspicious beginning, the notoriously touchy Lady Roxbury would condescend to grant him an interview at all.

"I . . . shall enquire, Your Grace," the old woman said reluctantly, and disappeared into the Marchioness's bedroom. The door closed behind her with an audible thump; her appearance of fragile old age was obviously illusion only.

Wessex turned and closed the outer door in the footmen's faces, then shamelessly approached the inner door, seeking to eavesdrop on the conversation within the Marchioness's bedroom. But it was a fruitless attempt; the door was too thick for even murmurs to reach him.

Gardner seemed nearly as surprised as Sarah to see her on her feet, though Sarah clung to one of the bedposts to steady herself.

"My lady," Gardner said, and sank automatically into a stiff curtsey. "I shall bring Dame Alecto."

No! The automatic flash of alarm sparked Sarah to feign a vitality she did not feel.

"Why?" she asked coolly. "I am perfectly recovered. Pray tell me, Nurse, who was that man?"

"I shall send him away at once," Gardner promised. "My lady, you are far from well. The stress of the accident—"

"That was several days ago," Sarah said. The confusion in her mind was as strong as ever, but so was the need to—not escape, precisely, but to be mistress of her fate. "And my . . ." She hesitated, but the ideas were there when she groped for them. "My *guests* will wish to see me, after all. Bring me my clothes."

"But my lady," Gardner protested again. Sarah said nothing, and after a few moments she saw the old nurse's indignation soften into defeat.

"Very well, Lady Roxbury. I shall send Knoyle to you so that you may dress."

A victory, but Sarah did not have the leisure to luxuriate in it. "And tell that man I will see him, once I have dressed," she instructed the nurse. Whoever he was, he might hold the key to the mystery that surrounded her.

6

A Masquerade in Shadows

❄ Upon being assured by Mrs. Gardner that the Marchioness would receive him the moment she was dressed, Wessex allowed himself to be conveyed by the house's butler to a bedchamber in the bachelor's wing of the house, where a servant took away his coat and boots to be brushed and polished, and Wessex made what repairs to his toilette he could with the time and materials available to him. Fortunately, when he was finished, the figure gazing back at him from the mirror far more resembled the Duke of Wessex than the madcap Chevalier de Reynard or any of his spiritual cousins. Thank God he had worn his signet ring, as befit a man of his station—his betrothed was rumored to be notoriously high in the instep, insisting on all observances due her exalted rank. Wessex gazed upon his reflection, drawing upon himself as surely as any role the trappings of his own life. As some might say, his real life.

Reflexively, his fingers caressed the stone of the massive

ring he wore on his left hand, and he smiled, for Lady Roxbury would never appreciate the true meaning of *this* signet.

At his practiced touch, the carnelian cut with the crowned salamander of the Wessex dukedom lifted up and out on an armature that had seemed, moments before, to be the rim of the bezel. Under Wessex's control, the engraved gemstone spun to reveal a device that only twelve men and one woman in the realm were privileged to carry.

In precise, exquisite enamelwork, an oak tree in summer foliage glowed against a silvery field. At its foot, a unicorn slept, its head upon the ground. In the branches, a crown in glory burned.

Boscobel—the King's Oak. And a symbol of loyalties that might at any moment be divided.

The League's founder had seen his father, Charles the First of England, executed by those for whom he ruled; had himself spent long years of penurious exile in all the courts of Europe while his birthright suffered beneath Cromwell's iron heel. When Charles Stuart had come into his own again he had been balked at every turn by Lords and Commons determined that the Crown of England would dance to their piping, and not they to that of any King.

And so Charles Stuart—King Charles II of England, Scotland, Ireland, and Wales—had danced; smiling and bowing and keeping his tongue behind his teeth as he painstakingly forged the sword to defend England against herself at need. The Boscobel League: twelve men and one woman, never more and never less—each new member chosen by his predecessor and approved by the King. Drawn from the highest and lowest in the land, loyal to King—or Queen—*before* Country.

It was by the decree of their Royal founder that the

League's numbers should not be greater—that the League should be funded from the Privy Purse directly—that each ruler, upon his accession, should be given one chance, and one chance only, to disband this secret weapon. Five kings had chosen to retain it, but the sword had always remained sheathed.

So far.

What Wessex had done in France had been done at the behest of his masters in the Order of the White Tower. But before he had pledged himself to them, Wessex had pledged himself to the League, and if his King so commanded, Wessex would betray England at the command of the Crown of England.

Or would he?

For now, the bonds of his oaths did not pull Wessex in opposite directions. Service to the Nation was still service to the King, and in his infrequent resorts to prayer, Wessex hoped that fact would never change.

But the possibility remained. Wessex stood between the Tower and the Oak—two holy and binding pledges—and lived with the nightmare that at any moment he might be called to break faith with one of them. When his other problems seemed too formidable, it was bizarrely soothing to think about this one.

There was a soft scratching at the door.

"The Marchioness will receive you now, Your Grace."

Dame Alecto had not made her appearance while Sarah's abigail dressed her under Gardner's supervision, but Dr. Falconer had, and bullied Sarah into submitting to another examination. As he held the listening tube against her chest, Sarah searched the doctor's face with as much circumspection as she could muster. This man was her personal physician. Why did he seem an utter stranger to her?

She did not remember him at all.

Carefully, Sarah kept her expression neutral. She was the Marchioness of Roxbury. This was Mooncoign, her home. As if it were a tale she had heard others tell, she recalled the particulars of her privileged life: orphaned as a child, she had been an autocrat from the time she learned to ride her first pony, and sole mistress of her fate by the age of sixteen.

"I find nothing amiss with Your Ladyship," Dr. Falconer pronounced with an air of great reluctance. "You were thrown clear of the wreck, and I have known you to take worse falls upon the hunting field—though I cannot say that your four days' sleep settled my mind overmuch."

He stared at her, his amber gaze fervent with mysterious meaning. "I warn you, should you regret your bargain, you will not find it as easy to unmake."

This was the second time he had mentioned a bargain, and Sarah still did not have the slightest idea of what he meant. She shrugged. "No bargain is easy to unmake, Doctor."

"Then on your own head be it," Dr. Falconer pronounced, as if he were judge, not physician. Gathering up his tools into their bag, he walked quickly from the room.

There. Now I have offended him, and I am sure I do not know how. But it would be better, perhaps, if he worried over offending me. . . .

The alien thoughts lay on the surface of her mind like smooth stones, and as she turned them over in her thoughts Sarah slowly became aware that Knoyle, the abigail, was chattering away, offering Sarah unfamiliar garments for her approval.

Knoyle knew her. And Knoyle was her personal maid. Why did she not know Knoyle?

"—and I may say, my lady, that the Duke is quite tolerably featured, for all he do go on glaring at one so!"

"He quite surprised me," Sarah said cautiously.

"Bursting in on Your Ladyship in that savage fashion!" Knoyle said disapprovingly. "What would his grandmother—who is your godmother as well—think of such behavior?" Apparently Sarah need not make any reply to this, for Knoyle sniffed critically and went on with her monologue. "And for all that your dear papa betrothed the two of you when you were born, such license—"

"I am to *marry* this Duke?" Sarah blurted, horrified.

"Your Ladyship must marry someone," Gardner pointed out imperturbably, "and the dukedom's lands march with your own. What could be more suitable?"

A stormy knot of rebellion formed within Sarah's bosom even as Knoyle pulled her corset-lacings tight. Though all else seemed oddly vague, she was quite certain she had never agreed to marry the Duke of Wessex.

But wait . . . Knoyle had spoken of a childhood betrothal. Perhaps the engagement was not so irrevocable as it had first sounded?

Knoyle left the room for a moment—Sarah could hear a whispered conversation with the maid whose job it was to take care of Lady Roxbury's clothing, and not her person. She turned to the nurse, who was coming forward with a shawl to place about Sarah's shoulders as she stood waiting in her stockings and petticoats, though with the fire on the hearth the room was already quite unseasonably warm.

"Oh, pray do not cosset me so, Gardner," Sarah protested. "I am far too old for that."

"You shall never be aught but the veriest babe to me," Gardner told her firmly. "T'was I who took you from the midwife's arms. Your dear mama would have no one save me to attend her—though there were some as said I was past my prime," she added darkly.

Sarah searched the old woman's face for veracity, suppressing a pang of despair when she found it easily. How could all those around her know her so well and she not know them at all?

"Here you are, my lady. In the first stare of fashion it is, and just such a gown as will put roses in your cheeks."

Sarah stared at the primrose-yellow gown of printed muslin that Knoyle held proudly over one arm. The neckline and the tiny puffed sleeves were threaded with bits of green ribbon, and knots of tiny floss roses trimmed the flounced hem and demi-train.

"Oh, how beautiful!" Sarah said. And beautiful it was, like a bird or a flower; purely ornamental and not at all for use.

Unresisting, Sarah allowed Knoyle to dress her and arrange her hair in a simple style, and Gardner to drape the cashmire shawl about her shoulders. When they were finished, a stranger stared back at Sarah from the chevalglass, a stranger with high-piled hair and an immodest expanse of skin exposed by the fashionable gown; someone Sarah did not know at all.

"And now," Knoyle said, "I shall just get the hare's foot and your jewel-case—"

"Oh, never mind that," Sarah said impatiently, turning her treasured ring round and round upon her finger. Now that her strength had returned, she itched to see the world beyond this room, and to discover what the Duke of Wessex was doing here, and how she might escape the clutches of their betrothal. "Where is this Duke?"

*　*　*

The house was not familiar to her at all, but Knoyle accompanied her as if expecting Sarah to need a stout arm to bear her up, conducting Sarah along unfamiliar corridors until she reached the library. Once inside, Knoyle stood beside the door as though hoping to emulate one of the suits of armor that Sarah had seen in the corridor, and Sarah gazed about the room with interest, stories that someone—who?—had told her resonating within her mind.

Family legend swore that, in the time of the martyred King Charles the First, before ever a Roxbury had walked these halls, this room had been not library but chapel to the manor's Catholic folk. Puritan storm and Glorious Restoration had destroyed most of the evidence of this—if ever there had been any—but what remained were three magnificent high-crowned windows in the north wall, the center one surmounted by a small but splendid rose window that had surely never been meant as any secular ornament. Sarah gazed out through the tiny diamond-shaped panes of the narrow windows at a world now red, now blue, now greener than grass, now a strange blank amber.

The room itself was filled with books and curios. *There, there are the antiquities your father gathered in Greece; the Canaletto King Charles gave your grandfather. . . .* She crossed to the shelves and took a book down at random. More books than she might read in a lifetime, here for the taking. Why did that astonish her so?

"Lady Roxbury?"

Sarah turned at the sound of the voice, automatically setting the volume in her hands aside. She clasped both hands before her, fiddling nervously with her ring. The Duke of Wessex was just closing the door to the library behind him.

"Your Grace," the appropriate title came to her lips

almost automatically. "What are you doing here?"

"Admirably direct." Wessex flicked a glance toward Knoyle, then crossed the room to where Sarah stood. "Send your maid away."

"I—I beg your pardon?" Sarah wondered if she heard him rightly.

"What I have to say is for your ears alone, Lady Roxbury. I won't have it repeated in every kitchen in—in England."

Sarah glanced toward Knoyle but received no clue there; the loyal abigail's face was a mask of righteous indignation that gave no hint whether Wessex's request might be reasonable. Sarah looked back at Wessex, trying to judge what sort of man he might be.

Face like a swordblade, and dark smudges of exhaustion beneath his eyes. His mouth bore the stamp of both temper and cold calculation, but some instinct prompted Sarah to grant his request.

"You may go, Knoyle."

The abigail fairly quivered with silent protest, and Sarah locked eyes with her, willing Knoyle to obey. After a moment Knoyle dropped her eyes and curtseyed before exiting the room.

As Knoyle left, Wessex made a cat-footed circuit of the library, lifting curtains to peer behind them and glancing into the chairs beside the fireplace as if to assure himself there was no one else present. Before Sarah could quite frame an objection, he had returned to her side.

"Victor Saint-Lazarre is one of your guests," Wessex said without preamble.

Victor Saint-Lazarre. The royalist, a ghostly voice prompted Sarah. "I know," she said.

"Why did you invite him?" Wessex pursued.

As Sarah herself had not the slightest notion, the question only increased her unease. As she wrung her hands, the too-large ring on her finger slipped free and went bouncing across the Turkey carpet, landing against Wessex's gleaming boot.

He bent and picked up the precious ring, and to Sarah's horror, she saw that in its fall the catch had come loose, and the stone had reversed to show its secret scene. When he saw the image, the Duke of Wessex stared at the unicorn beneath the oak as if he had been turned to salt.

She is one of us. An apprehension he had not known he felt lifted from Wessex's heart. He need fear no betrayal from Lady Roxbury—as a member of the Boscobel League, both her honor and her loyalty were above question.

Normally members of the League were unknown to one another—both members and candidates were masked at their election, and no list of the membership was kept. Wessex himself did not know who his fellows were. But if their common bond was not common knowledge, neither was it strictly forbidden for one member to reveal himself to another if need arose, and Wessex blessed Lady Roxbury's audaciousness in doing so. The revelation was safe enough, for the symbol meant nothing to anyone outside the League—and everything to those within it.

He glanced up and saw the Marchioness's wide grey eyes studying him expressionlessly. She could not *know* that he was also a member of the Boscobel league. She must be awaiting some hint of her gambit's success or failure, but she showed no evidence of any inner disquiet. Her face was the cool mask of a master gambler, and Wessex felt his spirits lift. With Roxbury to back his play, they could save Saint-Lazarre and take his would-be hunter without scathe.

"Your ring, Lady Roxbury. It is a pretty design," he added, turning the enamelled badge inward and clicking the bezel into place. "And it is one I have seen before."

"Have you?" the Marchioness said coolly, as if the matter were of no interest to her. "Perhaps you will be so good as to tell me what it is you felt you could not say before my maid."

His spirits bolstered by the knowledge of her trustworthiness, Wessex was blunt.

"That Victor Saint-Lazarre is to be murdered—here, tonight, in your house—by agents of the spymaster Talleyrand who are determined that a Royalist coalition shall not bear fruit."

"Murdered—in my house?" Her ladyship's tone was still cool, but the ghost of haughty indignation now informed it.

"Unless we two can prevent him. I do not know who the assassin may be, and if we are to take him alive we dare not alert him to our knowledge. That is why I came—because it is easy enough to claim that I have some business with you."

"Because we are betrothed." Now there was open disdain in her voice, and Wessex repressed an urge to shake the chit until her teeth rattled. Had the woman no sense of timing?

"Yes," he said shortly. "Though there is no cause to refine too much upon it, as we have been promised these past nine years and may go on unwed another sixty for all of me. But to business. Tonight you give a *bal masque*, as all the county knows, and I believe that is when the assassin will strike."

"He must be stopped," Sarah said automatically, then frowned, thinking. "But how?"

"Leave that to me," Wessex said. "All I ask is that you make it known I am your guest, and I shall contrive the rest."

*   *   *

For a moment Sarah stood silent before him, wondering what she should do. Something deep within her cried out that this was all wrong, all strange, all *alien*—but that inner voice was faint, muffled by the assurances of the doctor and the servants, by the very existence of Mooncoign itself. *I am Lady Roxbury,* Sarah repeated to herself, echoing what she had repeatedly been told since she awoke to find the world new to her. *I am mistress of Mooncoign. I am a loyal subject of the King.* The feeble cry vanished, muted by these pronounced truths. Reassured, Sarah lifted her head and stared into Wessex's midnight eyes.

"Tell me what you wish me to do," Lady Roxbury said firmly.

7

Ill-Met by Moonlight

Wessex gazed sourly down at the articles of punctilious Court dress spread out before him in the dressing-room of his country house. The elaborate costumes appropriate to a formal masquerade were commissioned weeks—if not months—in advance, and naturally Wessex, who had not expected to attend, had not done so. Formal dress would have to suffice him.

Wessex had spent a few hours mingling informally with Lady Roxbury's guests before riding back to his own ducal seat to dress—somehow—for the evening's masquerade. Roxbury's great house was filled to overflowing with guests who had been arriving for the past three days, swelling the ranks of the original houseparty and overflowing into the houses around. Even his own house was full. No other member of the Family was in residence, but Wessex supposed he must have extended an invitation to someone before he'd left for France—Wessex Court was well-populated with young bachelors of the ton who had taken advantage of the opportunity to remove to more spacious quarters than Mooncoign currently provided.

Wessex glowered in disapproval at the harmless garments. Tonight's *bal masque* was the perfect venue for an assassination—and Wessex had nothing truly suitable to wear for the occasion. Plain formal dress would be both conspicuous and unsuitable.

At least he could count on the Marchioness's support, even though she could not be quite certain he shared her membership in the League. He ought to enlighten her, but some strange reluctance held him back. A lifetime's habit of secrecy was too strong. But her revelation left him wondering—not for the first time—what secrets those he thought he knew were keeping as well.

A sudden rustling in the branches of the tree outside his open window made the hair on the back of Wessex's neck prickle. He slid his hand into a waistcoat pocket, easing his fingers around his pocket watch—an item that, in addition to telling time, could end time for some; it was a single-shot pistol to those who knew its secret. Moving cat-footed, Wessex backed toward the wall, holding the timepiece in his right hand.

"I say, Your Grace, you might give a fellow a hand up," a familiar voice complained. Wessex grinned to himself, relaxing, and went to help his partner in through his dressing-room window.

"What the devil are you doing here?" Wessex demanded, not unreasonably.

"Bringing your costume," Illya Koscuisko answered breathlessly-if-amiably.

His English was idiomatic but accented, though he spoke French, German, and his native Polish without flaw. He was in uniform, Wessex noted with a certain resignation—Illya's bearskin shako was tilted at an angle upon his head, and the eagle's wings wired into full extension and stitched to the back of his dark green, caped, and fur-trimmed, uniform pelisse scraped at the top of the window as he clambered into the room. Wessex caught the shako as it fell and tossed it into a corner.

"Traveling incognito, I see," Wessex observed.

"Ah, well, this rig-out should serve for a mere fancy-dress party, and if I'm not needed there I can always use it to terrify children," Illya said. His dark eyes flashed with self-mockery, and he ran his hand through his chestnut hair, most of which was short-cropped atop his head in the current mode. Longer side-locks were braided into long, silk-wrapped pigtails in the fashion of the Polish Hussar regiments.

In his native Poland, Illya Koscuisko was an aristocrat, and like the eldest sons of many aristocratic families, had found a career in the Army, joining the elite cavalry regiment whose uniform he still wore. Though his country had not truly existed since before he was born—having been sliced like a rich pie among Russia, Prussia, and Austria in three separate Acts of Partition—Illya Koscuisko was a fierce nationalist who longed for the return of Polish sovereignty, though not at any price. Unlike many of his countrymen—who, after Poland's final destruction in 1795, fled to France to seek preferment and promises at the French Court—Koscuisko had come to believe that salvation would come not from the Corsican Tyrant, but in a Europe free of him. Koscuisko had not followed his regiment to France, embarking instead upon a course of intrigue and resistance that had brought him first to Wessex's attention, and then to that of the White Tower. For five years now he had been Wessex's partner and closest friend.

They were an unlikely pair. Poland was the victim of three powers who were Britain's allies, and France, Britain's enemy, was widely thought to be Poland's salvation.

Despite twists of fortune that had delivered his titles and estates into the hands of others, Koscuisko was gay and outgoing, warm where Wessex was cool, genuine where Wessex was mannered. But in the end, like his partner, all Illya Koscuisko asked of life was the chance to play the Shadow Game, and to strike out at the tyrant who had redrawn the map of Europe more brutally than Czar Alexander ever had.

"My costume," Wessex said. "How could you possibly . . . ?"

"We have our little ways," Koscuisko said cheerfully. "But I dare swear you will deal more amiably with the little Roxbury and Talleyrand's pet if you wear this."

Warily—he had some experience of his friend's sense of humor—Wessex unwrapped the bundle.

There was a golden papier-mâché helmet with a nodding crest of scarlet egret feathers, a sweeping silken cloak in the same color, a breastplate and back, and several other light pieces of painted and gilded wood and leather, all cunningly crafted to mimic armor.

"It's a grand concealment for a brace of Mantons, any road—you'll never hide them in an unexceptional, Duke-about-town coat and knee-breeches," Koscuisko pointed out.

"So I am to be a noble Roman?" Wessex asked quizzically.

"*Ave*, Caesar," Koscuisko murmured, sweeping him a low bow. Wessex stepped back quickly out of range of the wings that cut through the air like feathery guillotine blades. They extended nearly a yard above Koscuisko's head, and at the gallop the wind flying through them produced a weird rustling moaning sighing sound that was quite disheartening to the enemy, or so Wessex had heard.

"I do wish you'd learn how to manage those things," Wessex remarked, staring pointedly at the eagle wings.

Koscuisko regarded him placidly from a pair of pellucid velvet-brown eyes.

"Oh, I manage well enough," Koscuisko said cryptically. "I shall even manage to skulk about Lady Roxbury's gardens all evening without being taken up by her gamekeepers."

"Let us hope that another individual will not be as fortunate," Wessex responded.

No one shall be murdered at Mooncoign. That determination provided Sarah with a certain fortitude during the hours that followed her conversation with Wessex. Dinner had been set forward an hour to give all the guests time to dress themselves suitably for the *bal masque*, and forty-five covers were laid in the Main Hall. Dame Alecto had returned from her mysterious afternoon absence and reassured Sarah that all would go well that evening, and indeed it had.

As if strengthened in her role by the expectations of her guests, Lady Roxbury presided over the table easily, falling as if by long practice into the character of witty and autocratic Marchioness.

The table-talk turned upon the recent betrothal of the Prince of Wales to Princess Stephanie Julianna of Denmark, a move that Prince Jamie's father hoped would end Danish neutrality and deny Beast Bonaparte a northern staging area for an invasion of England and Scotland.

"No nation, however much we value our sovereignty, must be allowed to conduct wholesale executions of its citizenry—much less behead its king. Still less may one nation be permitted to make all of Europe its empire, for in the natural checks and balances of nations and crowns are peace and freedom made," Victor Saint-Lazarre said.

After hearing Wessex's revelations, Sarah had arranged

to seat Saint-Lazarre upon her right hand at dinner, and had taken the opportunity to study him closely. A fair-haired, slender gentleman with blue eyes, Saint-Lazarre spoke words of peace and sense against the bloodbath that threatened to suck all Europe down into destruction.

"Indeed, sir—and is it true that the Corsican Tyrant is—as some would have him—an atheist?" the lady to Saint-Lazarre's right asked.

"He is worse than that," Saint-Lazarre replied. "He is a man who believes that he is the particular favorite of God, and chooses that there should be no one to gainsay him. In those lands where he rules he has driven the witches from their circles and the Fair Folk from their hills. In fact, he has banned the practice of the Art Magickal entirely."

There was a murmur of horrified disbelief around the table, and one woman reached slender fingers to touch the silver star that hung at her throat, as if to reassure herself that it was still there. But then talk turned easily to other matters, as foreign politics was not truly a matter of interest to the members of this company, save perhaps for Saint-Lazarre.

It was hard for Sarah not to warn Saint-Lazarre, or to search the faces of her guests for the mask of the assassin. But she must trust Wessex, or be willing to chart her course alone through the fearsome waters and treacherous shoals of this vast sea of uncertainty that threatened to drown her. At that prospect, even Sarah's iron resolve quailed. Anything was better than that. And Wessex had seemed so confident his plan would work—that the two of them could skulk among the revelers and take Saint-Lazarre's hopeful murderer just as hunters would take a fat deer. . . .

With the prospect of action, the fearsome voids in her memory seemed to close, or at least be covered over with laughter and talk, and Sarah was in high spirits indeed when she led the ladies from the table upon a general exodus to the dressing rooms, there to have the elaborate toilette of dinner removed and an even more outlandish garb substituted.

Sarah Cunningham regarded her reflection critically in her dressing-room mirror. Her light brown hair was elaborately dressed on the back of her head, with feathers and a rope of pearls braided through its strands. Her eyes were kohled and her cheeks were rouged, and a gilded mask— gaily painted and beaded in the fashion that the savages adorned their deer skins—waited to provide the finishing touch.

Her costume's overdress was sewn of thinnest buckskin, with fringe along the divided overskirt and all along the hem. Long tight sleeves puffed gently at the shoulders, and a long silk fringe was sewn in a line across the back, giving the effect of a cape. The petticoat, which showed in the front and at the hem, was of red silk with gilded passimenterie trim, and her dainty buckskin slippers were embroidered with colorful beads. A muslin stole, painted with barbaric designs and edged in squirrel fur, completed her costume. The modiste, who had come from London to add the finishing touches to the garment as it draped her illustrious client's body, had assured Lady Roxbury that her ladyship looked the very image of a wild Red Indian.

"Do I?" Sarah said cryptically, staring at the engraving in *Ackerman's Fashion Repository* that detailed the formal costume of the native race of England's far-distant American colony. A native sachem and his lady stood poised in the hand-colored engraving as though they might at any moment go for a saunter in Green Park. The Indian lady wore an outfit nearly identical to the one currently adorning Sarah's own person.

At heart Sarah suspected there was something wrong with this elegant image, though she could not fault Madame Francine's execution of the costume as portrayed in the engraving. And the famed modiste had been quite correct; the supple leather gown was indeed a very dramatic costume. Sarah thrust aside the last of her unease, and was prepared to descend to greet her guests when there was a tapping at the door to the dressing-room.

"See who it is," Sarah said to her abigail. Each time she gave an order it became easier: she seemed to more fully inhabit the life of the woman whose face she saw when she looked in the mirror.

A moment later, Dame Alecto Kennet entered.

"Dame Alecto," Sarah said, faintly surprised.

"I came to claim a moment of your time, Lady Roxbury," Dame Alecto said, smiling her faint imperturbable cat-smile.

"You are always welcome," Sarah said slowly. "But do you not dress for the ball? You need not wear a fantastical costume, of course—"

"I would be sadly out of place at such an entertainment," Dame Alecto said self-deprecatingly, "but I thank you for the thought. No, I have come to thank you for your indulgence of me these past several days and beg you will excuse me: my duties call, and I have been too long away from Bath. By your leave, I will take myself off this evening and spare your servants the work of finding room for me any longer."

"I am sure that if you desire to stay, it would be no trouble to me to accommodate you," Sarah said automatically. It was certainly odd for a guest to depart a houseparty in the middle of the night, though—so hints of overheard gossip among the servants told her—Dame

Alecto was known to be eccentric, and it was true that the Dowager Duchess wintered in Bath and might be supposed to miss her companion. But why should Dame Alecto leave now rather than tomorrow morning?

"Your manners are very pretty, my dear child, but your godmama would not thank you for pressing me to stay when she is wishing for my return. I did not wish to depart without wishing you well, and extending my best wishes for the success of your evening."

Was it Sarah's overheated imagination, or was there a double layer of meaning in Dame Alecto's voice?

"I admit I tarried here until I was quite certain you were entirely recovered from the shock you received in your accident," Dame Alecto went on. "And I am vain enough to ascribe much of your recovery to my own nursing. At any rate, I have left a batch of my cordial with your abigail, and if you continue to dose yourself with it, I make no doubt that you will outface the Season's challenges in the pink of health."

"I do hope so," Sarah said. She had swiftly learned that the Season as contemplated by the Marchioness of Roxbury was to be a busy one.

"Then we will see one another again soon," Dame Alecto said firmly, and on the heels of Sarah's automatic assent, took herself from the room.

How odd, Sarah thought—but it was a momentary consideration, swept away almost at once by the exercise of locating mask and fan and dance card, and arranging all these objects suitably about her ladyship's becostumed person. As she took herself off to Mooncoign's ballroom, Sarah gave no more thought to Dame Alecto.

Every window of the great house blazed with light this night; all the ground-floor rooms had been flung open to the Marchioness's guests, and rows of flaming torches warmed and illuminated the gardens as well. Sarah stood overlooking the ballroom that took up most of the West Wing's first floor. Curtains of blood-red velvet were drawn back to reveal windowpanes like a mosaic of black ice: within their frame the fugitive stars of torches illuminating the garden gleamed. Beeswax candles, dyed and perfumed, blazed out across the expanse of gilded and painted Chinese paper that covered what few walls the windows did not. The floor was black-and-white marble, patterned in a swirling knot that seemed to move of its own and was to overset more than one dancer this evening. Music sweet and fast filled the air from the velvet-draped dais where the Marchioness's own private orchestra, correct and slightly antique in powdered wigs and green-and-silver livery, bowed and blew like maddened automatons.

And for those who did not dance, there were side rooms open where cards, or punch, or even more hectic pleasures could be procured.

Will he come? Sarah pondered the question as she awaited the assassin as ardently as any woman might await a lover. She stood at the edge of a cluster of her guests; beside her was Saint-Lazarre's sister Isabelle, dressed as a French shepherdess. Despite the frivolous nature of her costume, Mademoiselle Saint-Lazarre was a quiet young woman who traveled with her brother out of necessity, not inclination, and did not interrupt Sarah's musings with idle chatter. The Marchioness of Roxbury's other guests were arriving; the music-master had looked to her before he began to play and Sarah realized it would also fall to her to lead the first figure of the evening.

At the thought, her head began to ache faintly, and she wished for the cordial that Dame Alecto had concocted for her. To distract herself, Sarah gazed about the ballroom, admiring the varied costumes her guests had chosen to wear this evening.

Here was a highwayman, deep-cuffed coat, tricorn, and pistols—Captain Stephen Price of the Royal Engineers, who had been her guest at dinner—there a noble of the Sun King's court—Saint-Lazarre; she had made sure to know what costume was his. Pharaohs, princesses, and playing cards; laurel-crowned Greeks and noble Romans filled her ballroom: this night, the Marchioness of Roxbury played hostess to the sun, the moon, and the stars.

The dancing was to begin at nine-thirty and it was nearly that now. Soon she must choose a partner with whom to lead out the first figure, but Sarah kept her eyes turned toward the staircase that led into the ballroom.

One of the curiosities of the house was that to enter the ballroom one ascended a staircase that took one halfway up the second story and passed through an archway to a landing where one appeared high above the ballroom, displayed to any spectators below as if upon a stage. Descent was accomplished by means of the six shallow steps that led to the ballroom floor. The whole arrangement guaranteed that every new arrival would be the center of attention at least once during the evening. A Roman general descended the stairway at the moment; he wore a scarlet loo-mask and carried a crested helmet beneath his arm. His crimson cape billowed behind him as he reached the last step and made his way toward Sarah.

"Wessex!" Sarah had recognized him only at the last minute. He should have looked ridiculous in such outlandish garb, but his stern expression saved him from such a fate. As she spoke his name, he made a leg and sketched her an elaborate bow.

"As you see, madame. Dare I hope that it is I you will choose for the inestimable honor of the first dance?"

Preoccupied by the knowledge that a murderer was

skulking in the shrubbery, Sarah had thus far resisted the blandishments of all the precipitous gallants who had begged to be allowed to write their names in her dance card. The sound of Wessex's mannered drawl sparked irritation. The man was far too self-assured. And while she could not recall ever having wished to marry him, the haste with which he had repudiated their betrothal irked her, as did the ease with which he contemplated murder. . . .

"Perhaps," Sarah snapped, unfurling her Indianpainted fan with a snap. She wanted to ask him about the assassin, but with so many people around, it wasn't possible for them to have any private words.

"I shall live in hope," Wessex murmured. "Allow me to felicitate you, Lady Roxbury, upon the . . . startling originality of your costume."

Though the words were spoken in tones of the deepest gravity, there was something about the set of Wessex's mouth, the glint of the black eyes behind the mask. . . .

"I chose it with the greatest of care," she announced, though in truth Sarah could not recall having seen the outfit before this evening, and something in her heart told her that it was not, despite the modiste's claims, an accurate representation of the native dress in the wild Americas. "I am excessively fond of it."

"And my admiration of it transcends my poor ability to express my feelings," Wessex responded. "But your guests, as you see, are ravenous for dancing, so if you would deign to oblige me—"

And so it was that Sarah, nearly without knowing how she did it, led off her ball with the Duke of Wessex.

Across the black-and-white floor, Saint-Lazarre was dancing with Lady Elizabeth Perivale, who was rail-thin and hoydenish. The one good thing about dancing, Sarah realized, was that the activity granted one a larger measure of privacy than did standing still. Though there would be waltzing later, for propriety's sake the ball began with a country dance, whose elaborate stately figures had not changed much from the court dances of Charles II.

"Will he be here?" Sarah demanded.

"Count upon it, ma'am—no assassin can resist a masquerade ball," Wessex replied.

But as the hour crept toward midnight, Sarah found herself almost wishing the so-far-absent assassin would make his appearance. She could not imagine how it was that everyone thought these affairs so appealing—for herself, Sarah found it monstrously flat. Lady Roxbury had attended so many balls since her first Season; perhaps that was *why* she found this supposed entertainment so very dull?

No matter; it still would not do for her to retreat to the library with a good book. But having spent the last two hours dancing with all who had claimed her—Wessex having made himself not-so-mysteriously absent as soon as the first quadrille had ended—Sarah was now weary enough to feel that she had earned the right to seek quieter pursuits. When Saint-Lazarre left the dancers to seek out the relative quiet of one of the side rooms, Sarah followed stealthily, catching the tail end of the conversation just as she arrived.

"Though it is true that England is a Christian realm, King Henry turns a blind eye to white witchcraft in his dominion, following his great-grandfather's example. The witches of England worked hard to place Charles II on his rightful throne, and his descendants have not forgotten," a man's voice said.

"And it is also true that your farms and flocks have prospered since you have become freer in your covenant with the Oldest People, but how can your prosperity excuse your blindness to others' misfortune?" she heard Saint-Lazarre say.

The salon had been reserved for smoking, and a blue haze hung heavily on the air, though the windows were open to the gardens beyond. There were half a dozen men present, including both Captain Price and Saint-Lazarre, their lavish masquerade costumes lending a freakish air of unreality to the talk. Sarah paused just outside the doorway to listen.

"You mean that we do not open our borders to every hellgrammite that seeks to cross them with a tale of woe as his passport?" a man dressed as Scaramouche said. "Saint-Lazarre, no man is more sensible to the troubles upon the Continent than I, but England must look to her own cares first. It is our gold that keeps Prussia and Austria in the field, do not forget."

Saint-Lazarre made some reply, but Sarah ceased to listen to him, for she saw faint movement just beyond the long windows, in the gardens below. And while it was true that her gardens were open to all this night, there was something furtive about that movement that set all Sarah's hunter's instincts a-tingle.

It took her only moments to make her way from the house unobserved and to reach the garden. The garden was another thing she did not seem to remember—almost automatically Sarah rubbed her head—but the architect's drawings had been hung upon the wall in one of the salons and Sarah had studied them, fascinated, for several minutes as she waited to go in to dinner. She ran quickly down the bank of lawn and across the apron of white stones, trying to hold in her mind the place in the garden where she'd spotted the stealthy movement.

Where was Wessex? Sarah felt unreasonably enough that this was *his* assassin, so he ought to be here to deal with it. As a party of revelers passed her—a tall redhead, a blonde woman in a costume that could charitably be described as exiguous, and a black-haired man with turquoise eyes dressed as a brighter buccaneer—Sarah shrank back into the shadows, congratulating herself on the fact that her costume was not all gold gauze and tinsel ribbons. It might look foolish, but it made it easy enough to blend into the shadows, especially in the dark. As soon as the threesome had passed around the corner—the lady apparently being possessed of a strong desire to see the ornamental water, and the gentlemen being nothing loathe to indulge her—Sarah continued on her way. She was just opposite the first-floor balcony that let out from the smokers' room when she heard a small noise behind her—the unmistakable sound of a trigger being cocked.

It had taken Wessex several hours to satisfy himself that the danger, whenever it came, would not come from within Mooncoign. Fortunately Saint-Lazarre had been a hunted man for many years—the price on his head was the staggering sum of ten thousand gold *napoleons*—and knew better than to parade himself as a tempting target for opportunistic would-be patriots. He had taken care to keep himself in the midst of crowds all evening, leaving Wessex free to spend his own energies on searching for the killer.

It was close to midnight: the full moon burned at midheaven, turning the sky from black to deepest blue and bathing the whole garden in misleading silvery light. For the thousandth time, Wessex pondered the possibility that deMorrissey's information might have been wrong: mistaken, or planted in such a way that deMorrissey had become an unwitting dupe. But where was the profit in that? Talleyrand already knew he had opponents in the Shadow Game; why expend such effort to neutralize one of King Henry's secret agents, especially when Talleyrand did not know which would be sent? No, it was simpler to believe that deMorrissey's warning was the unvarnished truth.

Now all Wessex had to do was find the man who had come to kill Saint-Lazarre.

Wessex stood upon the terrace that ran the length of the central wing of the great house. Saint-Lazarre was in one of the rooms behind him; Wessex wished he'd had enough forenotice to be able to garb himself in a costume that matched Saint-Lazarre's, then shook his head regretfully. There was no use brooding over the impossible. Better to concentrate on the job at hand: Talleyrand's political killer.

The ballroom was on the floor above, and through its open windows Wessex could hear the playing of the orchestra. The curtains fluttered constantly in the uprush of escaping heat, making the light that poured out over the garden flicker as if Mooncoign were burning. A scrap of woman's laughter drifted up to him, some happy reveler braving the heavy April dews in search of pleasure. He hoped that Koscuisko didn't trip over her. Wessex's partner was out there somewhere with a brace of pistols, a saber, and an ingenious line of blarney. And the Polish Hussar was Wessex's only backup. Foolish to attempt to protect a target with only two men, but at least they had the advantage of knowing where the assassin must go.

As he stared out over the garden, Wessex saw a flash of movement among the ornamental box-hedges. Someone was out there, someone who was moving much too fast and deliberately to be one of the party-goers. Without a moment's thought, Wessex tossed his Roman helmet aside and flung himself down the steps in hot pursuit. His long cloak fluttered behind him like the wings of a giant bat for a few moments before it caught upon some projection and tore free with a wrench.

The grass beneath his feet was slippery with damp, and Wessex gave swift thanks that his costume had allowed him to wear his riding boots. The convolutions of the ornamental plantings confounded him; Wessex turned the corner and found a dead end.

When he went to retrace his steps, the flitting figure was no longer in sight, but he had seen which way it had gone. Stepping carefully through the flower-beds—lest the crunch of his boots upon the gravel walk betray him— Wessex began stalking his quarry. As he moved, he began the process of extracting his pistol from its concealment behind his breastplate.

Firearms were chancy things; though Wessex would carry a cocked and charged pistol as readily as he would carry a lighted *bombarde*, he'd had little choice this evening but to charge his pistols before he dressed. The clicking sound as he eased the hammer back was loud in his ears. If the hammer fell now the pistol would discharge, sending a round lead ball the size of a cherry through the nearest solid surface with potentially lethal results.

He could see a figure up ahead, standing motionless in the moonlight. It was with a small pang that he recognized her.

Sarah, Marchioness of Roxbury.

Her memories might be temporarily mislaid, but with heart and bone and sinew Sarah Cunningham knew the deadly sound of a rifle being cocked. She froze where she was.

"A moment more, mam'selle, to stand where you are,

and I will bodder you no more, me." His voice held an unfamiliar accent, as unlike Saint-Lazarre's cultured French as black bread was unlike macaroons.

Sarah looked up toward the terrace, and to her horror saw Saint-Lazarre standing in the doorway of the smoking room, framed in the candlelight. The ice-blue satin of his costume made him a perfect target in the moonlight. In a moment he would step out onto the terrace with his companions, and the assassin would fire.

"Please don't do this," Sarah said desperately. Where was Wessex?

"Do no' worry, mam'selle," the assassin said. "It is no' your jewels nor your virtue dat I seek. One moment, and I shall be gone from your life, eh?"

"You cannot kill an innocent man," Sarah said. The conversation was beginning to seem slightly surreal to her. Of course the assassin could kill Saint-Lazarre. Innocent men died every day.

"But I mus'," the assassin said simply. "I 'ave been paid. But I mus' also ask myself, how is it dat you know so much of my business, eh?"

Saint-Lazarre hesitated in the doorway, still in shadow. It was not a clear shot, but perhaps the assassin wouldn't mind. There was a step on the gravel, and Sarah felt a hand upon her shoulder.

"Per'aps I mus' ask you to tell me."

Sarah turned to face him.

The assassin was a raffish, unshaven, disreputable-looking man in a moleskin coat, his uncombed chestnut hair falling into his eyes, but in one hand he held a gleaming Baker rifle by its black-oiled barrel. The Baker was the darling of the Riflemen and the terror of their enemies; though just as temperamental as Brown Bess herself, the Baker was accurate at more than three times the standard-issue Army musket's range. If the man knew how to use it, there was no possibility he could miss his shot.

"You an' Gambit, *ma chere belle*, we mus' 'ave words."

Smiling, the assassin laid the barrel of his gun upon her shoulder, staring into Sarah's eyes. In a moment he would fire. Sarah gathered herself to stop him.

But something else stopped him first.

"I daresay that I am not in your league, but I can shoot the pips out of a playing card at ten yards with one of these, and you are a deal closer," Wessex drawled. His speech was accompanied by the unmistakable sound of a pistol-cock.

Even at that moment, the rifleman tried to make his shot. There was a devastating percussion beside Sarah's head, but the assassin had not had time to aim and the ball went wild. She grabbed for the rifle, staggering backward when it came easily into her hands. An expert could make the Baker fire three rounds a minute, but the assassin had not had the chance to reload and the rifle was now useless to him.

Sarah staggered under the gun's awkward length as Wessex dashed past her, a fantastic figure in crimson and tinsel, following the assassin. She darted a glance up toward the terrace; it was filled with revelers, all now pointing down into the garden and shouting.

Sarah flung the rifle down and ran.

The only consolation was that Koscuisko must have heard the shot. Wessex did not know whether Saint-Lazarre had been injured; the killer—Wessex had heard him name himself Gambit—had not had time to aim, but Wessex had seen musket-balls do freakish things in his time. Taking Gambit alive would be what paid for all.

In minutes they had passed beyond the compass of the formal garden and its torches and into the darkness beyond, and still Gambit ran, though he must know now that his capture was inevitable. Roxbury would raise the hue and cry—the local Justice of the Peace was probably her guest tonight—and the whole county would be out, foot and horse, searching for him. Gambit could not escape.

Unless he had allies in the area willing to hide him.

Wessex was beginning to flag, and Gambit ran on toward the trees, fleet as a deer, though the distance between them had closed. Wessex still held his pistol in his hand, though by now all the powder had probably shaken from the pan. He might as well be carrying a club.

A club.

Wessex stopped. Gambit began to pull away from him. Wessex tossed the pistol in his hand up into the air, grabbed it by the barrel, and threw it like a belaying pin. The pistol struck the fleeing assassin between the shoulders, knocking him to his knees.

As he pulled himself to his feet, scrabbling in his clothes for a knife, an apparition on horseback appeared out of the shadow of an enormous oak. It was towering—monstrous, with a misshapen form and vast arcing wings that rasped against an overhanging branch with a sound like skeletal fingers. Gambit screamed.

Illya Koscuisko regarded him with bright interest, his saber drawn and pointing at the assassin's throat.

"Where the devil *were* you?" Wessex gasped in exasperation. He dropped to his knees, panting. The ridiculous breastplate and kilt of his centurion costume galled him everywhere.

"Finding his horse," Koscuisko said. His gaze wavered from the man at his horse's feet. "And we have company!" he added gaily.

Wessex staggered to his feet and turned to confront Sarah, who had been running with her skirts rucked up well past her knees but—seeing the horseman—had allowed them to drop to a slightly more respectable altitude. Her costume had fared as badly as Wessex's had; her high headdress of plumes and pearls had come askew, shedding its feathers, and she'd lost one slipper, her fan, and her stole.

"What are you doing here?" Wessex demanded.

"I *live* here!" Sarah retorted ungraciously. "And this man tried to *shoot* one of my guests!"

"I say we leave him to her," Koscuisko suggested. Wessex's mouth quirked. The situation was already preposterous, and the chit's absurd indignation only made things more laughable. He glanced at Gambit. He, at least, seemed to take the Marchioness's flash of temper seriously.

"Perhaps we should," Wessex said, matching Koscuisko's tone. "I dare say we can find a rope here about somewhere, and find a magistrate who will put the seal of approval upon the thing."

"Oh, now, Captain, you nevair do dat to Gambit," Gambit said coaxingly.

Wessex's eyes narrowed. In some circles he was known as Captain Dyer; was Gambit's use of the title pure chance—or had he been the true target of this trap all along?

"Who are *you*?" Sarah demanded, staring up at the fantastically garbed figure on horseback. Koscuisko doffed his shako and bowed low over his horse's withers, his braids swinging forward at the gesture, for all the world as if he were in a Piccadilly drawing-room.

"Illya Koscuisko, ma'am, and very much at your service." He smiled engagingly, and to Wessex's secret relief, Sarah smiled back. Straightening from his bow and sheathing his saber, Koscuisko dismounted from his horse and began to tie the assassin's hands behind him. The man's eyes glittered ferally, but he made no move to resist.

"Koscuisko's by way of being a friend of mine. Harmless, I assure you," Wessex added.

Sarah made a quick face of disagreement before looking back in the direction of the house. The orchestra's music could still be heard faintly in the distance, and the more adventurous sparks of the company were already in the gardens searching for the lone gunman. It was only a matter of minutes before they traced him and the others here.

"We must get him out of here," she said.

"Precisely our dearest ambition," Wessex said.

"His horse is back there in the spinney," Koscuisko added. "He's no Hirondel, but he should serve to get us away."

"Good."

Koscuisko tossed Wessex a bundled-up greatcape from the back of his saddle and Wessex swirled it about himself, covering his garish costume. He pushed Gambit roughly ahead of him; Koscuisko swung up onto his horse again, and in a moment the three figures had vanished into the night as if they'd never been there at all.

Well, really, Sarah thought inadequately, staring after them. She was not entirely certain of what she should feel; certainly arresting Saint-Lazarre's would-be murderer was the most important thing, but did Wessex constantly have to treat her as if she were an annoying encumbrance to be shed as quickly as possible? If not for her, the assassin would have succeeded, and Saint-Lazarre would be dead. . . .

As she brooded, staring at the oak, Sarah realized she was not alone. There was someone right in front of her, standing with his back pressed against the trunk, so still that Sarah could nearly believe that he had been there all along and she had just missed seeing him. For one brief final instant she tried to convince herself that the new-comer was one of the party-goers, and then, helplessly, surrendered to belief in the evidence of her eyes.

For the man was as small as a child—Sarah, no gian-tess, was fully a head taller than he. He was dressed in a sort of short deerskin toga, and his skin was stained dark in a dappled pattern that almost exactly matched the pat-tern of the moonlight through the trees. Around his throat he wore a torque of pure gold, with terminals of amber carved in the shape of acorns. His hair was long, and had leaves carefully braided into it, giving him a foliate mane that added to the camouflage effect.

He was barefoot, and carried no weapons that Sarah could see. But his eyes alone were enough to make anyone wary of him. They were as brilliant as open water in moonlight, and beneath their compelling gaze Sarah found herself completely incapable of moving.

"Sarah.. . . ." His voice was like the rustling of the wind through trees. "You do not belong here. Why have you come?"

Sarah could not have answered that question even if she had been able to speak. Suddenly she felt strongly that she did not belong at Mooncoign at all—but if she did not belong here, where else could she possibly belong?

As she struggled with that question, the stranger stepped closer, and laid his cool fingers upon Sarah's brow. Even in the chill of an April night she could smell a strange green scent wafting from his skin, bitter and sweet together.

"A summoning, that you may take the place of one who can no longer aid us," the fairylord decided. "You have come in her place to aid the land, though you will draw no health from it until you truly bind yourself to this realm's destiny. Beware, Mooncoign's lady!"

The creature's words had filled her with a thousand questions, but now, as Sarah filled her lungs to ask them, she had the odd feeling of rousing from a dream, though she had been fully conscious the entire time.

And the fairylord was gone.

The Fair Folk . . . she had heard them spoken of so casually this evening, though the very thought of them seemed strange to her. Was *that* what she had seen? And if so, why?

You do not belong here, he had said.

And Sarah had the terrible feeling he was right.

8

The Gilded Vixen (Cornwall, April 1805)

❊ Elsewhere in England, a few hours before His Grace of Wessex got his man and the Marchioness of Roxbury received such distressing intelligence, an interview of some importance was taking place.

At least, it was a matter of importance to one of the parties involved. The other seemed to be giving it very little of her attention.

"Now see here, my girl—" As if sensing that his tone was too martial, the Earl of Ripon broke off and summoned his rather meager resources of charm.

Richard Highclere was the Earl of Ripon, seventeenth in his line, and had succeeded to the honors and dignities of the earldom some twenty-four months before, following the death of his widowed elder brother, Guildford, on the hunting field. That brother Guildford's late wife had seen fit to present to the world only one chit of a girl accounted for Richard's sudden rise to consequence, and it might naturally be supposed that he would enfold the unwitting agent of this rise in an embrace of philoprogenitive loving kindness.

This was, however, not the case. For the new Earl of Ripon, having risen so high, looked to rise higher still . . . if the proper sort of marriage could be made by the proper person.

"Meriel," he said, cozeningly. Like his father and elder brother, Ripon was dark and heavy-featured, with something of a mastiff look about him. Though he had married to his family's best advantage some dozen years ago, Ripon and his Countess had no children. The girl he was now addressing was the family's current white hope for its future.

Meriel Jehanne Greye Bulleyn Highclere regarded her uncle and guardian with a steady blue gaze. She was seventeen years of age, and had the portrait-perfect match to her late mother's cream-and-midnight coloring. Though her father had been in his grave these two years and more, Meriel still wore the black of deep mourning, as much through the new Earl's indifference to her wardrobe as through any wish of her own.

"Now, child, don't take on so. You will like London— yes, and you will like Jamie as well. The two of you will make a famous match—"

"And there will be dresses, and sweetmeats, and places for your uncles at Court," a mocking voice sang out behind them.

The Highclere family had been a numerous one: in addition to the present Earl, there were four more brothers: two at present serving with the Peninsular Army, and the youngest in holy orders in the north of England. The remaining Highclere brother—next in age to the Earl himself—lounged in the doorway.

Despite his riding clothes, Geoffrey Highclere looked much as if he had just stepped from a pattern-card at a

Bond Street haberdashers. Only a claret-colored vest marred the monochromatic perfection of his black-and-white garb, and though his posture was the very image of indolence, he tapped a silver-handled riding whip against his boot with every evidence of irritated impatience.

Geoffrey was as blond as Ripon was dark, and spent his days gambling away his small allowance and running up a shocking array of bills with any tradesman foolish enough to extend him credit. Despite his elder brother's constant insinuations that an army commission would be an unparalleled opportunity to gain both renown and loot, Geoffrey remained stubbornly uninterested . . . and oddly in funds.

It was perhaps this quality of resiliency that had caused the Earl of Ripon to include his younger brother in his plans once those bright dreams had begun to blossom into something darker. A plot needed plotters, and Geoffrey Highclere had Prince Jamie's ear.

"Geoffrey," Ripon greeted his younger brother. Geoffrey sketched a mocking bow. "I thought the Court had returned to London."

"The court, yes, but the young prince remains in Scotland. For some reason he is not pleased with this Danish betrothal—" here Geoffrey shrugged, indicating his own incuriosity about the prince's objections "—and still less pleased that the wedding is being put forward to the fall. And how fares our little Madonna?"

"Don't blaspheme," Ripon said absently, then: "I had not thought the Prince's wedding would be so soon."

"Our glorious King desires Danish harbors for his Fleet, and Danish troops for the Alliance. A Danish princess for the Heir, then, follows naturally—if he does not marry into Denmark, after all, there are few enough royal houses who would have a Protestant prince—"

"A heretic prince," Ripon corrected, adding as if by

rote, "heir to a realm of pagans, apostates, and worse."

"—and the King will not indulge his sister's whims by marrying his house into the German states again this generation," Geoffrey finished. "So, once the treaty—I mean, the match—is made, it is best to seal the matter as soon as possible, before Bonaparte redraws the map of Europe once again."

He shoved himself away from the doorframe and sauntered into Ripon's study, drawing off his black riding gloves as he did so. Without asking his brother's leave, Geoffrey crossed to the table beneath the window and poured himself a large whiskey from the decanter standing there. The gelid gunmetal light of a Cornish spring shone full upon his face, turning his ethereal beauty from that of an archangel to that of Lucifer.

"At any rate, Jamie is at Holyrood, and so you find me here until such time as he deigns to grace Buck House and Town with his so-charming presence. We are not on such terms, he and I, to allow me to command him for my own comfort—he pays more attention to that damned valet Brummell of his!" Geoffrey added.

"You will have to try harder to gain his confidence," Ripon said quietly. His words were for Geoffrey, but his gaze was fixed unwinkingly on his niece.

The year might be 1805, but the memory of the great families of the realm was long . . . and those who had not changed their religion at the eighth King Henry's behest had found themselves in the minority in the acquiescent England that Charles II created upon his Restoration. England was now a tolerant kingdom, though a Protestant one, and the power that the Catholic lords had briefly wielded in Bloody Mary Tudor's day had been on the wane ever since.

"Prince James is not a strong-minded young man," Ripon said, staring at Meriel. "He is simple to manage—"

"If you say so, brother dear," Geoffrey murmured, addressing himself to his whiskey.

Determinedly ignoring his brother, Ripon continued to address his silent niece in a voice of portentous meaning, "And when the Prince takes a bride, she will be sure that her control extends throughout his household, eliminating undesirable influences—and returning England to the rule of the Old Religion of Holy Mother Church."

Meriel did her best to meet her Uncle Richard's gaze, but after a moment her own faltered, and she looked down, staring at her entwined fingers. She had known her uncle schemed—he had dropped enough hints during the past twelve-month that something dramatic was afoot—but never in all her seventeen years had it entered her head that she might be made a pawn in an intrigue of this magnitude! The Highcleres had always been intolerant of practitioners of the New Learning, as the Protestant sects had been called when they first sprang up, and Meriel had been taught to despise heretics and pagans just as she had been taught her Latin, her Greek, and her catechism.

But in the Old Earl's time, this enmity had been tacitly understood to be a private matter, not to be paraded upon the public stage. In the normal way of things, Meriel would have married into one of the other Catholic families of England and occupied her life with scholarship and childbearing.

But when her father had died and Uncle Richard had become the Earl of Ripon and head of the family, he was not so sanguine about the earldom's eclipse as Meriel's own papa had been. Now Meriel's beauty—which as a proper young lady she had been taught to modestly disregard, for vanity was a grievous sin—was suddenly a matter of great importance, for it was the lure by which the Earl of Ripon expected to entangle a prince.

"You will not fail me, child—will you?" Ripon was demanding of her now. "Once the ring is upon your finger, we can call an end to this useless war with France. The King is old, and his only son a useless fribble, ripe for rule by his betters. A Catholic England is no threat to Imperial France, but her natural ally—"

"Anyone would think the chit understood what you were saying—are you so desperate for an audience as all that, dear brother?" Geoffrey sneered. "You might as well talk to a parrot as to a girl—she cannot possibly have any interest in your plans. Can you, niece?" he asked sweetly.

"No, Uncle Geoffrey," Meriel whispered to her clenched hands.

"But you'll do your part?" Ripon insisted. "If I am to take you to London and put you in the Prince's way, I will not have your mouse-hearted missishness spoiling everything I have worked so long to bring about."

"Oh, she'll do what she's told," Geoffrey said, turning away from the window and slapping his crop against his high black riding boot. He glanced once at Meriel, and smiled. "I shall see to it."

In the spring, no one but the foolish and the desperate ventured forth upon the highways of England with any expectation of arriving anywhere at all, for the surfaces of even the main roads were neatly divided between axle-breaking stones and horse-crippling mud, rendering anything more than the passage of a rider on horseback a matter extremely problematical.

But possible . . . with patience, planning, and several good heavy coaches.

Jocasta Sybella Honoria Masham Dyer, Dowager Duchess of Wessex and grandmother of the present Duke, had no interest in the beauties of the English countryside. When her son Andrew was alive, she had endured the country for his sake, but when Andrew had vanished in France thirteen years ago, she had closed Wessex Court and begun to divide her time between London and Bath.

The practice of many years had enabled the Dowager Duchess to determine the earliest moment in the spring that the roads might be practicably navigated, and as soon as her lady-companion had returned from her errand in Wiltshire, Her Grace of Wessex had set forth for London. A week's hard traveling had seen the Dowager Duchess settled into the family's cramped and ancient townhouse that stood on Knightrider Street, within the shadow of St. Paul's and the sound of the Thames.

Although the word "Tenebrae" was picked out in letters of age-blackened silver above the lintel, the house's name was Dyer House; it had belonged to the Dyer family long before the dukedom had. Through the years, fashionable addresses had changed; Dyer House was almost within the City, and very far from Oxford Street and the western expansion that had made the open fields between Soho and Tyburn into the new resort of Society. But Dyer House had belonged to the family since time out of mind, and the Dyers were slow to change customs that suited them. Though the late Duke—Wessex's father, Andrew—had been a provident enough businessman that his son was now landlord to much of Piccadilly, the Dowager Duchess had resisted all blandishments to have a London residence built for her upon one of the spacious new squares. And so, though it lacked a few days of May, the Holland covers had been removed from the formidable Jacobean furnishings and the brightly polished knocker had been hung upon the door; the Dowager Duchess of Wessex was officially in residence.

*   *   *

"Where *is* the boy?" the Dowager demanded of her companion.

Dame Alecto Kennet smiled fondly at her mistress. Alecto had served as the Dowager's eyes and ears ever since Her Grace of Wessex had retired from the world— as well as performing those tasks from which the Dowager's rank barred her—and she was quite used to the older woman's moods.

"I'm certain he'll be here as soon as he feels himself presentable," Dame Alecto chided gently. "He must call upon the Horse Guards, after all, as well as speaking with those other gentlemen he thinks you to be in ignorance of."

The Dowager Duchess of Wessex laughed sharply. "Between the Horse Guards and the White Tower, I wonder that I shall see Wessex any day before the Season is over. Still, we must put the best face we can upon the thing, and it would be a kindness to let him know of our plans. Alecto, you have spent time with the girl—will she do?"

"I could not spend so much time with her as I should like," Dame Alecto responded slowly, gathering her thoughts, "for when Wessex arrived, I did not like him to see me, lest he wonder what I did there."

"Yes. It would have caused questions," the Dowager agreed dryly. "My grandson asks too many questions, and this one may still arise, if the matter of your visit comes up in conversation. . . ."

"Or if Dr. Falconer pursues his suspicions about Lady Roxbury's so-convenient recovery. The disobliging man attended Roxbury—he knew she was dying," Dame Alecto said. "Now Dr. Falconer suspects Roxbury made an unnatural bargain to save her life."

"As any might, who had the connections to do so," the

Dowager said. "Dr. Falconer can do nothing to hinder us, for he cannot possibly suspect the truth—that the Roxbury he knew is indeed dead."

The Dowager sighed, and pushed away the letter she was composing at the tiny chinoiserie writing desk that occupied one corner of her cluttered sitting-room. The Dowager was something of a jackdaw, and the room was crammed with exotic mementos of friends' trips abroad.

"Poor child. She was my goddaughter, and I must admit that I did not do my duty there. But we do not have time to grieve over what cannot be changed," she added briskly. "The Marchioness of Roxbury is needed, and England will have her, by fair means or foul."

"I think it will be only a matter of time until the girl forgets her old life in the world from which we took her," Dame Alecto said slowly. "The cordial I have concocted for her will suppress her old memories, and every day she will be prompted with the details of Roxbury's life. Soon she will know its every detail as though it had always been her own."

"And she will have Wessex, and continue the line," the Dowager finished. Though her face was serene, there was a faint note of worry in her voice. "He must not oppose me in this—our families have planned this marriage since the girl was born; the Conynghams have always had close ties to the Stuarts, and King Henry will want Roxbury to support him when Princess Stephanie arrives—he will want Roxbury to help the Princess make her way in society, and Roxbury cannot be Princess Stephanie's chaperone unless she is, herself, married."

"So the Duke of Wessex must marry his Duchess—and soon," Dame Alecto said. "And pray that the Oldest People will forgive the substitution of one Roxbury for another."

"They must," the Dowager Duchess of Wessex said.

"We had no choice—not if the Throne is to be preserved."

They ought to take pity on a poor man, Wessex thought groggily, *and not let the sun off its leash so early in the morning.* He might, in fact, have successfully rejoined my lord Morpheus, had Atheling not chosen that moment to ever-so-discreetly make his presence known.

Atheling was His Grace's most superior and long-suffering manservant, who kept His Grace's Albany rooms precisely as they should be kept, and His Grace's wardrobe perfectly fit to embrace any occasion from a Royal Drawing Room to a night spent steeplejacking across the roofs of London Town.

In addition to those undeniable proficiencies, Atheling also rejoiced in a singularly remarkable absence of curiosity.

But despite such a sterling and acquiescent disposition, Atheling knew his duty when he saw it. And so, surveying his master in his master's disordered bed, Atheling coughed.

Rather than movement, there was a cessation of movement beneath the thick woollen blankets. Encouraged, Atheling essayed a slight clearing of the throat.

"Very well, Atheling," the mounded counterpane announced. "I'm awake." There was a creak of the bedstead, and his grace made his delinquent appearance.

The night had been long and the play had been deep; he and Koscuisko had returned to Town with the assassin known as Gambit—revealed, when all was said and done, to be a man called Charles Corday, born in the French colony of Louisiana, who despite his ragamuffin appearance was a confidential agent high in Talleyrand's councils. The partners had left Corday to Misbourne's tender

mercies and decided to celebrate their success; weeks of
sleeping in ditches and sheltering beneath hedgerows were
still vivid enough in Wessex's mind to make the hells and
fleshpots of Town a powerfully seductive lure.

Wessex ran a hand through his hair, restoring it to as
much order as the current *mode* called for. He gazed down
at the bosom of his impeccable linen nightshirt as if he
could not precisely recall to mind the occasion upon
which he had donned such a garment, and then turned
his regard upon his valet with a levelness that was in itself
accusatory.

"Will Your Grace take tea or chocolate this morning?"
Atheling asked austerely. Wessex winced.

"My Grace will take an explanation of the *crise de coeur*
that causes you, my good Atheling, to cry the view halloo
through my bedchamber before two of the afternoon." An
unpleasant possibility took strong possession of his grace.
"I was not promised to anyone this morning, was I?"

"Indeed not, Your Grace; as Your Grace has often instructed me, I am to take measures to restrain Your Grace
from engaging himself to any party commencing before
the late afternoon. I shall heat the shaving water at once,
as Your Grace will wish to peruse the morning's post before breakfast."

His objective achieved, Atheling retreated from the
chamber. Unsatisfied curiosity finished the task of bringing
the young Duke to full wakefulness. *Now what could have
come in the post to warrant this display of amateur theatrics on
Atheling's part?* Wessex wondered.

Before he could arrive at any particular conclusion,
Atheling returned to the room with a basin and a can of
hot water, the case containing his grace's razors tucked
beneath one arm. Wessex swung his long legs out of bed
and reached for the dressing-gown laid ready to hand
upon the chair. He shrugged himself into it. Through the

open door to the dressing-room, a pier-glass caught slivered and angled impressions of the tall blond man with the swordblade face.

Atheling set the basin down upon the battered oak sideboard and placed the can beside it. He ladled a stoup of the water into a small bowl ready to hand, then labored soap and brush until the bowl was filled with stiff lather. When that was ready, Atheling poured the contents of the can into the waiting basin. Steam began to rise in opaque spirals, covering the mirror behind in a brief mist.

"If Your Grace will—"

"My Grace will not, Atheling. As you know." Wessex opened the case and picked up the razors.

It was an ongoing affront to Atheling's sense of fitness that his charge continued to insist upon shaving himself. All Atheling's pleas upon the subject were in vain, merely causing his grace to assure Atheling that Wessex dared not become used to Atheling's ministrations, lest he lose the barbering knack entirely and be thus forced to present himself at foreign courts unshaven.

Atheling believed none of this patent nonsense. He believed, merely, that his grace was obstinate, as his grace's father had been before him. On the other hand, such obstinacy was a character trait in which Atheling took secret pride, as only a most superior manservant could manage such a stubborn man.

When at last Wessex presented to his mirror and the world a clean-shaven countenance, he entered his dressing-room, where Atheling stood ready to assist him with such sartorial details as the rigging-out of a gentleman of fashion required.

The morning post, as yet, was nowhere to be seen. That, Wessex knew, would come with breakfast, and God help any man who attempted to remove things from what Atheling conceived to be their proper order.

So be it. His grace turned to matters of dress.

Contemplating an afternoon trot through Green Park, Wessex approved white doeskin inexpressibles and high-top oxblood Hessians with bullion tassels, the latter an exquisite product of Hoby's workroom. A shirt of dazzling white lawn, moderately pleated and ruffled, was eclipsed by a waistcoat of pale yellow Egyptian linen ornamented with buttons of Russian enamelwork that glimmered russet and scarlet against their demure backdrop. The cravat was a matter of some concern, but his grace favored a simple style and achieved it upon the first attempt.

Atheling cast an inquiring glance toward the repository of his grace's coats, only to be warned off with a small shake of the head. His grace would select his other accessories first, and with quick decision chose a watch, a fob, a dangling seal, and a small gold cravat pin, all of which were no more than the mere ornaments they seemed to be. He then slipped the ducal signet upon his finger and closed the shallow drawer with finality.

The choosing of a deep-pocketed coat of claret-colored superfine was almost an anticlimax, and indeed, Wessex regarded it only slightly. His sojourn with the Army had made him perhaps more cavalier about such matters of *tonnish* importance than his fellows.

Wessex turned a bleak eye upon the cabinet with its myriad niches, and for a brief fervent moment wished he were back with his men—fleas, bad water, chilblains, and all.

A discreet clearing of Atheling's throat called his grace back to himself.

"Breakfast, one supposes," said Wessex. "And the morning post at last."

His grace was not, customarily, a strong believer in breakfast, and if he had been he would certainly have, on this occasion at least, allowed the meal to wait upon the post.

With a strong cup of bitter chocolate at his elbow, and the prospect of buttered muffins in the not-too-distant future, his grace turned to the contents of the heaped silver salver with the keen interest of a hound on the scent.

The topmost letter, on lilac vellum insistently redolent of a lily-scent bordering upon the funereal, Wessex tossed unopened into the fire of sea-coals burning on the grate. He felt no compunction about doing this; Ivah only wrote to ask for money, and Wessex felt he had already subsidized her pleasures liberally enough. God knew a liaison with a woman of his own class was unthinkable, but there were limits to how far he would lower himself. Mrs. Archer was a good deal coarser than she had originally appeared in the social circles where she and Wessex had first met.

Wessex frowned over the matter momentarily, and then dismissed it. A parting gift, an intimation that the acquaintance would not bear furthering, would end the connection simply enough. His mind was already elsewhere as he turned to the next items.

Bills: from Tattersall's and Weston's, Asprey's and Talmadge's; from his cellarer, his tobacconist, his glovemaker. Wessex put them all aside, to be settled punctually at the quarter-day. The Duke of Wessex had an unaristocratic promptness about settling his accounts. Wessex's status as a player in the Game of Shadows meant his existence was at constant risk; he had no wish to burden his current heir—a scholarly and rather absent-minded cousin—with his debts.

If Wessex died without issue, that heir would inherit neither ducal debts nor ducal coronet; the ducal creation was entirely explicit that the title of Duke of Wessex might descend only through the direct line. But the family's earldom would continue, and the new Earl of Scathach would hardly mourn the omission of ducal honors; the earldom was both old and rich. The Scathach family seat, Lymondhythe, was nestled in the wild and beautiful Cheviot Hills, and his cousin and heir presumptive was already installed there by Wessex's own wish, not to be dislodged even if Wessex did manage in some unthinkable manner to produce an heir for the dukedom.

Wessex shook his head at the unwonted direction of his thoughts. There was something about wakening at odd hours that drove a man's mind to freakish fancies—that, and the recent unexpected meeting with his quondam betrothed. It was fortunate that Roxbury apparently had no more desire to lose her freedom than Wessex did to end it.

Now what was in this pile of paper that had so maddened Atheling?

Ruthlessly Wessex drove through the rest of the morning's post: cards of invitation to parties certain to be deadly dull; two thick bundles of letter that had come by hand after faring far in diplomatic pouches—

Ah. This was it. A faint sunny odor of orange blossom clung to the paper, just as it did to her clothes.

She did not write often, this remarkable woman who had been the center of Wessex's whole existence after his mother had died. When his unique gifts had called him to a wider stage, they had agreed that letters were very nearly pointless; he could not, for safety's sake, even hint to her of how he spent his days, and the circumscribed sphere in which she still moved would seem merely petty to him after his worldly journeyings. Instead, they chose to hold their feeling for one another a thing apart: not to buried in exchanges freighted with the minutiae of daily life, but to be savored on the rare occasions when they could be companionably together, as they had been before his father had followed his mother into Hades' chill kingdom.

Wessex paused on the verge of tearing open the letter from his grandmother.

Why should she write him here?

He had not been to Bath to spend Christmas with her; he had, in fact, been peculiarly elsewhere for Christmas. It was not their custom to announce their comings and goings to one another; in fact, though the billet had not been franked, placing her in Town, until this moment he had possessed every reason to suppose the Dowager Duchess to be residing in Bath, as was her unvarying custom during the winter months. In turn, it ought to have been impossible for her to direct a letter to his Albany rooms with any degree of certainty that he would receive the missive; Wessex had returned from France less than a week ago, and to his Town residence only last night.

Interesting. Interesting enough for Atheling to awaken him. Wessex tore open the packet and read his grandmother's letter carefully. His faint inquiring frown became a black glare of puzzlement and then a stare of stupefied horror as he read the brief missive first once, then twice.

The Dowager required his presence Thursday, at half-past two of the clock, for tea. There was no explanation for the request, extraordinary in its uniqueness, simply the unadorned summons.

And the Thursday she required him for was today.

"Atheling!" A spasm of sheer panic took momentary

possession of his grace. He rose to his feet, all thought of breakfast banished.

The manservant, still swaddled in the apron he donned to perform the more domestic of his duties, appeared in an instant.

"I have been mistaken," his grace said austerely. "This coat will not suit. And I shall not be riding today."

Sarah Conyngham, Lady Roxbury—which was to say, she reminded herself, Marchioness of Roxbury in her own right—gazed in exasperated amusement about the dressing-room of her London townhouse. Every available inch of the room was jammed with trunks, some of which hadn't been out of the Long Attic at Mooncoign since— so the servants had been happy to inform her—Sarah's grandmother's day.

Perhaps, Sarah thought, she had not adequately informed Knoyle of her destination. Perhaps the abigail had thought she was preparing her mistress for a journey to Timbucktoo.

It had been only three days since the masquerade ball at Mooncoign, but fortunately Sarah had not been forced to attempt to pack up an entire great household and shift it fifty miles north in that time. No, Lady Roxbury's annual move to Town had been on the servants' mind for many weeks, with many trunks, boxes, bundles, and packages sent forward at the first moment that the roads would permit.

Thus it had been easy enough on the morning following the ball, as soon as Sarah discovered that neither Wessex nor his companion Illya Koscuisko had delivered their prisoner to the County Magistrate nor returned to any house in the vicinity, to order her coach and depart for London *a l'instant.*

But the bumpy three-day trip to London in her own heavy coach had given Sarah time to consider the matter in more depth. Even if she did manage to find Wessex, what could she say to him? The man Gambit had undoubtedly already vanished into London's teeming thousands, no matter what fate Wessex had decreed for him. And whatever fate that might be, what did it matter to her?

That was the puzzle. Sarah had not been in the least enamored of Wessex upon their first or subsequent meetings, yet she felt a pressing need to see him again, though she could not precisely say why. She purely and simply felt an odd *compulsion* to be in his presence.

Odd, indeed. She had no fondness for the man, after all—and the Marchioness of Roxbury had no need to wait upon even the Duke of Wessex's pleasure!

Her feelings of uncertainty had been nearly banished in the excitement and frights of the evening of the ball and the bustle of removing to Town. Each day she grew more comfortable, more confident in her role as Lady Roxbury, and ceased to wonder at the strange blanks in her memory. Anything that she forgot, one of the servants happily supplied—as did her guests, each more eager than the last to finish her sentences for her.

So all was well.

Sarah regarded the toe of one sensible jean boot peeping from beneath the hem of her sober-colored morning dress. The stout grey-blue gown with its demure broidery of pimpernels worked upon the bodice was all very well for travel, but would not do as something in which to present herself before the dazzling flame of London Society and the glittering rowdiness of King Henry IX's Stuart Court.

Or even before her godmama.

The missive had been waiting when Sarah had arrived

at Herriard House. As new as Mooncoign was old, Herriard House stood far to the West in Picadilly, facing Hyde Park across Park Lane with a formidable Palladian *frontis* faced all in white marble. Behind it stood Grosvenor Square, and only a few minutes north was High Holborn, the road that ran between London and Oxford. From here Sarah could survey all of Society and could reign over that small insular kingdom with imperial dominion—providing always, of course, that Sarah took care not to alienate those even more powerful than she.

The Dowager Duchess of Wessex must certainly be counted among those potentates. Though Sarah's godmother had retired from Society upon the death of her son, she was still influential, and if she chose to oppose Sarah—

Oh, don't be a cloudhead, Sarah! The Dowager is your godmama; she has always been partial to you. Didn't she send Dame Alecto to you when you tangled your phaeton with the Bristol coach?

Didn't she?

But the rallying words failed to achieve their desired effect. Her memory remained frustratingly blank, and still weary from the rigors of the road—for her coach had arrived in London only a scant few hours before—Sarah picked up the billet of stiff, cream-colored vellum from her writing table and read it over once more.

"The Dowager Duchess of Wessex requests the favor of your presence at tea on Thursday, the 25th of April—"

Today.

At the appointed hour Wessex presented himself at Dyer House, alighting with formidable correctitude from a hired chaise, since his grace kept no carriage and would not stoop to the unpardonable solecism of presenting himself before his grandmother in his riding dress. The butler who opened the door to him was old and frail, a man who had grown old in the family's service—not as robust a party as the Duke could have liked to have seen guarding the portals of Dyer House. Nevertheless, His Grace gifted Langley with his greatcoat and curly-brimmed high-crowned beaver, flourished his amber-headed walking stick, and ascended to the first-floor parlor without comment.

Dyer House was dim even at midday. It took his grace a moment to see that there was someone besides Dame Alecto with the Dowager; another woman.

Then he recognized his grandmother's guest, and only long years of iron self-discipline allowed him to maintain a mask of well-bred composure. "Grandanne, Madame," Wessex said, bowing to both ladies.

Apparently not caring to conceal her feelings from him, Sarah, Marchioness of Roxbury, stared back at Wessex in horror.

"Ah," said the Dowager, "so here you are at last, Wessex. You are acquainted with Lady Roxbury, are you not? Yes, of course you are; you've been betrothed to her for—how many years is it now?" The Dowager paused, but neither Wessex nor Lady Roxbury found voice to enlighten her.

"Do sit down, Wessex, and I shall ring for Langley to bring us tea." The Dowager smiled.

Sarah could not refrain from glancing toward Dame Alecto, the Dowager's companion, as Dame Alecto sat inconspicuously in the corner of the Dowager's parlor. But Dame Alecto was as skilled at effacing herself as she was at being formidable, and Sarah was forced, willy-nilly, back into the conversation.

"I'm sure we shall all be looking forward to quite the

glittering Season," the Dowager was saying with determined obliviousness. "Especially with a Royal wedding to cap it at Christmastide."

"Princess Stephanie should sail in a month or so," Wessex agreed blandly. "I believe she lands in Scotland and heads to London by way of York."

In the half-hour since he had arrived, Sarah had come to dislike Wessex immensely for the easy facility with which he fielded each of the Dowager's conversational sallies; the man never seemed at a loss for words.

"Everyone will wish to entertain her," the Dowager said. "Even if Prince Jamie is not reconciled to the marriage, King Henry is much in favor of it, which will carry all. Naturally we shall invite her to your wedding ball; her attendance will set the seal on the King's approval of the match."

The rhythm of the conversation faltered and stopped dead as the for-once-nonplussed Duke of Wessex groped for a reply. Sarah, lulled by the cadence of a conversation she had not been participating in, was slightly slower to react, and when she realized what the Dowager had said, words failed her as well.

"I beg your pardon, Grandanne?" Wessex finally responded.

"Oh come now!" the Dowager answered imperturbably. "Nine years' engagement should be enough for any man—and you are three-and-thirty; it is high time that you married. There is just enough time to cry the banns and have you wed in June so that the celebration may not look *too* pointedly as if it is given for the Princess."

Wessex cast an expressionless look toward Sarah, who, oddly enough, found herself interpreting it as a desperate appeal for aid. But Sarah could not imagine what assistance she could be to him. Gardner and Knoyle had both spoken of Roxbury's betrothal to Wessex as something that was common knowledge, and what weight could the fact that Sarah found him a cold, unfeeling, hatchet-faced harlequin have in the face of Society's expectation?

"I do not choose to marry his grace," Sarah heard herself saying, as if from a great distance.

The remark ought to have pleased him—ungrateful man, he no more wished to marry than she did—but inexplicably Wessex cast a nettled glance in her direction and rose to his feet.

"It will not do, Grandanne," he said. "A childhood betrothal—who cares for that these days? Everyone knows that I have not been at pains to fix my interest with the Marchioness—"

"You were formally betrothed when the girl was sixteen; she was hardly a child then, or you either," his grandmother interrupted, adding ironically, "And everyone knows that you were very much in sight at Mooncoign this past week. I never thought you would be so behindhand, Wessex—stand up with the girl at Almack's; squire her about. There can be no lack of invitations once it is known that you are willing to accept them."

She might as well not have been in the room, Sarah realized. It was his grandmother with whom Wessex argued, not her.

"But I am not willing to accept them, Grandanne. A man in my station—leading my sort of life—has many things to think about besides becoming leg-shackled—"

"Yes," the Dowager riposted. "The getting of an heir to the dukedom, for one."

Wessex actually blushed, and stared fixedly at a point above Sarah's head. Sarah felt her heart beating faster: the two of them were about to carve up her future between them as if she were no one at all!

"I am not getting married," Sarah said again, louder. "To the Duke of Wessex—or to anyone else."

"But whyever not, child?" the Dowager asked mildly, able to hear Sarah when it suited her purpose to do so.

Such a speciously-reasonable question seemed to turn Sarah's brain to jelly. She stared at the Dowager, barely able to keep from goggling.

"Because it would seem most peculiar for a wedding to take place without the bridegroom in attendance," Wessex said brittlely.

"Or the bride," Sarah retorted hotly.

"But my dears, I have the guest list for the wedding breakfast already made up," the Dowager said, still in those same mild uninvolved tones. This time Wessex did not answer her, instead sweeping up his gloves and stick from the side table. "Grandanne, Your Ladyship. I bid both of you a very good day." He bowed with formidable correctness, turning and striding from the room before either of them could respond.

"Ah," said the Dowager, obviously pleased. "I think that went rather well, don't you, my dear? Men are like colts; they must be shown the harness and allowed to bolt from it a time or two before one can safely buckle them in."

9

The Prince Commands

❀ The Palace of St. James was located between St. James Park and Green Park, just south of Westminster and the Houses of Parliament, with Buckingham House to its east and the sprawling buildings of the Horse Guards on its western side. Its parks and lakes had been the resort of three centuries of England's royal house, ever since King Henry VIII had taken over the site of St. James Hospital to build his new palace here. St. James's red brick walls had watched over the martyred Charles I on his last night on earth, and ever after, the Stuart line had defiantly held court within those same red walls.

Though time had seen the erection of grander edifices to house the peripatetic Stuart line, nothing had supplanted St. James's splendor in the hearts of England's monarchs. Swans and peacocks strutted through its grounds, fashionable ladies paraded, and farmers still drove their cattle through its square to the shambles in London's West End. The madness upon the Continent did not penetrate here; within these precincts, it seemed a grave insanity to believe that the people could ever—again—rise up and butcher their rightful rulers in a senseless self-willed iconoclasm.

But in France, the people had. And the repercussions of that carnage extended even here, to this stately palace under an English heaven.

In a very grand apartment in the east wing of the Palace of St. James, the heir to the conjoined kingdoms of England, Scotland, Ireland, and Wales was dressing for an audience with his father.

"Oh, not that one, Brummell—Papa does not care for it by half!"

James Charles Henry David Robert Stuart, Prince of Wales and Duke of Gloucester—Prince Jamie to his friends, who were many—was nineteen years old, with the chestnut hair and flashing eyes that were evidence of his Stuart and Plantagenet ancestors. He was the youngest of five children, the heir and only boy, and the hopes of more than England reposed in him.

Though his father, King Henry, was hale and hardy, and might be expected to reign for many decades yet, Prince Jamie had ambitions to take his own place upon the world stage, and make his mark upon the new century. He had the devil's—or the Stuarts'—own charm when he chose to use it, though so far his father had managed to remain deaf to the pleas and blandishments of his Army-mad son.

"Oh, Brummell—have done," Jamie said excitedly to his valet. "The coat is well enough—I am nearly late for my interview with Papa!" He seized the coat—which a moment before had been so excoriated—and began dragging it over his shoulders willy-nilly. His valet winced, as if in personal pain, and moved to assist him.

" 'Well enough' will not do, Your Highness, especially

upon an occasion in which you wish to persuade His Majesty of something he does not wish to do," Jamie's valet said severely.

His name was George Bryan Brummell, and at six-and-twenty, he was barely older than the prince he served. Brummell had a florid complexion, curly light brown hair, and grey eyes, and even at such a young age had garnered a reputation as autocrat and *arbiter elegantarum* that was impressive enough to have brought him into Royal service.

"He *will* wish it," Jamie said, all-but-grumbling. "I do not see why I should be the only man in the realm not permitted to attend the fighting upon the Peninsula, when anyone else may go and be given a shilling into the bargain!"

"The price of a coronetcy in a Hussar regiment is more than two thousand pounds, Your Highness—as I have good reason to know," Brummell said austerely. The valet's past was something of a mystery—it was rumored that he'd been in the Army, but had gambled away his commission and had been forced to return to the family trade. "And Your Highness is far too intelligent not to discern what truly lies behind His Majesty's reluctance."

But Prince Jamie was not to be drawn with appeals to his common sense upon this particular occasion. Pulling himself free of his valet's hands and shrugging his coat ruthlessly into place, he strode over to the mantelpiece and caught up a gold-framed miniature portrait of a young blonde woman in ermine and pearls.

"Oh, *bother* the creature," Jamie said under his breath, glaring at the inoffensive Court image of Princess Stephanie Julianna, his hopeful betrothed. While he had known that such a match was proposed—he had been notified, if not precisely consulted—with the easy confidence of youth Jamie had been certain that Settling Day was far in the future. But not only had the actual betrothal been put forward, not two months before his father had informed him that the wedding itself was to be this September, putting a rude period to Jamie's carefree bachelor existence. And to Jamie's dreams of heroic action against England's enemies. . . .

He turned back to Brummell, unconsciously brandishing the princess's portrait. "While a man and a prince must marry, I am not yet twenty—there's years yet to do what must be done. Why must Papa insist upon this now? A mere betrothal would serve Mr. Pitt's policies just as well and me far better."

"And should Your Highness stop a bullet upon the battlefield?" Brummell inquired with the silky insolence that was both his trademark and his privilege. "If the crown should fall to your eldest sister's lot . . ."

"Oh, *bother* Maria!" Jamie said roundly, dismissing his eldest sister (who was married to a much disliked German princeling) out of hand. "What of *me?* I cannot be cabin'd, cribbed, confined—denied every man's birthright of high adventure!"

"No, indeed," said Brummell with a sigh. "One sees that Your Highness cannot." He crossed the room in the wake of his volatile charge and plucked at the shoulders of the coat of bottle-green brocade with matching silk facings, attempting once more to get it to hang straight upon the Prince's shoulders.

"You will be late, Your Highness," Brummell said quietly. "You had best go and lay your case before your father once more."

Jamie strode from the room, every inch a prince. A prince, but still a young one, and reckless as any of his hard-living ancestors. Unfortunately, this was an age in which the world had grown small, and recklessness of any sort had grave consequences indeed. Brummell only hoped that Jamie could learn that lesson . . . in time.

"But *Papa—?*" Jamie protested.

"Enough," King Henry snapped.

Henry had become King of England at thirty, when his father Charles V, a monarch as merry as Charles II and considerably more reckless, died upon a battlefield in the Low Countries. With his crown Henry had inherited a web of alliances that shifted with the wind, political ties to a Europe that seemed, in parts, scarcely to have exited the Dark Ages, and a brilliant, voracious, implacable enemy . . . Napoleon Bonaparte, the Great Beast who haunted Europe.

From First Consul to Emperor, the malignant Corsican genius had won every battle, moving from strength to strength across the chessboard he'd made of Europe, claiming countries like playing-squares. Bonaparte meant to have England too, and Henry meant to deny it to the tyrant, even if he must beggar his kingdom and sell all his children into slavery to do so.

The Danish alliance was a godsend—it would refuse Bonaparte the staging-ground for his invasion of Scotland, a country historically closer to France than to England. Never quite resigned to its union with England when James the sixth of Scotland had become James the First of England upon the death of the great Elizabeth, the unruly Scots might welcome a French force not as invaders, but as allies.

If that happened, Henry would have the Corsican Beast crouched on his northern border—and the North, as his family knew to its everlasting regret, was tinder for wildfire, ready to rise against the King in London at the slightest spark.

But with Princess Stephanie married to England's heir and the Danish–English treaty signed—joining Denmark with Russia, Prussia, and England in the battle against Bonaparte, and giving English ships free access to Danish harbors—one more chink in the island nation's armor would have been sealed, freeing Henry to make his plans for attack, releasing him from endless defense.

But Tsar Alexander of Russia and Prince Wilhelm of Prussia were not as sanguine as Henry. Both rulers suspected that the Danish match would be called off at the last minute, or that the so-far-neutral Danes would somehow twist the match to suit only their own advantage, and not England's. If England fell and the Triple Alliance crumpled, Prussia and Russia would bear the brunt of Bonaparte's victorious retaliation.

"But Papa, I—" Jamie tried again, and King Henry to cut him off.

"I said no, and I do not wish to discuss this matter—"

"I am not asking for a commission," his heir said bitterly. "For I know you will not permit me such à chance to distinguish myself! All I ask is your permission to journey to observe the fighting—Grandfather often did as much—"

"Aye, and much good it did him!" Henry snapped.

The young prince stared at his father in amazement; Henry was not often that sharp with him.

"I have made my decision, Jamie, and I will not change it. I forbid you to leave England. Review your regiments here at home all you like—or find something else to amuse you. But I will not send you to be slaughtered on a foreign battlefield."

There was a frozen moment of offended silence on the Prince's part, then he made a chilly formal bow and walked from the room without speaking.

The King sighed. He could have called Jamie back and

demanded an apology, but he knew too well the restrictions the young man was chafing under. The Tsar and the Prussian King's heir—both in the field—daily urged Henry to send his son to take a place upon the Alliance General Staff. And while such a post would be far from the fighting, Henry was reluctant to send his son and heir out of the relative safety of England. French ships patrolled the Channel like hungry sharks, and ashore, Bonaparte's methods of prosecuting his war were even less honorable. An even more overwhelming consideration was the fact that the Denmark Treaty was to be solemnized upon Jamie's wedding day—and without the Prince, there was no treaty.

But in comparison to the romance of the battlefield, meetings with his father's ministers, no matter how necessary to the government of the realm, held little charm. A king must know diplomacy; it was the backbone of statescraft.

Unfortunately, all too often a king must know war as well.

But not yet. Oh, God, not yet.

In the last fortnight Sarah had learned a great many things, including how scandalous all of London thought the Marchioness of Roxbury to be. It did not seem to her that she had ever noticed this before—certainly she did not feel like anyone who had spent the past several years weathering scandal—but it was undeniably a fact. Nice girls did not reside in their own townhouses with only the most minimal of chaperonage. Nice girls did not keep their own carriages. Nice girls did not ride out in Green Park at unfashionable hours, with only a lone groom in attendance.

Nice girls had vouchers for Almack's, the exclusive

waltzing club in Kings Street. And Lady Roxbury did not.

It was not that she lacked for invitations to parties. Ever since her arrival in Town, there had not been one day that had not seen Lady Roxbury engaged to what seemed an excessive number of parties. If not for the strengthening cordial that Knoyle scrupulously fed her every morning and night, Sarah was quite certain she could never have managed the endless social round.

But with her senses as finely attuned as those of a woodland hunter, Sarah knew that these parties, though quite glittering, were not quite the "right" parties: the ones to which the most respectable ladies of the *ton* were invited.

She was not sure she yearned for them—surely even more genteel entertainments meant even more boredom?—but the Dowager Duchess of Wessex was doing all she could to improve Sarah's standing among the guardian dragons of the Ton. Sarah was to be formally presented to King Henry at a Court Drawing-Room in a few weeks, and that same evening the Duchess would give a dazzling ball—to be held at Herriard House, since the Duchess's own townhouse lacked the necessary accessory of a ballroom—subsequent to which most respectable event, vouchers for Almack's would surely appear.

Sarah could only admire such dedication and energy—especially since she could not think of a blessed thing to do to stop it. Obligingly, she had ordered her presentation gown and her ball-dress, and hoped that something would occur to her to stop this whirlwind before it was too late.

At least Wessex had not forced his attentions upon her again, although if Sarah were being honest, she'd have had to admit he never *had* actually forced his attentions upon her. It was a most disagreeable thing, she told herself, to suspect the man of honorable intentions and to still not yet have received a proposal from him that she could decently refuse.

And she would refuse it, Sarah told herself, because there was not the least reason she could conceive of for accepting it. Like Wessex, she found it difficult to feel that a family agreement entered into when the principals involved were mere children carried much weight in the modern world of 1805. Of course, supposedly there had been a later, formal betrothal; supposedly she had been engaged to marry Wessex since she was sixteen years old ... *Then why do I not remember it—or him?*

No answer came to enlighten her. Very well, memory or no memory, she would refuse Wessex, however often his grandmother offered him to her. And then she would see out the Season, go back to Mooncoign, and ...

And what?

Abruptly Sarah felt a chilly sense of peril. The sense that she hesitated at the edge of a cliff was strong: one misstep would be fatal, and disastrous beyond her comprehension. But which way did the disaster lie? The memory of the *creature* she had seen in the garden on the night of the ball rose up unbidden in her mind: as certain as she was that such beings did not exist elsewhere, she was also certain that they did exist ... here.

But where is elsewhere? And where is here, if it is not the place where I was born? Sarah asked herself wildly.

"My lady?" Knoyle's voice sounded anxiously at her elbow, and Sarah realized that she had been standing wool-gathering on a busy London Street. So much for a morning's walk clearing her head of last night's cobwebs!

She was standing before the ornate green and gold double-doors of Hatchard's Bookshop in Piccadilly. One of the unalloyed pleasures of her sojourn in London was the opportunity to spend hours pouring over catalogs and visiting bookstores, purchasing any new volume her heart fancied. Every Wednesday she came to Hatchard's to look over new titles; the hours she spent in the hushed quiet beneath the bookshop's massive dome were some of the happiest in her recent memory.

And she *was* happy. The Duchess of Wessex was no ogre, merely an old woman who had sadly lost both husband and children before their time, and who meddled good-heartedly in her grandson's life perhaps more than she ought. That was all.

Squaring her shoulders, Sarah pushed open the door to the bookshop. Within, all was cool serenity; the golden light slanting downward from the dome, the circular counter beneath it, and the rows of books stretching off in every direction all acted to soothe Sarah's nerves. Without stopping to see if her parcel had arrived, Sarah drifted toward the shelves and began perusing the colorful spines of gilt and Moroccan calf.

She had spent some minutes in that agreeable pursuit when her attention was summoned insensibly by the presence of a young woman a few feet away. Sarah glanced up from beneath the brim of her bonnet, wondering what had attracted her attention to the stranger.

The young woman was dressed with Quakerish plainness; her round gown in plain lavender muslin the next thing to mourning apparel. But when she glanced up in pursuit of a volume, Sarah realized that any ornament would be entirely superfluous; the stranger was the most dazzlingly beautiful girl Sarah had ever seen.

Her flawless skin was the pale clear ivory of country cream, and the glossy hair that framed her face in smooth waves was so perfectly black that it cast faint blue shadows on her skin. Her long dark lashes—which owed nothing to artifice or kohl brush—framed eyes that were as startlingly green as if their color had come from a box of watercolors or a jeweler's window. In all, the young lady was a piece of perfection so arresting that for one ungracious instant Sarah thought that anyone that beautiful couldn't possibly be respectable. Instantly, Sarah dismissed the notion. Everything about the young lady—from her demure costume to the hovering presence of a middle-aged maid—bespoke complete respectability. In fact, Sarah thought, firmly returning her attention to her own selections, the lady was undoubtedly far more respectable than Sarah herself.

Which, Sarah reflected, only served her out for all the years the Marchioness of Roxbury had spent amusing herself at the expense of her responsibilities and position. For a moment Sarah's hand hovered over her breast, where her father's ring reposed safe beneath layers of silk, muslin, and buckram corseting. An odd flicker of disquiet disturbed her thoughts, as if some part of her was desperately attempting to remember something she had only forgotten at her peril. *My father's ring. . . .*

It was while she was caught up in that sense of *otherness* that Sarah took an unwary step backward, colliding with the object of her previous scrutiny.

"Oh!"

There was a patter of falling books.

Cheeks flaming, Sarah turned about to behold the fair stranger who had been the object of her curiosity.

"Oh—I do beg your pardon," Sarah gasped, stooping to help retrieve the scattered volumes. "It was inexcusably clumsy of me."

"It is nothing," the young woman said. "I dare say you were distracted by all the books—it is a failing of mine, I must admit; my uncle has taxed me with it often."

"For good or ill my faults are mine to indulge without anyone else's censure," Sarah said frankly. "I am the Marchioness of Roxbury, and I promise you that I do not always trample my fellow bibliophiles."

"I am very pleased to make your ladyship's acquaintance." The young woman's alleged pleasure sounded actually sincere. I am Meriel . . . Bulleyn, of—oh, nowhere in particular! Stopping for the Season in London—" Miss Bulleyn seemed about to say something more, but bit her lip and desisted.

"Then we shall be friends," Sarah said, obeying a sudden impulse. By now she had collected all her new acquaintance's selections again and handed them over to her. "I will admit, I should be glad of a friend in London."

"You, Lady Roxbury?" Miss Bulleyn said, plainly unconvinced of this possibility.

"I," Sarah said with a smile. "No one has so many friends that they may not be glad of a new one." And truth be told, those who had presented themselves at Herriard House over the past several weeks had not been such persons as Sarah could bring herself to be easy with. Fast and fashionable without a doubt, and more or less above reproach, but these glittering ornaments to fashionable life who comprised the Marchioness of Roxbury's inner circle were not close friends, and Sarah yearned for someone in whom she could confide. "I should be glad if you would be my friend."

For a moment it seemed as if Miss Bulleyn studied Sarah coldly through those green cat-eyes. But it must have been a trick of the light, for the moment passed, and Miss Bulleyn smiled warmly.

"Then I shall be glad to be your friend, Lady Roxbury."

"Oh, please!" Sarah said impulsively. "If we are to be friends, you must call me 'Sarah,' and I will call you 'Meriel.' A pretty name, and most unusual."

"It is a Cornish name," Miss Bulleyn said, with some reluctance. But her reluctance vanished in the next moment and she smiled. "And now, do let us go away, if you are quite finished with your investigation of the new offerings—for if we stay much longer, I cannot answer for what more I may buy."

"I wish we might go for a drive in the Park," said Sarah, whose open carriage had followed her upon her expedition to Hatchard's and now stood waiting at the corner. "But I am promised to Madame Francine, who is fitting my presentation gown. I am to be presented at Court in two weeks, you see, and I am told that the proper sort of gown is of the highest importance." Sarah linked her arm through Meriel's, and the two ladies strolled along the sidewalk, their maids, with respective bundles, following behind.

A flicker of envy crossed Miss Bulleyn's features at Sarah's words. "It must be a splendid thing to have such a beautiful gown! I was to be presented at Court; but then Papa died, and my uncle and the rest of the family did not approve of such a frivolous expenditure," Miss Bulleyn said, her voice kept neutral with an obvious effort.

"How perfectly dreadful!" Sarah said instantly. "Everyone knows that a Court presentation is the surest way to gain the *congé* in the very best circles—and I am told that is of the first importance for a young lady. Perhaps your uncle will reconsider."

"No," said Miss Bulleyn with sad finality. "Uncle Richard has other plans for me. But I should so like to see the dresses. . . ." She sighed.

"Well, you shall see mine at least—if you wish it," Sarah decided. "For I see no reason that you should not come with me to Madame Francine's—your uncle can hardly forbid you to have *any* friends in Town, can he?"

"No," Miss Bulleyn said, brightening instantly. She smiled, revealing perfect white teeth and an enchanting dimple. "My uncle could hardly object to my knowing you."

Madame Francine had been born plain Sarah Franks in a small Midlands village, and had, by dint of industry, talent, determination, and the generosity of a noble lover, become one of the leading dressmakers to ladies of the *ton*. In the few weeks Sarah had been visiting her—having found, to her faint mystification, that the Marchioness of Roxbury had always patronized an establishment of which Sarah had no conscious memory—she had discovered that Madame Francine not only knew all the gossip about everyone in the Polite World, high and low, but that her fashionable designs came straight from Paris, having paid as little heed to borders and tariffs as had her *on-dits*. Madame Francine had done as much as anyone to make Sarah feel comfortable in Town, and when Sarah entered with her new friend, the modiste called for tea and cakes and exerted her exotic charm to the utmost.

Miss Bulleyn was easy to confide in, and long before Sarah's fitting was ended the two young women were fast friends, and Meriel was in possession of an invitation to call upon Lady Roxbury at any time. Wary both of male fortune hunters and the threat of marriage to the Duke of Wessex, it did not occur to Sarah that there might be any clandestine reason for a female to seek out Lady Roxbury's acquaintanceship, nor to consider the uses that might be made of such acquaintanceship.

On that same May day that was the scene of so many other interesting meetings, a visitor came to Wessex's Albany rooms.

The young Duke had kept a low profile since the occasion upon which he had been summoned into his grandmother's presence, both to avoid the endless social engagements which he found wearying and to give himself some time to consider the thorny problem his dearest grandmama had set him.

The trouble was, he could not think of any good reason *not* to marry the Marchioness of Roxbury—at least, no good reason that his grandmother would accept. He and Roxbury had been betrothed for years, after all; she was suitable—from all he knew of her, Roxbury was not the sort to require a husband dancing attendance on her with loverlike devotion. He could go his way and she could go hers, and so long as she refrained from presenting the dukedom with any cuckoo's eggs, he would account himself one who had got off lightly, no matter what her conduct.

But in spite of his hopeful self-encouragement, Wessex did not wish to marry at all. Wessex knew his way of life to be too uncertain, the compromise of his honor in service of king and country too great, to make him a decent husband for any decent lady. He suspected a taint in the Dyer blood; why else would two dukes in succession have succumbed to the dark lure of the Shadow Game? In black midnight moments, Wessex swore the dukedom would end with him.

But it was impossible to offer those most excellent reasons to his loving grandmother.

And if I did wish to take a wife, it would most certainly not be a woman as disturbing as Roxbury. . . .

Disturbing. Wessex was about to trace this interesting thought back to its wellspring when there was a tapping upon the door.

"Mr. Koscuisko, Your Grace," Atheling said. Illya Koscuisko did not choose to bedeck himself in his full uniformed splendor on most of his sojourns about Town, for to do so—in addition to imperilling every fan-tod in Piccadilly—would merely call attention to the fact that though he had chosen to absent himself from it, his regiment had chosen to serve England's sworn foe.

A faint air of disapproval hung about the valet like the ghost of London fog; he did not approve of the mercurial foreign fellow who called upon his master at all hours and led Wessex into escapades that were a trial to his wardrobe.

"Send him in." Wessex shoved the litter of bills and *cartes de invitation* into his desk, and waited expectantly.

He was not long disappointed. Illya Koscuisko, resplendent in the latest of London *mufti*, insinuated himself into Wessex's sitting room as languorously as his volatile nature would permit, retaining his hat, gloves, and stick against Atheling's half-hearted attempts to possess them. Even in civilian clothing, Koscuisko's taste was far from the sober and quiet idea of London's *bon ton*. On this particular occasion, Mr. Koscuisko had outfitted himself in primrose-yellow pantaloons whose xanthic hue precisely matched that of his glazed kid gloves. His Hussar's braids were bound in matching ribbon, and dangled upon the bosom of a silver-buttoned embroidered violet velvet waistcoat that was a wonder and a delight to all who observed it. Over this amazing garment he wore a dashing coat in coquelicot brocade, and crowned his sartorial confection with a curly-brimmed beaver brushed to glistening perfection. A diamond pin to secure his lace-trimmed cravat; an assortment of fobs and seals to begem his waistcoat; an enamel-headed sword-stick to brandish in martial fashion; and an earring in one ear completed the dashing and wholly awe-inspiring picture he presented.

"Good God," Wessex said mildly.

Koscuisko beamed. "Colorful, is it not? I daresay I shall

look quite the exotic foreigner at Lady Jersey's party this afternoon."

"No one," said Wessex with stark honesty, "could possibly mistake you for anything else. But what brings you here? Not, of course, that I am not happy to see you—"

"But if we are much seen together in London someone will begin to wonder what business Captain His Grace the Duke of Wessex has with a lowly layabout expatriate with a taste for flash company," Koscuisko said equably. Without waiting for an invitation, he sprawled upon the battered leather couch beside Wessex's desk and picked up an unloaded pistol Wessex had been using as a paperweight.

"Half of a Judas pair, is it?" he asked with interest, peering into the barrel. Though the pistol looked precisely like its ordinary mate, it was designed to fire backward, not forward—killing the duelist instead of the person at whom he aimed.

"I took it off Warltawk's man in Calais last spring," Wessex said. "Malhythe's false flag operation nearly did for the Underground cell there, as you'll recall."

"At least it encouraged the Home Office to stay out of the White Tower's business," Koscuisko said pacifically. "Since while they do what they do very well, half the time it isn't worth doing in the first place. But I've spent the morning with Lord Misbourne getting my orders, and I'm perishing for a drink."

"You know where it is," Wessex said unfeelingly, and Koscuisko abandoned the rigged dueling pistol and went in search of revivification. A quick search revealed the decanter—half buried beneath the litter of bachelor living—and once the volatile Pole was in possession of a large glass of brandy he returned to the couch to regard Wessex mournfully out of velvet-brown eyes.

"I may as well give you all the gossip, since you will

undoubtedly hear it anyway, though not from me—I am to take ship for Copenhagen on Friday."

Koscuisko announced this as though his destination were Antarctica, instead of Denmark. "I am to go and amuse England's future Queen until she sails—and afterward, I suppose."

Wessex frowned. It had been settled—before he'd gone to France that last time, and gotten himself entangled in *l'affaire deMorrissey*—that *he* was to be a member of Princess Stephanie's escort. "And when did you learn this?"

"It's common knowledge," Koscuisko said mendaciously. "You'd know it, too, if you'd trouble to read your mail."

Extracting a folded billet from his jacket, Koscuisko flipped the packet to Wessex, who snatched it out of the air. The paper was heavy with the weight of a sprawling wax seal, which Wessex deciphered without difficulty as King Henry's own private signet. The missive did not appear to have been opened.

Breaking the wax, Wessex read the few brief lines written in the King's clear careful hand. It was precise yet uninformative: as the King wished most particularly for Wessex's presence in London for the next two months, he was withdrawing the invitation he had extended to Wessex that he should make up part of the Danish envoy.

Wessex carefully lit the paper at the candle upon his desk; when the paper was burning well he shied it at the grate, where it struck in a shower of sparks and ash.

"No need to ask if Misbourne's read this," Wessex said crossly. He had been counting on the Danish envoy to remove him from the influence of his grandmother's machinations; he wondered now whether she had extended her influence to the Palace itself to keep Wessex in Town as she attempted to make this match she was so set upon.

"Read it?" Koscùisko asked with a laugh. "For all either of us knows, the man wrote it; it would amuse him to force me to play the common seaman for the next two months; tell me it would not! But to be fair, he's set you a pretty puzzle to keep you amused while I'm enjoying a life of luxury and debauchery at foreign courts: Saint-Lazarre has disappeared."

"Vanished?" Wessex came fully alert. "Not dead?"

"Dead if you like," Koscuisko said agreeably, "but four days ago he was alive and taking a moonlight flit with some obliging gentlemen down Norfolk way. Our man there had no orders to keep Saint-Lazarre in the bosom of Mother England, so he let him go. . . ."

"But it's a damned smoky thing for the man to be doing," Wessex agreed, "and on a smuggler as likely to dump a passenger in the middle of the Channel as land him on the other side. The Admiralty would have put him over for the asking."

Providing, of course, that the Admiralty had also thought Saint-Lazarre's mission worth pursuing.

"So we must assume that our Victor did not ask," Koscuisko finished. "But why not? Bosom companions, natural allies . . . England has every reason to wish to help Saint-Lazarre at his hobbies."

"I don't suppose that M'sieur Corday had any light to shed upon the subject?" Wessex asked politely.

Koscuisko grimaced. "We have been most explicit in our requests, but our friend Gambit does not seem to be forthcoming with his answers." He shrugged. "I supposed Lord Misbourne will have to ask Talleyrand if he wants the fellow back—that, or send him back to the colonies, which will only keep him out of the way for as long as it takes him to reach Louisiana. The colony is Royalist, of course, and His Majesty's Royal Governor would hardly cooperate with one of the *sans-culottes*, but young master

Gambit isn't likely to be all that forthcoming about who's paying him when he acts the distressed traveler."

"And the governor is in the unenviable position of being in rebellion against his *soi-disant* Emperor but not necessarily upon terms with England," Wessex finished for him. "Still, one supposes there might be a certain amusement to making Gambit Corday walk all that way."

"It isn't up to us," Koscuisko reminded him. Wessex could tell from his friend's abstracted tone that Koscuisko—like Wessex—was occupied with the pretty puzzle of what could possibly be important enough to draw Saint-Lazarre back to France, where every man's hand was against him and his capture could be a highly profitable affair. What information could he have gained— and not shared—from among the Royalist factions with which he was in touch that could possibly have motivated this clandestine flight?

"But I must be off upon my rounds—I need to tell one lady that I'm leaving her for another," Koscuisko announced provocatively. "And there is packing to see to and old haunts to, er, haunt before the *Endeavour* sails." He drained his glass and got to his feet, reclaiming gloves, hat, and stick with easy grace. "At any rate, you may console yourself with the knowledge that while I suffer along before the mast I shall be forced to be a very pattern-card of virtue, and nothing at all of interest can possibly happen."

"No," Wessex agreed, rising to his feet to see his comrade out. "The fun will start when Princess Stephanie arrives, and King Henry must persuade Jamie to accept his bride."

But consideration for a parent's feelings was very far from Wessex's mind a fortnight later when he attended upon

King Henry on the evening of the Court Drawing-Room.

Wessex had managed to put from his mind until that very morning the knowledge that he was promised to the Dowager Duchess of Wessex's ball this evening—a ball thrown at Herriard House to celebrate the Marchioness of Roxbury's belated presentation at Court. But once he'd unfortunately remembered that interesting fact—with the aid of Atheling, who wished to know if his master would wear ball dress or regimentals for the momentous occasion—it had refused to leave his mind. He'd spent the morning at his desk in Bond Street (for the members of the White Tower Group had as many despatches to read as any other political, and Misbourne did not encourage the removal of such sensitive material from the premises) and his afternoon at White's; but as the shadows of evening had drawn nigh he had returned to his Albany rooms to dress, and then had made his way to St. James Palace.

He'd been ushered into the King's presence at once, but this caused no comment, as it was publicly known that King Henry frequently sought Wessex's advice upon matters pertaining to the Army. And so King Henry had; for three-quarters of an hour the two men, monarch and subject, discussed the difficulties of supplying an army across a stretch of water over-amply supplied with eager French men o'war, the delicate awkwardnesses of precedence caused by a battlefield cluttered with kings, archdukes, and princes, and the notorious unreliability of the irregular troops that were more harm than help to Lord Wellesley's Peninsular Army.

"Your young friend Koscuisko has arrived safely in Copenhagen," King Henry said, "and has found everything much as I expected that he would."

Of course Koscuisko had not been forced to sail upon the *Endeavor* as an able seaman, but neither had he sailed under his own persona, that of Illya Koscuisko, late of His

Polish Majesty's Household Guard, a charming, scapegrace fellow with a taste for low company. Such a presentation would not gain him access to Princess Stephanie's suite, nor would it be in the least likely that such a raffish fellow would attend on such an important occasion in the first place. Wessex knew Koscuisko had adopted any of half a dozen disguises while aboard the warship, to vanish as soon as she made port and reappear in Denmark in yet another guise.

"And that is, Sir?" Wessex asked politely, though his innate caution warned him that His Majesty was making his way slowly toward the reason he had called Wessex into colloquy this evening.

"Oh, disorganization and delay—the French envoy, that turncoat Saint-Germain, is naturally doing all he can to sway the Prince Regent from his agreement. But Sir John is a diplomatist I trust absolutely to talk his way around any obstacle, and so I imagine the convoy will be on its way here only slightly behind schedule. Which brings me to the matter I particularly wished to raise with you, Wessex."

Every sense was sharpened to a fever pitch of alertness, but Wessex did his best to give the King no sign of his apprehension.

"As you may be aware, Prince Jamie is . . . perhaps not entirely reconciled to Princess Stephanie's arrival," King Henry said with odd tentativeness.

Wessex stiffened. While it was common knowledge that Jamie abjured the match, what was common knowledge was not necessarily a subject for common gossip. "I am certain that the Princess is all that is amiable," Wessex said a bit stiffly.

Henry smiled. "I am glad to hear you say so, but you know that everyone will not agree. Mr. Fox is already calling for appeasement, and the Prince's Party cannot like a move which they will only see as a drawing of new factions into an old war."

Assuming, of course, that the Danes jump the way we wish, Wessex thought to himself. Aloud he said: "I am certain that time will persuade them that they are misinformed. Prince James is of quite an age to marry, and Denmark . . ."

"Is very far away, and this poor girl will be all alone here among us—and I am afraid that Society's view of the suitability of the match will be very much informed by whether or not the *ton* approves of the Princess . . . which is why I wished to speak to you privately this evening."

Unconsciously, Wessex braced himself for the blow.

"I mean to appoint the Marchioness of Roxbury to the position of Mistress of Robes—"

Now Wessex could see where this was going, and cursed himself for not having had the foresight to stow away upon the *Endeavour*, or visit the Cannibal Islands, or shoot himself. The position of Mistress of the Robes was a high-ranking one in the Royal Household . . . but it could not be held by an unmarried woman.

And King Henry was still speaking.

"—I mean the Princess to be all the fashion; I will not have another arrangement beneath my roof like Maria and her German Georgie—the man can't even be bothered to learn English; he's hissed everywhere he goes. Princess Stephanie will arrive in England by mid-July, and I should take it very kindly if you and the Marchioness had wed by then. Roxbury has cut a dashing figure upon the Town for years, and you are hardly an inconsequential fellow, Your Grace—the two of you can sponsor the Princess in English society, and make certain that all goes well for her. I need you to do this for me, Rupert."

Wessex's heart sank, but he could hardly refuse the

King in such a small matter when he had given up so
much more than his honor in England's service. If a Duke
and his Duchess would be of more use to the King than
an unmarried Duke and the freewheeling Marchioness of
Roxbury, Wessex would marry the chit. The Royal command had been given, and it did not occur to Wessex to
disobey.

But Wessex's tainted line ended with him; he would
breed no more spies to follow him. That vow Wessex
would not break.

"I will not fail Your Majesty," Wessex said, bowing
slightly. He wondered if the Marchioness would be as
agreeable to the King's behest—but he had seen the tal-
isman she carried; as a member of the Boscobel League,
one of that elite cadre sworn to serve the interests of the
King, she must be, once she knew it was the command
of the King himself.

Henry saw Wessex's faint hesitation and mistook its
cause.

"My dear Rupert," he said, smiling, "is it possible that
you think Roxbury will refuse you? I grant the girl has a
high enough opinion of herself, but the family has always
been a great friend to the Crown—to save you the worry,
I'll ask her myself. On your behalf, of course." King
Henry smiled.

Sarah could not repress a last flutter of nervousness as she
regarded her reflection in the gilt-framed mirror. The archaic presentation dress, a peculiar anachronistic confection of wide-sprung hoops and towering headdress,
gleamed with white satin, silver tissue, and enormous jewels of price. The design had been copied, in the same
fabrics but in a modern line, for the ball-dress she would
wear later this evening. Sarah only hoped her nerves

would get her from here to there. Fortunately, the Presentation was a very formal affair; she, along with perhaps a dozen other hopeful damsels, would be ushered into one of the palace's withdrawing rooms to await the arrival of King Henry. There, each of them would be presented to the King and have the opportunity to make their bows. It would all be over very quickly, so she'd been told.

Out of consideration for her rank and precedence, she had been given a private chamber to wait in while she put the last finishing touches on her costume, and she and Knoyle had needed every minute to affix the egret-plume headdress—too high to survive a trip in the carriage—shake out the yards of ice-white satin that made up the voluminous skirt of Sarah's gown, and finish sewing and pinning the Roxbury diamonds to every available surface of the costume. Sarah glanced in the mirror. She was pale with tension, and glittered as though her gown were sewn of ice, not silk. Only a few more minutes now, she could see by the ormolu clock on the nearby table, and they would call her to attend the King.

By rights, Sarah should have made her bow to the King at the same time she had made her bow to Society, eight years ago. She could not at the moment recollect why it was she had not done so then, though the stress of doing so now was undoubtedly the cause of the strange and disturbing dreams she'd been having of late. Perhaps once this evening was over, the dreams would vanish, too.

If they did not, she did not think she could stand it. If she had not had Miss Bulleyn to confide in, the last few weeks would have been quite unbearable.

Sarah had wanted to invite Miss Bulleyn to her ball—and had, in fact, broached the subject to her friend. But Meriel had brushed aside all Sarah's hopeful suggestions, saying only that her uncle would certainly not approve—and would certainly find out. Sarah found herself nourishing quite a healthy dislike for Mr. Richard Bulleyn, wherever he was—any man who would deny his niece such a harmless and respectable entertainment as a ball given by the Dowager Duchess of Wessex for her god-daughter was certainly no one that Sarah could be fond of, and the future he was shaping for his niece by keeping her so secluded from Society was certainly not an enviable one.

Not that Sarah's own future looked that much brighter. She sighed. Despite her triumphs, she was thinking of returning to the country just as soon as the ball was over. The city was no place for her; whatever she was seeking, it was not to be found here.

The melancholy tenor of her thoughts was interrupted by a tapping at the door. Knoyle rushed to open it. A footman in formal palace livery—gold-laced suit and powdered wig—stood in the doorway.

"Lady Roxbury? King Henry has sent me to conduct you to the Withdrawing Room."

The Drawing-Room was crowded and overheated; the last glimmerings of dusk were still in the sky, though the candelabra that lined the walls had already been lit and the heavy scent of burning beeswax filled the air. Sarah concentrated on standing so still that her diamonds barely flashed in the sweltering air, and took the position that the liveried footman showed her to without complaint, or any attempt to find a more favorable one.

The salon's walls were draped with thick falls of red velvet, interspersed with brilliant gilt-framed mirrors, and the floor beneath Sarah's diamond-sewn slippers was a polished checkerboard of colored marble. On the gilded and painted ceiling above, plump and glittering cherubs surrounded depictions of ancient kings—finding swords beneath altar stones, drawing them forth from anvils, receiving them from ladies rising up out of lakes. The three chandeliers sparkled with candles and cut-crystal lustres until the light was nearly enough to hurt Sarah's eyes. To rest them, she glanced about herself, careful not to move from her appointed place.

Most of the other ladies present were far younger than Sarah's own advanced age of five-and-twenty, and all were so nervous—even though they were, as Sarah was not, accompanied by at least one hovering female relative—that Sarah felt herself grow calmer in simple self-defense. There were a number of gentlemen of the Court also present in the room, and as Sarah looked up, she saw that one of the spectacularly-uniformed Hussars standing near the window was the Duke of Wessex.

He was wearing a short blue jacket encrusted with the distinctive silver lace of the eleventh Hussars, and a bearskin-trimmed pelisse was slung over one shoulder. Cherry-red trousers were tucked into gleaming gold-laced tasseled Hessians, and his plumed shako was tucked beneath one arm. The uniform looked unfinished without the sword that should have hung at his waist—since Wessex could not come armed into the King's presence—though he was still wearing the sabretache embroidered with the regimental honors slung from his belt. In uniform, Wessex cut a dazzling and martial figure far removed from the languid and chilly harlequin with whom Sarah was acquainted.

He saw her across the room and seemed to become utterly still, much as a leopard who had sensed the presence of an unwary hunter. For a moment his black eyes burned into hers—

Then he glanced away, without so much as the felicity of a common bow in passing.

Sarah's eyes flashed dangerously. So he thought to ignore her, did he, and pretend he didn't see her, as if she were some cast off, importunate mistress?

The situation would not have been so appallingly irritating had not the last several weeks given Sarah a very good sense of her own importance—and if not for the fact that she had sensed some strange bond between herself and Wessex from the very first. It seemed so much more of a betrayal when all her instincts told her that they ought to be friends—and they weren't.

She glanced away, and when she looked back, Wessex had disappeared behind another pair of gorgeously costumed officers. She had almost made up her mind to pursue him when a footman bearing a long ivory stave entered through a hidden door and thumped his shaft upon the marble floor, summoning the attention of all.

"His Royal Majesty, Henry Charles James Arthur Christian, King of England, Ireland, Scotland, and Wales!"

The king's image was, of course, to be seen on every coin from golden guineas to copper ha'pennies and in a number of the pictures that hung in the Royal Academy as well, but this was the first time that Sarah could remember laying eyes on the living man. He was not as tall as she had expected, and the bright chestnut hair that marked the Stuart line had faded and darkened with age, but even without crown and royal robes, Henry was every inch the king, and Sarah found herself responding to that aura of kingship with an almost unconscious reverence.

King Henry moved slowly about the circumference of the room, stopping and greeting each person there. At its simplest, a Royal Drawing-Room was an opportunity for the people of England to see that their monarch was hale and whole, something that would stop the rumors of illness and even death that tended to run rampant in troubled times.

A number of gentlemen of the court followed the King, and Sarah was faintly irritated to see that Wessex was among them. She had not known that the Duke was an intimate of the King, and the knowledge vexed her for some perverse reason.

At last the King reached her place in the tableau, and Sarah gracefully sank down into the Court curtsey she had rehearsed for so many hours. Her hoops made a faint thump as they struck the marble floor, and then collapsed neatly upon themselves, folding the white satin and silver lace of her skirts as if it were the sugary whipped-cream decoration at the top of a ornate dessert. She bowed her neck, and the egret-feather headdress bowed with her until she could see the tip of the feathers dangling in front of her nose. Then she looked up, and was astonished to see that the King was holding out his hand to help her rise.

She had not looked for such a particular mark of favor; placing her gloved hand into his, she allowed him to help her to her feet.

"And how do you find London, Lady Roxbury?" King Henry asked, a twinkle in his eye. Sarah smiled in return. She could not commit the incredible social solecism of looking away from the King to see where Wessex was; wherever the Duke might be, she knew that he saw her.

"It is an interesting place, Your Majesty," Sarah replied.

"But not so interesting as Mooncoign, eh, Your Ladyship?" the King said with dismaying insight. "You must tell me something about it."

Almost without thought Sarah found herself describing the glories of the Wiltshire downs to King Henry, who seemed completely enchanted by her depiction, until abruptly Sarah realized she was rattling on like the veriest greenhead.

"But Your Majesty will not wish to hear about such things," Sarah finished lamely.

"*Au contraire*; it is utterly delightful—but it only serves to convince me that we must do more to amuse you here in London—and perhaps you will take pity on Princess Stephanie when she arrives, and show her about the Town?"

"Of course," Sarah replied quickly. The plight of the Danish princess—to be sent so far from home to seal a treaty, betrothed to a Prince who didn't want her to come at all—had touched Sarah's soft heart as soon as she had heard of it.

"Then that is settled—and it will be good for the Princess to have the guidance of a young married lady of unexceptionable connection. You must on all account send me an invitation to your wedding breakfast; I shall be delighted to attend."

"Your Majesty is too kind," Sarah said automatically. Only long practice kept her features immobile as King Henry released her hand and moved on.

Married lady? Automatically she looked around for Wessex, only to find he wasn't there at all.

10

The Prince of Our Disorder

✳ **M**y dear, the King was all that we could have hoped for! He engaged you in conversation for quite ten minutes—your success is assured," the Dowager Duchess of Wessex assured her.

Sarah glanced away from the mirror; Knoyle was putting the finishing touches on Sarah's second full-dress toilette of the evening. "Yes," Sarah said slowly, "I suppose that it is." But social success somehow seemed more irrelevant than ever. King Henry had spoken as though her marriage was a certainty, the date set and settled—and in the face of the King's expectations, what could she say?

"Poor child," the Dowager said. "You already look all in—and you must see in the dawn, you know, or the gossips will make heaven above knows what of your absence. But come along—there will be just time for you to swallow a bite of supper before you must greet your guests."

*   *   *

The ball was all that the Dowager had predicted and Sarah had dreaded. All of London was there, and ready to meet her—with, it seemed, one exception.

The Duke of Wessex was nowhere to be found.

Sarah was dancing with the Earl of Ripon, rather against her wishes. She knew the Earl only by dinner-table reputation; the Highcleres were a Catholic family which had for generations held a grudge against the Stuart line for turning to the Anglican faith and forsaking the Old Religion. Though they made their way in Society, the Highcleres could be counted upon to oppose any policy of the King's—from the continuance of the Continental war to His Majesty's liberal dealings with the American colonies.

But if the Dowager Duchess thought it good to invite Ripon to Sarah's ball, the Marchioness of Roxbury could do no less than dance with him. And she did have to admit that Ripon did not tax her with his politics on what was, after all, a purely social occasion.

Yet there was something about the Earl that Sarah could not like—not quite a lean and hungry look, perhaps, but something just as dark—

As if it could be anything to do with me! Sarah told herself brusquely. She was still seething at Wessex's absence and knew that she was seeking other targets for her anger.

The music spun down to its end, and the couples who had made up the set looked to the sides of the dance floor in unconscious pursuit of their next partners, but before the dance could reach its natural conclusion, Ripon dragged Sarah to a halt as he stopped in amazement.

"Geoffrey!" he muttered.

But the eyes of the jumbled dancers were not upon Ripon's younger brother, but his companion, now making his grand entrance into the ballroom as if the entertainment had been given in his honor.

Jamie, Prince of Wales, had arrived—and he had not come alone.

Slowly, Sarah and Ripon moved to the edge of the dance floor. The Prince of Wales had not been invited, although of course all the Royal Personages had *de facto* invitations to any entertainment they might choose to grace with their presence. But Prince Jamie's interests ran with an entirely different crowd than that of the reclusive Dowager Duchess of Wessex—and tonight's guest list had been drawn very much from the Dowager's set.

Sarah recognized none of the half-dozen male sparks of fashion attendant upon the Prince, save by reputation, but almost certainly the blond man at whom Ripon stared so fixedly was Ripon's ne'er-do-well younger brother Geoffrey. The man on Jamie's other side—dark angel to Geoffrey's golden one—must be the notorious Lord Drewmore, a man whose exploits were too scandalous for even gentlemen to talk of. And the woman on his arm, whose bright yellow curls owed far more to Art, Sarah was certain, than to Nature, was someone she thought she knew. . . .

Caroline Truelove was the young relict of Sir Arthur Truelove, who had distinguished (as well as extinguished) himself upon the field of honor less than three years before. His young and beautiful widow had made her way through most of the available European capitals and all of Sir Arthur's money in her progress toward England and the loving bosom of her husband's family. But that assemblage—Sir Arthur's younger brother having inherited both the baronetcy and the guardianship of Sir Arthur's two young sons—was inclined to be far less indulgent of

Lady Truelove than her late husband had been. Balked of any attempt to enlarge upon her widow's jointure and quietly discouraged from seizing her boys to accompany her upon her peripatetic round of house-parties, Lady Truelove found her natural volatility of spirit drew her, like a leaf upon the bosom of the river, into the whirlpools of fast company and high living in the company of a dangerously raffish crowd.

In fact, Sarah recalled seeing Lady Truelove at Mooncoign not so very long ago, though she was quite certain that the Dowager had not invited her tonight. Lady Truelove was wearing a low-cut gown of Paris green silk adorned with knots of diamonds at the shoulders and decolletage; in Herriard House's chaste Palladian ballroom she looked far less respectable than an opera dancer upon the Covent Garden stage.

"You had better go and greet your guests," Ripon snarled in Sarah's ear, and she shot him a murderous look. *How dare you speak to me as if this disaster-in-the-making were my idea!*

Music began to play once more as Sarah headed for the Prince's clique. The Dowager must have told the bandmaster to begin again, and Sarah was grateful to the cover of respectability that the music afforded, for as she approached, she could see that Prince Jamie was rather the worse for drink. His cheeks were flushed and his eyes glittered brightly and he looked entirely too dangerous for Sarah's peace of mind.

"Lady Roxbury!" the Prince of Wales cried gaily as he saw her. "How splendid to see you here—and here is His Grace of Wessex! What a demmed fine fellow you look in all that regimental lace—what a pity to waste such a uniform on a fellow who might go overseas whenever he chose and doesn't."

Sarah risked a quick glance behind her. Wessex was

standing behind her in the same dazzling dress uniform he had been wearing at the Royal Drawing-Room—she wondered when he had entered, as she had not seen him do so—smiling as though he had not just been called a coward by the Prince of Wales.

"Indeed it is, Your Highness," Wessex said genially, stepping forward, "but as the Eleventh is the Prince's Own Regiment, if the uniform offends Your Highness, you have only to change it, you know."

The idea seemed to amuse Jamie; he laughed, and clapped Wessex upon the shoulder. "For a chap who spends all his time hanging about m'father, you're not such a dull dog after all. Kate, say hello to His Grace."

Lady Truelove smiled at Wessex in the fashion of one who knows she will not be chastised whatever her actions; the expression made Sarah long to slap the woman—she was not certain why she'd ever found Lady Truelove an amusing companion, but vowed to cross her off the list of Lady Roxbury's acquaintance at once.

"I'm honored that you should choose to attend my ball, Your Highness," Sarah said, taking command of the situation. Though Geoffrey Highclere had stuck close by the Prince's side, his other companions had wandered off to sample the delights of the ball. "Perhaps Your Highness would care for some refreshment?"

"Splendid notion!" Jamie beamed.

At least some of the sets were returning to the dance floor. Perhaps the Prince's inebriated and totally unexpected entrance could be smoothed over, Sarah thought hopefully.

But her plan to divert the Prince—and whisk his disreputable companions from public view—was doomed to failure. As Sarah conducted the Prince through the ground-floor rooms that had been opened for the ball,

Jamie began, inevitably, to attract just such an audience as Sarah had hoped to avoid.

"Is it true we are to expect an Interesting Announcement this evening, Lady Roxbury?" Lady Truelove asked with a giggle. "I vow, there is nothing I like better in all the world than the chance to wish someone very happy."

Sarah hoped her expression did not too patently display her disbelief; Lady Truelove looked rather more like the sort of person who would revel in her acquaintance's *mis*fortune. And was she hinting that she, as well as half the world, expected Sarah to announce her engagement—or rather, the date of her marriage—this evening?

"Well, you shan't be felicitating *me*, Your Ladyship," Jamie said abruptly, reeling to a stop. One of the hangers-on had brought a glass of champagne. Jamie gulped the liquid as if it were water and beckoned for more. He glanced about himself and then sprawled upon the nearest sopha, and Lady Truelove promptly disposed herself beside him. There was nothing for Sarah and Wessex to do but stop as well.

"But I had understood you were to marry, Prince Jamie," Geoffrey Highclere drawled from his position at the Prince's elbow. "Some deadly dull Danish cart-horse, wasn't it?"

Jamie's color deepened to a maroon that even the amount of drink he had imbibed could not entirely account for.

"The devil I shall!" he exclaimed loudly, his fiery Stuart temper slipping from his control. He struggled to his feet again, his angry glittering gaze sweeping the assembled guests—and not all of them were the Prince's cronies. "Princess Stephanie may sail for England, or Hell, or wherever she likes, but I shall not marry her! No Stuart Prince shall be—"

"Sold for an advantage England could as easily gain

upon the battlefield?" Mr. Highclere said helpfully.

"Precisely, Geoffrey!" Jamie said, pleased with his crony's cleverness. "So let the Danes look to their best interests, lest the British Lion—"

"More wine, Your Highness?" Wessex asked with ruthless politeness.

There had to be some way to break this up, Sarah thought with growing desperation. Suddenly, inspiration struck.

"Mr. Highclere," she said abruptly, "*do* favor me with this next dance, won't you?"

Sarah locked eyes with Ripon's younger brother. Geoffrey's pale eyes burned into hers, but the forms of the Polite World had been invoked, and Highclere could no more ignore Lady Roxbury's request than he could sprout wings and fly. He bowed slightly, favoring her with an avaricious lupine glance.

"As you command, Lady Roxbury."

Exerting every wile that imagination could devise, Sarah kept Geoffrey Highclere by her side for the next quarter of an hour, though the man's presence made her feel oddly endangered. It was with intense relief that Sarah spied Wessex returning to the ballroom, and could finally allow her impatient companion to conduct her to a chair. The moment she was safely disposed, Highclere strode from the room with almost indecent haste, and Wessex watched him leave with a rather chilly smile.

Sarah started to her feet, alarmed.

"Oh, do let him go, Lady Roxbury," Wessex drawled. "I am devastated to tell you that His Highness has already moved on to his next engagement, and the hopeful Mr. Highclere will seek his quarry in vain."

"Thank heavens," Sarah said in relief.

She discovered her fan, looped about her wrist on a tinsel string, and plied it vigorously to conceal the force of her feelings, then glanced around for Lord Ripon. She did not see Geoffrey's older brother anywhere, which was an additional mercy.

"So all has been tidied away, for the moment," Wessex said. "Unfortunately, the Prince's intemperate remarks will be all over London by dawn, which brings me to . . . Lady Roxbury, may I have the favor of a private word with you?"

Sarah rose slowly to her feet, wondering how on earth she could avoid this interview. Only a fool would be unable to guess what subject Wessex wished to raise; and it would lead to a discussion that Sarah very much wished to avoid. Reluctantly, she raised her glance to his face, and against her expectations, he smiled.

"Yes, I know; you do not wish to grant me such a favor, and in fact you wish me entirely at the devil. But we do not either of us have the luxury of behaving as private persons, so if Your Ladyship will do me the honor . . ."

His hand was beneath her elbow; moved as much by the force of his personality as by his grip upon her arm, Sarah let Wessex lead her from the dance floor. Though so far as she knew he had never been here before, Wessex seemed to know her house better than she did herself, for in a few moments they were on the narrow servants' stair ascending to Sarah's small private parlor on the second floor. He conducted her into the room with a little more force than courtesy and closed the door behind them.

"You wished to speak to me, my—Your Grace?" One of the frightening blank spots in her memory had suddenly appeared, carrying with it forgetfulness of proper forms of address that Lady Roxbury must have known from her cradle. But the bobble was only momentary and Sarah doubted Wessex noticed. She crossed the room and seated herself in the large comfortable chair in front of the fire. By her standing orders, there was a fire of sea-coals burning, taking the edge off the chill of the May night, but Sarah was not comforted.

Away from the watchful eyes of the other revelers, Wessex's face was set in harsh lines, as if there were a painful duty before him, and Sarah could guess what it was.

"Your Grace—" she began.

"Be quiet," Wessex said sharply. "There are some things which—I believe!—you do not know. And you will learn them tonight, Lady Roxbury.

"Prince Jamie has for some time been surrounded—in spite of King Henry's efforts—by a faction composed primarily of those who still regret the loss of Charles II's Catholic younger brother James as England's king. You have danced with one of its leading architects this evening; the Earl of Ripon is one of those who believe that England should stand with the Catholic kingdoms of Europe, and abandon its policy of tolerance and emancipation." Wessex stared broodingly into the fire's heart for a moment before continuing.

"The Prince's marriage into the house of Schleswig-Holstein-Sonderberg-Glucksborg would be a great blow to their plans; as you have seen, Ripon's supporters do all that they can to keep Jamie dissatisfied with the match his father has made for him. What few people know is that Ripon has his own candidate for Princess of Wales: his young niece, a girl who has been carefully schooled for her role in his machinations. It is said that Ripon plots to entangle Prince Jamie with this girl past his ability to free himself; to cause a scandal great enough that the Danish Prince Regent will withdraw both his sister and the treaty of alliance."

"I see." Sarah's hand went involuntarily to touch the

small hard lump that was her father's ring, tied securely into the bodice of her ball-dress.

"I doubt you see all of it, Lady Roxbury. Should the Danish marriage fail, England would lose an important ally. And should Prince Jamie go on to marry Ripon's niece, Ripon would gain such power at Court as to be able to further his ultimate ambition—to withdraw England from the Triple Alliance and force her to make a separate peace with Bonaparte."

"But—But—" *But this is impossible.* "But Ripon's niece must be a Catholic—"

"And you will be wondering how such a marriage could be made in the face of the Act of Succession," Wessex finished. "Depend upon it, madame, if Ripon's plans go as he wishes them to, the King must allow the match, or see the Throne rocked by such scandal as it cannot easily weather."

"And so the Earl wins either way," Sarah said, slowly puzzling out the political tangle Wessex had presented her, "because he wants to put an end to the Alliance, doesn't he, and if there is such a—a turmoil here in England . . ."

"Our beloved allies will bolt like frightened coach horses," Wessex agreed. For a moment he gazed once more into the hot flames, his face expressionless, and when he spoke again it was nearly as if he spoke to himself alone. "That must not happen. If Prince Jamie can be brought to a sense of his responsibility; if he can be kept from entanglement with Ripon's brat . . . but most of all, if Princess Stephanie can make herself agreeable to the *mobile*, to the English people, then public pressure on her behalf will force the Prince to behave appropriately."

Wessex took a deep breath before adding, "In the face of Prince Jamie's displeasure, the Princess will need advocates and partisans—and you, Lady Roxbury, cannot sponsor her in society as an unmarried woman, nor can I associate with her without my attentions seeming far too particular for the delicate measure we must tread."

Then Wessex fell silent, and much against her will, Sarah thought about what he had said. She did not much care for Ripon, and somehow felt about Prince Jamie as an elder sister about a younger brother whom she saw heading into disaster. Princess Stephanie she did not know at all, but the thought of a young woman traveling to a strange land and an unknown fate struck a deep chord somewhere within her, so that Sarah felt she needed to do whatever she could to help the Danish Princess find happiness in England and her marriage.

Marriage. It all came back to that, in the end. Marriage, and the Duke of Wessex. Sarah did not doubt that Wessex was telling her the simple truth—that without this marriage, she could not do anything to aid either the Prince or the Princess. Was this what the Old One had meant that night in the garden at Mooncoign when he had told her that she must make herself a part of this world—or die?

"So you wish me to marry you?" Sarah asked. Wessex's tone had implied that it was almost a formality—something to be done for the look of the thing, nothing more. And King Henry wished her to marry him, even if Wessex seemed less than enthusiastic about the matter himself.

"Yes," Wessex said baldly.

He had hardly been able to bring himself to say the words that made their marriage inevitable—he must remember upon some future occasion to thank the Earl of Ripon for providing him with such a textbook illustration of how vitally necessary it was. In some sense, Wessex would be taking a far more public role in the fight against

England's foes than ever before, if he and his Duchess
were to lead the faction in Society that opposed Ripon's
isolationist schemes. At least he was not being asked to
perform a task beyond his strength. It would be one more
masquerade, that was all. Another part to play, and the
Duchess of Roxbury only another partner in the Game of
Shadows. *So now I corrupt her, too—*

"All right," the Marchioness said. She shrugged, as if
the matter were not of very great importance.

Wessex felt a spasm of something similar to relief. She
was even more cold-blooded than he, it seemed: this marriage would not disturb her ladyship in the slightest. *And
perhaps she will develop a taste for the Shadow Game. . . .*

Recollecting himself, Wessex pulled off his dress glove
and removed the ring. He'd tucked it over the tip of his
little finger for safekeeping, the gorgeous uniforms of the
Prince of Wales's Own being undersupplied with pockets.
Taking the ring between his thumb and forefinger, he held
it out to her.

"You'll want this, then. It's traditional." There. The
thing was done past all unmaking.

The thick circle of rose-gold gleamed between the Duke's
fingers; Sarah took the ring with as much caution as if she
were being offered a poisoned chocolate.

It was an old piece, the rose-gold of its surface worn
with time and many hands. The ring was a salamander
in flames; the tail of the salamander circled her finger,
glittering with the red of the flames and tiny yellow diamonds set to represent sparks. The face of the jewel was
the creature's body, set with tiny golden pearls meant to
represent its knobby hide, surrounded by carved ruby
flames. Its head was set with a tiny diamond, and the gem

winked in the candlelight as Sarah turned the ring in her fingers.

A betrothal ring. She'd agreed to marry him, hadn't she? But somehow Sarah could not bring herself to put the ring on her finger.

Abruptly Wessex seized her left hand. She was still wearing the jewels she had worn for her presentation; he drew a large ring with an onyx table set with marquise-cut diamonds from her finger and replaced it with the salamander in flames.

Done! a tiny voice seemed to cry out within Sarah's mind. *Done past all undoing.* She stared at the metal salamander circling her finger as if the little creature might bring itself to speak at any moment.

"What do I do now?" she asked numbly.

"I think," said Wessex grimly, "that it would be best if we announced our Joyous Event—and gave your guests something else to talk about this evening."

11

The Property of a Lady

❊ If anything, being Officially Engaged was less devitalizing than simply being abroad in London had been. People, Sarah reflected with a new cynicism, knew what to think about the Marchioness of Roxbury now. And if it was rumored that the Duke of Wessex was getting damaged goods—well, at least Sarah did not have enough of an affection for the unspeakable man to care!

She had not had a recurrence of her headaches in the fortnight since her marriage date had been announced, but she had finally been forced to admit to herself that her "little lapses of memory" were nothing of the sort.

For try as she might, she could not truly remember anything at all before her awakening at Mistress Bulford's after the coach crash. Mooncoign—where she must have grown up—was as unfamiliar to her as London. The Marchioness's circle of friends were people Sarah had no memory of ever meeting. She reread the Marchioness's careful diary entries, and could not imagine ever having written them.

Sarah did not much like the woman she met in those pages, either. Vain, arrogant . . . Sarah could not even be properly ashamed of her previous behavior, since she could not manage to believe in her heart that the woman represented in the pages of the little red-bound diaries was anything to do with her. Was *this* the woman the high-nosed Duke of Wessex thought he was marrying? It hardly mattered, Sarah thought with resignation, since Wessex had made it clear that their marriage was a social formality only.

She would not think about that. It would be enough that she was doing what she could for the Crown. Her family had always served the Stuarts. . . .

The sidestepping of the mare beneath her brought Sarah's mind abruptly back to the present day. Her personal life might be a hopeless tangle, but she had many other things to be thankful for!

May had turned into June, continuing bright and warm; and Sarah had taken advantage of the delightful weather to go riding every morning. At her orders, her groom waited for her at the park gate, and in the gently rolling wooded environs of Green Park, the strange dissonance between her surroundings and her expectations seemed to vanish.

And at this hour, the park was also an excellent location to meet with someone who did not wish to be seen.

A few minutes' trot brought Sarah to a secluded clearing just off the edge of the trail. It was watched over by a statue of Apollo, and anyone in the clearing would have been visible to anyone passing along the ride—but Fashionable London preferred to take its exercise in the afternoons, and the morning sun was just clearing the rooftops of Piccadilly. The spire of Christ Church winked golden in the distance as Sarah turned her delicate-footed mare into the clearing and waited.

She had just reined in when she heard the quick rhythm of hoofbeats on the path behind her, and Meriel Bulleyn cantered into view.

Miss Bulleyn wore a neat and very modern black habit cut *à la Hussar*, with double rows of silver buttons glittering upon the jacket's impeccable broadcloth bosom. Her gleaming beaver hat was swathed in veils to preserve her anonymity, but the horse she rode was enough to make her stand out in any assemblage—its coat was as black as Miss Bulleyn's own hair, except for a silver mark in the center of his forehead like a fairy's kiss. As Meriel reined it to a halt it danced and bowed, indicating its displeasure at stopping.

It was beyond Sarah's understanding why Meriel's uncle would present her with a mount the equal of which could hardly be found in the Royal stables—and then insist she keep herself out of Society.

"Good morning!" Miss Bulleyn called. Her own groom, Sarah knew, waited around the bend of the trail; either he was more loyal to Meriel than to her guardian, or wicked Uncle Richard saw no harm in these early morning meetings. "How do you do this morning?" Meriel continued, flinging back her veils.

"I vow I am run off my legs with everything to do with the wedding—and the Dowager tells me that my bridegroom is in a foul temper, because he means to buy a house for us to live in—Dyer House is far too small and the Dowager Duchess has lived there for years—nor would I ask him to turn her out of it—and by no stretch of will or imagination can a new house in the West End of the grandeur he proposes possibly be ready in time for our wedding." As she spoke, what had loomed as a catastrophe Sarah suddenly saw as the trivial crisis it truly was. Sarah felt her spirits lift, and smiled at Meriel.

Meriel laughed in return. "He will have to learn to live
with disappointment—and upon a short rein, as all hus-
bands must! Have you not got a house of your own, after
all?"

"So I do," Sarah said, "and you must come and see it,
Meriel. I vow, when I have so many good things in my
life it burns my heart to see my dearest friend skulking
about in corners. I am to be the Duchess of Wessex, an
intimate of the King! How can your uncle possibly object
to your seeing me?"

"He . . . is very pleased that I have made your acquaintance, but—oh, do not ask me to explain—I would give
anything to attend the fêtes you describe to me, but I
cannot. Not yet!" Meriel cried.

"Not yet?" Sarah's puzzlement made her pry when she
did not wish to, but the look of anguish on Meriel's face
made her wish she had not. "Well, I will content myself;
I ought not tease you, Meriel, I know!"

"You are far too good to me," her friend said in a low
voice. "If you knew what I truly was, you would not be
so kind."

"If you were Old Nick himself I should still love you,"
Sarah declared stoutly. "Come, a good gallop will shake
you out of these blue megrims!"

The Duke of Wessex's wedding drew closer with each day;
he regarded it with the same fatalism with which a man
might view his execution. The unpleasant event would
occur no matter what he did; therefore he might as well
occupy his time until the fatal day with what diversions
he might.

To that end, Wessex frequented his clubs, spent a suitable amount of time at the Horse Guards, attended his

boxing club and his fencing salon, and rode in Hyde Park at the fashionable hour. He saw little of his betrothed (which suited him, he told himself) but had constant reports of her from their mutual acquaintance.

Such urbane delights must be supposed to please; Wessex permitted himself to seem idly amused by life in London. But every few days, he found occasion to stop by the building in Bond Street, arriving through one of its assorted entrances, and one afternoon, there was a summons from Lord Misbourne awaiting him.

Wessex crushed the paper between his fingers and replaced it upon Charteris's silver salver. The butler bowed and retreated, and then dropped the crumpled wad automatically into the closed stove that served to dispose of all of the White Tower Group's waste paper.

Wessex got to his feet, glancing about the paneled room that looked so much like the library in an ordinary gentlemen's club. The others who were there did not even glance up from their reading; two of them Wessex knew by name, and the other was a stranger to him, but within these precincts they were all equals, and all equally anonymous.

He sighed. There was as little point in postponing the moment as in wondering why Misbourne had summoned him. He turned from the room, heading down the corridor to the padded red leather door of Misbourne's office.

"She's meeting Ripon's niece nearly every day. In Green Park," Baron Misbourne said.

Wessex blinked, momentarily off-balance at this rather unconventional greeting. Misbourne shimmered in the chamber's radiant gloom like some deep-sea beast being drawn toward the surface in a net.

"Good afternoon, Lord Misbourne," Wessex said equitably. A lethal instinct made him hazard a guess at Misbourne's meaning: "Lady Roxbury?"

"Has become quite the bosom-bow of Ripon's whelp," Misbourne said, fixing Wessex with a pale baleful eye.

"Don't blame me," Wessex snapped. "I'm only marrying the woman."

"And thus her conduct is none of your concern. Quite so. But her motive is," Misbourne reminded him.

Wessex frowned, realizing that he'd still formed no very complete picture of his betrothed's character. On the one hand, he knew she was a member of the Boscobel League, but as that secret could not be shared even with Misbourne, it was of no use now. Nor did Roxbury's membership in the League preclude any amount of intrigue with Ripon's niece, especially if Roxbury were playing a deep game of her own at the King's behest.

"There could be any number of possible motives," Wessex pointed out, which was only the truth. "And what is Ripon doing?"

"Nothing." Misbourne's answer was comprehensive. "He keeps his niece very close and does not seem anxious to make the *ton* a present of her existence; she goes nowhere and sees no one . . . save Lady Roxbury."

"Interesting," Wessex said, with a composure he was far from feeling. He was possessed of a sudden swift desire to grab Roxbury and shake her until the truth rattled out from between her lying lips. He'd thought he could trust her—he'd thought he didn't have to think about her at all—and now look what she'd done. He became aware that Misbourne was watching him closely.

"Is there any news from Denmark?" Wessex asked.

"No more than one might expect." Misbourne answered him readily. "Koscuisko tells us that they still expect to sail by the end of July, when the sea is at its calmest. The Prince Regent is still attempting to redraw the treaty so that the Danes are obligated to nothing, but Sir John continues to forestall him at every turn, the wily old fox."

Wessex smiled faintly. Sir John's nickname in political circles was "The Little Bulldog" for precisely this quality of unswerving tenacity.

"What must be a matter of more concern is the Princess's reception when she arrives. Prince Jamie's intemperate behavior increases with each passing day, and there are rumors that an open break between the Prince and his father is all but inevitable."

And an open break between King and Prince would give Jamie a chance to form his own party—or, more likely, have it formed for him by the likes of Ripon. At least Jamie had not yet been beguiled by Ripon's niece. Wessex was certain that Misbourne would have mentioned such a disastrous development.

But no. Ripon's pretty catspaw was spending her days in the company of Wessex's betrothed.

"I may be able to whistle the Marchioness to heel," Wessex said slowly, "or at least gain her attention. I doubt she'd obey any order I gave, but if I were to object to the connection between her and Ripon's niece, the ensuing brawl might at least lend the matter a publicity that Ripon seems unwilling for it to have."

Misbourne regarded Wessex for a long moment, his grey eyes as bright and pale as glass.

"No," Misbourne said at last. "The vixen is out of her earth. We must see how she runs," Misbourne said.

12

The Marriage of True Minds

On June 15, 1805, at the Chapel Royal in St. James Palace, Rupert St. Ives Dyer, Captain His Grace the Duke of Wessex, took in holy matrimony Sarah Marie Eloise Aradia Dowsabelle Conyngham, Marchioness of Roxbury. The groom was formidably correct in a dove-grey waistcoat, biscuit-colored knee-breeches, and a dark blue coat; the bride was resplendent in cloth-of-silver. The King himself presented the bride to her groom, as the Marchioness was an orphan and—by the sheerest of technicalities—His Majesty's ward.

Though the wedding party itself was quite small, one hundred and fifty covers had been laid for the wedding breakfast that was held at the Marchioness's own property of Herriard House. Every delicacy and novelty that a small army of cooks could provide had been produced for the delight of the guests, including a small rainbow of jellies, and ices in every flavor imaginable.

By popular consensus, it was a very merry occasion.

Rather sourly, the Duke of Wessex wished that Illya Koscuisko was here to enjoy it. In fact, he wished that Koscuisko were here in his stead, and that he himself were at the devil.

This was a mistake. Regardless of his grandmother's wishes—or his monarch's—Wessex should not have married Roxbury. He'd known it the moment he entered the chapel and saw the girl standing beside the altar, an opulent and gleaming ghost in a dress that made her look as if she were formed of ice and steel. She had looked as stricken as if she were to be shot, and his sympathy with her feelings had made Wessex smile encouragingly at her. He could not tell if she had noticed.

Then had come the ceremony, and every word of it had hammered home the awful finality of what he was doing. Once they two were wed, only an Act of Parliament could undo the marriage again.

But once begun, there was no stopping the ceremony—and then the thing was done, and when Wessex kissed his bride, her lips were as cold as the ice her gown so resembled. Fortunately, she was not given the time to speak her mind about their wedding as the party dispersed from the church steps into breakfast-bound carriages, and afterward, Wessex had seen to it that she had no chance to approach him again. Tonight the happy couple were to sleep at Dyer House, as generations of Dukes and their Duchesses had before them, but—as Wessex's partner often said—they would burn that bridge when they came to it. Meanwhile, there was enough champagne flowing to drown the entire Imperial Guard in, and Wessex vowed that he would founder on it.

If he did not quite manage that, he succeeded in drinking enough to insulate him nicely from the wedding toasts that he was forced to receive. Possibly he even smiled at his bride. But while Wessex had often been a ready executioner in the service of King and Country, he'd never taken any joy in it. And by any honest account, he was ruining his new Duchess's life quite thoroughly. After all, she had married a spy, the lowest of the low. If his clandestine activities for the White Tower Group ever came to light, it would not be the hero's laurel that awaited Wessex but the martyr's crown—and an eternity of shame for his family that its head should have behaved in so thoroughly despicable a fashion.

And if that were not bad enough, his unfortunate Duchess was married to a man who had not the slightest intention of continuing his tainted line. She could, Wessex knew, gain an annulment if she could prove that (and if he had made enough enemies of the right sort in the interim). Perhaps, in a few years, that would be a way out for both of them, though that scandal, too, would be killing.

And then again, he could die.

Wessex felt his spirits lift. That possibility hadn't actually occurred to him before, but in his line of work it was a very real one. If he died, his shameful secrets could die with him, his widow could respectably remarry, and his grandmother need never know what a creature her grandson had become. Under the influence of far too much of the finest vintage champagne, Wessex became convinced that his death in action was the best of all possible outcomes, solving all his problems in the neatest fashion conceivable.

He would have to arrange it.

Just as soon as Jamie was safely married, and that damned treaty signed.

But first, he had to manage to get through his wedding night. . . .

*   *   *

Sarah, now Duchess of Wessex, sat bolt upright in the bridal bed, just as she had been left, watching the heavy bedcurtains sway gently closed from where Knoyle had let them fall a moment before. Light from the chamberstick that had been left burning on a side table winkled through tiny pinholes in the ancient fabric, and could be seen as a·thin slice of light where the faded scarlet silk had not quite been pulled shut.

She heard her abigail's steps fade as the woman left the room, and when that sound had vanished completely, Sarah could still hear all the other sounds Dyer House made as it settled upon its foundations. The sound of her new husband ascending the stair to join his bride, however, was not among them.

Secure now in the knowledge that Knoyle would not return and catch her behaving in some mysteriously unbridal fashion, Sarah pushed back the curtain and slipped out of bed. Her cashmire shawl lay across the back of a nearby chair; she picked it up and swirled it about herself.

The rooms of Dyer House were tiny, and though this back bedroom was one of the grandest the house could boast, its ceiling gorgeously painted with a daylight view of the dome of St. Paul's wreathed in cherubs and heavenly light, that same painted ceiling slanted dizzyingly down toward the windows in the back wall, making Sarah feel almost as if she needed to duck her head to reach them. The window's antique catches were tricky things, but after a moment's work Sarah flung the windows open and leaned out.

The night air was heavy with the river damp, and fog had curled in off the Thames, misting the air around her and·making the ground impossible to see. It was very late; a full moon rode the sky like an argent tea-tray, its light striking the fog and turning familiar shapes into the terrain of a frosted unreal otherworld out of which anything might come. Outside the narrow windows that opened onto the house's tiny back garden all of nighttime London could be heard going about its occupations as it readied itself for the morning. Sarah could hear the clip-clop of horse's hooves on the cobbled streets, the faint distorted cry of the Thames boatmen plying their river trade . . .

Where was Wessex?

Inexplicably, Sarah felt deserted. It was not that she had a *personal* interest in her new husband, of course. Her emotions were most certainly not engaged; that would be foolish, when by his every word and gesture he had indicated that theirs was to be a marriage of convenience only; the convenience to be King Henry's. But even so, it was slightly embarrassing to misplace one's bridegroom upon one's wedding night.

Suppose he did not mean to come at all?

That would suit her just as well, Sarah declared to herself, but she would like to know at once, and not have to lie awake wondering if her sleep would be disturbed by the sudden arrival of a stranger in her bedroom. Which was certainly what His Grace of Wessex was to the former Miss Sarah Cunningham of Baltimore. . . .

No. She was—she had been—Sarah Conyngham, the Marchioness of Roxbury. *Lady* Roxbury. She was the mistress of Mooncoign, and Mooncoign was hers, hers and her daughters', so long as the Pledge were kept.

Roxbury had sworn. But she *had not sworn. And she was not bound to the land.* . . .

Sarah rubbed her aching head, feeling a sudden wave of utter weariness crest over her. Her day had started before dawn, and it was now nearly midnight. She was as tired as she could ever remember having been, and her nightly dose of strengthening cordial had been forgotten in all the excitement, the bottle left behind in her bedroom in Herriard House. No wonder she was so confused that not only who she was, but where she ought to be was scattered and obscured in her mind.

A breeze purling in through the window made the flame of the chamberstick dance and swirl. The painted London on the ceiling seemed to tower and shimmer above her, as if at any moment the image might alter into another landscape entirely. Sarah groaned and closed her eyes tightly, leaning her head on the cool painted sill. She'd eaten very little at the wedding breakfast—fine name for a party that had stretched on until a scant few hours ago!—and drunk several glasses of smuggled French champagne to make up for it. No wonder she felt unwell.

Sarah slunk across the room and sat down in the chair, drawing her feet up beneath her to save them from the floor's chill. Cocooned in her cashmire shawl, she contemplated events. If he wasn't here—never mind "why" just now—where was he? She'd lost track of her new husband during the festivities at Herriard House, but he'd known she was going to Dyer House—he'd insisted upon it, in fact; some fugitive flare of *amour propre* in His Grace rebelling against beginning his marriage beneath his wife's roof. Around the time the lanterns were lit, Sarah had been happy to leave for Dyer House at the Dowager's urging, and naturally had expected Wessex to follow at once—the man was such a painful pattern-card of virtue that Sarah had assumed he would do precisely as anticipated upon every occasion.

Except, apparently, upon this one.

But as the hours had passed, and Sarah's elaborate wedding toilette had been dismantled, Wessex still had not arrived, and somehow she could not bring herself to ask the Dowager where her grandson—Sarah's husband—was.

Which thought brought Sarah back to this room, to an aching head and a rapidly increasing sense of unreality.

It didn't look as if Wessex was going to put in an appearance any time soon, or perhaps at all; Sarah was certain that Langley had long since barred the outside door, so unless the man could scale the wall to Sarah's third-floor window, he was doomed to spend the night on the street. Which was where (if nowhere worse) his bride wished him, if anyone were interested.

The candle had burned more than halfway to its socket when Sarah sighed and shook herself, and climbed stiffly back into bed. Why had he not come? He'd insisted upon this marriage—he'd offered her his ring and his name— why make a fool of her?

Why?

The rose-pink room was filled with candles and mirrors, and with tables draped in white linen cloths upon which decks of gaudy pasteboard and rouleaus of golden guineas vied for pride of place. Fortunes had changed hands here upon the turn of a card, and men whose families had been destroyed by the tables had slunk from these precincts to end their lives in the waters of the Thames or the privacy of their own libraries. The room remained unchanged.

The establishment was called Garvin's, and the man in the corner had been there since midnight. An empty decanter of whiskey sat at his elbow, and he was one of the few patrons in the salon who had not taken the opportunity to exchange his fashionable coat for one of the linen dusters provided by the establishment for the comfort of its patrons. It was now after four o'clock of a new spring morning, and he was still there, playing as mechanically and as desperately as if faro were his only hope of salvation. Onlookers thought it odd, since His Grace of Wessex had been winning consistently since he sat down.

In a lull in the play, a sharp-eyed servant whisked the

empty decanter away and replaced it with a fresh one.
His Grace affected not to notice.

Garvin's was only one of several clubs to which His
Grace of Wessex belonged, and by no means the first he
had visited since he left Herriard House several hours before. His original destination had been his Albany rooms,
as a satisfactory compromise between the company of his
well-wishers and the company of his new-wed bride.
There Wessex had shed his wedding garments for something less gaudy, and by the time he had done that, it
seemed an easier thing to seek the company of intimate
strangers in clubland than to go and make the acquaintance of his wife. Eventually and inevitably he had arrived
at Garvin's.

Garvin's was a unique establishment for a number of
reasons, two among them being that it admitted both
women and foreigners. The man believed to be its
owner was a thoroughly disreputable Irishman named
O'Donnell, whom few of Garvin's members would have
considered receiving in even a bachelor establishment that
aspired to respectability. It was said that O'Donnell had
killed a man with his fists, though no one was quite certain
of where or when this interesting event had taken place—
excepting always His Grace of Wessex, who had his own
ways of knowing a great many interesting things. It was
also said he had a partner, a woman, but no one knew
anything about her, either, including Wessex.

For that matter, no one knew why the club was called
Garvin's, or where O'Donnell had gotten the funds to
open it, and O'Donnell did not enlighten them. This air
of mystery in no way lessened the club's attractions; it may
well have increased them, as its patrons either relished the
self-created illusion of danger or felt that a man with such
a cloudy past would turn a tolerant eye upon their

equally-occluded presents. In this, too, O'Donnell did not enlighten them.

The ground floor of Garvin's was a series of private rooms available to members by appointment. It was the only area to which nonmembers were admitted, and then only when accompanied by a member. It was also the only floor possessing visible windows, and those windows were heavily barred, though Garvin's was located very near the best part of town. The first floor held the windowless gaming rooms—faro, whist, roulette—as well as a salon in which gentlemen who wished to drink in peace could do so. The second floor was a fencing salle, where those so inclined could practice the deadly art of the blade against one another or under the auspices of the dueling master whom O'Donnell kept always upon the premises. The quite-illegal boxing matches that Garvin's occasionally hosted for the delectation of its members were held upon the second floor as well.

The cellars of Garvin's were extensive, and contained a target range of sufficient length to accommodate those duels among members that could not be resolved through diplomacy or the sword. Though Garvin's kept no kitchen (members might partake of bread, cheese, and cold meat if desired), it had an extensive catalogue of wines and spirits stored beneath the street as well—conveyed to its cellars, or so it was rumored, by the same conjectured Thames tunnel through which many a duel's survivors were alleged to have been smuggled to the Continent or to a ship bound for the Americas. Most of the members were not completely certain whether or not such a tunnel existed; the uncertainty added to Garvin's mystique.

But the two things that Garvin's offered most of all to its clientele were absolute privacy and complete freedom from interruption. Its precincts were as sacrosanct as those of a medieval church. Bailiff, Redbreast, or private revenger, no one save Garvin's own members ascended above the ground floor, and once inside, even members were as likely as not to be chucked violently into the street did they venture to annoy another member.

Which was why it was so particularly surprising, on this very early June morning, that His Grace of Wessex was to be interrupted in the midst of his twin pursuits of deep play and heavy drinking.

The man who entered the gaming salon was almost painfully nondescript. That he wore evening dress—dark blue coat matching breeches buttoned at the knee, white silk stockings, black pumps—seemed almost an oversight. This self-effacing personage was hardly the sort that any hostess would invite to ornament an evening party; he had the sort of face that was forgotten almost before it was noticed.

Forgettable or not, he ought not have been able to pass the footman at the door below, much less ascend to these sacrosanct altitudes.

As he crossed the room, the self-effacing gentleman began to be noticed—for where he was, if not for who he was—and gradually the quiet conversation from the ranks of the gamesters ceased. As the ripple of quiet reached him, Wessex looked up into the spreading pool of silence and saw the intruder.

With great care, Wessex lay down his hand of cards and refilled his glass. He watched the quiet gentleman approach, but even after the man's destination became obvious to all, Wessex did nothing to indicate he was aware of the fact, other than to watch the man's advance with a steady implacable gaze.

At last the visitor reached Wessex's elbow.

The rest of the room had returned to its pleasures, once its inhabitants were certain that it was not their privacy that was to be infringed upon. The other gamesters at

Wessex's table, the intruder's target being determined beyond all doubt, set down their cards and waited for the Duke to deal summarily with him.

"There is someone who wishes to see you, Your Grace," the gentleman said.

"Then let him tell me himself."

Wessex was not precisely in his altitudes, but in the last several hours His Grace had drunk sufficiently deeply to have gained a certain implacable recklessness. It was the sort of condition in which a man might fight a duel over a comment about his tailor, were such a comment to be offered.

"Alas, the gentleman is not a member," the other replied.

"Then let him apply," Wessex said reasonably.

"Unfortunately, his business with Your Grace cannot wait upon the application process."

"I understand that O'Donnell can act in the absence of the Members' Committee, if necessary," Wessex responded unhelpfully.

"It is possible that Mr. O'Donnell would not welcome this gentleman's membership," the stranger said.

Wessex regarded him narrowly, patience gone. "It is more than possible that I shall shoot you if you do not go away."

"The gentleman's business with you is urgent, Your Grace," the gentleman persisted. "Will you not come?"

Perhaps it occurred to His Grace at this moment to wonder how the stranger had made it this far without outcry, or perhaps he simply tired of the verbal fencing match. Without answering, he stood and swept the pile of yellow-boys on the table before him into one of his pockets, and indicated that the interloper should precede him.

*   *   *

The chill predawn air was cold on Wessex's face as he stood on the doorstep of Garvin's. The night fog was at its thickest, but even so, he could see the lamps of the heavy carriage standing in the street a few doors away. Instinctively he stopped, his hand going to the concealed pocket in his jacket.

"There is no cause for alarm, Your Grace," the man said, turning. "I come on business from the Palace."

"So any man might say." And there were more factions in the Palace of St. James than King Henry's.

"But few of them would carry this."

The emissary reached into his pocket and withdrew a slender wallet. Flipping it open, he allowed Wessex to see the badge it contained. Gold and enamel glinted colorfully in the light of the cresset-basket burning beside Garvin's green door.

Wessex strode past the man to the standing coach, and flung open the door.

"Your Majesty."

King Henry was in a towering rage; Wessex could see that much from the hot glitter of the King's eyes and the high color spread across his cheekbones.

"So, Wessex. Is this how you would serve your King?" Henry demanded.

Wessex was abruptly, entirely, and unpleasantly sober. With the force of a sudden revelation, it occurred to him that he ought, perhaps, to have gone home. Hours ago.

"I made no secret of what I wished for with this marriage—that the Duke and Duchess of Wessex, leaders of the *ton*, should ease Princess Stephanie's admission into the ranks of English society. May I ask how the Duchess's reputation is to be enhanced by the knowledge that her husband has spent their wedding night at his clubs rather than going home to her bed?"

The King's tone was arctic. Wessex could not think of

any explanation he was willing to even attempt to provide.

"It will not be enhanced, Sir," Wessex answered in a low voice.

"Then, perhaps, this is the opening gambit in some deep game you play? Is the *ton* possibly to be moved to compassion by Her Grace of Wessex's plight? How could any woman deserted by her husband upon their wedding night be other than an object of pity, after all? And you have made the matter so very public."

And so he had, Wessex thought in despair. Had his wits utterly deserted him, that instead of going to ground, he had made the knowledge of his absence from Dyer House a present to half the Polite World? Even if those he had played against tonight at Garvin's said nothing of his presence there, that was not the only place he had been this evening.

There was nothing he could possibly say.

The King gazed fixedly at him, and Wessex was possessed of the sinking feeling that King Henry understood everything of what had happened here tonight, even those things of which Wessex himself would prefer to remain ignorant.

"Do you think you can repair matters?" the King asked evenly.

"I *shall* repair matters," Wessex vowed. Tonight's folly could be smoothed over, with determination and his wife's assistance. He had not made a good beginning, but with luck they could still produce a convincing charade. He would be the uxorious and attentive Duke, and Sarah his gracious Duchess.

At least in public.

"Then there is no more to be said," King Henry pronounced. He tapped his cane upon the ceiling, and Wessex felt the coach begin to move off. *Of course,* he realized.

It would be best to conceal the bridegroom's time of arrival at Dyer House as much as possible.

But the journey, short as it was, was far from pleasant.

She was Sarah Cunningham, and in her deepest dreams she was passing through a wood that had never known axe or forester; she moved like a carp through the river, an animal at home in the place for which it had been created.

She no longer wore long gowns of muslin, or brocade, or calico over stockings and corset and petticoats. Her hair was not dressed high on her head with ribbons or jewels. She did not carry a painted fan, and move with the whisper of satin slippers over marble floors.

No.

The dream-Sarah's braided hair hung down her back, heron feathers braided into it at the temples. Her face was painted with hunting magic in red and yellow and white, and she wore the beaded leather smock and leggings of a warrior of the People. In her left hand she carried a musket in its fringed and beaded sheath.

She was Sarah Cunningham of Baltimore, of a country that had owed no allegiance to mad, bad King George of England in all the years of Sarah's lifetime.

But no! It is Henry Stuart who is King, not George of Hanover!

No. She might be a backward Colonial, ignorant of the ways of the Great Power to the East to which her country had been so lately subject, but even she knew . . .

But the memory-within-a-dream balked her; memory of an opulent presentation gown far finer than anything that could be found in the entire state of Maryland, and of a regal man who smiled at her as he raised Lady Roxbury from her curtsey.

But that was not true; not real. It could not be.

She was Sarah Cunningham of Baltimore. She was! There was no Roxbury, no Marchionate.

And to fall back into that elegant fantasy would destroy her.

Her vision cleared. She was Sarah Cunningham, daughter of Alasdair Cunningham, foster-daughter of a Cree warrior. This was what was real. She stood very still, inhaling the sharp green scent of the summer woods. The wind was blowing toward her, away from the prey she hunted.

As if by her thoughts she had ill-wished herself, the wind shifted, and suddenly she could smell the rank scent of decay. There was something behind her; something monstrous and evil.

And it was moving toward her.

Sarah stood frozen to the spot, unwilling to believe, until she heard the sound of crackling underbrush, as something heedless in its power began moving deliberately toward her. Hunting her.

Sarah began to run.

The sound behind her grew louder, and now the choking stench of the monster that pursued her was all that she could smell. Wildcat—boar—without knowing what followed, Sarah feared it as she had never feared any earthly peril. If it caught her, a disaster worse than death would be her portion.

As she ran, the forest began to thin, but instead of the cultivated fields · and white-washed frame houses that made up Baltimore in the first years of the new century, she broke out onto an endless vista of close-manicured green.

This is Mooncoign..

She stopped, disoriented enough to forget, for a moment, what pursued her. New memories warred with old, and try as she might, Sarah could not reconcile them. She had been journeying to England—She had taken ship in Baltimore—

No. She had been born at Mooncoign. . . .

Both could not be true.

"But they can."

Sarah spun around. The voice had come from behind her, and as she turned she thought wildly that it was the monster itself, given human voice. Then she saw the speaker, and for an instant believed that it was one of her Cree brethren who spoke—but this stranger, for all that he dressed in the skins of animals and carried a tall spear, had the rosy-fair skin of an English child.

His hair was a white, lime-stiffened crest over his skull and down his back. Rings of blue paint around his eyes gave his gaze the staring intensity of an owl's, and around his neck he wore a gleaming tubular collar of pure gold. As he regarded her serenely, she realized that she had seen him before.

In Mooncoign's garden, the night of the masquerade ball.

"How," Sarah asked, falteringly. "How can both be true?"

The stranger smiled, as if she had passed some unknown test merely by asking the question, and held out his hand.

Sarah set her hand in his.

The dream shifted. Now she and the stranger were walking through the paths of Mooncoign's formal garden, and the great house itself reared up before them, its white facade blue with the chilly spring twilight of weeks before. Sarah still wore her beaded buckskins, but the stranger now wore a fantastic archaic costume in green velvet and a brazen mask ornamented with sweeping golden antlers. He gestured toward the house with one gloved and jeweled hand.

"It begins here. But where does it end—ah, me; there

is the riddle. And not mine to solve, Sarah Cunningham—but yours."

"Mine?" Sarah echoed, startled. The juxtaposition of her suppressed self and the undeniable reality of Mooncoign was illuminating that baffling netherland of memory: there had been Baltimore, then the ship, then the coach.

And Dame Alecto in both—in Baltimore, and here.

"The same woman, but not the same person," her guide said. Now he wore a leopard's skin over black Elizabethan velvets and a mask to match, and stared wisely out at her from behind the jeweled eyes of the cat.

"You're talking in riddles," Sarah said angrily.

She'd forgotten that she was dreaming, but she had not forgotten the loathsome beast that had chased her out of the wood. If it were not a trick of this smiling, elegant gentleman—something she was not prepared to rule out—then it might return at any moment.

"Riddles are my nature," the stranger replied, "for I am the Master of the Horn Gate and the Ivory. But here is your answer, Sarah—look."

Sarah looked. They were in the shadow of the house itself, now, and she could look in through a ground-floor window and see an opulent room with a fire burning upon the hearth, and over the hearth, a painting of a woman in antique gems and velvets.

"That is my bedroom," Sarah said. *At least, it is the bedroom of the Marchioness of Roxbury, and everyone says that I am she.*

"Is it?" said the stranger. "Then why aren't you in the bed?"

Sarah looked. A young, brown-haired woman lay in the great carved bed, her slender form elevated upon a mound of pillows.

"But I am in the bed," Sarah said in growing confusion.

Through the glass of the window she could see herself plainly.

Just as she had seen herself in the moments before the mail-coach had crashed. The sun had been rising—

—setting—

—the stranger had been driving a gig—

—sitting inside a coach; and she had—

"Stop!" Sarah groaned, turning away from the bewildering scene at the window. "How could I be in two places at once?"

The same woman . . . but not the same person.

"Ah," said the stranger. "A question I can answer." He plucked at Sarah's sleeve, and led her away from the window.

The ornamental water had been added to the grounds by the last Marquess of Roxbury, Sarah's grandfather. But which Sarah? Following her guide, Sarah began to dimly realize that all that she thought she knew of Mooncoign— or of London society—she had been carefully taught in the weeks that followed her accident.

And her own memories had been hidden from her.

Sarah leaned forward, gazing into the still, silvery surface of the lake. Though she could feel the presence of her companion's body beside her, the surface of the lake reflected only her.

Instinctively, Sarah tried to turn toward him, to reassure herself with her own eyes that he still knelt beside her, but his hand upon her cheek prevented her.

"No, Sarah. Gaze into the water, and see the truth."

Sarah leaned forward, and the mirrorlike surface of the water darkened until it seemed an endless void opening beneath her feet. In its depths she could see a flicker of light, and as she stared at it the flickering took on form and color.

Figures. Pictures. Scenes. And at the center of each one was Sarah.

Sometimes it was as if she gazed into a mirror. Sometimes she did not recognize herself at all. It was the present that she saw—but an infinity of presents, ranging from the nearly familiar to those so alien that Sarah hardly recognized them. Here she was in the dress of a Cree maiden, a baby in her arms and a tall warrior at her side. There, she slaved still in her cousin's house in Baltimore. And again, another Sarah stood beside the Duke of Wessex—

"I will not look at any more!" Sarah cried, dashing her hand across the surface of the water and spoiling the mirror. "What does it mean? They are all me, but . . ."

"But they are all in their proper places, Sarah Cunningham of Baltimore, and you are not," her companion said. "You have been brought from your own world to take the place of one who failed—and yet who dared not fail. For a creature stalks *this* world—"

In the distance, Sarah heard a faint savage howl. Though the day had been sourcelessly bright, it seemed now as if a cloud passed over the sun. The day seemed darker now, and colder.

The sound came again. Instinctively she connected it with the creature that had chased her.

"That is what you must help to destroy," her companion said gravely. Sarah opened her mouth in automatic protest—they had risen to their feet, her companion's uneasiness communicating itself to her—but the wailing came again, closer this time, and now it seemed as if she could smell the foul rankness of the hunter once more.

"Go," the other said, pushing her toward the trees. "You must flee, Sarah; I will hold the beast back while I may, but it is not my blood that it hungers for. Remember all I have told you—and remember, too, that you do not yet belong to this world. If you cannot make yourself a part of this land, you will die, Sarah, and the Great Work will remain undone!"

"But—But—" Sarah sputtered. Half-hints and impossible truths—what was she to make of them?

Her companion now was garbed in silver armor, a red cross blazing like rubies upon the shining white damask of his stainless surcoat. He lifted a sword that flashed so brightly in the light that she could not tell whether it was forged of gold or silver, and raised his shining shield.

"*Go!*"

There was a crashing sound, as of something forcing its way through the ornamental hedges at the far side of the house, and Sarah surrendered to the urgency in his voice and to her own fear.

She ran. And as she ran, she heard an unfamiliar voice shouting for her to come back, come back, and a high keening sound, as of a stormwind whipping through the treetops.

Wessex cautiously opened the door to his bedroom. The early summer dawn thrust a ghostly illusion of light through the narrow windows, allowing him to make out the shapes of the familiar room even without the hood-winked lantern that he held.

The bedside candle had burnt itself out, filling the pewter receiver with a white pool of beeswax. At some point the window had been opened and not relatched; when it was closed the slant of the house had caused it to drift open again, filling the room with morning chill.

Wessex reached into his pocket for the object he carried, and advanced cat-footedly toward the silent bed. The lantern was well oiled; there was no betraying squeak as he opened it and allowed a ray to fall through the opened bed-curtains onto the bed's sleeping occupant.

His wife lay pillowed against white linen like a Renaissance angel in disarray. Her braided hair lay loosely against her neck; her lashes brushed her unpainted cheeks, and the whitework-embroidered lawn of her nightdress made her look absurdly young. Disturbed by some dream, she frowned. Asleep, she possessed what was to Wessex's eye a curious purity, almost an innocence.

And her life, her fate, and her reputation were now in his keeping.

I will never hurt you, he vowed, gazing down at her, and a fatal quirk of honesty made him silently amend the words to: *I will hurt you as little as I may.*

But he had come here on a specific mission, and he wanted to fulfil that charge without wakening her. He set the dark lantern down carefully on the table beside the chamberstick and drew the package from his coat pocket.

Ruby and gold flared in the lantern-light, caught in a web of glittering flame. The necklace held a heart-shaped ruby the size and color of a ripe cherry, surrounded by diamonds as clear as winter's first ice. On each side of the ruby a diamond-encrusted heart led to the wide gold chain. For almost two hundred years his line had presented the Heart of Flame to Dyer brides as the Morning Gift.

He turned it over. The back of the flanking hearts was plain polished gold, on which the intertwined initials of generations could be seen. A new set of initials now shone bright upon the old gold, graven by steady expert hands at Rundell and Bridges: *R* and *S*, ornately intertwined. Rupert and Sarah.

Careful not to waken her, Wessex set the glittering necklace on the pillow next to Sarah, and picked up the lantern once more. A moment later he was gone as if he had never been there at all. The door closed softly behind him.

Sarah did not wake.

Moving like a specter through his own house—it was his mother's residence, but that was an inconsequential distinction—Wessex reached the library and eased the door shut behind him. He drew a breath of relief; no one would disturb him, and he would disturb no one, here.

In his father's day, this had been the study, and a strictly masculine preserve. The heavy mahogany desk and sideboard remained from that time, and books still lined the mellow oaken shelves, but the Dowager and her lady-companion had since made their own stamp upon the premises. There was a needleworked footstool beside the deep chair that faced the fireplace, and a wicker sewing basket, half-spilling its freight of embroidery, lay upon the seat cushion.

Wessex set his lantern down upon the desk and rummaged in the drawer for a rolled spill. Finding one, he lit it at the lantern's flame and used it to light first the candles on the mantel, then the elaborate candelabrum that stood on the library's long center table. The room filled with light, the illumination banishing its aspect of ghostly disuse.

There was a fire on the hearth, ready-laid for morning, and it kindled quickly, radiating a welcoming warmth. Wessex searched out the brandy decanter and poured himself a generous glassful. Langley kept the decanters filled; the Dowager might use this room, but she would not materially change the way it had been when her son was alive.

Automatically, Wessex looked up to the portrait above

the mantelpiece; a LeBrun portrait of his father as a young man, wearing the satin and lace of a vanished age and swaggering with a rapier upon his hip. That swashbuckling dandy had died a dozen years ago, in a fatal, foolish attempt to save the Dauphin of France from the Terror, but Grandanne lived in patient waiting, as if some day Andrew Dyer might walk back in the front door—even though a dozen men had pronounced him lost in France and a Chancery Court had ruled that the title should pass to his son.

Still, somehow, Grandanne thought against all reason and sense that Andrew might someday return, and sometimes Wessex felt as if she were right; as if the *soi-disant* certainties of his life were only a masquerade, their foundations built upon shifting sand.

He shook his head, dourly amused at his own fancies. He needed either more liquor or not to have drunk what he already had; with a quick, brutal gesture he raised the glass of brandy to his lips and half drained it.

He had not meant to give Sarah the Heart of Flame at all. A petty gesture, he knew, as if having lost the game of freedom he could not bear to capitulate utterly. For the Heart of Flame was a gift between lovers, and he and Sarah were not lovers, nor would they ever be: he had married her at the command of the King, and at the same command she had accepted him.

But he had given Sarah his name and his title, and she was entitled to all of the jewelry that went with them. There was no reason for him to withhold any of the traditional gems simply because the act of their presentation was a lie.

He emptied the glass and refilled it again, knowing that the liquor was a substitute for steadiness of nerve, and tomorrow he would have to learn to face his wife without its aid.

Tomorrow and for the rest of his life.

Wessex sighed, and carried his glass back to the fire. As he passed the stool, his foot struck something that lay upon the carpet and set it skimming across the floor. Intrigued, Wessex stooped and picked it up. A sketchbook, bound between boards of gold-stamped buckram. He carried it back to the chair and sat down, automatically moving the workbasket as he did so. Neither Grandanne nor Dame Alecto sketched, to his knowledge. He wondered whose it was.

The pages were filled with careful, intricate drawings, some of them finished in watercolor and ink. Obviously the sketchbook of a young lady of fashion, the contents were very much what one would expect: bowls of fruit, studies of flowers and horses' heads, drawings of long-limbed ladies in elaborate gowns, apparently copied from Ackerman's Repository.

But there were other drawings, harmless enough in themselves, but oddly disturbing to Wessex. The deck of a ship, carefully executed but oddly generalized, as if the artist were attempting to reconstruct something from memory. A Colonial settlement, its crude whitewashed buildings scattered along a stretch of unfamiliar coast. A woman churning butter. Another sitting at her spinning wheel.

And then page after page of Aborigines, wild and splendid in their feathers and paint. The artist had spent a great deal of time on these subjects, rendering every detail of their barbaric costumes and wild surroundings with scrupulous care . . . and accuracy. Wessex had reason to know the drawings were accurate, as he and the volatile Mr. Koscuisko had spent some six months traveling with the People in the American colonies during one memorable adventure.

But it would be an extensive search to find any

woman—even one born and bred in the Colonies—who had as intimate an experience with the Cree as this artist seemed to possess. Who was she?

There were some letters interleaved with these pages, and from them he discovered the name of the book's owner: Sarah, Marchioness of Roxbury.

His wife.

Surely this was not possible. If Sarah had traveled to the American Colonies Wessex would know . . . and if she had not, he did not think she could have drawn such detailed and precise images.

For the first time, Wessex began to wonder precisely who it was that he had married.

Sarah ran from the Terror that pursued her through a landscape that grew increasingly more unreal, until its very unreality drove her out of sleep and into waking.

She was lying in an unfamiliar bed in an unfamiliar narrow room. Golden morning light turned the mural of aerial London spread across the ceiling to glitter and fire.

She was in Dyer House, and yesterday she had married the Duke of Wessex.

Sarah groaned, rolling over. She'd thought, for a brief dazzling moment, that it was all part of the dream.

The dream! But even as she tried to grasp at it, those memories filtered through her fingers. There was something she'd learned—some truth that she needed to remember. . . .

But it was gone.

Sarah pounded her hand against her pillow in frustration, and yelped as something cold and supple slithered against her wrist. She jerked away, sitting upright and opening her eyes.

There was a necklace lying in the bed, where it had

fallen from the pillow. Confused, Sarah picked it up, wondering if in all the confusion of yesterday she could possibly have worn such a thing to bed.

No. This was none of her jewels. Sarah stared down at the ruby heart cradled in her hand as understanding came to her. The Duke of Wessex had been here, sometime while she slept, and left this.

Sarah turned the glittering prize over in her hand, and gazed at the intertwined initials engraved upon the back. A pretty token; an opulent bribe, intended to buy her compliant silence on the subject of his absence the night before. To buy . . . as if she were a tradesman, a servant, a common prostitute walking the London streets. As if there were no honor between them, or even duty, but only an acquiescence that must be bought.

Sarah ground her teeth in irritation rapidly turning to fury. Wessex must not think his dukedom a very worthy thing if that was the sort of person he was willing to have for his Duchess. Pure furious anger swept away all the ambiguity and uncertainty of the last several weeks and the last clinging cobwebs of her strange dream. Wessex had offered her a mortal insult, and Sarah was going to make him very sorry that he had.

The yellow-and-white breakfast parlor on the first floor gave one a fine view of the bustle of the street below. The Duke of Wessex regarded it with a baleful disinterest. The fine china cup before him held strong black coffee instead of his usual morning chocolate; even with Atheling's sternest measures and a great deal of ice-cold well water, Wessex felt as brittle as the delicate cup he held.

He had come down to breakfast as if everything were perfectly normal; he had greeted Grandanne (the Dowager was a notorious early riser, and her grandson was not

surprised to see her up and doing at an hour when most
of Society still clung to its bed) and told her that Sarah
was still asleep. So far he had told nothing but the truth;
if the conclusions he wished his grandmother to draw
were not precisely the truth, that was merely another sin
upon his far from lily-white conscience.

If the Dowager had anything to say about the lateness
of Wessex's arrival at Dyer House or his choice of ma-
tuinal beverage, she made no comment. The morning
light sparkled upon the linen and silver, and upon the
bright spectacle of oranges filling the colorful Export Ware
bowl on the table. The Dowager placidly ate her mar-
malade and toast and drank her tea as if this were any
ordinary morning, and Wessex realized that he had made
yet another miscalculation in this whole disastrous affair.

He had undertaken to enact a masquerade with the aid
of an only somewhat-willing partner; well and good. But
it was borne in upon him that unlike his many other im-
personations, he had no idea of what this one entailed.
How was he to carry off before the eyes of the *ton*—and,
a slightly more urgent question, before the eyes of his own
grandmother, a far more critical audience—the illusion of
an ordinary marriage?

He was saved from further consideration upon that
head by the entrance of his Duchess. Sarah swept into the
room as regally as if she were making her bow before
Royalty, and stopped beside Grandanne's chair to drop a
kiss upon the Dowager's cheek.

"Good morning, my dear. How radiant you look," the
Dowager said placidly.

"Thank you, Godmama," Sarah answered.

She was dressed in a pale pink morning robe trimmed
with ribbons of darker pink, and the Heart of Flame was
a vivid blaze about the base of her throat. She looked

across the table to Wessex, who had stood when she entered the room.

"Rupert," Sarah said calmly.

Of course she had every right to use his Christian name—they were more than mere acquaintance, they were married—but Wessex found himself slightly nettled by her cool assumption of her new status. However, he bowed over her hand in the fashion that had charmed countesses and courtesans in half the capitals of Europe, and conducted her to her seat.

"I trust you slept well?" the Dowager asked, as a footman stepped forward from his post beside the door to pour tea for Sarah. "Sometimes it is difficult to do so in a strange house."

Sarah smiled at Wessex, color rising in her cheeks, and raised her cup to her lips. "I slept entirely well," she said.

The ring that held the device of the Boscobel League glimmered upon Sarah's finger, made to fit by a plug of beeswax inserted between the finger and the band. Gazing at his new-wed bride, Wessex felt himself relax. She had agreed to his terms, then, and would help him play out the game. Married by the King's command, theirs would be a *marriage blanc*, with no sordid tangle of bodies or passions to mar it. Sarah would have a Duke's ransom in jewels.

But no Duke.

13

A Singular Duchess

It was exceedingly fortunate, the Duchess of Wessex told herself on a fine June morning precisely one week after her wedding day, that her husband had been called from Town on Royal business of the most urgent. Fortunate because if he were not there to see it, he was not there to rebuke her for removing back to the comfort and familiarity of her own home—fortunate, too, that his absence carried with it a ready-made justification for such a move that even the highest sticklers must accept.

The move back into her own house gave her a breathing space while she considered how she was now to manage her life. For King Henry and the still-unknown Princess Stephanie of Denmark's sake, Sarah must present the world with the illusion of a happy marriage. And that meant that she must see Wessex every day. They must live in the same house.

But not yet, Sarah told herself with craven relief. Her husband was off to the fen country, and she was left in

Town, to sample the delights of being Wessex's Duchess without suffering the inconvenient presence of the Duke.

Those delights were both powerful and pervasive, but Sarah possessed a sense of standing apart from the pleasures of Society. Others might desire these things, but she did not.

The puzzled looks of her servants and of her acquaintance told Sarah how very much she had changed from the Marchioness of Roxbury that they had known. But she was *not* that woman, and in her troubled, restless nights, Sarah wondered if she ever had been. Only Mooncoign seemed real, and not the ritual and the pomp that surrounded it—and certainly not this London life of endless revelry.

At least she had made one true friend in her time here. And Sarah had discovered, to her delight, that a ducal coronet seemed to carry enough weight with Meriel's wicked uncle to overcome his prohibition against Meriel's going forth into any form of society whatever—for Miss Bulleyn had been granted permission to call upon the Duchess of Wessex today to drink tea.

Nervously, Sarah fluttered about the drawing-room, as if Herriard House's small army of servants had not already engineered all domestic matters to perfection, and as if Cook did not have an array of tasty dainties prepared in the kitchen, awaiting Sarah's call. She paused to peer out the window, inspecting the carriages that passed on the street below. A glance at the clock upon the mantlepiece told her that she could not expect Miss Bulleyn for a quarter of an hour yet, so there was no use looking out for her carriage.

It occurred to Sarah that she was not even sure where Miss Bulleyn lived. They had always met in secluded public places, by arrangement, each new meeting fixed at the close of the previous. But that near-clandestine arrangement would cease as of today, Sarah vowed. If Meriel's uncle could afford to set at naught the wishes of a mere Marchioness, he would find the desires of the Duchess of Wessex a different matter entirely.

The sight of a familiar figure in the street caused Sarah to emit a highly unduchesslike squeak. It was all she could do to compose herself in a slightly more ladylike fashion until Buckland came to announce her young visitor.

Miss Bulleyn was a figure of flowerlike perfection in white muslin and a deep-poke bonnet. The ribbons that trimmed bonnet and dress alike matched the deep green velvet spencer that she wore, and tiny emerald drops glittered in her ears. She had the same Otherworldly beauty as—

But as soon as the thought formed it vanished, leaving Sarah momentarily confused. She shook off her confusion to hug Meriel in greeting, a salutation that was warmly returned.

"How well you look!" Meriel said. "Marriage agrees with you."

"The absence of my husband agrees with me," Sarah responded with tart honesty, and Meriel's green eyes danced with answering amusement.

"Then I will be glad for you that he is gone—but he is twice a fool to leave you so hard upon the heels of your wedding." Meriel untied the ribbons of her bonnet and set it aside, and then began calmly removing her crocheted cotton gloves.

"It was not of his own choice." Perversely, Sarah felt the need to defend her new husband. "It was by the King's order. Something to do with the Army," she finished vaguely, suddenly realizing that though she had thought Wessex's explanation pedantic and boring in its length, he had actually told her nothing at all.

"And when the King disposes, what can his loyal subjects do save obey?" Meriel said.

It was undoubtedly not Meriel's intent to make the simple statement sound so scornful; Sarah decided that her nerves were playing her false after so many sleepless nights. While she had no idea what Meriel's politics might be, certainly there was no malice in her friend. Sarah smiled to herself, shaking her head. Meriel's caustic words were no more than the truth, anyway: what could any of them do in the face of King Henry's commands? She had married Wessex because of them, after all.

"But I hope he does not make you too unhappy," Meriel went on.

"The King?" Sarah said blankly, and Meriel laughed; a silvery peal of affectionate mirth.

"Your *husband*, looby! Although, if you are thinking of the King when you ought to be thinking of him . . ."

"Indeed," said Sarah with exaggerated piety, "I should be very wrong not to think of the King on every possible occasion."

As she had hoped, Meriel laughed.

At first the visit passed smoothly, with the two women chatting of their common experiences: books, shopping, plays they had attended. They did not have many acquaintance in common—for though Sarah was not much fond of Society, she was a figure in it, while so far as she could tell, Meriel did not go out at all. Sarah tried to extract from her friend the promise that she would visit again, but Meriel's response was odd; not precisely evasion, but almost one of guilt. At last she said:

"I see I may not put it off any longer, but I pray you, Sarah, that for the friendship we have shared, you will not hate me for what I am about to do." From a pocket in her dress, Meriel withdrew a small velum envelope folded over a square of stiff pasteboard.

Highly puzzled, Sarah took the mysterious billet. Opening it, she pulled out the little square of pasteboard and read almost with incomprehension the invitation written upon its smooth white surface.

"The Earl of Ripon requests the Favor of the Duchess of Wessex's Attendance at a Ball to be held upon the Occasion of the Presentation to Society of his Niece, Lady Meriel Jehanne Bulleyn Highclere. . . ."

"Your wicked Uncle Richard is the Earl of Ripon?" Sarah said in astonishment. Which meant, her mind informed her with pedantic thoroughness, that Meriel was Ripon's niece and, further, that her dear friend Meriel was the woman Wessex had said was intended to entrap the Prince of Wales into marriage at the bidding of some looming Catholic conspiracy.

"Yes," Meriel said in a low voice. "When I knew who you were, I did not want you to know, for your husband and my uncle are political enemies, but Uncle Richard insisted . . ." Her voice trailed off.

Sarah looked sideways at Meriel. It was hard to imagine anything more ridiculous than that Meriel should be entangled in such a dark plot—but Wessex had said it was true, and whatever Sarah might think of the man, he was not given to flights of gothic imagination. If Meriel were indeed tangled in such a coil, surely she would need a friend to help her find her way free.

"Oh, Meriel, *pray* do not look so Friday-faced! I do not care two pins for any quarrel that Wessex and Ripon may hold," Sarah said, with more heat than accuracy. "We two are friends, are we not? And I hope we shall remain so."

"Then . . . you do not mind?" Meriel asked in a low voice.

Sarah hesitated, choosing her words with care, for to tell Meriel she did not "mind" was to extend a *carte blanche* over Ripon's contemplated treasons, and that she could not do. Disgusted with her husband Sarah might be, but she was loyal to the King, and it had not even occurred to her to doubt the wisdom of the Danish treaty and the wedding that was its price. Sarah decided her first action must be to extract a promise from Meriel not to be a party to any plan to entrap the Prince of Wales.

But Sarah would never know whether her common-sensical approach would have enjoyed any particular success, for at that moment the door opened, and Wessex strode unannounced into the parlor.

Wessex checked at the sight of Lady Meriel, but by then it was too late, for his guest brushed past him. A heartbeat later James, Prince of Wales, came face-to-face with Lady Meriel Highclere.

She swept him a deep curtsey, looking up from beneath her raven's-wing lashes into Jamie's face.

"Duchess!" Jamie said tardily, never taking his eyes from Meriel's face. The Prince hurried forward, raising Meriel up out of her curtsey. "Dash it, Wessex, you never told me that your wife's friends were such charmers!"

"Your Highness, may I present Lady Meriel Highclere? She is the niece of the Earl of Ripon," Wessex said austerely.

Sarah stared at Wessex, surprised out of her mortification. How had he known who Meriel was?

"Yes, that is right," Sarah said lamely. "She has just come to—to drink tea," she finished, whisking Ripon's invitation behind her back.

As if on cue, Buckland entered the room, carrying a heavily laden tea tray. Sarah flicked a glance at the mantle clock. It was four o'clock, and Sarah had asked that the tea be brought in now, but—oh!—her timing could have been better . . .

"Well," the Prince said heartily, "I must say that tea seems like a fine idea—and with such delightful company, too. But I must take Mr. Highclere to task; Geoff never told me he had such a handsome niece."

"You will turn my head with your compliments, Your Highness," Meriel murmured. A fetching blush rose into her ivory cheeks, and she clung to Jamie's arm as if unable to stand by herself. "I know that you are widely accounted a connoisseur of many things, so that your praises must be held to be far more sapient than those of lesser men."

"Ah, well, a man in my position does have his opportunities," Jamie said, happily swallowing this piece of outrageous flattery without a blink. "But do sit down, Lady Meriel," he finished, conducting her to a chair beside the tea table and seating himself beside her.

Filled with a looming despair, Sarah sank back down onto the sopha. She tried not to look in Wessex's direction—of all the times for the man to come back, why did he have to return *now*, and in such company?

And what must he be thinking, to find her entertaining Ripon's niece? It was true Wessex had not forbidden the connection when he had told her of his suspicions regarding Ripon's plans, but then, he had not *known* of the connection—or had he?

Sarah did not choose to wonder—at least, not at this fraught moment. She poured tea for her future sovereign, her guest, her husband, and herself.

And then realized, with Meriel and the Prince deep in the most animated of exchanges, that Propriety demanded that she make some sort of conversation with Wessex.

*   *   *

There had been a hint of Saint-Lazarre's business, a hot enough lead that the King had been willing, even after the furious upbraiding he had given Wessex less than a day before, to set Wessex upon the trail; the source was one of Wessex's own contacts. Such promising information turned neglect of his new bride into a positive duty.

And so Wessex had saddled Hirondel and ridden for the fen country to tease his informers out of their taciturnity. What he had learned there had been enough to cause him to follow the trail across the Channel, to spend three days in a French port impersonating a Breton fisherman on the run from the Army. He had barely escaped impressment by a French shore party, but Wessex had no desire to spend any time at all fighting for La Belle France in a naval capacity, either from the rigging of a man o'war or from the decks of a prison galley, and had taken that near miss as his signal to find his way back to England. His news was too important to risk losing, and he was the only one who knew it.

On a bitter January day twelve years ago, the King of France had been guillotined by a bloodthirsty Convention. Louis-Charles, the Dauphin of France, had been a child only seven years of age.

Louis-Charles—King Louis XVII from the moment the blade fell upon his father's neck—spent only a few more months in the company of his mother and elder sister, the fourteen-year-old Marie-Therese, before being taken away into "more secure custody" at an unknown location. By Christmas, his mother, his sister, and his aunt were dead . . . but no one was sure where the young Louis-Charles was.

Wessex's father Andrew had died trying to find out. In the wake of King Louis's execution, Andrew, Duke of Wessex, had gone into France at the White Tower's behest to try to save the rest of the French Royal family, especially the vital heir to the House of Bourbon. But Andrew had vanished without a trace, without any hint of how close he was to the completion of his mission. And the whereabouts of the young King remained a mystery that baffled all of Europe.

A band of *emigrés* that succeeded in escaping France a few years later carried the story that the boy had died in prison, but this tale had been seen by the Great Powers as a fairly transparent attempt to consolidate France under Napoleon by causing the Royalists, through Louis-Charles's supposed death, to acknowledge the *emigré* Comte de Provence as King Louis XVIII knowing that the Comte's unreformed Bourbonist sympathies would win French supporters not for the true king, Louis-Charles, but for the devil they knew—Napoleon.

The Comte de Provence, however, had refused to assume the title of King upon the rumors of Louis-Charles's death, instead challenging the French to produce the body of his nephew or even a reliable witness to his death. But no one was able to present Louis-Charles, dead or alive, and the succession was deadlocked.

So matters had stood for the next ten years. Belief grew that the young King must be dead—for surely, if he were alive, he would have appeared, even if only to be paraded as a suppliant puppet at Bonaparte's Imperial court. And if he *were* alive; Louis-Charles's arrival on the political stage would galvanize the Triple Alliance to renewed energy and spur the Royalist factions to consolidate and fight effectively for the one King of France everyone must acknowledge without question: the son of Louis XVI.

Thus, everyone grew to assume Louis-Charles was dead, but no one was entirely certain of it. And now this.

Saint-Lazarre thought the Young King was alive. More, he thought he knew where Louis-Charles was. Saint-Lazarre was suspicious and cynical, but whatever information he had gained had been enough to convince him. That was why Saint-Lazarre had disappeared so suddenly from English society, and why he had vanished into France without a word to anyone.

Truth or compelling fraud, this news could overset the chessboard of Europe, and the players of the Shadow Game must be warned at once. So Wessex had made his way back to England, reclaimed his horse and his own identity, and ridden for St. James Palace.

He'd made his report twice: once to King Henry and once to Baron Misbourne, each of whom had plied him with endless questions. Such information could not be taken at face value: it must be sifted, weighed, checked as much as possible. But if it were true—if there were even a possibility that it was true—someone must go to France to pick up Saint-Lazarre's trace, to reach the Young King before Saint-Lazarre moved him to yet another hiding place . . . and to make certain that King Louis would await the restoration of his throne in England, and nowhere else.

But Wessex would not be the man charged with carrying out this delicate task. King Henry had been most explicit in that regard. Wessex's place was in London, dancing attendance upon his wife and preparing the way for the arrival of the Danish Princess, not adventuring upon the Continent.

And so Wessex had returned at last to Dyer House, only to discover that his wife was not there. That his wife, free as you please, had removed to Herriard House once more, just as if their wedding ceremony had never taken place.

For himself, Wessex would have been just as happy to leave her at Herriard House—but fresh from the King's presence, the King's strictures firmly in mind, Wessex was not at all doubtful as to where his duty lay. It had been

pure bad luck that he had fallen in with Prince Jamie on
the way.

He'd seen the Prince coming out of one of his clubs in
the company of Mr. Geoffrey Highclere, and a desire to
preserve the young Prince from that gentleman's poison-
ous counsel had led Wessex to detach Prince Jamie and
bear him off toward Herriard House. Jamie had conceived a certain affection for Wessex's new Duchess, and
was easily persuaded that he ought to tender his felicita-
tions. Wessex had thought it would be all for the best, and
would give him a breathing space while he thought of
what to say to his new wife.

As it happened, he was now in no doubt at all of what
he wanted to say to his wife. Unfortunately, it was not
such information as any gentleman of breeding could convey to any female whatsoever.

"And how do you find the weather here in London?"
the Duke of Wessex said to his Duchess.

The next quarter of an hour passed with painfully exact
courtesy between Wessex and his wife, while Jamie and
Meriel were very merry indeed. In the midst of all her
other emotions, Sarah was conscious of a sense of seething
betrayal. She had thought Meriel a girl of sense and sen-
sibility, too wise to fall in with her ambitious Uncle Ripon's silly plan to attach Jamie to his faction by entangling
him with a Catholic heiress.

Apparently she'd been wrong. For Meriel was playing
the part of a vivacious, empty-headed charmer, and doing
it with enough conviction to cause Sarah to wonder if she
had ever known Lady Meriel at all.

At last Jamie rose to go, and inevitably, Meriel rose to
her feet as well, exclaiming that she was late for an appointment. There was a brief flurry of bonnets and hats,

and then the Duchess of Wessex was alone with her husband.

Hesitantly, she risked a glance at his face. His black eyes glittered with anger, and his mouth was set.

"I shall ask you only one question, Your Grace: do you know what you have done here today?" Wessex said.

Anger gave her answer a fearful precision. "*I* did not bring the Prince of Wales here. Was that the reason for your return, Your Grace? To thrust him into the midst of this Catholic plot of your own devising?"

Wessex recoiled as if he had been struck, and his face filled with a white fury.

"How could you?" he said in a strangled voice. "How *dare* you? Is this how you serve the King and the League— by playing at petty plots of your own, like a spoiled child with his nursery toys?"

"How dare *you*?" Sarah responded just as hotly. "You call me a child—you have no idea of my character, of anything about me!"

"There you are wrong," Wessex said in a deadly calm voice, the worse for his obvious anger. "I have every notion of your character, and would to God I did not! You are spoiled, luxurious, and wilful—you betray a sacred trust for your own idle amusement—"

By now Sarah was not entirely sure of what Wessex was talking about, and it frightened her. "Idle amusement!" she countered, grasping at the parts of his speech she thought she did understand. "Meriel is my *friend!* She does not love her uncle in the least, and certainly she would not do such a thing as you suggest to please him—I know you wish to think her at the heart of Ripon's plotting, but she is not such a fool as that!"

"Is she not?" Wessex snarled. "She gave a perilous good imitation of it here today, Madame! Tell me, what freak of distempered nature inspired you to invite her beneath this roof?"

"It is *my* roof, Your Grace, as you are at such pains to re-mind me."

"Should there be the sort of scandal that Ripon will not scruple to brew, the Danish Prince Regent will not hesitate to withdraw both the Princess and the treaty—"

"And does the Prince of Wales not know this?" Sarah demanded with icy archness.

"Jamie is a young and volatile boy—not yet a man—and his father, our King, set both of us to guard him from just the sort of foolish error that he is about to commit, thanks to *you*."

"Then he is too much of a fool ever to be crowned!" Sarah cried, and froze in horror at the audacity of her own words.

"Do you play at kingmaking, then, Madame?" Wessex asked, very softly. "Oh, beware, Your Grace, if that is the direction in which your appetites have led you."

Their quarrel had veered into deeper and more dangerous waters than Sarah was prepared to navigate, and Wessex now seemed less an infuriated husband than a dangerous enemy whose presence placed her in mortal peril.

"I don't know what you're talking about!" Sarah cried. "I never wanted to marry you in the first place, and I wish I'd never been born!"

She grabbed the nearest thing to hand—the porcelain sugar bowl—and flung it at Wessex's head. As he almost automatically caught the china missile neatly in his hand, Sarah ran from the room.

After setting down the sugar bowl upon the nearest flat surface, Wessex walked over and closed the door, very quietly. He had never been less sure of his ground, and in his position, such uncertainty was dangerous.

What was Sarah's game? Was she loyal to the Boscobel League, or did she seek to bring down the League and destroy the King? In befriending Lady Meriel, was her intent to fall in with Ripon's plans, or to turn his pawn to her own use? Wessex paced, trying to think beyond the disaster of the moment. That Sarah was hunting her own line of country was clear—but it was also clear that for the moment Lady Meriel was coursing the game the Earl of Ripon had set her at, whatever Sarah's plans for her might be.

Should he keep his Duchess in Town or bundle her off to Wessex Court to bury her there, far from Town and its temptations? A man might do as he liked with a wife— this was one of the joys of marriage, so the wits said— but on the other hand, it must be admitted that the fatal introduction of Lady Meriel to Prince Jamie already had been made. If Lady Meriel had cultivated acquaintance with Wessex's wife in hope of just such an apparently accidental introduction, then Lady Meriel's use for a maddeningly stupid but not actively treacherous Duchess of Wessex had just ended. But if Lady Meriel were a mere catspaw, and her grace a scheming puppeteer . . .

His metaphors hopelessly mangled, Wessex's attention was drawn to a scrap of white pasteboard sticking out between the arm and the cushion of the sopha. He drew the card out as carefully as though it were the fuse of an unexploded bombard and inspected it carefully.

An invitation to a ball that the Earl of Ripon was giving on behalf of his niece.

Fascinating. Enough so, at any rate, for Wessex to once more alter his opinion of his wife's actions. Now, he had to admit, he had absolutely no idea what game she played. Why did she want to go to Ripon's ball enough to attempt to conceal the invitation from her husband?

And—far more to the point—why would Ripon invite her?

Sarah fled to her room as ardently as she had ever run from the Terror-beast that stalked her half-remembered dreams. She'd assumed that Wessex would make it easy for her to enact the shadow-marriage, but after today she realized there could be no easy peace between them. With a feeling very similar to panic, she reached the safety of her room and slammed the door.

Since Wessex showed no inclination to follow, Sarah quickly calmed in the privacy of familiar surroundings. A warrior of the People never surrendered to panic; fear was the Way of the Bear, and caused one to lose one's path . . .

For a moment two Sarahs—Sarah Cunningham of Baltimore, and the false Lady Roxbury she had since become—quarreled for possession of the young woman's body. Then once more Sarah's *self* slid from her grasp, to hover tantalizingly out of reach. But this time it left one certainty in its wake.

They all want me to play Wessex's Duchess, and lead Society upon a merry dance. But I don't know how. I'm not the woman they think they've bought and paid for. . . .

Sarah sank into a chair, wringing her hands. The mirror on the dressing table mocked her with her own reflection: a serene, self-assured noblewoman in a gown of old gold and blue; a woman not pretty, perhaps, but strong-featured and strong-willed.

And not the Duchess of Roxbury. Though I suppose I am the Duchess of Wessex, since I married the Duke, but I am not the Duchess he thinks I am. . . .

Her muddled memories betrayed her; Sarah could hardly imagine by what feats of falsehood and impersonation she had been set in the Marchioness's place, but here she was. As for where the Marchioness was—or who Sarah had been before this insane masquerade began—she had the teasing feeling that she knew these answers, and that they were only awaiting the proper moment to reveal themselves.

She took a deep breath, and her old plucky common sense asserted itself. Other things did not matter so much, now that Sarah knew who she was not.

But what was she to do now?

She could not stay in London. She could not endure this masquerade one moment longer. She had been willing to be Wessex's ally from the first moment he had asked for her help, but it seemed that all he did was demand her cooperation even as he pushed her away. And now he was furious—it was true that Meriel's introduction to Prince Jamie was a disaster, but as Sarah had pointed out, it was a disaster of Wessex's creation, not of hers, and it was a thing they could have repaired together, had he only been willing to cooperate.

She was tired of being the only one who tried to compromise! An end had to come sometime—let it be now. She would go back to Mooncoign and leave Wessex to manage his affairs without her.

She doubted he'd mind.

Wessex was still brooding over the billet from the Earl of Ripon when Buckland opened the door once more. The old retainer's face was worried.

"Your Grace? A Mr. Farrar to see you. He says his business is urgent."

If Wessex had been any other man, he would have commended Mr. Farrar to the devil with a hearty good will, but in the profession he followed, one did not lightly dismiss unfamiliar visitors.

"Send him up, Buckland. And get someone to take away all of this," he added, waving a hand at the tea tray and sugar bowl.

Mr. Farrar was a neat gentleman in a self-effacing bottle-green coat. Wessex had reason to know him, though not by that name.

"Good Lord!" Wessex exclaimed. "Toby! What are you doing here?"

"It's a delicate matter—and a bad one, Your Grace. I'm sorry for the Christmas pantomime, but Lord Misbourne did not wish to entrust anything to writing, and so he thought it best to send me."

The man Wessex knew as Toby—though that was no more his real name than Farrar was—was not a member of Society, though he could certainly pass for a gentleman, and had. If he were someone Wessex was likely to encounter in private life, Misbourne would not have let Wessex know of his existence, for what a man does not know he cannot reveal, even under torture. For Wessex, "Toby Farrar's" existence began and ended in the hallways and libraries of the house in Bond Street.

Yet now Toby was here. And a situation or a summons that could not be entrusted to a curt "see me" encoded in a tailor's bill delivered by an unwitting lackey was a serious situation indeed.

"Tell me," Wessex said.

"Princess Stephanie's vanished." Toby said flatly.

The Danish embassy had not been to sail until the end of July. Instead, it had embarked a month early in strict secret—reasonable enough, as a ship containing a member of the Royal family of neutral Denmark would be a rich prize indeed. The two ships—*Queen Christina* and

Trygve Lie—had sailed four days ago. One of the ships had reached Roskild. The other had not.

"Captain Koscuisko says that they lost *Queen Christina* in the fog—says it was thick enough that Old Boney could have moved the entire Household Cavalry ten feet off the starboard bow and they'd have been none the wiser—the ship was gone when the fog lifted, and hadn't made port before them."

Princess Stephanie—the key to the vital treaty—gone! "How old is this information?" Wessex asked.

"No more than thirty-six hours, Your Grace. It was sent by heliograph to Scotland, and by pigeon from Edinburgh," Toby said.

Wessex didn't bother to ask if the information was good. That was something one never knew. They must assume it was, and deal accordingly.

"Who knows?" was his next question. And how long until everyone did?

"The crew—the portmaster in Roskild—King Henry—Baron Misbourne," came the curt reply. "Koscuisko says it looks to him as if *Christina* was not interfered with in any way."

Which meant that her absence was intentional—on someone's part—and suspect.

"Do we have any notion of why the *Queen Christina* disappeared?"

Toby Farrar pulled a disgusted face. "Lord Misbourne says, 'Go and see.' "

14

Dance with the Devil in the Pale Moonlight

A fortnight later Sarah, Duchess of Wessex, attended the ball given by the Earl of Ripon to present his niece, Lady Meriel Highclere, to Society.

That fortnight had been an awkward period. When Sarah had finally mastered her inner turmoil to the point that she was ready to confront her husband and explain why she intended to return to the countryside, her husband wasn't there. Neither was he at Dyer House, at the Albany House rooms she had discovered that he still maintained, or at any of his clubs. Two days later, a hasty message from Wessex himself—addressed both to her and to the Dowager Duchess, and sent to Dyer House— explained that urgent business with the Regiment had called him away, and that he hoped they were not too inconvenienced by the abruptness of his departure.

It was so preposterous a missive that Sarah had hardly known whether to laugh or to cry. But with Wessex gone, she didn't need to leave Town to avoid him—and she did want to keep an eye on Lady Meriel.

Keeping an eye on Lady Meriel wasn't especially difficult, because everyone Sarah met was wild to tell her what Lady Meriel was doing. She was seen in the company of the Prince. They had gone riding. They had gone driving. He was expected at her come-out ball. He had thrown over Caroline Truelove and his other flirts. He had gone to her uncle's house and stayed all afternoon.

Rumors. Gossip. Worries. And Meriel would not answer Sarah's messages, would not meet Sarah at any of their appointed places. Sarah had even gone to call upon her in person, only to be told mendaciously that Lady Meriel was not at home.

And so, in the end, the Duchess of Wessex went to the Earl of Ripon's ball.

Sarah's coach—the crest on its side was still that of Roxbury, not of Wessex—rocked and complained. The old-fangled conveyance was hung on leather straps rather than set on the modern leaf-springs, and consequently provided a jarring ride, but it was enormous and well-made, and when at rest, provided a haven of unequaled comfort—and this evening, it spent most of its time at rest.

The gilded leather curtains were buttoned away from the windows to provide more air; Sarah folded down the window and looked out. They were nearly to the corner, well-wedged in this vast crush of conveyances; another half an hour and she would have reached the door. Already she could see the Earl of Ripon's London establishment looming ahead, nearly medieval in its splendor. The house soared over its neighbors like a great beast intent

upon choosing its prey, a gothic facade faced with dark
Cornish stone and ablaze with torches. Though the worst
heat of the summer was yet to come, the sultry July night
made Sarah glad that her ball-dress was of the most modern—and lightest—mode; muslin and silk instead of stiff
brocade and velvets. Her hair was dressed simply, with a
low cockade of egret plumes set in diamonds, and her
etherial-blue ball-dress was composed of yards and yards
of aerophane crepe sewn with sequins and trimmed in
rosettes of silver tissue. She did not wish to outdazzle Meriel, whose night this must be held to be, but neither did
she wish to look like a Duchess grieving over her absent
Duke—and she fancied she did not.

Reflexively, Sarah touched the ring hidden at her
bosom. She could not wear it, of course—the low-cut neck
of her gown prevented that—but she had been able to
persuade Madame Francine to make a small pocket in the
bosom of the dress where the ring now resided. Its hard
weight reassured her, even while it raised new questions
of its own.

The ring had belonged to her father. Sarah was certain
of that. But the ring had most certainly not belonged to
Lady Roxbury's father—and yet the first time Sarah had
met the Duke, Wessex had recognized the ring and its
device. Which meant that the ring held meaning—
perhaps the key to her entire history—and Wessex knew
what it was.

The coach lurched forward with a jolt, disrupting her
thoughts. The line of carriages was moving again, bringing her closer to the house.

Captain His Grace the Duke of Wessex—traveling of necessity under his own dignities and title—stood at the railing of His Majesty's ship *Widowmaker*, bound for the

northernmost possession of the British Crown: the Orkney Islands. Atheling had accompanied his master on this journey, for on this anomalous occasion Wessex was acting as a representative of King Henry and could not afford to be anything less than splendid.

Passed from Denmark to Scotland by the queen immortalized in history as Lady MacBeth, the Orkneys were largely the resort of isolated fisherfolk for whom life had changed little in the past thousand years. Roskild was the largest town in the island chain, and the only harbor deep enough to anchor a ship of any size. *Trygve Lie* had made for this anchorage, and now Wessex followed in his turn. He'd sailed from London on the tide, and the *Widowmaker* had headed north, hugging the English coast (much to the distaste of her captain) in order to avoid provoking the French ships lurking in mid-Channel like pelagic sharks. A journey that would have taken a man on horseback more than a week was accomplished in four days of expert sailing, and at dawn on the fifth day *Widowmaker* sailed into Roskild harbor on the morning tide.

This far north, the sun was already high in the sky at an hour when even honest tradesmen would still be abed. It therefore gave Wessex a certain ruthless pleasure to leave the Captain to present his credentials to the harbormaster while he sought out Illya Koscuisko.

The Polish Hussar (who was not, so far as any of the inhabitants of the town was prepared to testify, either Polish or a Hussar) had taken a room in the lesser of Roskild's two hostels, an inn set far enough away from the harbor that it could not quite be confused with the flash kens that catered to common seamen, but one which did not by any stretch of the imagination cater to such gentry as might inexplicably find themselves in Roskild.

Wessex had never been to the Mermaid, but he had been to a thousand places like it; though the front door was still stoutly barred against the terrors of the night, the kitchen door stood open to let the heat of the day's baking escape, and Wessex walked quickly through the kitchen to the steps that led to the first floor.

There were two doors on the floor above, and from behind one came a thunderous snoring. Wessex opened the other.

Illya Koscuisko lay sprawled atop his disorderly bed in a state of absolute unconsciousness, one hand stuffed beneath his wadded pillow. His mustache had been shaved, and his hair had been trimmed out of its fantastic Hussar style and bleached a nondescript blond. He wore a shirt and pantaloons unbuttoned at the knee and looked like any of a hundred students, refugees, or remittance men.

Wessex closed the door behind him. The click of the latch almost masked the sound of the pistol cocking. He turned back.

Koscuisko had raised himself up on one elbow and was pointing a pistol at Wessex's head. When he saw it was Wessex, he raised the barrel and set the gun aside.

"You should dress better, my friend. In that villainous coat I was sure you were a Frenchman." Koscuisko ran a hand through his hair, wincing slightly as his fingers encountered its coarse bleached texture.

"If you thought I was likely to be a Frenchman, you ought to have locked your door," Wessex reproved him.

"I'd rather been hoping one would come along, you see," Koscuisko confided to him. "Where's the point in leaving one's self open to overtures if no one makes them?"

Koscuisko got to his feet and began searching about the disorderly room for his boots and a bottle of brandy.

"And no one has?" Wessex asked.

"We have been singularly blessed by an absence of any adversarial nationals whatsoever," Koscuisko said, and added a long phrase in his native tongue. From experience, Wessex knew that the translation was something on the order of: "the Devil sends peace when one is already bored"; it was one of Koscuisko's favorite sayings. "For myself, I cannot explain it." He shrugged, and sat down to put on his boots—which, being the shabby down-at-heel footgear required by his persona, gave him no difficulty whatsoever.

Wessex looked about the room, but there was no other furniture besides the bed and the table beside it. He settled for leaning against the wall.

"You were, you know, supposed to be on the ship with the Princess," he observed conversationally.

"And so I was—I was doing a very pretty job of being a Dutch physician who'd prevailed upon the kindness of Sir John to secure myself a place on the first ship bound for England, I'll have you know. But Her Highness shuffled me off onto the second ship just before we sailed—said she couldn't fancy that Van Helsing fellow above half, and it was too close to sailing for me to come up with anyone else.

"I wasn't worried at the time—checked out the crew of the *Queen Christina* while we were in port, and they were all disgustingly loyal; not a traitor among them. No last-minute changes, either. The only drawback to my being on *Trygve Lie* was that I wouldn't be close to the Princess, but Sir John would be, and he'd make a better report of the Princess's mood to the Palace than ever I would. And then the *Christina* vanishes clean as you please, half a day before we're to sight the Scottish coast."

The plan, Wessex knew, had been to keep close to the English coast—just as *Widowmaker* had—in order to avoid French attack.

"And that's all you know?" Wessex said in mild exasperation.

Koscuisko threw up his hands. "There's nothing more *to* know," he said, a faint wail in his voice. "No one on the *Tryg* was expecting the Princess's ship to vanish—you can believe I made sure of that—and nobody aboard has the slightest idea of where she's gone."

"We must assume," Wessex said reasonably, "that she's gone *somewhere*. And if it were any place in the least desirable, we would have heard by now."

"Which leaves France," Koscuisko said glumly.

"Which probably means France," Wessex agreed. "We daren't put off telling Prince Christian that we've lost his sister—we have to assume he's heard already—so *Widowmaker* and I are bound for Copenhagen now. I'll sniff around the Danish court and see if anyone knows more than he should."

"I'll go with you," Koscuisko offered instantly.

"No," Wessex said firmly. "You're bound for England. Prince Jamie's got himself entangled with Ripon's girl, and you've got to pry her away from him."

"Me?" Koscuisko said blankly. Then he smiled. "Well, it's worth a try. Is she pretty?"

"More than you deserve, my son. So make yourself beautiful and be on your way."

"Her Grace the Duchess of Wessex!" the bewigged footman shouted as Sarah reached the top of the stairs.

The Earl's ballroom occupied the second floor of his townhouse, three stories above the London streets. Sarah could not help comparing the room with that at Mooncoign, and wondering if the differences between the two betokened differences in character as well.

Mooncoign's ballroom was lavish—everything gilded and grand, meant to be impressive. But Brookstone (Ripon's townhouse was named for one of his secondary titles, Viscount Brookstone) was meant to overwhelm—not with itself alone, but with the consequence of the family that had caused it to be built. The Highclere arms were repeated everywhere, like trophies of captured enemies, and the mirrors reflected the Waterford chandeliers into an infinity of heartless dazzle that struck the eyes like a thrown challenge.

Sarah had meant to come early, hoping to get Meriel off in a corner where she could quiz the girl about her true plans, but the crush of carriages in the street had delayed Sarah's arrival until well after ten. The ballroom was already filled with people, and in the arctic glitter of the crystal and mirrors, Sarah could see neither Meriel nor Prince Jamie. Perhaps the Prince had not come, which would be ideal—

"Your Grace, how pleasant it is to have you join us." The Earl of Ripon materialized at her elbow.

"Yes, isn't it?" Sarah shot back, biting down an even more caustic reply. She wondered if Ripon really believed in the success of his scheme to make Prince James a puppet king upon a shadow throne, and if the man had for one moment stopped to count the cost.

"And your husband?" Ripon pursued. "The Duke?" As if Sarah might have forgotten who it was she'd married barely more than a month before.

Sarah tightened her grip on her fan. "My husband does not care for your company," she said boldly. She might as well send all her bridges blazing to heaven upon this one occasion; her attempts to personate a pattern-card of virtue had brought her nothing but failures, so perhaps the opposite would serve her better.

"Alas." Ripon did not seem especially devastated by this observation. "Perhaps we can persuade you, at least, to a better opinion of us."

I doubt it, Sarah thought, but this at least she did not

say aloud. Instead she allowed Ripon to lead her along the edge of the ballroom floor and into another room, where he procured her a glass of iced champagne punch and bowed himself off, leaving her in peace. With a duplicity that surprised even its owner, Sarah spent the next half an hour dissembling to her fellow guests and promising dances she did not intend to dance before setting off in search of Lady Meriel. Ripon had outdone himself—half the Upper Ten Thousand, it seemed, had crowded into these rooms tonight.

A quick scouting of the rooms flung open to the entertainment satisfied Sarah that her quarry was not anywhere present, but it was inconceivable that Lady Meriel should be absent from the ball being given to establish her in Society. It was barely possible that Meriel was still in her rooms; Sarah set out to discover the actuality.

She was able to make her way out of the ballroom without difficulty, but once on the floor below, Sarah was adrift in a strange house with no idea where Meriel's rooms lay. She shrugged philosophically, pulling her crepe shawl higher about her bare shoulders. She must search until she found it—it was unlikely, with everyone attending the ball on the floor above, that she'd startle anyone but the servants, and eccentricities in the Quality were only to be expected. A few vails, liberally bestowed, should ensure that Ripon did not hear of this excursion. Toward the back of the house, she found another staircase and began to climb.

The first few doors she opened on the third floor led only into darkened bedrooms and parlors—none of them showing any signs of extensive occupation—and Sarah began to think her idea a particularly shatterwitted one when she turned the corner and saw light leaking from beneath a closed door. Perhaps Meriel was within.

But she could hardly walk up to the door and knock,

Sarah realized. What reason would she give?

She'd just realized the ill-conceived nature of her mission when the door she had been contemplating swung open abruptly.

"There's no one there," the Earl of Ripon prophesied.

"I know there's no one there!" Geoffrey Highclere snarled. "Just your mewling catspaw of a niece, a houseful of servants, five hundred guests—" *A courier from France.* . . .

With an effort, Geoffrey reined in his temper. There was no sense in alienating his so-helpful brother, especially since the original plan to entangle the Prince of Wales had been Ripon's idea.

But Geoffrey's French masters had battened upon it, particularly that white spider Talleyrand, secret master of France, and suddenly it was Geoffrey's business to make sure his brother's plot achieved its full flower—without, of course, letting Ripon know who took so much interest in it. Because Ripon was loyal to England, after his fashion—and any power that Ripon tore loose from the Crown he meant to bestow only upon Ripon.

But when a thing was struck loose from its moorings and floated freely, it might end up anywhere at all. . . .

"You worry too much, Geoffrey," his brother rumbled. "Meriel is weeping in her abigail's arms after the lesson you gave her earlier, and everyone else is at the ball. As I should be—Wessex's Duchess has favored us with her presence, and it would not do to neglect her."

"Wessex!" Geoffrey all but hissed. The courier had brought word from Geoffrey's French masters that Wessex was becoming a dangerous annoyance—the man, Geoffrey had discovered, was more than he seemed. "He meddles in our plans at every turn."

"How can he?" Ripon asked reasonably. "Wessex has gone to the country once more."

"He has not gone to the country," Geoffrey said. "He has gone to Denmark—Princess Stephanie has vanished; her ship did not reach landfall in the Orkney Islands."

"What?" Ripon was thunderstruck. "When you told me you had urgent news, I thought it was to do with our cause."

Your cause, dear brother, Geoffrey amended mentally.

"And so it is. Do you think France uninterested in any matter that could make England once more her natural ally against a sea of inhuman creatures and heretics?" Geoffrey said smoothly. "And so she has acted to aid us: Princess Stephanie will never reach Edinburgh."

The rumors of the Danish Princess's disappearance were already drifting from the Palace like smoke, and the courier had brought Geoffrey confirmation of them— though it was possible, his informant had told him, that the account of Princess Stephanie's disappearance was merely a Banbury tale to explain why the Duke of Wessex was traveling to the continent in such unseemly haste.

"Vanished!" Ripon smiled. "Then we have more time to make sure of the Prince. You need not have been so harsh with Meriel this evening at all."

"We may not have so much time as you think," Geoffrey said slowly. He hesitated over how much to tell his brother, drew a deep breath, and called upon all his powers of inventive diplomacy.

"My . . . sources believe that Wessex's real mission has nothing to do with Princess Stephanie. That it is only a convenient excuse for those who know that the Duke is King Henry's agent. It is believed in fact that Wessex is on the trail of Louis XVII. It seems that the Young King may be alive, and if he is, Wessex means to bring the boy to England and set up an opposition government."

Ripon mulled this over while Geoffrey wondered if his brother would take the bait.

"It is possible," the Earl said. "Did not Wessex's father go to France to rescue the child—and fail? Or—wait! *Did* he fail? If the old Duke were able to spirit the boy into hiding with a loyal Royalist family . . ."

"Then the son could stand ready to complete what the father could not," Geoffrey said. "And once the Young King is in English hands, Imperial France will be seen as weak enough to defeat. England will never sue for a separate peace . . ."

"And our cause is doomed." Ripon frowned. "Wessex must be stopped."

"He isn't here—*brother*—to be stopped," Geoffrey pointed out. "How do you propose to neutralize him?"

"I have a plan that might amuse you, Geoffrey," the Earl said. "It will involve travel upon the Continent. . . ."

Sarah retreated around the corner just as the door opened, and her common sense asserted itself in a mighty surge. If she wished to present herself as the voice of Reason, skulking around the hallways of other people's houses was *not* the way to do it.

She was very glad to have made such a decision when she heard Geoffrey Highclere's mocking drawl. He had undoubtedly chosen this occasion to present his brother with yet another selection of his duns, for all the world knew that Mr. Highclere's pockets were emphatically to let.

As for where Meriel was, a perfectly reasonable explanation presented itself upon reflection. The girl did not yet have much experience of Society, and was in the midst of conducting a scandalous romance. What was more likely than an attack of nerves was delaying her appearance? The reasonable thing to do was to return to the dance floor and take the opportunity to ask Lord Ripon about it when she saw him again.

But Reason was not to be her ally—this night or any other—Sarah reflected irritatedly several hours later.

Her dressing-table was lit by one lone candle, and she sat before her mirror in a grey watered-silk combing-coat lavished with ecru lace, still damp from the ablutions that had removed the makeup from her face. She had sent Knoyle to bed as soon as the abigail had unlaced her dress and unpinned the jewels from her hair, and it had taken the better part of an hour after that for Sarah to finish preparing herself for bed.

She inspected her reflection in the mirror critically. Neither an intriguer nor the society leader King Henry had wanted her to be; she had not managed so much as a private word with Lady Meriel all evening, and seen much to dismay her.

For Prince Jamie seemed more than simply dazzled by Meriel's beauty. The young Prince seemed dangerously—foolishly—recklessly—besotted with Meriel. And Meriel was playing him as if she were a damsel in a courtly romance, requiring outrageous and public proofs of his devotion.

If Wessex had still been here, Sarah would have swallowed her pride and gone to him—this disaster was too large a thing for her to stand upon her hurt pride if there were any help she could seek. But Wessex was gone away, and she did not know if anyone knew how to reach him.

Sighing, Sarah set down her hairbrush. If the Marchioness of Roxbury had possessed numerous allies, plain Sarah Cunningham had none. Which meant that though she was filled with a sense of responsibility for the impending ruin of the Danish treaty, she was completely powerless to affect matters—

No! I will not accept that! Meriel had been Sarah's friend, and there must be some way still to reach her.

Perhaps tomorrow Sarah could discover what it was.

She was Roxbury. She was Mooncoign. The ancient promise and ancient bond beat in her blood, and from behind the sleep-pierced veil of her amnesia Sarah understood it: she was the champion of the Oldest People, the human warrior set to guard their lands from the intrusion of those who would seize them. That was the responsibility that the Other Sarah had forsaken; the one that she—the Other's doppelgänger—had so carelessly taken up. She, like her predecessor, had rashly believed that there was no enemy to fight.

And she, like her predecessor, had been wrong.

The Sarcen Stones loomed high and grey above her, the pillars of a city without walls. In the waking world the stones were rough-hewn things, but in this dream Otherworld they were tall silvery pillars of gleaming rune-covered crystal. Sarah stood in their midst, before a block of stone through which was thrust an ornate and glittering sword. It was a ceremonial sword—far too large for any human being to wield. A sword for a giant.

But she was expected to wield it—to draw it from the stone and carry it against the enemies of the People. Against the Terror; the beast that paced just beyond their borders.

They were watching her. Out of the corner of her eye she could see them, standing among the pillars which bordered the circle. Rank upon rank of the Oldest People, their bodies nebulous and insubstantial as mist, waiting for her to keep her promise.

Only she was not the one who had made the promise. Another had promised for her—had plucked her from her own familiar world to keep a promise she had never made.

Despite this, Sarah would not fail them. The fight was just, and she was ready to take her part in it. But when she steeled her nerve and reached for the sword, she could not grasp the jeweled hilt. It slipped through her fingers each time she tried.

"You are not a part of the land."

It was the man who had shown Sarah her other self in Mooncoign's lake, but now, instead of green velvet and golden horns, he wore a suit of cloth-of-silver that glowed so brightly that she could barely look at him. Around his brow was a chaplet of rubies, and as she watched they swelled and broke, running down his face—not rubies, but blood.

"Until you make yourself a part of the land you cannot serve it. Nor will it nourish you. Do not fail us, Sarah. . . ."

"Wait!" she cried. "I don't understand!"

Sarah sat bolt upright in her bed, heart racing. She gazed wildly about the bedroom—only the faintest of light filtered in through her windows, left open and uncurtained in the summer heat.

"I don't understand," she whispered, but she had no chance to chase after the wisps of the dream. A shadow moved between the window and the bed and she realized she was not alone in the room.

"Shhh!" an urgent voice hissed, just as Sarah drew breath to cry out.

"*Meriel?*" Sarah whispered in disbelief.

The phantom drew closer to her bed. It was Lady Meriel, clad in a long black domino over the white silk ballgown Sarah had seen her in earlier this evening.

Sarah flung back the coverlet and scrambled out of her bed.

"What are you *doing* here?" Sarah demanded, more harshly than she intended. She moved toward the table, intending to light the candle waiting there, but Meriel was there before her.

"No!" she hissed in an urgent undertone. "No light! Someone might see!"

"Who?" Sarah demanded, instantly alert. She pulled the windows shut, then drew the heavy brocade draperies over them.

"Uncle Geoffrey," Meriel said in a low voice. "If he should see a light—"

"It is all right now, Meriel—no one can see us," Sarah said. The heavy damask draperies would certainly shield the light of a single candle from observation by the street below—even if there were an intruder lurking in Sarah's back garden.

"But he will know that I am here," the other girl said miserably. "Uncle Geoffrey always knows everything—it is he who said I must scrape an acquaintance with you, that your loyalty to the King would provide a good blind for—for what he would do. He said you were cold and over-proud—but you were always such a friend to me. . . ." Meriel's voice faltered and she could not go on.

"Never mind that now," Sarah said hastily. She abandoned the candle to cross the room and take Meriel by the arm. Even through the thin silk of the domino, Meriel's flesh was icy. "The important thing is whatever brought you out like this—it is the middle of the night."

Meriel managed a shaky laugh. "It is nearly morning, and I am meant to be found with the Prince at Vauxhall Gardens in one of the private boxes—to what end you may well imagine! Uncle Geoffrey got the Prince to come away with him when the party was over, and has put laudanum in his flask. Then when he was insensible I was to go to him, and allow myself to be discovered with him—" The younger woman's control broke, and she dissolved into a fury of silent weeping.

A spark of resolute anger kindled within Sarah, even as she urged Meriel to sit down on the edge of the bed. It was a shabby trick to play on both Jamie and Meriel, and if Jamie did not panic and marry her—If the King did not give in to the scandal—Meriel would be ruined all the same, and all for her uncles' greed and ambition.

"But you have not gone to Vauxhall," Sarah said, her tone half-questioning.

"Uncle Geoffrey sent the carriage for me," Meriel said, her voice filled with grim triumph, "but I did not let the door latch, and when it was stopped behind a brewer's wagon down near the docks, I slipped out and let it drive on without me. But then I did not know where else to go, so I came here."

"You walked all that way?" Sarah was horrified. She had heard tales of the bands of roving young noblemen— Mohocks—who spent their nights serving up mischief to anyone unlucky enough to be abroad. And down near the river even greater danger abounded—Meriel had been lucky indeed to reach Herriard House, instead of having her throat cut—or worse.

"I had no choice," Meriel said. In the darkness, she was only a faint shadowy shape, and for a moment Sarah wondered if she were still dreaming. Everything seemed so unreal here in the dark.

But it *was* real. For one brief pure moment, Sarah wished Wessex were here. As cold and calculating as the man was, she was certain he would know exactly what to do in this situation. Shoot Ripon and Mr. Highclere, perhaps, but certainly he would know just how to whisk Meriel out of her wicked uncles' reach.

Unfortunately, Sarah had not the least idea of where he could be found. Perhaps the Dowager Duchess . . .

"I know it is too dreadful of me to burst in on you this way," Lady Meriel said ruefully, as if only now realizing what she had done. "But I shall only be a charge upon you for a short while longer. I have had more than enough time to consider what I would do—Uncle Richard's plans have been no secret to me this past twelvemonth and more!—and I know, now, that I must go where he will never find me."

"Where?" Sarah asked, fearing the worst. "Meriel, don't be afraid—I can take you into the country, to Mooncoign—"

But Ripon was likely to trace Meriel there easily. Ripon need only present himself at Sarah's door and demand her return, and Sarah—or her servants—would have little choice but to comply. And try as she might, Sarah could not think of where else Meriel could go once she had run away from her guardian.

"No!" Meriel said, her voice rising above a whisper for the first time. "I shall go to Mama's family, in Spain. He dare not follow me there, and they will take me in—"

"Spain! Meriel, have you lost your wits?" Sarah gasped. Only last December England had declared war upon Spain, and Spain was now a French vassal state, its exiled nobility fighting frantically—as was all of Europe—to free its people from beneath the Corsican boot.

"My mother's family is there," Meriel said. "I know my aunt Maristella very well, and until my uncle Richard forbade it I would write to her every week. She will take me in—and I will be done with both my uncles and their plots."

Sarah tried to argue Meriel out of her mad plan— travel halfway across Europe in the middle of a war? But English ships continued to call at still-neutral Lisbon, in nearby Portugal, and from there Meriel could probably find an escort to take her to her mother's family. Even the candles that Sarah finally succeeded in lighting did not shed the light of Reason on the discussion.

"Sarah, I have no choice!" Meriel burst out at last. "I

do not dare go home again—do you know what my Uncle Geoffrey will do to me? No?"

Meriel flung off the domino and tugged wildly at the bosom of her ballgown. Delicate silk and lace parted, opening the neckline far enough for Meriel to push it and the chemise beneath down a few inches. She turned her back to Sarah, and in the candle's glow Sarah could see an ugly red welt marking Meriel's skin above the line of her corset.

Lady Meriel had been whipped.

"Your uncle did this?" Sarah said, aghast.

"Uncle Geoffrey," Meriel said. "I did not wish to fall in with their plans—to see the Prince last night—but if I do not do as they wish, Uncle Geoffrey says he will make me disappear to where no one will find me . . . and I believe he will. I have money," Meriel went on, pulling a pocket from beneath her skirts that clinked heavily, "and my mother's jewelry. It will be enough to take me to Madrid," Meriel said stubbornly. "And there are those who will help me, once I reach Dover. I know those whom Uncle Geoffrey deals with—they have no loyalty above gold, and I have gold."

This put an entirely new complexion on matters, Sarah realized. She was not satisfied of her own ability to hide Lady Meriel— not if the Earl of Ripon and Mr. Geoffrey Highclere wanted their playing-piece back. But to leave Jamie to be entangled in a web of Ripon's spinning was unthinkable—not the least now that Sarah had seen what they were capable of.

What to do . . . what to do . . . ?

"You cannot continue to wear that," Sarah said decisively, gesturing toward Meriel's torn and mud-draggled ballgown. "Let me ring for Knoyle, get you a suitable gown, and have the coach put to—"

"*No!*" Meriel protested.

"But Meriel, however else will we get to Dover?" Sarah said simply. "You say you have friends there, but I think you need friends here as well."

It was still an hour before dawn as Sarah and Meriel entered Sarah's well-sprung yellow-paneled traveling coach. Unlike the ceremonial monster in which Sarah had journeyed to Lord Ripon's ball the night before, the yellow coach was a swift, smooth-riding beauty, which would whisk its passengers to Dover in only a day.

Knoyle, her face a mask of expressionless disapproval, sat on the seat facing Sarah and Meriel, bandboxes crammed with the most vital necessities tucked to either side of her on the yellow velvet seat. A large hamper full of cold delicacies—for every English traveler knew the unreliability of the *table d'hôte* at English posting inns—occupied the floor between the travelers' feet. All three women were swaddled in thick warm shawls—despite the summer weather, the morning was cool—and looked like so many bundles of laundry.

The door closed, and Sarah heard the coachman crack his whip out over the ears of the team leader. A moment later the carriage began to rock over the cobbles in front of the house. Behind her, Sarah heard the hoof-clatter of the outrider's mount as he took up his position.

It was hardly a covert or unremarked departure, but to travel without a coachman, a footman, and an outrider was to invite disaster along the way. And Knoyle would be needed, not only to preserve Sarah's reputation on the return trip . . .

But so that she cannot be taken and questioned—however unlawfully—while I am gone. A quality that Sarah had not realized that she possessed made her soberly estimate the danger they were in, and not hold lightly Ripon's power to do harm. He knew that she was Meriel's friend—once Meriel had vanished, Ripon would wish to see what Meriel's friend knew about it, and somehow Sarah was not as sanguine as, as—

—*as the real Duchess of Wessex would have been*—

—that her rank would protect her from Ripon's curiosity. The man was already conniving at High Treason, after all—what was one duchess more or less to his plans? Once Meriel was safely away—and Sarah intended to satisfy herself of that before she abandoned her friend—Sarah intended to lie low at Mooncoign behind a wall of stout footmen until she could locate Wessex—

—*and explain to him how wrong he was about Lady Meriel's character, though I must own he was right about the rest of her family,* Sarah admitted mournfully. *Accursed man! Where* is *he?*

The Amalienborg Palace in Copenhagen was a severe and formidable grey stone building facing an enormous square. The *Widowmaker* had arrived the day before yesterday, but it had taken until today for Wessex's credentials to work their way up through the labyrinth of protocol that surrounded the strait-laced Danish court and win him an interview with Prince Frederick, who was regent for his father, Christian VII. King Christian had for years been subject to such fits of rage and melancholy that the government of the country had eventually passed to his eldest son, Frederick.

Prince Frederick was Princess Stephanie's father, and Wessex did not relish being the bearer of the news that her ship had disappeared without trace somewhere in British waters.

The Amalienborg was of recent construction, its classical marble facades presenting a chill and imposing vista.

Wessex's self was equally chill and imposing: his blue uniform coat and its silver lace gleamed as if they were made of metal and enamel, and the finish on his black Hessians glittered like glass. He carried a dispatch case beneath his arm.

At the door of the palace, Wessex was met by a functionary in Court livery, who took and inspected his documents before allowing him inside. Another courtier, adorned and slightly antique in slippers and powdered wig, was waiting; he turned and strode away without meeting Wessex's eyes, carrying a gilded staff of office before him.

Wessex followed the courtier, his boots echoing upon the polished marble floors as he walked along a corridor of columns and mirrors. The infrequent bronze doors that interrupted the pale sweep of the walls were flanked by strapping guardsmen in ornate uniforms.

The documents he had presented yesterday—returned to him so he could present them more formally today—should be his guarantee of a private audience with Prince Frederick, but Wessex had not lived as long as he had by making any assumptions. While he would certainly receive a hearing today, he might not see the Prince for several days yet. There was still the Court Chamberlain to get past, Wessex reckoned, and a smattering of Gentlemen of the Bedchamber at the very least—the Danish court's protocol was far more elaborate than that of the relatively freewheeling Stuart court that had sent Wessex as its emissary. If it would not be in the worst of taste to take a lead from regicidal France, Wessex might even suppose that the very winds of Liberty and Equality that had fanned the flames of the holocaust in France blew more gently on England and her American colony. Certainly as the years passed, Great Britain and her dominions seemed to have less and less in common with their Continental kindred.

But these were ruminations for another day. For some minutes his guide had been leading Wessex deeper into the palace and up several flights of steps. Wessex judged they were now some distance from the ceremonial spaces of the palace.

So it was to be a private interview, then.

The courtier stopped before the most elaborate door they had passed yet. The Danish Royal arms, carved and gilded, were set into the center of the door, and as the courtier stepped toward the door the guards standing beside it turned smartly to and thrust the two halves of the door inward. Wessex's guide snapped to attention, becoming nearly a statue, and Wessex, guessing his role in the play, walked past him.

The walls of the small windowless room were elaborately draped with dull gold velvet, and even the ceiling was hung with the stuff, pinned and pleated in elaborate sunburst folds that radiated from a central rosette. The thick soft cloth that covered the walls and ceiling deadened all sound and gave a curious sense of disassociation to the room's inhabitants, and though Wessex knew it was just past two in the afternoon outside, it could be midnight here, or any other hour . . . just as anything might be hidden behind those all-enshrouding folds of velvet. The predominant color in the Aubusson carpet that covered most of the floor was the same soft amber, and the only furniture in the room was an enormous desk whose top was a single slab of semiprecious green malachite, and the thronelike chair behind it, occupied by the man Wessex had come to see.

And the Prince Regent did not wait alone. With a sensation as of a knife twisting in his gut, Wessex recognized the Regent's companion.

The Marquis Donatien-Alphonse-François de Sade had been an inmate of the Charenton lunatic asylum until the Glorious Revolution released him. The unsavory rumors that surrounded his name to some extent explained Napoleon's tolerance of him, for the Marquis de Sade was thought by England to be a diabolist as well as a deviant, and in the apostate court of the Emperor Napoleon, such black arts could be more than useful. Ever since the time of Louis XIV and the affair of the Marquis de Montespan and the Chambre Ardente, it had been known that the etheric magnetism more vulgarly known as the Art Magickal could be a powerful weapon—especially in the hands of those who, unlike the Wicca, the Jews, and the Christians, were not bound by either ethical or religious precepts. The worship of Lucifer, that fallen angel, was a peculiarly French vice, and de Sade was a master of that and many other vices, that much England was sure of.

But what was de Sade doing here, in pious, straitlaced, *Protestant* Denmark? While at the moment Denmark was still neutral, that neutrality would end the instant the treaty was signed, making de Sade liable to arrest and unceremonious banishment at the very least. And de Sade did not know that the most vital component for the treaty's signing—Princess Stephanie—was missing. The disaster had happened less than a week before: news traveling through normal channels could not possibly have reached the Danish court yet. So de Sade could not know.

Or could he?

The courtier followed Wessex into the room, precise as any well-drilled ranker in the Duke's own regiment, and announced him.

"His Grace the Duke of Wessex begs leave to approach Your Most Christian Highness."

Privately, Wessex did not beg leave of anyone to do anything, least of all foreign monarchs who were not even—as yet—England's allies, but he supposed he would allow the statement to stand.

"Your Highness," Wessex said. He advanced to the front of the desk and made his bow, then indicated the case of his credentials that the servant had placed upon the table between them. The lion and the unicorn of England, stamped in gold upon its flap, flanking the Royal arms, gleamed brightly in the room's candlelight as Frederick opened the pouch and withdrew a document heavy with seals and written in King Henry's unmistakable raking script. There had not been time to commit the details of the disappearance to paper, even if the King had been willing to do so, so Wessex, like a messenger of old, carried the true message in his head.

As the Prince studied the document, Wessex studied the Prince. Prince Frederick shared the pale, hawklike good looks of the rest of the Danish Royal family. His light blond hair was swept back from a high widow's peak, and his broad forehead and piercing blue eyes gave an impression of keen intelligence. He was dressed in a uniform of pale blue satin, which, Wessex guessed, must be that of one of his regiments, though Denmark was primarily a naval power and it was the Danish navy that England feared Napoleon gaining as a weapon against the Triple Alliance.

Neither King Henry, who had dealt extensively with Prince Frederick in arranging for the now-endangered treaty, nor Wessex, who had read the briefing book the White Tower kept on the Danish Prince Regent, knew much about the man himself. Denmark had played a remarkably close hand these past two decades in navigating through the sea of alliances and entanglements that had marked the map of Europe in the wake of the French Revolution, and even now she was far from wooed to England's standard.

And now Wessex must tell Denmark's ruler that his daughter had vanished, an event that the Frenchman de Sade would be quick to turn to England's discredit.

"So you are the Duke of Wessex," Prince Frederick said, in his ponderous, accented English.

Wessex inclined his head. De Sade emitted a faintly audible sneer. His eyes glittered fervidly, reflecting the flame of the candles, and his gaze flicked back and forth from Frederick to Wessex. The diabolist was dressed in ornate black and had powdered his pale skin until he looked like a convict . . . or a corpse. His face was fleshy and corpulent, and his body had the bloated unconvincing obesity of the invalid or the drunkard. His hands were long and slender, making a shocking contrast with his black and ragged nails (normally of the most cold-blooded temperament, even Wessex did not like to contemplate what use those sullied hands were put to), and the Marquis's fingers were crusted with massive rings whose stones shone in the dim candlelight of the windowless room as if they were open sores.

"I had hoped that we might speak privately, Highness," Wessex offered as his opening gambit.

"I do not think you will say anything I would not wish my good friend the Marquis to hear," Prince Frederick said disapprovingly.

Wessex kept his eyes on the Prince and his face expressionless, but from the corner of his gaze he could see that de Sade gave every appearance of wriggling with delight at Wessex's discomfiture, rubbing his hands together so that the rings he wore clicked together like abacus beads.

"Then I am sorry to have to convey to you King Henry's deep sorrow and regret in so public a fashion, Your Highness. He is desolated to be forced to inform you that Princess Stephanie's ship has disappeared, and she and all aboard her are missing."

Wessex had spoken so bluntly in part to judge the reactions of his auditors to the news he bore, and in this he was not disappointed. The Prince Regent's face went absolutely white, confirming Wessex in his belief that the Prince had not known about this in advance.

But de Sade certainly did not seem to be particularly surprised by the news of the Princess's disappearance. His face was slightly flushed beneath its coating of greyish powder, as if he fed upon the Prince Regent's palpable distress.

"Missing?" Prince Frederick said. His pale eyes, unfocused by the sudden shock of the devastating news, fixed themselves now upon Wessex, and there was an angry light in their wintery depths.

"Her ship disappeared a day's sail outside of Roskild, while still in Danish waters," Wessex said again. Roskild was the northeasternmost port that Britain could claim, and her influence did not extend appreciably far beyond it: as Wessex had said, the princess had vanished in Danish waters, for what that was worth.

"A very pretty illustration of how the English treat their allies," de Sade said. He spoke in French, as if all the world should be expected to know that tongue.

"Be silent," Prince Frederick snapped in the same language, without looking at the Frenchman. The Marquis emitted a small displeased hiss and rocked back on his heels.

"You will please tell me what occurred," the Prince said to Wessex in his labored English. "And where is Her Highness my daughter?"

"Your Highness," Wessex said, bowing again, and proceeded to explain at great, diplomatic, and ultimately pointless length what little the English knew: that the *Queen*

Christina had sailed from the Copenhagen harbor toward the port Roskild (where she and her sister ship were scheduled to rendezvous in any case if there were any trouble on the voyage) and had disappeared in a fogbank before she reached it.

"And this is the *security* you haf provided for my poor daughter?" The Prince Regent's accent was thicker now with the stress of this information, and his face had darkened with the characteristic rage of his royal line.

"The security for your daughter disappeared with her," Wessex pointed out. "Along with a number of British diplomatists. Naturally His Majesty has sent ships to search for the *Christina*, and hopes that he can count upon Your Highness to do the same. However—" Wessex nodded toward de Sade "—there are some elements that might complicate His Majesty's ability to carry out such a search."

"I do not care." The Prince got stiffly to his feet and did his best to glare down at Wessex, who, unfortunately, was taller than he by several inches. "You vill find my daughter and return her to me—and *then* perhaps we vill discuss the matter of this treaty further."

"I am sure His Highness would not choose to make a dangerous enemy lightly," Wessex said confidingly in French, as though making a casual comment to de Sade about the weather.

Prince Frederick stopped in the middle of turning away and stiffened as though he had been struck. His already florid color deepened alarmingly, and for a moment Wessex feared that the Prince Regent would explode into the same sort of extravagant fury for which his Royal father was noted.

"Find my daughter!" the Prince roared, swinging back toward Wessex. Without waiting for any reply he strode to the door concealed behind the velvet drape in the back wall, thrust the hangings aside, and strode out through the secret door. There was a faint dull impact as the concealed door closed, and suddenly the room seemed much smaller.

Wessex stood as he had been left, watching the dull gold velvet swing slowly back into its original position. His message had been delivered, and some small amount of information had been gained. Now Wessex was free to make what further inquiries he could, but his finely-honed instincts warned him already that there was little enough for him to find within the walls of the Amalienborg.

"Oh, Duc d'Anglais, I think you handled that so very well," de Sade said softly in French. The little man moved toward the desk, though the Prince had given neither of them leave to go . . . or, in fact, to move at all.

"Do you think so?" Wessex answered pleasantly in the same language. "I thought that perhaps my approach lacked something of subtlety . . . but no. I bow to the perceptions of one far better versed in these matters than I. It was well handled."

"Well! It speaks a civilized tongue," de Sade said, concealing his astonishment at Wessex's response.

"Alas, French has forfeited that claim in recent years, for a language must be held to partake of the virtues of those for whom it is their native tongue," Wessex said in tones of regret. "But perhaps at some time in the future," he added kindly.

"Mock if you wish, English Duke! But France shall have the last laugh as we bury you English. The Emperor is one in ten thousand—such a man will not be born again for a century! What he proposes shall come to pass—and he proposes that France shall be the master of Europe. In his lifetime he will redraw the map of Europe," de Sade gloated.

"And when he dies, we shall simply redraw it once

again," Wessex drawled, unimpressed with de Sade's rhetoric. "I do not think that you can refine too much upon your ability to make away with one ship. A ship is not, after all, a nation. Or even a regiment."

Though Wessex was not completely certain of French complicity in the matter of the *Christina*'s disappearance, this meeting with the perverse French magician might yield valuable information. De Sade must have been at the Amelienborg before the ship sailed . . . could he somehow arranged for the *Christina* to disappear? Or did he simply know who had made such arrangements?

But oddly enough, braggart though he obviously was, de Sade did not rise to this particular bait. He smiled his reptilian smile at Wessex and the gems on his fingers glittered wetly as he worked them about his fingers.

"Oh, let us be frank with one another, English Duke. The little princess is far less important than that which you have actually been sent to find. We know who you are, you of the White Tower. The English King's hellhounds—and you think France unaware of what game he has set you to course this time. Is it here, I wonder? Or have you simply come to divert suspicion while others do your hunting for you?"

Wessex did not allow one iota of the baffled amazement he felt to appear on his face—nor the chagrin that de Sade knew him for what he was: a spy.

"My very dear Marquis," he said lightly. "You should know that an Englishman's greatest joy is the hunt. As for the location of the covert I draw, perhaps it will amuse you to attempt to discover it, M'sieur le Marquis."

"What is de Sade doing here?" Wessex asked without preamble, striding into the library of the small, nondescript house situated on a back street near the center of the city.

Sir Gavin's residence—it was nothing so grand or definite as an embassy or an office—was indistinguishable from the houses which surrounded it here in this quiet side street. Unlike London, which had constantly been renewed, phoenixlike, by the series of fires which had swept away the construction of previous generations, Copenhagen was still very much a medieval city, narrow and grey. The Augustan sweep of the Royal family's rebuilding fervor had not extended to the city itself; in most quarters buildings of stone and timber stood much as they had three centuries before.

Sir Gavin MacLaren studied Wessex for a moment without answering. MacLaren was a tall, spare Scot, whose ancestors had fought for the Stuart line during Cromwell's Great Experiment in the seventeenth century. His good-humored Presbyterian virtue stood him in good stead amidst the austere ardor of the Danish court, and for many years he had been King Henry's representative to this most difficult of political posts—not so much an ambassador or official representative as a solver of problems great and small. And the disappearance of the Princess was a very large problem.

"De Sade has been here for the last three months, replacing the previous ambassador, an odd notion in itself," Sir Gavin finally said. "I have been unable to uncover what he may be doing here, other than supporting French interests, of course. There is, unfortunately, no way for me to get rid of the cursed creature," Sir Gavin added, shrugging. He gestured toward the sideboard, where a row of decanters gleamed in the pale northern light. "And he has not—yet—done anything unspeakable enough to make himself *persona non grata*—odd in itself, as Frederick is notoriously puritanical."

"Fine talk, coming from you," Wessex said with a grim

smile. He crossed to the sideboard and poured himself a whiskey.

"Ah, hadn't you heard, Your Grace? Even virtue can become a vice if pursued with sufficient extravagance," Sir Gavin assured him.

"But why is he here?" Wessex persisted, leaning back against the sideboard and unbuttoning the high, silver-laced collar of his dress uniform. "De Sade is a voluptuary, a dabbler in philosophy and the Black Arts. He might be of some use in Paris as a blackmailer and gossip-monger, but why send him here to offend the Danes?"

Sir Gavin shrugged without moving from his comfortable seat. "There's certainly no sign of de Sade's line of country here. The Old Races are strong in the countryside, you know, and they've never accepted any part of the White Christ's pantheon."

"And it's just as unbelievable that a Black Lodge is operating at the Danish court itself. But if not for de Sade's special talents, why send him here?" Wessex brooded.

"Have you considered the possibility that he is not the only warlock the French have sent—only the most visible?" Sir Gavin asked.

"Naturally. But whether he is working alone, or as part of a group, I need to know why he is here," Wessex said.

And why he thinks I am here.

15

Summoned as to Tourney

Despite the fact that they were under the constant threat of being overtaken by the Earl of Ripon, the hours of the journey passed with aggravating slowness. Both Sarah and Meriel were too overwrought to engage in small talk, and Meriel did not encourage any discussion of her future plans, so in the end the two fugitives simply stared out opposite windows in silence as the countryside rolled by.

The horses were changed every two hours, and at noon they stopped for an hour at a coaching inn in order to partake of the contents of the hamper in comfort and safety. The inn the outrider selected was quite clean and comfortable enough for Sarah to be almost sorry that they had brought their own provisions. The ladies were able to secure a parlor for their private use, and the landlord's wife contributed hard cider and strong coffee to their collation, and an upstairs room so that they could refresh themselves a bit from the rigors of their headlong journey.

But that peaceful interlude was over far too soon, and once more they were on the road.

"You will have to tell me where you are going sooner or later," Sarah pointed out reasonably. "Unless, of course, you expect John Coachman to drive us right into the sea."

The very thought drew a muffled giggle from her companion.

"Oh, no, Sarah. It is just that—I have been planning this for so long, and it is my only chance. . . ."

And it is so hard to trust anyone, when everyone you meet may be an enemy, Sarah thought sympathetically.

When they stopped again to change horses, Meriel at last told Sarah where they were going—not to Dover, but to a small fishing village several miles down the coast. By the time they reached Talitho (driving slowly to spare the horses, as the possibility of a change was much less off the main coach road) the sun had set and sea-mist had begun to creep in toward the land. The lanterns on the sides of the coach, lit at their last stop, burned with a dim warm glow.

The village of Talitho was a small isolated hamlet tucked into a fold of the coastline, and seemingly unchanged for centuries. There was a church and an inn anchoring the two ends of the brief high street; Sarah's coach passed the one and stopped at the other.

Sarah pushed open the door to the coach and leaned out, grateful to be stopping *anywhere*. She could smell the sea in the air that she breathed, and was eager to get out of the coach despite the misty rain that fell with soft soaking insistence.

The footman brought the step and placed it on the ground, and Sarah disembarked. Behind her came Meriel, looking disheveled with the rigors of the day's travel but still radiant, like a rumpled rose.

"Simon, go and see if there is a private parlor we can have," Sarah said. "John, take the coach around to the stable and unharness the horses. We must have a fresh team if we are to go any further tonight."

She wasn't sure yet whether to ask about rooms for the night, for the inn was very small, but lodging could certainly wait until they'd recovered somewhat from the journey.

"Well, Meriel," Sarah said, turning to her companion as the coach rolled away. "We have arrived at your destination safe and sound. What do we do now?"

Meriel shrugged slightly, weariness etching lines of strain on her face in the light from the coachlamps. Sarah took Meriel's arm, and the two ladies, followed by Knoyle, proceeded toward the door of the inn, only to be met by the liveried footman.

"Beg pardon, Your Grace, but the landlord says that the private parlor is already reserved—for Lady Meriel, Your Grace."

Who knew we were coming?

Sarah glanced toward Meriel. The girl's face was drawn and frightened. Meriel had not made this arrangement herself, then.

In that sudden premonition of disaster, Sarah wished for a weapon. In her imagination, she could feel the weight of a long gun in her hands, and did not doubt her ability to shoot, even to kill. The last shreds of the glamourie that Dame Alecto and the Dowager Duchess of Wessex had set upon her when they brought her to this alien England was lifted by catastrophe, and Sarah realized at last who she was.

I am Miss Sarah Cunningham of the United States of America, and this is not my world at all—

But both shock and questions must wait upon current danger. Her warrior's instincts awakened, Sarah realized that they dared not walk into this trap. She clutched at Meriel's arm again; they would go back to the coach and leave. It was the only way.

"Simon—" she began, but the footman was already moving aside to make way for the man behind him.

"That's right, Lady Meriel. The coffee parlor is already reserved for you and your little friend. It's wet and it's late. So why don't you come inside? Especially in consideration of the fact that I have a pistol in my pocket and I'm not in the least afraid to use it."

With the light of the doorway behind him, neither woman could see the speaker's face. But once heard, the voice was unmistakable.

It was Geoffrey Highclere.

The last ten days had been interesting, if one were of a temperament that could find intense and utter boredom interesting, and Wessex, alas, had been forced years before to admit that he was just such a person. Any absolute condition was so rare as to be peculiar, and the peculiar was the Duke of Wessex's line of country.

Even the frantic sea-hunt for Princess Stephanie, whose disappearance was gradually becoming common knowledge, lacked any sense of suspense, because no one really expected to find either the Princess or the *Christina* after so long a time. The sea did not easily give up her dead, and unlike the land, disaster at sea left no evidence behind. And if the Princess had washed ashore anywhere along the coasts of the British Isles, Denmark, or her Baltic neighbors, he would know about it . . . which left only one coastline upon which she could have made her landfall: France.

Initially Wessex had ruled that country out—July was calm sailing weather, so the missing ship could not have been blown off course. The Captain and crew were all trustworthy and loyal, which ruled out mutiny. And if there had been pirates, one source or another would have let slip that information. There was no way for the *Christina* to have reached a destination so far off course.

No natural way. . . .

But they lived in an unnatural age, and though Wessex half-disbelieved in the Art Magickal, he could not afford to leave it out of his hypotheses. On the island once called Logres, the Oldest People had constructed passages that led to Otherwhere, connecting disparate places and times, so the thing itself was not impossible. Could not the same sorcery that Christian magicians used to summon demons from their proper sphere be used to annihilate space and time and cause a sailing ship to vanish from the coast of Scotland to reappear off the coast of France?

Assume that it could. And suddenly de Sade's appearance at the Danish court became much more comprehensible—to attempt to sway the Prince Regent in the direction of France by any means fair or foul—but more to the point, to somehow use his arts to bespell the *Queen Christina* so that the Princess, captured and held safe in France, became a hostage to ensure Prince Frederick's new pro-French position.

Wessex wished that Koscuisko were here, and not safely back in England. The Polish Hussar was a jack-of-all-trades, and more than once had saved Wessex's skin and his own through the use of some scrap of arcane knowledge he'd managed to pick up in the course of his vagabond career. Koscuisko would probably be able to tell Wessex if de Sade had the capabilities the Duke had imputed to him—at the moment, Wessex's shatterwitted theory had all the respectability of a blind and desperate guess.

Of course, there was the heartening fact that someone had tried to kill him just yesterday.

He'd been walking back to MacLaren's house very early in the morning. A wearying day spent presenting the public face of England's solicitude for her hopeful ally had been followed by a slightly more interesting evening party given by a Baron Anderssen, at which Wessex had sifted gossip, hint, and innuendo. He'd thought nothing of walking home alone afterward, for the moon was nearly full and the streets of the Danish capital notoriously safe. He'd taken a small candle-lantern with him to light some of the darker corners of the streets he would have to traverse, bid his host a warm farewell, and was on his way.

And he'd been followed.

Even with as many bottles as Wessex had drunk that evening—for it had been an exclusively masculine gathering—he detected the presence behind him almost at once. Two men; either very eager or not very skilled. In less than ten paces more he had made up his mind what he would do about it, and began feigning the sloppy gait and wandering attention of one far more intoxicated than he actually was.

A block later the narrow street opened out into a small square of the sort that had a pump and trough at its center. Wessex had stopped at the trough and splashed cold water on his face, then gone on . . . leaving his lantern behind.

As he'd hoped, the invitation was too good to refuse. He'd barely reached the street at the far end of the square when they attacked.

"Can I help you, gentlemen?" Wessex asked, drawing

his sword and turning on them in one practiced moment. He blessed the happy accident that had let this happen while he was in uniform; he need not deploy any of his more clandestine weaponry against these bravos when his saber was ready to hand.

There were two of them—neither, from the look of him, a Dane. The taller one looked to be Irish; he carried a stout cudgel and seemed more than willing to use it. His companion was shorter and darker; he had a pistol thrust into his waistband and held a dagger with a very keen edge to its glittering blade.

Wessex recognized him. It was Charles Corday— Gambit—Talleyrand's assassin.

"*Allons!*" Gambit snapped at his companion. The Irishman began to move forward, swinging his shillelagh back and forth in front of him in experimental swipes. Wessex retreated warily. His saber was the finest Sheffield steel, but the stout stick in his opponent's hand could snap the blade with one blow.

"Sure now and it's a terrible thing, but its Your Lordship's life we'll be wanting, so you'd best be making up your mind to lie down at once, so says Sean O'Brien."

"I tell you what, O'Brien," Wessex answered back easily. "Throw down that twig and tell me who sent you, and I promise only to thrash you severely."

Sean O'Brien threw back his red-maned head and roared with laughter. "Sure, and it's a rare waste to have to kill you, me Lordship," he said. But there was no regret in his voice, only anticipation, and his small eyes were cold. Without further warning, he charged.

But Wessex wasn't there. Like an acrobat evading a maddened bull, he slid aside and allowed the force of O'Brien's first ferocious rush to pass him by. His blade flashed in the moonlight, and O'Brien went down with a roar, hobbled by a cut to the thigh.

Wessex looked for Gambit, his eyes probing the shadows. He'd resigned himself to having only one man to question, but to his faint surprise Corday hadn't bolted. He stood in the mouth of the alleyway, the pistol Wessex had seen held in both hands.

"You are not so drunk as you appear, *cher*," Gambit Corday said reprovingly in his heavily-accented English. The barrel did not waver, even in the uncertain light: the uniform of the Eleventh Hussars had been designed to be visible at all times, and Wessex made an easy target.

"And you are nothing like a Dane, Frenchman," Wessex answered. O'Brien was getting to his feet, and in a moment Gambit would fire.

"And I am not French. I am Acadian, me," Gambit said proudly, and then fired with one lightning movement—

—straight into O'Brien's chest.

The Irishman fell back with a roar, blood fountaining from his wound for a few brief seconds as his heart beat its last. The noise would summon the watch—Wessex intended to be far from here when that happened. He glanced back at Gambit.

An Acadian—a settler in Acadie, one of the New World colonies that had once been French, but had been ceded to England almost a century ago. Her inhabitants had not taken kindly to the change in government and had been dispossessed as a result. Most of them had gone south to settle in the still-French Louisiana Colony, though Wessex knew that the children and grandchildren of the Acadians still mourned their lost homeland.

"We 'ave been on opposite sides before, but now I t'ink we are on de same one, me," Gambit said to Wessex. "W'at you look for—maybe it better dat you find it, eh? You put it back where it belong, an' nobody bodder wit' us over de sea."

Wessex drew breath for a reply, but Gambit had already vanished. Wessex could hear the rattle of shutters opening in the windows above the streets, and knew he had little time to waste if he was to escape undiscovered. He turned to the body at his feet.

First de Sade, now Gambit. Their presence argued a major clandestine operation being staged on Danish soil, but Wessex could not imagine what it was—or why Gambit had felt the need to save him when his orders had obviously been to see Wessex dead.

O'Brien had little of value about his person, and nothing in writing. It was possible that the man had been unable to read. But he apparently had been able to count very well . . . he was carrying ten Imperial golden eagles with Bonaparte's laurel-crowned image on their face.

Wessex pocketed the money and took to his heels. A few minutes later he was safely within doors at MacLaren's house, being helped out of his uniform coat by a silently-disapproving Atheling.

"Have mercy, man," Wessex protested. "I didn't get a spot of blood on me."

"Your Grace is perhaps mistaken," Atheling murmured, drawing Wessex's attention to a smudge on his scarlet trousers that was beginning to turn brown as it dried. "But I daresay that I can save them, Your Grace."

Wessex waved this aside; God knew Atheling had been given ample opportunity to learn every method known to manservant of removing blood from clothing.

"May one ask if any events of unusual interest have transpired this evening?" the valet pursued.

"Nothing," Wessex said shortly.

Except that two men—paid in French eagles—had been sent to kill him tonight. Except that one had killed the other rather than fulfil his commission. And that Gambit, though in the pay of France, styled himself an Acadian

. . . who wanted Wessex to find what he was looking for, and then put it back where it belonged.

Wessex had a hunch Gambit hadn't been referring to Princess Stephanie—but what *had* the man meant?

Wessex had not the slightest notion. It was all very mysterious.

Things were looking up.

There had seemed no recourse but to do what Mr. Highclere said or be shot on the spot, so Sarah had dismissed Simon and she and Meriel had gone into the parlor Mr. Highclere had reserved for them. Meriel was white to the lips and shaking; if Sarah had needed any further proof that this had not been a trap of her friend's devising, Meriel's shock at seeing her uncle provided it.

The coffee room already had a collation laid out in expectation of their arrival: pasties and cheese and a steaming pot of coffee. A vigorous fire blazed on the small hearth, and despite herself, Sarah felt cheered—and hungry.

She knew who she was, now, but her orderly American world had been turned inside out: she had been thrust into a strange mirror-image of an England she barely recognized, a world populated with spirits and woodkin. Any daughter of the People knew that they shared the world not only with the Speaking Animals, but with the Firstborn of the Great Spirit—but Sarah Cunningham of Baltimore had never expected to see proof of that, let alone find herself forced to masquerade as her own strange twin in a world that held such creatures openly.

But despite the unbelievability of her whole situation, Mr. Highclere presented a far more urgent threat than mere magical oddity. However strange and unreal this new world might be to Sarah Cunningham, Mr. High-clere's gun was tangible enough.

Reality and masquerade blended; bearing Meriel with her, Sarah swept past him just as the true Duchess of Wessex would have done and seated herself upon the long bench that ran around two sides of the room. Behind them, Geoffrey pulled the sliding door of the coffee room shut, sealing them off from prying eyes.

"Now that you've got us, Mr. Highclere, what do you mean to do with us?"

With a detached clinical interest, Sarah heard her voice wavering between the broad vowels of Baltimore and the clipped English way of talking she had learned as the Marchioness of Roxbury. It was as if she had slumbered these past months, and now was awake . . . but to what end?

Geoffrey ignored her question, pouring out coffee for both of them and behaving as if he were any host.

"Can I tempt you to a bit of the ham, Your Grace? The cook has a delicate hand with pastry, but I daresay you'll want something more filling than apple tarts after your long journey. There's bread from the morning's baking, and several kinds of fish, I'm afraid, but what can one do this close to the ocean? Why, Meriel, I do believe you don't look at all well. . . ."

"Enough of your roundaboutation," Sarah snapped. "Kindly state your business with us, if you please!"

Mr. Highclere looked somewhat taken aback—American forthrightness, Sarah realized, did not go down at all well with the English nobility. But he quickly regained his composure, and smiled at both of them.

"Why, I've come to congratulate my little niece on showing some spirit and sense at last, Your Grace. Dick *would* take a maggot with his notion of making the Prince marry into the Old Religion and turn England back into the fold of the True Faith, but I know Jamie better than he does—our Jamie might marry the girl, but he'd never mind her. And marriages can be unmade, one way or another."

"Wh—what do you mean?" Meriel stammered, regaining enough of her composure to speak at last. "I could not divorce him!" Her hand went to the base of her throat, as if searching for the beads of an absent rosary.

"No," Mr. Highclere said with a vulpine smile, "but you could die, my dear. The King would see to that—he and his hatchet-man Wessex."

"King Henry would never be so base," Sarah scoffed. She picked up the coffee before her and sipped at it cautiously. The warmth lent her vitality and courage. "Drink your coffee, Meriel. I'm sure that Mr. Highclere will get around to explaining his purpose eventually."

"It is me that he wants," Meriel said in a low voice. She cradled her cup in her hands, looking miserable.

"You're quite wrong in that," her uncle told her genially. "As I said, Dick was right out in his notion—I went along with it because it would pretty well queer the Danish treaty, but with the Princess gone missing there's not much more need of that. There's still Wessex to consider, though—a man of truly annoying habits."

Though she was not herself in charity with Wessex, Sarah did not wish to allow anyone else the liberty of criticizing her husband.

"I am certain that no one here has any idea of what you mean," she said coldly. "The Duke of Wessex is a man of irreproachable character."

"My so-dear Duchess," Mr. Highclere said. "You wound me far more than I can say. Did I reproach him? I merely pointed out that he is a murderer and a spy in the King's service. I do apologize for distressing you—if indeed I have done so—is it possible that you did not know about your husband's secret life?"

Wessex an agent of the King! Sarah's mind shied away from the implications of the information. It explained so much—and nothing.

"That is—" *That is none of your affair,* Sarah had meant to say, but somehow the words tangled on her tongue.

"But you don't want me anymore? I'm free to go?" Meriel interrupted, her voice full of hope. She took a deep swallow of her coffee.

Mr. Highclere's smile widened still further. "Now sweeting, did I say so? Dick's plan may have failed, but there's still a world of uses for a girl like you. . . ."

Sarah tried to set her cup down, but the table jarred it loose from her numb fingers and it jounced across the surface, spilling coffee in a dark fan across the table.

Drugged. She wanted to shout out the word, but no words would come. She tried to stand, but she no longer had any sense of her body. The world blurred, and Sarah did not even know when she crossed the border into unconsciousness.

The first of July had seen Illya Koscuisko arrive in Edinburgh, where the young Dutch artist Jan van Harmenz who had debarked the hired fishing boat vanished, and a cheerful French *emigré* named Jean-Marie took his place for just long enough to claim a safe-house and send a brief report by carrier pigeon to London. Jean-Marie saw Koscuisko over the border, where the Polish Hussar could at last resume his own identity and make his way at a less-than-breakneck pace back to London and a certain house on Bond Street.

He spent the next week being carefully debriefed of everything he had seen and heard in the last month, and learned that the Danish Princess was still missing, and that Wessex in far-off Copenhagen was no closer to finding a solution to the mystery. From more public channels, he learned that the Prince of Wales was conducting a scandalous and unsuitable flirtation with the Earl of Ripon's niece and that Wessex's Duchess seemed to smile upon the match, since she had accepted an invitation to Lady Meriel's come-out ball.

Koscuisko wondered what Wessex made of all this. He knew his partner's guarded heart well enough to know that Wessex had not intended to marry and would not have done so if the King had not commanded it, but the little Roxbury who was the Duke's choice of bride Koscuisko did not know at all. It did not even occur to him to wonder if she could make the Duke happy . . . but he did wonder very much if she could be trusted.

In the service of his curiosity Koscuisko changed his coat once again, becoming Davy Vaughn, a young ostler in Baron Misbourne's service who was looking to find another post due to a quarrel with His Lordship's head groom. He was taken on at Herriard House provisionally, and thus had every excuse to loiter about the household and hear the gossip that servants always had about those they served.

It was Davy Vaughn who searched the Duchess's rooms quite thoroughly while she was at Lord Ripon's ball and failed to find even one scrap of sedition, and it was Davy Vaughn who, loitering in the garden well past midnight, saw the startling spectacle of a gently-bred young maiden in domino and ballgown scale the trellis to enter the Duchess's rooms. All of Davy's cleverness was not sufficient to gain him access to what transpired thereafter, but from his privileged position in the stables, he was aware that the Duchess's traveling coach was summoned and put to before the sun had even begun to consider rising. And for a long journey, too—the coach-footman was provided with musket and shot, and an outrider was given two charged pistols and enough gold to secure many days' changes of horses at the coaching inns of England.

And so it was that as the Duchess of Wessex's coach rolled away from her front door, Davy Vaughn slipped out of her life forever, having discovered that the Duchess's midnight visitor was none other than Lady Meriel Highclere, Prince Jamie's dangerous *inamorata*.

An hour later Illya Koscuisko claimed his stubborn, heavy-boned grey from the stables in Bond Street, and was away down the Holborn road in pursuit of Wessex's Duchess before the sun had cleared the church spires.

A traveling-coach is not the world's fastest form of transportation, and Illya Koscuisko, on horseback, could easily have caught up with and even overtaken the vehicle early on, had he so wished. He was, however, much more interested in where the Duchess and Lady Meriel were going—and why—so once he was certain that he was on their trail he hung back, sparing Spangle as much as possible. As the sun climbed higher, the coach left Holborne Road for the Dover Road, and Koscuisko began to believe that a journey of some length was contemplated. But there was only one likely destination when one embarked for Dover. . . .

He followed the coach throughout the day, staying out of sight and riding across fields to avoid coming to their attention. So certain was Koscuisko that Dover was their destination that he nearly lost them when they turned west, away from the bustling port city. By now night had fallen and a soaking drizzle had begun, so Koscuisko was willing to follow the coach more closely, but he was relieved to find the coach stopped in Talitho. When he was sure of their destination, he rode back up the road a ways and coaxed his tired mount to perform its favorite trick, and made his formal entrance into the lives of the landlord and his goodwife as a wet and irritable traveler leading a very lame horse.

The stableboy led the grey—who, with the soul of a thespian, was nearly bowing now with each step—back toward the stables, promising poultices that would have the animal ready to run in the morning. Koscuisko turned his attentions to the inn.

"I will of course require a private parlor," Koscuisko said haughtily. The persona he would use on this occasion was one that had served him well many times previously, that of private secretary to a gloriously-nonexistent Duke.

"Of course, sir," the innkeeper said, and escorted his esteemed (and open-handed, for Koscuisko had tossed him a yellow-boy along with the demand) guest to the private parlor at the back of the inn.

As Koscuisko passed through the common room he glanced about surreptitiously for men in the Duchess's livery, but saw no likely prospects.

The landlord rolled back the sliding door. A fire was already burning and the room was warm. Koscuisko touched the surface of the table and found it slightly damp, as if fresh-wiped. There'd been another occupant of this room, he'd be willing to bet—and that recently.

"Is this your only private room?" he demanded. "Have you nothing better?"

The innkeeper stuttered and stammered his way through a speech extolling the parlor's virtues; Koscuisko cut him off with another sovereign.

"Bah! I am going to the stables to see what those lunatics you doubtless employ have done to my horse—I shall expect dinner to be ready for me when I return."

Koscuisko strode from the common room of the inn. The inn had no other parlors, and the town had no other inns. He had seen the carriage stop here, and it and its occupants hadn't been out of his sight more than half an hour.

So where were they?

His spirits lifted momentarily when he entered the stableyard and saw the muddy yellow-paneled coach with the Roxbury crest on its doors standing empty, but it was only the small elation of being proved right. He still had to locate the Duchess and her subversive ladyship. And as much as he needed to do that, he must find out what time the tide ran tonight, and who was sailing on it.

Entering the barn, he found Spangle much recovered, a hot bran mash in his nosebag and a groom working over him. When he saw his master, the grey picked up his right fore and began pecking at the ground with it, as though the hoof was too sore to put down. Koscuisko smiled. It had taken months to teach the animal that trick, but it had been worth the effort. There were times when it was worth real money to have a horse that could "go lame" on command.

The grey was crosstied between two beams, because every other stall in the barn was full. Six of the inhabitants were match bays, the excellent and high-mettled horseflesh of the Duchess's equipage. One was the outrider's chestnut, and the other three stalls were filled with local animals.

"See here, my good man," Koscuisko barked. "What d'ye think you're about, leaving the animal to stand in the draft like that?"

"I'm sorry, me lord," the ostler said, obviously willing to err on the side of the conservatism in the matter of Koscuisko's rank. "But h'it's only for an hour or so. 'E'll have a warm bed for the night."

"An hour?" Koscuisko affected outrage. "Turn one of those nags out and put my horse in." He started toward the stall that held the outrider's chestnut.

"Begging your pardon, me lord." The ostler's voice was anguished. "But those 'orses belongs ter the Duchess of Wessex."

Koscuisko stopped, as if struck by the force of the argument.

"The Duchess of Wessex is here?" he said. "And her servants?"

"I dessay young Simon might be about," the ostler offered. "The others is all inside, a-having of their dinners. Hi! Jemmy! Go on up to the loft and fetch down Her Grace's Simon."

The ostler's apprentice, so addressed, came away from the horse he had been grooming and began climbing the ladder to the loft.

"Are you mad?" Koscuisko demanded in tones of outrage. "Do you think I came out here to chatter with the servants? Just go on about your business and see that he's hale to travel in the morning." With a swirl of his greatcape, Koscuisko stalked from the stable.

But he did not go back into the inn. Instead, he stood on Talitho's High Street, looking up and down. He could smell the scent of the ocean, and the riper scent of trash fish left to rot on the beach even through the veils of soft rain that gave the landscape a misty, unreal quality. It made visibility difficult, and though he strained his eyes, he saw no sign of light except the vigil lights in the church up the hill and the lanterns hung at the front of the inn.

The coach was here. The horses were here.

The Duchess was not.

Lady Meriel awoke to violent rocking and the overpowering smell of fish. She opened her eyes and then wished she hadn't, for the action brought on a headache that made her gasp in protest.

"Awake, are you?" There was the sound of a lamp chimney being removed, and then a sudden wash of light over the rocking walls of what Meriel realized must be a ship bound for France.

But why? Uncle Richard was fanatic about the restoration of the True Faith to England, but France had not been a Catholic country since the Revolution banned all churches nearly twenty years ago. Uncle Richard would never ally himself with the Emperor.

But Uncle Geoffrey would. Uncle Geoffrey would do anything that would cause someone else pain.

Having little choice, Meriel rolled over on the narrow bunk and sat up. The flare of pain on her welted back anchored her further in consciousness. She looked up.

Uncle Geoffrey was standing beside the hanging lantern he had just lit, looking like a rose-gold Satan. Meriel flinched involuntarily at the sight of the riding crop in his hand.

He laughed. "Oh, you've earned yourself a proper hiding, my dear, but at the moment I'm minded to be pleased with you. I'd never have winkled Wessex's Duchess out of her burrow half so neatly, and, I'm forced to admit, she's of a lot more use to me at the moment than you are."

"But you're certain you will find a use for me later," Meriel said bitterly. "How did you find us? We were not followed—I made sure of that."

Geoffrey laughed again. "I hadn't the least need to follow you, my poppet: I've read every letter you've posted since your dear father died and Dickon hatched this cloudwitted scheme to make you Queen of England. Knowledge is never wasted, so I've found, and what an inventive little plotter you are! So once the carriage turned up at Vauxhall empty, I just assumed you'd bolted for Auntie and set my course accordingly. Your precious blockade runner doesn't give a fig what cargo he carries, you know, so long as the price is right. And I've found over the years that gold is always right."

Meriel hung her head. It had all been for nothing, and the brief illusion of freedom she'd cherished was only that. But in the midst of her despair, a faint spark of defiance kindled and swelled within her. More than she wanted her own freedom, she wanted to deny her tormentors the prize they sought.

"So you want the Duchess," Meriel said, making certain she sounded cowed and bitter. "But why?"

"Because the Duchess has a Duke," Geoffrey said. "And at the moment, he's a most inconvenient one."

It was nearly midnight when the three of them were rowed ashore on the French coast. Sarah still slept heavily, for Geoffrey had given her more landanum a few hours into the voyage, something Meriel had not been able to prevent. Now Sarah lay on the sandy shore bundled in her traveling cloak, while Geoffrey waited for a response to the message he had sent from the ship. He still carried the hoodwink lantern in his hand, as if he thought to have further use for it.

Meriel crouched beside Sarah's slumbering form. Geoffrey had not bothered to drug her—one unconscious female was burden enough, he'd said. Meriel knew that he was certain she was cowed into submission, and she meant for her uncle to go on thinking so.

She also meant to run at the first opportunity—although she knew any apparent opportunity would only be the illusion of a chance. Geoffrey had only to run her down to capture her once more.

Therefore she must run when he was not able to follow. And she still had money, gold coins in the pocket in her petticoat. Uncle Geoffrey had overlooked that.

*   *   *

To Meriel's disquiet, their signal was answered by men in French uniform. The French Captain did not seem at all surprised to see such strange and ill-assorted arrivals on the beach at this hour, and spoke for some time to Geoffrey in a French too low and rapid for Meriel to follow, though she knew the language well. The party was then brought to what was probably a local inn; the landlord, yawning and unshaven, provided hot soup for Meriel and whiskey for Geoffrey. Their respite was brief, however; by the time Meriel had finished the cup of broth, a carriage had arrived, and once more the little party was on the move.

The miles passed slowly. As the sky lightened toward dawn it began to rain. This was unusual weather for July, but Meriel blessed it; rain would help to cover her escape. As they traveled on, Meriel stared out the window, wondering where she was. She was too young to have memories of France in happier times and so had no hope of discovering their location, but that did not dissuade her from her plans in the slightest.

The sun was well-risen when the coach jolted to a stop in front of an inn of the sort that catered to travelers. The rain had recently stopped, and the dampened countryside was shrouded in veils of steam. The country here was pretty and rolling, and in the distance Meriel saw the spire of a church. There would be a village nearby, then.

She did not try to feign sleep, for Uncle Geoffrey would see through that ruse and it would make him suspicious. Instead, she concentrated on projecting an air of abject fear and dejection—it was not hard, for she could not see much future for herself along any course she pursued. Spain and the dubious support of her mother's family was

very far away, and there were many perils set in the path
of a young girl on her own.

Still, she would not let Uncle Geoffrey win.

The coach rolled to a stop. There was bustle and rocking as the team was unhitched and led away; the mounted
French soldiers who accompanied them took the opportunity to reconnoiter the taproom with an eye to refreshment and comfort. Geoffrey stretched, and leaned over to
inspect his sleeping prisoner. Sarah's hands were icy and
her breathing was slow, but Meriel believed that the dose
of laudanum was not fatal.

Satisfying himself that Sarah would not move, Geoffrey
pushed open the door of the coach.

"I'm off to breakfast. As for you, poppet, wait right
here, or Uncle will be very, very angry."

Meriel hung her head and did not answer. But as soon
as her uncle was gone, she pushed open the door on the
far side of the coach and slipped out. Her borrowed traveling boots slipped and squished in the inn-yard mud, and
she clutched at the frame of the carriage for support.

She did not like to leave Sarah a helpless prisoner in
Geoffrey's hands, for she well knew his implacable cruelty.
But her uncle had claimed that Sarah was necessary to
some plot he was hatching against the Duke of Wessex,
which must mean that he would not harm the Duchess.

Meriel had to believe that.

Carefully she closed the door of the coach behind her.
The main road was at her back, and behind the inn she
could see the hedgerow that flanked the country lane.
Throwing the hood back—she dared not look as if she
were skulking, should anyone notice her—Meriel began
walking toward the hedge.

She was nearly there when she was seen, by a soldier
who preferred to take his beer and bread in the fresh air,
even if the weather was damp.

"Where are you going?" the soldier asked in French, but his tone was curious, not sharp.

"I have a necessity," Meriel replied in that same language. When the soldier took her meaning he looked away, begging her pardon as the color rose in his cheeks. Meriel walked briskly past him, in the general direction of the privy.

If Uncle Geoffrey knew his niece so well, then equally Lady Meriel knew her uncle. Unwilling to share his information, intent upon keeping others in the dark as much as possible, why should he tell them that he did not trust his niece, and that she must on no account be allowed to escape?

She'd gambled and won. Now let her luck only hold for ten minutes more. . . .

The angle of the building now concealed her from the curious soldier, and Meriel picked up her skirts and began to run. She reached the hedge and scrambled through it, blessing the ever-practical Sarah for insisting on the nigh-indestructible *Cotton de Nimes* traveling dress that she wore, and the stout boots that were on her feet. Swathing her cloak tightly around her and gathering a fistful of skirts, Meriel hurried in the direction of the village.

She could not get far before she was discovered; but Meriel knew that Uncle Geoffrey had urgent business elsewhere, and she thought she could manage to hide until her uncle could no longer afford to search for her. She hurried through the town, assessing every building she saw in light of her needs. She could rely upon no one to help her escape, for anyone might betray her to Geoffrey.

At last, nearly despairing of finding a haven, Meriel reached the old church at the edge of the village. For an instant she considered seeking Sanctuary at its altar, then dismissed the foolish romantic notion. That custom was centuries dead, and even if it were not, Geoffrey Highclere did not respect man, God, or devil.

But the church was attached by a walled garden to the residence of its *abbé*, and at this hour of the day the garden was deserted. Meriel opened the little gate and stepped inside, glancing fearfully toward the house. But no one had seen her.

Flitting through the garden like a feral ghost, Meriel found sanctuary in a gardener's shed at the foot of the garden. Gingerly she pulled open the door, fearful of spiders, but even spiders were not as terrifying as her uncle. She slipped inside and closed the door behind her, then groped through the darkness until she found an empty corner. There she crouched down and settled in to wait. And as the slow minutes passed and nothing happened, Meriel fell asleep.

"You can come out now, you know. He's gone."

With a gasp, Meriel snapped awake, heart hammering. The little hut was stiflingly hot now, but a cool breeze wafted in through the open door, and slanting golden afternoon light filled the dusty shed. A figure stood silhouetted in the doorway, but her dazzled eyes could not make him out. As she struggled to her feet she became tangled in her cloak, and fought the cloth as if it were a living thing.

"It's all right," the stranger said, taking her arm and raising her to her feet. "He's gone. He was looking for you, wasn't he—the ill-tempered *Anglais* with the golden hair?"

Meriel could see him now. He was a young man, near her own age, dressed in the plain simple clothing of the country burgher. His toffee-colored hair was pulled back in a short queue, and his blue eyes regarded her inquiringly.

"He's gone?" she asked, wanting to be sure of the most important thing first. She spoke in French, as he had addressed her in that language.

The stranger smiled. "He has gone hours ago, Mademoiselle. I waited for you to emerge, and then I began to think that you meant to spend the night in Jacques's shed, and that certainly could not be allowed."

Meriel shook out her skirts and attempted vainly to brush some of the dust and dried mud from her draggled cotton gown. Her mind was working frantically, trying to decide whether this was salvation or yet another form of trap.

"If you knew I was there, why did you not tell him when he came looking for me?"

The stranger laughed. "Because I did not like him, Mademoiselle! And *Père* Henri—I suppose I should say the *Abbé* de Condé, but he has lived here for so long that everyone in Trois Vierges calls him *Père* Henri—did not know you were here, so he was not forced to perjure his soul with lying, which is a very good thing," the stranger said piously. "But now the *Anglais* is gone and I may present you to *Père* Henri, so that we may all decide what to do. This is a very bad man you are running from, Mademoiselle, is it not?"

"He is a devil," Meriel said with feeling. "If he should find me again, he will kill me."

"Alas," the stranger said. "There are many devils in France these days—but *Père* Henri is very good at making sure that they do not find those whom they seek. And now I shall present him—poor man!—with someone else to hide. Only—who shall I say that you are?"

Meriel hesitated. But she very badly wished to trust someone, and this engaging young man seemed as though he might be an ally. Still, she hesitated for a long moment before she replied.

"Meriel . . . Greye. Yes. Tell him that. But who are you?"

"You must call me Louis," the stranger said, smiling a little bitterly. "It is forward, I know, but I have had no other name in our glorious Republic these dozen years."

16

The Lion in the Oak

As soon as Wessex had walked into the Parisian cellar, he'd known that this was a trap. He did not recognize any of the members of this Underground cell—and he'd been forced to use the cover of M. de Reynard in contacting them, knowing that the Red Jacks had blown that *nom de guerre* months ago and that in all probability they would know him for an English political agent. And so, it seemed, they did.

"Come in, M'sieur de Reynard . . . or whatever your real name is," the leader—a brunette who must once have been beautiful but who now was merely striking—said. "Do not try to leave—you will be dead before you do."

"I've come for information," Wessex said evenly. "I am not one of the Red Jack's dogs."

"It does not matter whose dog you are, if you are not ours, *hein?*" the woman said. "You will tell us what you know, and then . . . we shall see."

"If I knew anything of interest, I would not have come

to you," Wessex responded. In his persona of the Chevalier, he wore a saber at his hip, and carried a number of other little surprises about his person, but he did not wish to kill anyone here tonight, much less attract undue attention. "Can't we behave as reasonable people? My people have always supported the Restoration of the true government of France—you have worked with us before."

"Times change," the hard-eyed brunette said. She seemed upon the verge of a drastic decision, when suddenly there was a small commotion from outside the door, and Victor Saint-Lazarre walked in.

He appeared taken aback by the sight of Wessex.

"Zette! What are you doing?" he demanded.

"What I must, Victor," Zette replied stonily. "Do you think we dare to trust our so-called allies at this time of all times? They would steal the bone themselves—"

"Be quiet!" Saint-Lazarre snapped. "Can we behave like the *sans-culottes* and hope to save France at the same time? This man is a friend—"

"This man has no name," Zette noted dryly. "He says he is the Chevalier de Reynard—but the Chevalier de Reynard does not exist; he is a shadow cast by an English spy."

"I know this man," Saint-Lazarre said, gazing steadily at Wessex. "I will vouch for him. He means us no harm and has done me a very great service." He turned his attention to Wessex. "What have you come here for . . . m'sieur?"

So Saint-Lazarre was willing to keep his secret. Wessex spared a moment to feel relief. But Saint-Lazarre knew he was the Duke of Wessex, and now knew him for a spy. Try as he might, the Frenchman could not keep the expression of distaste from his face, for a spy was the lowest of back-alley skulkers, and to find that a nobleman had descended to such a level . . .

"I came to see if the rumors that the Tyrant was behind the disappearance of Princess Stephanie of Denmark were true. Her ship has vanished, and I do not believe that she is dead."

"The little Princess who was to have sealed the treaty," Saint-Lazarre said. "She is gone?"

"Her ship has vanished." Wessex admitted only what the whole world knew. "And the Marquis de Sade is discovered as the Tyrant's emissary at the Danish court. What can he be doing there, I ask?"

"De Sade is a foul name indeed," Saint-Lazarre said, shaking his head in disgust. "But we cannot help you, m'sieur. The Princess is not in Paris. And I advise you to go home, Englishman. France will determine her own destiny without England's help."

And so Wessex had left Paris. But he had not gone home.

All his instincts assured him that Princess Stephanie had been kidnapped, and the only power that could wish to abduct her was Imperial France. But the Princess had not vanished alone. A Hundred-Gun Ship of the Line carried over eight hundred men as its crew; over a thousand men and women had vanished with the Princess, and Wessex did not believe that Bonaparte had executed them all . . . the little Corsican was too canny a gamesman to have done that.

They must be somewhere. To search all of France for them was like searching for a needle in a haystack. But where better to search for a needle than in a haystack made of needles?

*   *   *

The medieval walled city of Verdun bestrode the road to
Paris like an angry colossus, but the colossus was a tame
giant in the pay of La Belle France. Within the city's walls
lay all those who did not swell the numbers within French
prisons—enemy soldiers on parole; neutrals who could
not be allowed to pass; others who, though prisoners, had
not been judged enemies of the state.

If Avery deMorrissey had been able to escape from the
place, Wessex mused, he himself should certainly be able
to get in. He lacked the papers that would allow him to
enter the city's guarded gates as a bureaucrat or tradesman upon lawful business, and had little interest in entering Verdun as a prisoner. The only remaining
possibility was a clandestine entry that eluded the sentries,
and Wessex was considering how he might effect one
when his attention was caught by the sound of hoofbeats
on the road behind him.

Dismounting, he led his horse off the road into a small
stand of trees. They would not conceal him completely,
but it might serve to screen him from casual attention.

A few moments later, a lone rider on a neat-footed grey
gelding came trotting up the road. The man was in uniform and cut a fantastic figure, from the leopardskin sad-
dlepad beneath his saddle to the arcing eagle's wings that
thrust skyward, making a faint keening sound as they cut
through the air.

Wessex stayed where he was. He was too far away to
recognize the rider—and many of those who wore that
uniform now served Bonaparte—but the Andalusian gelding was impossible to mistake.

Illya Koscuisko reined in. Spangle stopped, bowing and
prancing.

"I do hope it's you cowering there in the bushes, my
dear fellow. I'd hate to have to shoot another in a series

of minor French bureaucrats in order to cover my traces,"
Koscuisko said.

For a long time Sarah had only come near the surface of
wakefulness before being forced down again into darkness
by the sick-sweet taste of laudanum. In her mind, her
drugged state became the insensate period just after the
carriage accident, when she had been reshaped by careful
instruction into the semblance of the Marchioness of Roxbury.

But now that shaping had fallen away, and having been
caught so once, she could not be beguiled so again. She
was Sarah Cunningham of America—and it was that peculiar stubborn independence of mind, forged in the aftermath of a war this world had not experienced, that
allowed her to force herself awake at last.

The drug still anchored her body in the bed like the
press of a heavy hand, and her head felt made of lead,
but at last she could open her eyes and think . . . after a
fashion.

Geoffrey Highclére had found her and Lady Meriel in
Talitho, drugged them, and brought them . . . where?

The room she lay in had the same impression of heavy
stone and hint of damp that Sarah associated with the
chapel at Mooncoign, only here the sensation was magnified a thousandfold. The bared plaster upon the walls
was stained with moisture, and in places the plaster had
flaked away to reveal the grey shapes of dressed stone
beneath.

The ceiling was crafted of massive age-darkened beams,
adding to the sense Sarah was gaining that she lay within
the walls of some medieval fortress. When she at last managed to lift her head, she could see that a window—the
sole source of light in the room—was set deep into the

opposite wall. Two cross-bars blocked off that avenue of escape.

Groaning, Sarah levered herself into a sitting position. The room contained only the bed she was on—a thing of delicate curved and gilded and enameled wood that looked jarringly out of place in this rude medieval keep—and a rough wooden table upon which sat a carafe of water and the ominous blue bottle of laudanum.

The upright position brought with it lightheadedness and thirst. She was still wearing her traveling clothes, down to her cloak and shoes, and wondered how long she had lain drugged. Her hair felt sticky and disheveled, and her feet had swollen as she lay abed until they ached like a bruised tooth. Using the frame of the bed, Sarah dragged herself to her feet, wincing at the pain. The room reeled savagely around her, but she was determined to prevail. At last she managed to make her way over to the barred window.

She was in a castle.

Outside her window, the tower wall dropped sixty feet to a stagnant moat almost overgrown with water lilies. The landscape stretched soft and green, verdant with summer growth. In the distance she thought she might be able to see the spire of a village church, but she couldn't be certain.

England . . . or elsewhere? Meriel had planned to go to Lisbon—

Where was Meriel?

Still light-headed and groggy, Sarah turned and looked around the room. No Meriel. Sarah shook her head, trying to clear it. Mr. Highclere had meant to bring both of them with him. Was Meriel being kept somewhere else?

Sarah ran her hand through her light brown hair, dislodging the last of the pins and sending it cascading down her back in a tangled mass. Could she get out of the room to find out? Sarah studied the stout, iron-bound oaken door with misgivings. She wasn't certain she even had the strength to drag the heavy door open—and what if it was locked?

She was spared having to make that discovery. There was a rattle of keys (so it *was* locked!) and a groaning of unoiled hinges as the massive slab swung inward.

A young woman dressed in country homespun entered, carrying a large wooden tray containing a bowl and a pitcher. Behind her came Geoffrey Highclere, neat and immaculate in Revolutionary black. He looked like an elegant ferret, and Sarah felt even more disheveled and grubby by contrast.

The servant uttered a distressed squeak at the sight of Sarah on her feet, and scurried over to the table to set down the laden tray burden. Mr. Highclere merely smiled.

"So you're awake then, Duchess? Well it saves me the trouble of wakening you."

"Where is Meriel?" Sarah demanded with Yankee bluntness. If he expected fits or vapors, Mr. Highclere was going to have to look elsewhere for them.

He smiled, obviously about to spin her some faradiddle, and Sarah's frayed patience snapped. "And the truth, if you please, Mr. Highclere! I am in no mood for one of your Banbury tales."

"You ought, you know, to be more conciliating," Mr. Highclere pointed out in hurt tones. "After all, you are my prisoner."

Sarah's only response was an unladylike snort.

"Oh, get out, girl, and go tell the Monsignor that he can talk to her now," Geoffrey snapped in French.

The frightened maidservant bobbed deeply and scuttled from the room.

Sarah faced Mr. Highclere. Her heart was fluttering frantically, but she knew that her face was an expressionless mask, and that such a Sphinx-face would unnerve him. Her enemy was a soft city-dweller, and he would not survive a day in the boundless forests of her homeland. If she could only escape from this keep, she could vanish into the French countryside beyond his ability to trace her.

"You may think you have the upper hand, but the Monsignor won't care for that. He'll break you the same way he shells a walnut; he has but to tighten his fingers—"

"And then he can eat me," Sarah supplied helpfully. "Well, while I must admit it sounds a useful party-trick, Mr. Highclere, I can hardly see that it is of the least use here. You are a traitor to England, Mr. Highclere, and while I have some passing sentiment for traitors and revolutionaries, I cannot approve of the way you have treated Lady Meriel," she said firmly, returning the conversation to the matter she most wished to know.

"It is nothing to the way I would have treated her," Mr. Highclere snarled, "and I hope the chit is dead in a ditch somewhere. She bolted from the carriage at the first stop—abandoning *you*, my dear Duchess—and I have not the least idea where she is now."

"How *very* too bad for you," Sarah said commiseratingly.

Mr. Highclere's face darkened with rage, and he moved toward her, hand raised. Sarah stood her ground, braced for the assault. She had been a warrior of the People, and if Mr. Highclere expected an easy conquest, he was quite misled. Sarah expected to be the victor, and once he was immobilized, she would escape.

But her plan—and Mr. Highclere's—was forestalled by the arrival of a dapper young man in an immaculate unfamiliar uniform.

"Monsignor Talleyrand will see you now, M'sieur Highclere. And Madame *la Duchesse*, as well."

*   *   *

Sarah did not know that Charles-Maurice de Talleyrand-Perigord held the nickname in some circles of the Black Priest (only partially due to his unwilling flirtation with holy orders), but she might have coined it herself upon reflection; though the fair hair had since gone to silver and he was entering his sixth decade, Talleyrand still had the sweet-faced innocence of a kindly village priest. He had escaped the Terror by becoming its instrument, and when the wheel of bloody Revolution turned, he had gone on to become an instrument of Imperial terror instead.

He was dressed in a black coat like any clerk, his hands sheathed in black kid and a black stock tied about his throat (some said he wore black because it showed the blood less than a white linen cravat would—but fortunately Sarah had not heard these tales). He sat in a plain wooden chair behind a plain wooden table in a room upon the ground floor of the keep. An inkwell, pens, and paper stood on the table at his elbow, as if he were a law clerk preparing to take a witness's statement.

Sarah gazed about as she was brought into what once must have been the grand salon. It was a chamber thirty feet by sixty, and had been beautiful once, but now the salon held the same air of vandalism and neglect as the rest of the building—a pale area on the bare wooden floor showed where a rug had once been, and many of the panes of the row of long windows had been mended with parchment, casting the room into a dolorous golden gloom. The ornamental plasterwork had been damaged, and the wall-coverings ripped away. Someone had taken a hammer or a crowbar to the immense white marble fireplace, so that its frieze of satyrs and cupids now stood eyeless and maimed. No fire burned upon the hearth now, and despite the season, the echoing room was cold.

"Good afternoon, Madame *la Duchesse*," Talleyrand said in flawless English as Sarah was brought to a stop before his desk. "I trust you hád a pleasant journey?"

"Oh, *do* stop all this play-actor foolishness," Sarah burst out in exasperation. "You know very well I did not! I was kidnapped, and drugged—and if you do not know what a head so much laudanum gives one, I shall be happy to enlighten you upon that much, at least!"

"Madame has spirit," Talleyrand observed. "Such spirit as others have had, when first they came before me. Not afterward."

"If you brought me here only to kill me," Sarah observed with some asperity, "allow me to point out that you have very many other people available to you for this exercise, much more easily obtained than I. You went to a great deal of trouble to get me here."

"But you are here now," Talleyrand observed passionlessly.

"Yes," Sarah agreed. "And I should like to know why?"

"You did not explain?" Talleyrand asked Mr. Highclere.

"I thought—That is to say—" For the first time in their unwanted acquaintance, Sarah saw Mr. Highclere at a loss for words.

"You did not think. Very good, Monsieur Highclere. I do not ask all of my agents to think. You may go now. I wish to speak to the Duchess privily, and then I shall have another commission for you."

From the corner of her eye, Sarah saw dark color mount in Mr. Highclere's face, but he seemed unwilling to cross the man he had called Monsignor, and after a moment Geoffrey Highclere managed to master himself enough to nod stiffly and stalk from the room.

"And now we may be comfortable, madame," Talleyrand said, as if Sarah were not left to stand in front of him, without even the refreshment of the bowl of gruel that the maidservant had brought to the room. "And I shall explain matters to you."

Sarah was tired. She was afraid, and becoming more so at the minute, for she could sense that Tallyrand was a far more dangerous man than Geoffrey Highclere. But her face showed nothing of this—she was cornered and at this man's mercy, but she would do as the porcupine and the skunk did in such situations.

She would bluff.

"I do not require your cooperation, so you may set your mind at rest upon that head," the Black Priest said, when Sarah said nothing. "What I require is that your husband come to heel and cease his quixotic quest."

Talleyrand got to his feet and began to pace, speaking as if he were lecturing a hall of students.

"You may perhaps not be aware that for some years the Duke of Wessex has been King Henry's chief political agent, a meddler without portfolio in the affairs of sovereign nations: killer, blackmailer, thief—"

"He is, after all, English," Sarah said, a faint ironic note of explanation in her voice. "But pray continue, sir. I collect that you have brought me here to transform my husband's character?"

Talleyrand stopped, and what seemed an expression of genuine amusement transformed his fallen angel's countenance.

"In a manner of speaking, my brave one. In the past few days I have been made aware that Wessex's latest adventure is a strike against the secret heart of France. Monsieur *le Duc* wishes to accomplish his father's commission and discharge the duty that the late Duke his father died attempting to fulfill. Such filial feeling is often admirable, Madame *la Duchesse*, but in this case I must deplore it. France's affairs must be left to France, and if

the Duke of Wessex does not see the wisdom in this, I am
desolated, dear lady, to tell you that your life will be for-
feit."

Sarah's heart sank, though her face did not show it.
She'd known there was something smoky about her husband's character—and frequent absences. But to hear his
crimes and his profession laid out so baldly . . .

"It would make more sense, surely," Sarah offered in a
steady voice, "for you to murder my husband. If you had
a desire to accomplish your objective, I mean." She forced
herself to stand as still as ever she had stood while on the
hunt. This, too, was a hunt of sorts . . . only who was the
hunter, and who the prey?

"I will admit, madame, that here we touch upon a small
difficulty," Talleyrand said, stopping in his endless pacing
to face her. His back was to the window, and his black
coat was spotted with gold and silver light falling through
the glass and parchment panes of the windows. His silver
hair was haloed in metallic fire, and in that moment he
seemed less like a man than like some inhuman instrument of Fate.

"For you see, at the moment we have no method of
placing this small matter before the Duke your husband.
We attempted to settle the matter of his inconvenient life
in Copenhagen, but we have received recent word from
Paris that the Duke of Wessex is still most troublesomely
alive—though, alas, still incommunicado. And while he
remains so, it will be a matter of the most difficult to
explain to him that he must surrender or receive your
pretty head in a large box."

Even Sarah could not keep from flinching at the particularly brutal image Talleyrand's words conveyed. Defiantly, she walked around the table and sat down in the
chair he had vacated. She folded her hands in her lap and
raised her chin boldly.

"He will be a difficult man to convince," Sarah said after a moment. "He does not love me, you know." And even as she said that, a tiny part of her deep inside cried out that it did not matter, because she loved him, the man she had crossed universes to find. . . .

Talleyrand walked over and stood directly before Sarah, gazing down at her with a stern fond expression, as if he were her father confessor.

"My dear Duchess, no wonder you look so, as the English say, blue-deviled. How could any man spurn a lady of such vivacity and breeding—not to mention undoubted wealth? Truly this Wessex is not a civilized man. But do not concern yourself: Wessex will certainly wish to preserve your life, for you are his wife. I would hesitate to term this a matter of honor, something which no spy has, but certainly his pride would be touched upon if I were forced to kill his Duchess. Alas, madame, it is a weak reed, but it is all we have to rely upon, you and I."

Sarah's head hurt; she was tired, thirsty, and beginning to be hungry. And she was becoming very weary of this man's pretense that the two of them were allies of any sort.

"You cannot possibly suppose that I believe I will escape this chateau alive?" Sarah scoffed.

"Perhaps not, madame, but you will hope," Talleyrand said at last. "As we all must hope, in these dreadful uncertain days."

Without waiting for her reply, he went to the door and knocked at it. It opened, and the same young soldier who had conducted her to this room came to lead her away.

"How did you get here?" Wessex demanded of his errant partner. "And more to the point—why? Did Misbourne send you? Has the Princess turned up?"

Koscuisko shrugged, looking oddly uncomfortable. "No, and no, but I can assure you that Ripon's guns have been rather neatly spiked as well. Lady Meriel is here." Koscuisko seemed to gather his forces. "And so is the Duchess of Wessex."

For one appalled moment Wessex thought Koscuisko meant his mother, then he recollected that it was Roxbury who was Duchess of Wessex now.

"She's in France?" he said rather blankly.

Briefly, Illya Koscuisko put Wessex in possession of such information as he'd managed to piece together: the Earl of Ripon's ball; Lady Meriel's midnight visit to the Duchess of Wessex; their flight to Talitho; Geoffrey's Highclere's sudden arrival.

"I tracked down the blockade runner he used too late to stop the sailing, but there's no doubt it's Highclere who made all the arrangements. And I'd lay a monkey the Duchess didn't mean to make the trip—not and abandon her coach and servants. I found the maid in an upstairs room—drugged—and she told the tale that they were running from Mr. Highclere. If that's the case, they didn't get very far."

"*Women!*" Wessex swore in furious exasperation. His mind was working rapidly. "If Highclere has made for France, it does seem to argue that his heart isn't quite with his brother and the cause of the Old Religion."

"Or that the plot had blown up—especially if the lady wasn't as willing to play as she was previously advertised— and Highclere was looking for a new paymaster. He's quite the loose fish by all accounts," Koscuisko said.

"Where did he take her?" Wessex asked hopefully, but his only answer was a rueful shrug.

"I waited for Captain Crispin to return and had him land me and Spangle at the same location, the good Captain being a man of remarkably elastic principles when hard coin is at stake. But we were a day behind them, and the trail went entirely cold in a little village about a day from here. So I decided to take a cold cast, and since they might as well be held here at Verdun as anywhere . . ."

"Here you are," Wessex agreed. "And I'd had the same thought, regarding the Princess and her suite. Shall we try our luck? Providing, of course, you have a plan to get both of us past the city gate."

"Well, as to that," Koscuisko said modestly, "I always have a plan."

The Lieutenant of the Emperor's newly-formed *Bataillon Polonais de la Garde Impériale* rode up to the gate at Verdun with the fury of a young nobleman who had lost his day and was late for his dinner. To be asked to present his papers was an insult. He and M'sieur le Chevalier were attached to Talleyrand's own Department—it was impertinence even to question them. Did the gentleman—and the Lieutenant used the term with all due disbelief—wish to send for his officer to meet the Lieutenant with sabers in the woods nearby?

The outrageous bluff worked. Cavalry officers were frequently detached from their regiments to serve as couriers and messengers, and it was known throughout France how highly Bonaparte valued his Polish troops, who added style and spirit to what was, at this moment in time, the most broadly based multinational army in the world. In the end, the guards saw what they expected to see, and Wessex and Koscuisko passed through into Verdun.

"It won't work for long," Wessex told his partner, as they rode up the street to their assigned billet.

"I didn't think you wanted to stay long," Koscuisko replied with elemental simplicity.

Verdun was a city with every appearance of being under siege. Its wealthier residences had become boarding houses for those who had the money to make their incarcerations comfortable; the less fortunate were crammed into every crowded corner of the medieval city. Every necessity of life was sold at a premium, and to find one's self without money was to be tumbled into a life of an unspeakable level of squalor.

The tension of the city's inhabitants was a nearly tangible thing, composed of narrow streets and patrolling sentries, of a high wall and fates held in far-off Imperial hands. When the war was over, the internees could leave Verdun. But whether they would find a homeland to return to was another question for a day many of them might not even live to see.

Wessex and Koscuisko checked in at their billet—despite the oppressive crowding of the internment city, the provision for traveling officers was much what it would have been anywhere in France— stabled their horses, and went on to a café to plan their next move.

"Well?" Koscuisko said bluntly, once he had been supplied with coffee and cognac. He spoke French, though any other language would not have been out of place here in this cosmopolitan city of refugees.

"You astonish me," Wessex said mildly. "We are in Verdun, and in desperate need of gossip. Where else ought we to repair?"

There was a moment while Koscuisko digested this.

"Ah. I see. We are to visit Helicon, then."

Wessex smiled.

*   *   *

Germaine de Staël, Baronne de Staël-Holstein, had been born in 1766 to a life of wealth and privilege. An internationally acclaimed authoress, salonniere, and reigning Toast of Europe's intellectuals, she had been banished from France by the Revolution and from Paris by the Directory. When that government fell in its turn, Madame had returned at once to the Paris she so loved to become that most French of paradoxes: an ardent Royalist who embraced the ideals of the Revolution.

In the name of both these loves, she had opposed every step Bonaparte had taken toward the golden laurel crown of Empire, and when, two years before, he had forbidden Madame to return to Paris, she had taken up residence in the walled city simply to spite him. From Verdun she ran one of the most notorious underground presses in all of Europe; according to rumor, its pamphlets and essays drove both Napoleon and his unscrupulous handmaiden Talleyrand (satirized in the novel, *Delphine,* which had occasioned her banishment) to utter distraction. Yet Bonaparte dared not make himself appear altogether ridiculous by moving publicly against a mere woman, one who, moreover, was a daughter of a hero of the Revolution, banker Jaques Necker.

And so Madame de Staël recreated her famous Paris salons here in this subjugated city, mocking the Emperor with her very existence.

It took Wessex and Koscuisko about an hour to reach Madame de Staël's house, making their leisurely way through the streets of the city. Verdun as it had become reminded Wessex of an Eastern city: crooked, crowded, and desperate. The butler who opened Madame's green-painted door was formidably correct in coquelicot satin livery and powdered horsehair wig. The man did not so much as raise an eyebrow at Koscuisko's fantastic uniform, and took Wessex's card in to his mistress without a murmur. A moment later he was back to say that Madame would see them both.

Wessex preceded his friend into Madame's ground-floor salon.

The room had been painted with fantastic murals and furnished out of the *Arabian Nights*. *Trompe de l'oeil* vistas recreated Madame de Staël's beloved Paris, while the room itself was strewn with divans and cushions and contained ornaments of the most fantastic nature, including an enormous green parrot chained to an ivory perch and a tiny black monkey dressed in a copy of the servant's livery which sat upon Madame's shoulder.

Now nearing her fortieth year, Madame de Staël was still a commandingly handsome woman. Though the lustrous black curls turbanned in an Indian shawl were touched with grey, she still retained the opulent figure and round white arms that had made her known as much for her beauty as for her formidable intellect. She extended a hand as Wessex entered.

"Reynard!" she cried, in her hoarse beautiful voice. "So you are *not* dead!"

Wessex made a profound leg and bowed over Madame's hand, kissing it thoroughly. "Reports of my death—as so often—have been greatly exaggerated, Madame. As you see, I journey instantly to your side to dispel them."

"Willingly or no," Madame responded, darting a glance at his companion.

Wessex made the introduction, and Koscuisko launched into a voluble flood of Polish. Wessex could not follow their conversation, but apparently Madame was well enough versed in that language to be able to blush in it. She shook her head, laughing.

"Abominable boy!" she declared in French. "But it is good to know I am still read."

"Madame knows that her greatest triumphs are still before her," Koscuisko responded gallantly, "and one hears rumors of a masterwork to come—a German history?"

"Young flatterer!" Madame declared roundly. "Yes, I am still writing—much as That Man in Paris would wish that I were not. But come! We shall have tea, and you may tell me all the news of the larger world which I am denied."

For fully an hour conversation turned upon events in Paris and the Continental war. Madame was not so uninformed as she would have herself appear, and her reputation as the foremost *conversante* in Europe was well deserved. The discussion ranged from the rights of man to the necessity of government, touching occasionally upon the inequities suffered by Verdun's internees. At last Wessex turned the conversation toward the purpose of his visit.

"Shocking indeed. One wonders how much longer the Corsican can expect to send people here without allowing any to leave. One feels there must be some limit to the numbers poor Verdun can accommodate," he said.

"Indeed," Madame said, cutting a sly unbeguiled glance toward the man she knew as the Chevalier de Reynard. "Not three weeks past we were forced to accept a positive deluge of *Anglais* whose ship was blown ashore near Calais. And what is most infamous is that it was a Danish ship, and though Denmark trades freely with France, her officers were likewise imprisoned, her men impressed, their ship impounded. It is more than shocking—it is infamous!"

"Infamous indeed," Wessex agreed smoothly, though his heart was racing with the excitement of a fresh scent. "But no doubt a temporary annoyance? Once the Captain applies to the Danish ambassador, his release and that of his crew are assured, are they not?"

"So one would think, M'sieur le Chevalier, though the post from Verdun is read by the commander of the garrison, and letters are often stopped. Yet if I were to tell you that this was a consular vessel carrying members of the Royal family of Denmark to a meeting in England to seal a treaty that would bring Denmark into the Grand Alliance that opposes my poor France while she languishes in the grip of that madman . . . ?"

"Then I should not be surprised that Bonaparte holds this ship and all who sailed in her, for where Denmark goes, the rest of the League of Armed Neutrality will surely follow," Wessex said. "Russia has already done so."

"And Denmark dares not take the opposite side of a Russian quarrel, lest the Tsar use the excuse to gobble her up—so!" Madame said, snapping her fingers to illustrate her point. "But they do not hold *all* those who sailed upon this ship. So it is said," Madame finished. She selected a sweetmeat from the tea tray before her and offered it to her costumed monkey. The little creature took the sugared walnut and bounded away with the tidbit, retreating to the top of a gilt-framed mirror to devour its treasure.

"If it is said, Madame, I make no doubt that it has been said to you," Wessex said gallantly. "For everyone knows that you are the eyes, the ears, the conscience of France. I do not doubt that it would be most diverting to make the acquaintance of these folk. But only if they are entertaining. Saving yourself, Madame, who are an oasis in a desert, I find myself nearly dead of boredom."

"My poor Reynard!" Madame cooed, and laughed her throaty laugh. "You will be more than bored once you have spent a few weeks here."

"Alas," Wessex said lightly, "I fear that my sojourn here is much briefer than that. I vow that I have come only to see you."

"But my dear man—" Madame said, and stopped. "You will be leaving Verdun?"

"Almost instantly," Wessex said. "If the Jacks do not find me here, of course."

Madame made a *moué* of distaste at the mention of the Red Jacks. "If it is as you say, there is a trifling commission you can discharge for me, if you will. In return, I promise to alleviate your boredom, if you will do me the honor of dining with me this evening. And bring your handsome friend, of course."

Extending one glittering, bejeweled hand, Madame achieved the yellow velvet bellpull and rang it vigorously.

Wessex was already standing. "It will be the greatest delight of my heart, Madame. You may depend upon it."

By any standards—let alone those of embargoed Verdun—the meal that evening was lavish, beginning with clear soup and sherry and proceeding to the highest pinnacle of the gastronome's art. They were seven for supper, and Madame had not stooped to the empty conventionality of a balanced table. She was the only woman present.

Koscuisko had shed his uniform for an evening suit of an even more peacock splendor than his Hussar's garb, and even the Chevalier de Reynard had found it incumbent upon himself to blossom, in part, through the good offices of his fellow internees, in an aubergine silk coat, oriental brocade waistcoat, and dove-colored breeches ornamented with steel-cut buttons. The party might have been any gathering in any metropolis—but there was always the undercurrent of tension peculiar to the walled city.

And as Madame had promised him, Wessex was amused.

The party consisted of Wessex and Koscuisko, and four

others: Captain Rytter, formerly master of the *Queen Christina*; Lord Valentine Grant, the engaging redheaded scion of one of England's noblest families; a Belgian divine named Poirot; and Sir John Adams, King Henry's envoy to the Danish court. Dinner was conducted in French.

Wessex studied Sir John closely, thanking his lucky stars that he and Sir John had never formally met. It would not do for Sir John to know him as the Duke of Wessex when he was here upon the pretext of being the Chevalier de Reynard—but then, even if Sir John should recognize Wessex, the old fox was far too sly to tip his hand. King Henry's envoy had this very year achieved the Biblical threescore and ten, but his gadfly vigor showed no sign of abating. He had been born in England's North American colonies, and his forthrightness and persistence had seen his rise in the Foreign Service to this most delicate of all posts. If Sir John was in any wise discomfited by this abrupt change in his fortunes, Wessex could discern no sign of it.

And Captain Rytter's presence at Madame de Staël's table was living proof that Wessex had been right. The *Christina* had been somehow waylaid, and shipwrecked on the inhospitable shores of France.

It was not unreasonable that conversation should dwell upon such an unfair misfortune, and so Wessex learned that the *Christina* had sailed into a fogbank, only to sail out of it upon the coast of France, hundreds of miles from her last position.

"And I am afraid the French did not believe anything of my explanation," Captain Rytter said regretfully. "For we were taken and boarded over our protests, the men impressed and the rest of us sent here to Verdun. I am afraid that the *Kronprinz* must consider this an act of war; Denmark is neutral and to violate her flag is an act of arrant piracy."

"And so he will, should he ever happen to hear of it," Lord Valentine said. The youngest son of the Duke of Hurley, Lord Valentine had been encouraged to leave home at an early age and never return, as his politics were quite at odds with his father's. "But I daresay Boney don't want him to know. If anything'd make the Danish lion lie down with Britannia, snabbling the Prince Regent's daughter off the high seas would do it."

"But we are fortunate that he did not," Captain Rytter said. "The Princess was aboard the *Trygve Lie*, and we have heard nothing to say she did not reach port safely."

Wessex kept himself from looking at Koscuisko. His partner had been aboard the *Christina*'s sister ship and was prepared to swear that Princess Stephanie had not been on the *Trygve Lie*. Instead Wessex looked toward Sir John, who, of all the rest of those gathered tonight at this table, must know that Captain Rytter was lying.

"Indeed, though it was impossible to persuade our friends of that as well," said Sir John blandly, in his fluid diplomatic French. "The Princess's ladies-in-waiting and gentleman ushers were aboard the captured ship, and a detachment of her regiment, but they were wholly unable to produce the Princess, no matter how diligent their search. Captain Rytter, of course, told the French she was not aboard." He shrugged. "I dare to swear their powers of comprehension were not above ordinary."

"So Princess Stephanie has made her way to safety," Koscuisko agreed cheerfully. "What a very good thing, to be sure."

At the end of the meal, Madame de Staël rose promptly.

"I shall leave you gentlemen to—briefly—punish the port, as I know that Sir John and Lord Valentine are English and would fall into despair if this custom were not followed. But I shall expect you to be brief, and the Chevalier I shall take away to bear me company while I wait."

Wessex obediently rose and followed Madame from the dining salon. However, she did not conduct him to the grand salon, but rather to her private study on the floor above.

"Are you most certain, M'sieur le Chevalier, that you will be leaving Verdun within the next few days?" Madame de Staël demanded.

"I think I can promise you absolutely that I shall be away by the end of the week. To prefer one place over another becomes tedious over time, do you not find?" Wessex said smoothly.

"Then I will give you this. It is a manuscript that I wish to see published—in France."

From a secret compartment in her desk, Madame withdrew several thick sheaves of paper inscribed in a fine copperplate script. She piled the pages together, forming a bundle nearly a foot thick, and began making it fast with red waxed string. "It is my latest work—based upon my journeys in Italy. *Corinne* will show the world that I am not to be forgotten!"

"If you can obtain the imprimatur. The Minster of Police will surely have something to say about that," Wessex observed mildly.

Madame threw back her head and laughed. "And so he should, if he knew that it was by my pen! *That!* for Fouché—I have it in mind to let him know that this is by my hand only after the edition has been circulated, and see how he weathers the charity of his Corsican master! But first the manuscript must be taken to a publisher and prepared for press."

"Dear lady," Wessex protested, slightly alarmed.

"Oh, do not fear, Monsieur le Chevalier, I do not have you in mind for my go-between. I have for some time been in correspondence with a certain religious gentleman possessed of a noble and open mind; you have but to take this parcel to the village of Auxerre and give it into the hands of the innkeeper there; *Père* le Condé will call for it in good time—and I shall be spared the tedium of recopying it when the so-tiresome commander of our lovely city loses my package, as he has done so often before. Will you help me, M'sieur le Chevalier? It would seem you have been sent by the very Spirit of Liberty to aid me."

"When such a beautiful—and formidable—woman makes such a gracious appeal, what can any man do but lay himself down in her service?" Wessex answered grandly. He needed Madame de Staël's help—though she had been of great assistance to him already in gaining him access to Sir John—and he relished the opportunity to tweak the noses of the bureaucratic butchers who were currently stifling the life of the mind here on the Continent.

"Then I will wrap this with my own hands for you against its journey," Madame said. "I dare not trust the manuscript to my maid—there are spies everywhere, and many within my own household. But for now, we have the whole of the night before us, and I have invited a few of my particular friends to call. Let us banish care."

The party broke up long past midnight, after a glorious evening of Olympian wit and sparkling talk. Some twenty members of Verdun's society—free-thinking men and women both—had made the walls ring with epigrams and laughter, and even Wessex had been able to lay his cares aside for a while.

He had not been so rash as to attempt to approach Sir John at the gathering, but as housing was a frequent subject of discussion, it had not been difficult to discover where Sir John lived. Wessex had made plans to visit that location as soon as it might be arranged.

As Wessex was making his good-byes, Madame handed him a large, oilcloth-wrapped bundle.

"Your books, Chevalier. Be sure to return them to me soon," Madame said.

"You may depend upon it, my dear *Baronne*," Wessex said. "In fact, I shall exert myself to return them a thousandfold."

When Wessex returned to his billet, Illya Koscuisko was there before him, lounging on the bed in shirt and trousers.

"You've been shopping, I see," Koscuisko said, indicating Wessex's package.

"Something that may be as damaging to Bonaparte— in the long run—as a couple of companies of heavy artillery," Wessex answered, setting the oilcloth-wrapped bundle containing Madame de Staël's manuscript down on his bed. "We are encouraged to bring it to a little town named Auxerre."

"I know the place," Koscuisko said. "A village about one hundred and eighty kilometers outside Paris. Madame has friends there who will surely help her work see print. But is this quite the direction we are bound in, one wonders?"

"I shall know better once I have seen Sir John," Wessex said. As he spoke, Wessex began changing his evening finery for the more sober coat and breeches he had worn that day—but he did not put the coat on immediately.

First he turned the garment inside out—it was lined, not in silk or satin, but in soft black moleskin that ate the light. There were small black horn buttons on the reversed lapels as well, and when Wessex had put the coat on and buttoned the collar into place, he was wearing a sort of black tunic closed high up to the neck. He turned the cuffs down over his hands, and then the dark moleskin tunic covered his white shirt completely; he would be invisible in dim light.

The boots Wessex donned were rubber-soled, permitting a noiseless movement and a certain ease in scaling the walls of buildings.

Koscuisko rummaged about his luggage and produced a curiosity: an unfringed shawl of black gauze. Sheer enough to see through, the shawl's swaddling folds would dim the whiteness of Wessex's skin and the brightness of his blond hair, allowing him to become even more a phantom of the night. Wessex thanked Koscuisko with a curt nod and began swathing himself in the veiling.

"And what am I to do, while you are frightening the amiable Sir John out of several years' growth?" Koscuisko enquired.

Wessex paused to slip a long knife into one boot and to wrap a primed pistol carefully in his handkerchief before sliding it inside his coat.

"You, my son, will be figuring out some way to get yourself and both our horses out of the city again—not forgetting Madame's parcel—without raising the view halloo. There's an inn a few miles west of here—I'll be there by dawn."

"And if you aren't?"

"Then for God's sake take Madame's package on to Auxerre for me, and then get home as quick as you can. Misbourne needs to know that Princess Stephanie's entourage is here in Verdun. The captain was lying—she *was* on that ship—and I hope Sir John can tell me why. But the information that she is here is of vital importance."

"And what of the Duchess?" Koscuisko said. "Highclere has kidnapped your wife."

For a moment Wessex's face went very still, but when he spoke his tone was unchanged. "Get the information to London and the manuscript to Auxerre, there's a good fellow. I'll join you as quickly as I can."

But for all his cavalier dismissal of his Duchess's fate, Wessex could not stop thinking of the woman he had married as he made his careful way across the rooftops of Verdun to a meeting with King Henry's envoy.

The deep game his wife had been playing had proved successful—she had turned Lady Meriel and drawn the girl away from Prince Jamie's side. Sarah, Lady Roxbury—now Duchess of Wessex—was a member of the Boscobel League, sworn to serve the person of the King before her country or her crown, and so she had done. The king was safe from the assassination that Lord Ripon must surely have contemplated once he felt Prince Jamie was safe in his marital trap.

But now Sarah was in danger, imprisoned somewhere in France. Kidnapped by Ripon's ill-mannered younger brother—had Geoffrey Highclere somehow discovered who she was?—and spirited away for reasons unknown.

Sarah might already be dead.

Wessex set his jaw. He dared not think about that now. If he did not find Princess Stephanie, the Danish Treaty would collapse. Denmark would become Bonaparte's foothold on the Scandinavian countries; the Tyrant's bridgehead from which to launch a Russian invasion.

That must not be.

Over the last several years Wessex had made it his business to know the streets of Verdun very well indeed, and he found Number Ten Rue de la Paix without trouble.

Even in the summer's heat, the rooftops of the city were largely deserted, owing primarily to the sentries' habit of shooting at anything they saw moving there. Their muskets did not have such range as to make it likely they would hit anything beyond three hundred yards, but even a spent bullet could kill.

And so the rooftops remained empty.

Sir John, as one of the latest whom the poor city must somehow find room for, had been given an attic bedroom, and the shutters of his windows were open against the heat of the night. Wessex made short work of descent from the rooftop through the open window.

The room was empty.

"I have very little worth stealing," Sir John Adams remarked from behind the wardrobe. He was in nightshirt and cap, with a fireplace poker clutched in one hand. "Your countrymen have been remarkably efficient."

"Not my countrymen, Sir John," Wessex drawled, straightening from his crouch and turning to face the envoy.

"You're English!" Sir John exclaimed, his eyes first widening, then narrowing as he recognized his dinner companion from earlier in the evening.

"King Henry sent me to discover what happened to the *Queen Christina* and Princess Stephanie," Wessex said. "It's a pity I can't show you a Royal Commission, but I left that with Prince Frederick in Denmark. He was as cordial as you may imagine."

"And what brought you here?" Sir John said, his tone cautious.

"I was possessed of the liveliest curiosity as to why Bonaparte should have despatched the Marquis de Sade as envoy to the most straitlaced court in Europe," Wessex said. "It occurred to me to imagine that his reputation for sorcery may not be entirely undeserved."

"That fog was a thing of the devil, right enough," Sir John muttered. Gathering his dressing gown from a nearby chair, Sir John swathed himself in its folds and sat down. "And you've come here—why? After this evening's masquerade, 'Chevalier de Reynard,' I can hardly imagine that you are here to treat with the garrison commander for my release."

"I'm afraid not," Wessex agreed, "though I will certainly tell the King that you are here in Verdun, and perhaps pressure can be brought to bear. For that matter, His Holiness will not approve of Bonaparte's employing sorcerers, and even these days, France is still very much a Christian country. But what I wish to know is, where is the Princess?"

Sir John sighed, and seemed to age years in seconds.

"I only wish I knew," John Adams said.

"When we came out of the fog," Sir John continued, "at first we were not at all certain of where we were. The navigator shot the sun, of course, but it was some time before any of us could believe what the ship's instruments told us. By then we had been sighted by a French patrol, and the outcome of *that* was only a matter of time. The *Christina* fought well—I will give Captain Rytter that— but she was outgunned, three against one.

"By the time she struck her colors and stood to for boarding, it was late afternoon. The women had been belowdecks for hours, with a couple of *Kongelige Livgarde* there to defend them—we sailed with a full company: sixteen men.

"The French must have thought we were a spy ship, or a particularly foolhardy smuggler. They swarmed over us; there was some fighting hand-to-hand. It took the French Captain nearly an hour to restore order. He seemed con-

vinced that we were leaving France, having taken on passengers; when we managed to make him understand that
we were a consular ship that had somehow found herself
in French waters I do not think he believed us, but he
was so relieved that the Dauphin was not aboard that—"

"The Dauphin!" Wessex could not keep from exclaiming. "King Louis? Ridiculous; the boy died years ago."

"So I had always understood," Sir John said, waving
his hand to dismiss the matter, "but the Captain seemed
obsessed with the notion that we had the Lost King somewhere in our luggage. At any rate, by the time order was
restored and I was free to go and attempt to explain to
the Princess what had happened . . . she was gone."

Wessex waited, but there was no more.

"Gone?" he said at last. "Gone where?"

"Vanished, my dear boy," Sir John said. "Vanished
from plain sight and the midst of her entourage. When
the Captain and I went below to escort the Princess up
on deck, she was not there."

Then where am I supposed to look for her? With a significant
effort of self-control, Wessex kept from speaking the words
aloud. Every instinct told him that Sir John Adams was
speaking the truth—at least as Sir John knew it.

"And none of her entourage were able to tell you where
she had gone?" Wessex finally asked.

"My dear young man," Sir John said, "I have exerted
my wiles on kings, tsars, tyrants, and princes—but it is
quite beyond me to impose order on a dozen weeping
women all wailing in Danish and of the unshakable opinion that they are about to be sold into the Grand Seraglio
of the lustful Turk! I have spoken to several of the women
since, of course, and their story remains the same: they
don't know where the Princess is, or where she could have
gone."

"They're lying, of course," Wessex said.

"I imagine so. But there is one thing of which I am certain, and that is that the French have no more idea of Princess Stephanie's location than I do."

"That is something at least. Very well, Sir John, I will leave you to an undisturbed rest. I shall convey to the king news of your situation as soon as possible."

"There is a letter I have written to Lady Adams, which I should be most obliged if you would convey to her for me. Dear Abby! If she were only with me, I dare swear we should have routed those Frogs."

Or at least would now know where Princess Stephanie was, Wessex thought dourly. He accepted the neat wax-sealed billet from Sir John and tucked it into his coat beside the pistol.

"I shall convey your letter—and your regards—to your lady as soon as possible," Wessex said. "But now I must bid you farewell, for it has been a long night already and I have still to break out of this cursed city."

Sir John chuckled at that. "Then be on your way, my nameless friend—and I hope we shall meet again under more pleasant circumstances!"

17

The Once and Future King

The small bedchamber was tucked up beneath
the eaves of the country house, and from its open windows
Lady Meriel could see the riotous abundance of the Abbé
de Condé's garden and the beautiful grey stone of the
small church beyond drowsing in the golden evening light.
The little village of Trois Vierges looked just as it might
have appeared a hundred years before, as if neither the
Terror nor the new Empire had been able to harm it.

The room smelled of lavender and fresh linen—
Madame Carmaux had been all that was kindly and efficient when Louis had come into the kitchen trailing Meriel like some stray kitten. It was Madame Carmaux who
had bundled Meriel off to the guest room with a bowl of
soup and a glass of sherry, and announced firmly that
Louis and *Père* Henri's inquisition must wait until the little
maiden had set herself to rights.

Now Meriel was clad in a borrowed dressing gown, the
housekeeper having taken away her clothing to make it as

presentable as womanly possible after its adventures. Meriel had gladly taken the opportunity to refresh herself; to wash her face and comb out her long black hair before braiding and pinning it up once more. And the thick nourishing soup had done much to restore both her equilibrium and her spirits.

She turned away from the window to regard herself in the green-turned, fly-spotted mirror that graced the door of the enormous mahogany wardrobe. An etherial *fantome* returned her gaze.

Lady Meriel was aware of her own beauty—she had been raised to be constantly aware of it, first as a spiritual obstacle to be overcome and then as a lure to entangle young Prince James in her uncle's web. Now, as she studied herself, Meriel wondered if there were anything more to her than this accident of comeliness. For the fresh beauty of youth would fade with time, and then what would she have left?

Who would she be?

There was a knock upon the door, and Madame Carmaux entered, with a bundle of clothing over one stout arm.

"Ah. A little soap and water soon puts things to rights, eh, mademoiselle?" the housekeeper said, laying out her burden on the bed.

"Yes, indeed," Meriel agreed warmly. She smiled at Madame Carmaux. "I am very grateful for your hospitality."

"It is of the most improbable that you are one of the Black Priest's spies, being English as you are," Madame Carmaux said. "If, of course, the blond English was indeed your uncle, as he swore himself to be to the good father."

Meriel sighed, knowing that she would have to explain herself sooner or later—and servants were apt to be much more concerned with propriety than their masters.

"He did not lie," Meriel said with a sigh. "He *is* my uncle, but he is a very wicked man. He will surely return to search for me again."

"As to that, no doubt he will find what he deserves," Madame Carmaux said placidly. "But there! I am an old fool to worry you so when a good dinner awaits you. But I must tell you that your dress will not be ready for you until tomorrow—and perhaps some of the stains will not come out at all," the housekeeper added darkly. "I have brought you some of my daughter's clothes, which will suit you for tonight."

Madame sorted through the bundle she had brought, laying aside a nightcap and gown for later use, and flourishing a slightly old-fashioned dress of sprig muslin with a wide deep neckline, a ruffled lawn fichu, and a warm woolen shawl.

"You are very kind," Meriel said again.

"It is a sad thing to be hunted like the hare in the spring," the older woman said. "I shall send Jeanette to you to help you dress, then she will bring you to *Père* Henri's study."

When Meriel knocked and entered, she did not see the Abbé de Condé at first. Tall leaded-glass windows were open into the garden. A white cat drowsed on the sill in the last rays of evening sun, and the enormous carven oak table that dominated the room was covered with books and papers. Sudden tears prickled in Meriel's eyes. Somehow this room reminded her of her father and her home, and of how safe she had once felt. Sternly she suppressed the traitorous emotion. Lady Meriel had long since learned that she had no one to depend on save herself.

"Ah, there you are, my child. Come in, and let me look at you."

The Abbé de Condé was a tall, slender, regal-looking man, with swept-back silver hair that owed none of its color to wig or powder. It was impossible to judge his age, but whatever his years, his piercing blue eyes were as keen and sharp as those of a much younger man. The Abbé wore a black soutaine, its hem sweeping the floor, and a large gold cross upon his chest. The ring of his office circled the first finger of his right hand; a violet stone glinted dully in the dim light.

"Are you a believer, child?" the old priest said.

"I . . . yes, Father. I am a Catholic," Meriel said diffidently.

"And what brings you to my garden?" he continued.

Meriel was attempting to bring the tangled threads of her story into some semblance of order when there was a knock on the door.

"Ah," *Père* Henri said. "That will be Claude with the candles."

But it was not Claude with the candles. It was Louis, the young man who had found her in the shed, who entered. Louis carried a massive candelabrum in each hand; he set them down on the table.

"Marie says you will go blind entirely, working here in the dark," Louis said. He lit the candles with a spill kindled at the room's one lamp, and once the candles were all alight, settled himself upon the edge of the table with every air of intending to remain.

"Louis—" the Abbé said warningly.

"I found her," the young man said stubbornly, "and—I should very much like to hear what Mademoiselle has to say."

"I don't mind," Meriel said. "I have little to hide."

*   *   *

But if she had little to conceal, the household was her opposite. For there was a great secret here, Meriel realized later, when the small household was seated at dinner. When he had heard her story, *Père* Henri had agreed that of course Meriel must stay with them until such time as her aunt Maristella in Madrid could send for her. Of the fate of her companion—Meriel had been reluctant to mention that Sarah was the Duchess of Wessex, and neither Louis nor the Abbé de Conde had pressed her upon any point—they had been unable to speculate, though the Abbé had promised to make discreet inquiries as to Geoffrey Highclere's destination. But it was quite impossible, so the priest assured Meriel, that she should send a message to England.

"We are at war with England," *Père* Henri had said mildly. "And we dare not draw attention to ourselves here in Picardy. We are not so far from Paris as all that, and the Emperor might at any time remember that he is only a friend of the Church when she comes bearing gifts."

Meriel had hung her head, unwilling to press the issue though determined that she would find some way to aid her friend. But tomorrow would be soon enough to think of that. For now she was willing to be diverted by the far more agreeable mystery of young Louis.

Everything about him bespoke aristocratic blood—blood as blue as de Condé's, who had been a prince long before he had become a prince of the Church, as so many younger sons were. Meriel knew that it was de Condé's induction into holy orders that had saved his life when so many of the rest of France's Royal family had died. Though many members of the Church had died in the bloodbaths that had characterized the nineties—for the Jacobin mob had drawn little distinction between princes

of this world and the next—those with quiet country par-
ishes far from Court, such as de Condé's, had weathered
the storm of atheism until Napoleon had found it politic,
as First Consul, to court Mother Church once more.

But that did not resolve the puzzle of Louis.

Marking the strong resemblance between him and the
old priest, she wondered if he were in fact the Abbé's
natural son, but the words Louis had spoken to her in the
garden still teased at her mind.

"I have had no name in France these dozen years."

No. Not a by-blow. Something more magnificent, and
far more dangerous.

Meriel was not willing to construct such a fabulous cloud-
castle without more proof than her own wild surmises,
however. There was a great distance between knowing
that Louis had the look of the Bourbons about him and
deciding that he was Louis-Charles, the lost boy-king who
had vanished amid the bloody chaos of the Revolution.

It was more likely, in fact, that Louis was not the true
Dauphin at all, but merely a young man groomed to impersonate the heir to the throne of France; a pawn for the
French Royalists to use in another of their so-far-fruitless
series of countercoups.

She had never thought she would bless all those tedious
frightening hours spent sitting quietly while her uncles
wrangled about plot and counter-plot; of the Catholic support they could expect from Scotland and the possibility
of a separate peace with France. But those long hours had
left her able to see the Matter of Europe as a great chessboard, its playing-pieces interlocking in infinite combina-
tion. To return the lost King of France to the chessboard
of Europe would dissolve old alliances and make new
ones. Louis XVII's importance was so great it hardly mat-

tered whether he actually existed or not. . . .

And so Lady Meriel bided her time, through the soup, the fish, the roast, the savory, the sweet, and at last the cheese, keeping her own council and turning over in her mind how she might prove—or disprove—her theory.

When she excused herself from the table and went into the garden, Meriel was not surprised to find that Louis sought her out not so very much later. Her beauty was her currency, and Meriel could wield that beauty as a soldier might ply his sword.

"I came to see if . . ." Louis began.

"Your Majesty," Meriel said, sweeping the startled young man a deep curtsey. She glanced up at him from beneath her lashes, knowing that the light from the house fell upon her face and turned her skin to lambent cream.

Louis drew back as if Meriel had transformed herself into a viper upon the spot. "How—How did you—" he stammered.

"You have the look of your uncle—if he *is* your uncle," Meriel said. She rose gracefully to her feet.

"A cousin, not an uncle," Louis said. "A distant cousin, who endangers himself by sheltering me." He regarded her unhappily. "Perhaps you are one of the Black Priest's agents after all. Have you come to number the days of my life, then?"

Abruptly Lady Meriel lost all appetite for the game she was playing with him.

"I have no desire to harm you . . . Your Majesty. But I have no taste for plots and secrets, and if you are entangled in one I will not remain here. There are things I did not tell your cousin the Abbé earlier."

To her own surprise, Meriel found herself confiding the whole of the truth to Louis—about the plot her uncle Ripon had hatched to snare Prince Jamie of England, of her flight with the Duchess of Wessex's help—

"Wessex!" Louis exclaimed. "I remember the Duke of Wessex—he came when I was just a boy, to save me from the *sans-culottes*. Is this his daughter, then?"

"The wife of his son, I think, for I have heard that the old Duke disappeared in France years ago. My uncle Geoffrey thinks the current Duke is a political agent for the king, and has taken Sarah as a hostage for his good behavior—only I do not know what it is that he is doing that Uncle Geoffrey has taken in such dislike," Meriel finished faintly.

It was such a relief to tell the whole truth to someone at last that Meriel hardly cared at this moment whether Louis was the rightful King of France or not. She thought that he might be—the reason for the old Duke of Wessex's disappearance was certainly not a matter of public knowledge. But if the son were a political agent, it was not unlikely that the father had been as well.

"Do you think the Duke will come to France to rescue his Duchess?" Louis demanded eagerly. Meriel stared at him, baffled.

"I . . . suppose he will. Uncle Geoffrey must have some notion of how to reach him," Meriel said uncertainly. But was that true? Why, even Sarah hadn't had any idea of her husband's whereabouts!

"Then perhaps he will aid me, as his father tried to do," Louis said. "Listen, *ma petite*—you know who I am."

"I know who you wish me to believe that you are," Meriel answered cautiously. Louis dismissed such equivocation with a wave of his hand.

"The *soi-dissant* rightful King of France—as if France can ever again be what she was," Louis said with wistful scorn. "Even if the Tyrant died tomorrow, how could I bear to rule those who killed all my family? No. If France will have no more of kings, then this king will have no more of France."

"You don't want to be king?" Meriel asked cautiously.

"I am the king," Louis corrected her gently, "but I do not wish to rule. Perhaps the English Duke can help me."

"He will take you to England, to live under King Henry's protection and form a government in exile," Meriel said with bitter cynicism. "Is that the help you want?"

"Should you like such aid, in my place? No, *ma petite*, I have said I am done with France. If the Duke of Wessex can smuggle me out of this country which once was mine, I will take the first ship I can find and go to the New World. They do not care so much for old blood there, and there the world is wide. There, at last, I can make my own fortune."

Meriel gazed at the young king, dazzled by the audacity of his vision. Shyly, she extended her hand. "I hope you may achieve your dream, Your Majesty."

"You must call me Louis, my brave one—the Emperor would be very cross with you if you insist upon giving me a title long since revoked." The young man smiled slightly at his own joke. "But the first thing that falls to us, I think, is the rescue of your friend."

"Could de Sade have spirited Princess Stephanie away just as he did the *Christina*?" Koscuisko asked idly.

Kosciusko and Wessex rode southwest, toward Auxerre and away from the grim walls of Verdun. Madame de Staël's manuscript was in Wessex's saddlebag, and the letter from Sir John Adams was tucked inside his coat. There was no point in concealing either document. If they were stopped, the two of them would have more troubles than a mere set of seditious papers could place them in.

"To what location? The man is too foolish to be playing a double game, and I would bet my soul that the lady isn't in Paris. Sir John said the Princess was gone by the time the French took possession of the *Queen Christina*."

"But gone where? Not to England, not to France, not back to Denmark. . . ." Koscuisko appeared to ponder the matter for a moment. "Where?"

"That's the question," Wessex said.

"Well," Koscuisko amended. "One of them, anyway. I can think of half a dozen more."

"Who is de Sade *really* working for? Where did he gain the right to call upon such power? Why did Gambit think letting the Irishman kill me would harm the cause of Acadian independence?" Wessex recited, ticking the points off on his fingers.

"Why did the French Captain think that the *Christina* had the missing Dauphin aboard? Is Ripon as well as Highclere working for the French? And why does Highclere think it necessary to kidnap your Duchess?" Koscuisko added helpfully.

"A question that I hope soon to put to Mr. Highclere," Wessex said broodingly, "but at the moment all trails seem equally cold. And why the Young King? The poor child has been dead these twelve years."

"Well, *someone* thinks he's alive," Koscuisko said. "And if Princess Stephanie continues missing, that means farewell to the Danish alliance, and hello to Citizen Bonaparte's perfect staging ground for an invasion of England."

"In that case," Wessex replied, "I think it is almost obligatory that we provide M'sieur L'Empereur with something to distract him from such an attractive notion. A Found Dauphin seems about right as a diversion, don't you think?"

"To be sure. But at the moment we are in rather awkward circumstances ourselves, particularly should someone wish to ask questions about our holiday at Verdun."

Wessex considered this. "As you say. I have no papers save as the Chevalier de Reynard, and I dare not present them, for I fear that the Chevalier's usefulness is at an end. It is too bad: I shall miss the fellow."

"He was a good deal more amusing than present company," Koscuisko said provocatively, "but if Reynard's dead there is no use wailing over him. You shall have to become someone else. Now, my friend, who shall it be?"

Four days later Citizen Orczy of the Committee for Public Safety arrived—with his escort, a galloper from the Garde Polonnaise—in the city of Amiens. Citizen Orczy went directly to the Golden Cockerel, where he took the best room in the inn, was rude to the landlord in the way that those of high station traditionally were, and closeted himself in his rooms immediately.

The Pole, after the fashion of *his* kind, immediately took himself off, announcing that the Cockerel was by far too tame for his tastes, and a few hours later was to be found dicing in an accommodation house which had been set up on the former premises of a cobbler, from which device the place had taken its name of The Red Boot. As accommodation houses provide nothing for their customers beyond tables, chairs, and some very bad coffee, the Pole had brought his own brandy and his own dice, and was throwing left hand against right and disliking the results extremely. The Pole looked a villainous sort of fellow, and in a foul mood beside, but as the brandy was in plain sight, it was perhaps not surprising that, after three-quarters of an hour or so, he was joined by a fellow whose smock and clogs proclaimed him a local tradesman.

The man sat down and essayed some pleasantry about the weather, which was ignored by the Polish Hussar. The tradesman made a number of other casual remarks—all ignored—until the attention of the accommodation house's other inhabitants drifted elsewhere, since a quarrel did not seem to be forthcoming.

"I perceive you are a fishmonger," the tradesman said at last.

"No, but I can tell a hawk from a handsaw when the wind blows from the White Tower," Koscuisko responded.

"What do you need?" the tradesman said, leaning closer.

"Travel papers for myself and a friend. I have his particulars with me, and I'll need the papers as soon as I can get them. I'll also need information, but you may have to send abroad for it."

"Have you anything to pass to the White Man?" the tradesman asked, using the field agent's name for Baron Misbourne. Amiens was a large enough city that the White Tower ran a station there—the contact was known as the Bishop—and its field agents knew the contact procedure—though not, of course, who the agent was. Even now Koscuisko did not look at the well-disguised Bishop of Amiens, learning as little as he could about the man, so that he would have little to betray if he were caught and questioned.

"Andiron sends," Koscuisko began, using his and Wessex's code-name. Each team of field agents had a code-name, and each individual agent had one as well. Koscuisko was Eagle; Wessex was Lion. But it was not important that the White Man know which of them had sent this message, only that it came from a trustworthy source.

"The crew of the *Christina* is interned in Verdun. The Princess disappeared from the ship and is still missing. Andiron believes that Charenton"—the code-name by which they denoted the Marquis de Sade—"is responsible."

"So that's your hare," the Bishop said respectfully. "You'll need this then: Saint Lucky's been captured by the Jacks and is sleeping in the Tuilleries. 'Tis said he was dolphin-fishing when he got the office."

Koscuisko drew a deep breath, concentrating on keeping his face blank. He threw the dice again, then pushed the cup across to his companion.

"Try them if you like—they're sound enough," he said in the faintly imperious tones suitable for a Hussar condescending to address a tradesman.

So Saint-Lazarre was taken by Talleyrand's secret police and being held in Paris. That was disaster enough, but that Saint-Lazarre had been captured while attempting to get to the missing Louis-Charles nearly beggared belief. Worst of all, Tallyrand would be sure to break Saint-Lazarre, given enough time, and then everything the man knew about Royalists still operating in France would be endangered.

"The frogs were fishing for dolphins in the Channel and drew a *Queen* instead," Koscuisko murmured.

The disguised Bishop darted him a startled glance, then recovered himself and threw the dice. Both men inspected the results. Koscuisko laughed, and clapped the apparent tradesman on the shoulder. He passed the bottle and, when it was returned, took a drink himself.

The tradesman spent another fifteen minutes throwing the dice against the Hussar, and among the winnings that changed hands at the end there was a small folded scrap of paper. Koscuisko shoved it into his pocket along with the small hoard of greasy coin and wandered unsteadily from the accommodation house.

Wessex had intended to stay circumspectly in his room at the Golden Cockerel until Koscuisko had met with the

Bishop of Amiens and received Citizen Orczy's proper documentation, but once his partner was gone, the Duke found himself too restless to remain in one place. Despite his discipline, his mind kept turning upon Sarah. Where was she, and what was happening to her?

It was entirely his fault that Sarah was in danger. If he had not married her, she would not have become a target for Ripon's vengeful plots. The mere Marchioness of Roxbury did not fly high enough for Ripon, nor was she so closely placed to the Crown.

But the Duchess of Wessex was so placed, and with the Duke's anonymity becoming more compromised by the day, the time would soon come when there could be no place for Wessex on the chessboard of Europe.

Such thoughts disturbed him—the more because there seemed no escape from them. But there was escape from the small inn, and so Wessex tucked a pistol in his pocket and went to walk about the town.

His steps soon took him in the direction of the church. Amiens was not a cathedral town (although, Wessex reflected sardonically, it was the seat of quite another sort of Bishop) but the Popish church was quite grand enough for all practical use. Vaulting gothic arches led the eye skyward to battlements encrusted with saints and gargoyles, remaining despite the best efforts of the atheistic Revolution to overturn them.

The more pragmatic Bonaparte had restored Holy Mother Church and her privileges to the country that had fought so desperately to throw off her yoke. Bonaparte gave lip service to freedom of conscience, but in truth, the highest power in the land was the Imperial Eagle, and even the Church must bow to that. Even the Powers of the land itself fled before the great beast Bonaparte, causing disturbances in the Unseen World whose repercussions spread like the lake-ripples from a thrown stone.

Thinking his bleak thoughts, Wessex found himself gazing at a tiny shop that stood almost within the church's shadow. It was such a shop as would never have existed so openly in Royal France, where the kings had made the promises and treaties they must but commended their people wholly to the mercies of the Church. But at the dawn of this new century, the Church's power to dictate was much circumscribed, and such things as this shop flourished.

Willing to be distracted, Wessex crossed the square toward the shop. It occupied a small narrow building, and the age-old symbol of an open hand inscribed with the symbols of the palmist hung above its door.

Wessex opened the door warily, and a tiny bell rang sweetly as he did so. The narrow shop was fragrant with the scent of stolen Church incense, and the walls were covered with gaudy broadsides detailing the phrenological map, the signs of the zodiac, a prudently unattributed horoscope, and other tools of the prognosticator's art. A curtain divided the back of the shop from the front, and as Wessex looked about, a woman came forward through the curtains.

She was not dressed in Gipsy tawdry as he had half expected, neither was she some ancient crone; instead, a woman only a few years older than he was regarded him calmly. She was dressed in neat, plain, sensible clothing, and her blue wool shawl was pinned at the neck with a scarab-shaped brooch of red carnelian, the only exotic thing about her.

"Good afternoon, monsieur," she said. "Do you seek advice from Madame Fabricant?"

"Is that what you sell?" Wessex asked. "Advice?"

To his surprise, the question made the woman laugh merrily. "Oh my! Monsieur, you know what sort of shop this is. I sell what people wish to buy—but you do not look as if you need me to petition the Good Mother for health or wealth or love. So it must be the future you wish to know."

"I had rather know the present," Wessex found himself replying, "if your skills extend to that, mademoiselle."

"Your Grace is too kind," the woman said, turning to pass through the curtain again. "But I did have a husband once, though he is dead now."

Wessex stood as if rooted to the spot. Was the title she had given him just empty flattery, or did she indeed have the Sight?

Or was she one of Talleyrand's agents, warned to look for the Duke of Wessex along the road to Calais?

No answer came; Wessex shrugged to himself and followed her though the curtain, one hand inside his coat and resting on the butt of his pistol.

Behind the curtain the shop was dark, lit only by a large pillar candle that stood upon a massive brass holder in the shape of a monkey. The walls of the room were lined with cabinets of polished mahogany, whose myriad of small drawers reminded Wessex of an apothecary. Just as in an apothecary, there were jars of herbs and flasks of colored liquid, but no apothecary would have a statue of the Blessed Virgin upon the wall, and before her a small table upon which rested a small votive in a red glass jar in the midst of a tumble of less recognizable objects.

Dominating the room was the table upon which the pillar candle rested. The table was covered with a green oilcloth drape, and in addition to the candle, its surface held a large crystal ball and a deck of tarots pillowed upon a red silk kerchief. Smoothing her skirts, the shop's proprietor seated herself at the far side of the table and gestured for Wessex to take the other chair.

To do so would place him with his back to the curtain. Wessex did not move.

"Why did you address me as you did, Citizeness?" he asked. "I am no aristocrat, but a proud citizen of France."

She glanced up from beneath her lashes, and the candlelight seemed to gather in her eyes, making them glow like an animal's.

"I shall call you what you wish, Citizen," Madame Fabricant said with a shrug, "but I will not say I do not see what I do. I have the Sight, as my mama did—we are from the Languedoc, and the Old Blood runs strong there—and I have known for days that one would come for whom I had a message."

"And I am that one?" Wessex asked. His voice was skeptical but civil.

"Do you want the message or not?" Madame said tartly. "I was to tell you this first: *I am the key for every lock.*"

Wessex went very still. He knew the Roxbury motto as well as he knew his own family's—this was either a trap, or a true sending. Without responding, he went back through the curtain to the shop, and occupied himself for a few minutes closing and locking the door and pulling the shutters across the window.

When he was done, the shop was so dark that he could see the thin line of candlelight that leaked out from beneath the curtains between the front room and the back. He dragged the curtains open and tied them securely.

"Very well, Madame," Wessex said. "Deliver this message you say that you have for me, and I shall see you properly compensated for your troubles."

"How cautious you are," the sorceress mocked. "You are a man who is no stranger to trouble, so I think. You are not the client I would have chosen, but I do not turn away any who come to my shop. It is bad for business," she added with a very French shrug.

Wessex smiled sourly and seated himself opposite her at the table. The candlelight collected in the crystal ball, showing him the whole room turned upside down.

Madame Fabricant took his hand and turned it palm upward. She gazed into his palm intently, as another of her ilk might stare into a bowl of water or ink.

"Monsieur is married?" she asked after a moment.

Ridiculous that the question should pain him so, as if an escape route he had not noticed before was closing even as he gazed upon it. But escape from what?

"You tell me," Wessex said.

Madame Fabricant made a face. "So cautious! Very well, Your Grace. I see that your wife is in danger, over stone and water, but not far from here. She is guarded by Time itself, and her danger will only increase once she has France in her charge. She relies upon you to aid her, so you must follow the setting sun until you come to the ancient regime."

"You must admit that the message is a bit vague," Wessex drawled politely.

"It is what I have been told, Monsieur *le Duc*," the fortune-teller snapped. "Go west without delay—or you will lose your wife . . . and your heart."

Lady Meriel sat on a little stool placed beneath one of the trees in the garden, using the strong summer light to work on a shirt she was making for Louis. It had been five days since she had come to the Abbé and stumbled upon his great secret, and though she worried constantly about Sarah's fate, the days had passed like something outside of time, like a beautiful dream out of which she must someday awaken. Here she could be herself, not an actress in a wicked masquerade, playing out a part written for her by someone else.

And Louis was a part of that dream.

Louis could not be for her, Meriel told herself firmly.

For Louis was the true King of France, and reject his birthright though he might, others would force him to take it up as soon as he declared himself.

Meriel set another stitch in the shirt, reproaching herself for her foolishness in giving her heart to a man who—no matter how much he loved her in return—could never marry her. A king must have a princess, and, though the blood of kings flowed in her veins, Meriel was not one such as Louis would be forced to accept as his wife.

Let us have this little time together then, before they take him. Oh, Blessed Virgin, surely that is not too much to ask of You?

Louis would return soon. He had gone to the village—*Père* Henri was a member of the Royalist Underground, and through him, Louis could reach those who had eyes and ears in every part of the land. Already they had discovered that Meriel's uncle Geoffrey Highclere was in Talleyrand's pay. If they could only discover where Uncle Geoffrey had taken the Duchess of Wessex, they might be able to rescue her, and then the great burden of guilt that Meriel carried would be eased.

She continued sewing—she was happy enough to take up what work of the household she could, and a basket of whitework lay at her feet, awaiting attention—but could not keep herself from glancing toward the road every few minutes, hoping to see Louis's return. When she saw him at last, walking up the road with his wide-brimmed hat in his hand and his white shirt open at the throat in the country fashion, Meriel surrendered to her impulse and put the shirt aside, running to greet him.

They met at the gate, where Louis set his hat upon Meriel's head and kissed her soundly. He smelled of clean linen and sunlight, and Meriel's heart swelled with present joy and future sorrow.

"Marry me," Louis said instantly.

She laughed, because it was a familiar demand. "No,

and no, and no again! I've told you, Louis—one so great is not for such as I."

"I have renounced my throne," Louis reminded her, coming through the gate and closing it behind him with his free hand. His other hand was on her waist. "I am no one greater than Citizen Capet, and Citizen Capet wishes very much to marry a pretty English girl."

"Louis, don't tease me," Meriel begged. "Renounce what you will—no one, English or French, will leave you in peace. You are too important to them."

"Too important to their games," Louis corrected bitterly. "They are like children with toy soldiers, forgetting that these toys of theirs bleed and die. It is different in the New World. We can be free there, Meriel. Wessex will help us."

"Against his King's wishes?" Meriel asked. "Oh, let us not quarrel now, my love, but tell me: what news do you have of Her Grace?"

"I only spoke to a messenger," Louis said, "a drover who had come to town. But he brought word of a meeting—at the ruins of the chateau that is about five miles from here. He says that if I will meet their leader there, he will have news of the Duchess."

"It is too dangerous!" Meriel said.

"And that is why we will not say a word of this to *Père Henri*," Louis said firmly. "When we have certain knowledge of where your uncle and Her Grace are will be time enough to involve him. He has risked too much, hiding me here as he has, for me to worry him now."

"But if you should—" Meriel began.

"These people are friends," Louis cut her off gently. "They believe in France and the King—not in that opportunist who has lately crowned himself Emperor in Paris. They will not betray me, though they do not know who I truly am. Now, we should go in. If we hurry, we can be married before Madame Carmaux has supper upon the table."

"No," Meriel said, smiling back at him.

But her fears would not be put to rest. In some ways she was wiser than Louis—though he had been in danger since he had been a small boy, he had always been surrounded by those who wished him well. He believed in happy endings.

Meriel did not.

And so, when Louis left the house a few hours after dark to keep his appointment with the Underground, Meriel followed him.

The moon was only a couple of days past full, and still provided enough light for Meriel to find her way. Louis carried a dark lantern, but did not need it to find his way over familiar roads.

The chateau had burned many years ago, during the riots that had plagued the countryside as the Glorious Revolution took hold. The great house had been looted before it was set ablaze; now only a few walls and charred timbers remained to mark the spot where it had stood, since all else had been carried away by the people or masked by Nature. The gatehouse had been pulled down entirely, its stones carried away by the villagers to repair their own homes and barns. Even the iron gates had gone for Bonaparte's cannon. The sweeping lawns had turned to wild meadows; the formal gardens had become a wilderness of thorn and bramble.

Now Louis used his lantern to find his way, and Meriel—who had lagged far behind, both from fear of discovery and because her skirts did not allow her to keep to his pace—saw its tiny golden spark bobbing on ahead of her. As she tried to follow, she stepped into a rut and fell full length.

She froze where she lay as Louis, yards ahead, looked around for the source of the sound. As she lay sprawled in the dirt, her outstretched hand touched another rut in the ground, twin to the one she had tripped in.

Wagon tracks. But who would be taking a wagon up to the ruined chateau?

Louis moved on. Meriel rose to her knees, tracing the shapes on the ground by touch. New marks—the ground was still moist. The wheels that made the tracks had been very wide, and the wagon heavy; the tracks were deep.

Meriel got to her feet, her heart hammering with more than exertion. Gathering up her skirts in her hand, she began to run after the bobbing lantern light.

Let her be wrong. Merciful saints in heaven, let her be wrong!

She had thought to catch Louis before he entered the ruin, but the darkness caused her to misjudge the distance between them. When she stopped to catch her breath, she saw that he was almost to the chateau itself.

What if she were wrong? If Louis were truly coming to meet the Underground leader, she would frighten the man away if she cried out, and then they might never have what information about the Duchess of Wessex he possessed.

There was little time to weigh her options—she must choose between her lover and her friend. But though her heart broke at her own betrayal, Meriel did not find the choice hard.

"Louis!" she cried as loud as she could. *"It's a trap! It's a trap!"*

Louis turned. She saw him raise his lantern high, saw its golden beam fall across his face as he looked for her. And then the ruin blazed with light, as though the aban-

doned chateau had been set afire once more, and soldiers
were shouting and running from their places of concealment.

"Run!" Louis shouted as they grabbed him. "Meriel—
run!"

She hesitated for only a moment, then, fleet as a white
deer, turned and ran.

She stopped for nothing. Shots were fired past her, but
she felt nothing. She held her skirts as high as she could
and ran as though Hell's mouth had opened behind her,
ran until she reached the church door and rang the bell
that summoned the priest to midnight emergencies.

When *Père* Henri came Meriel could not speak. She
crouched at his feet, gasping for breath and fighting the
nausea and faintness that gripped her.

"Louis!" she finally managed to say, gesturing back the
way she had come.

As if she had summoned it, a black coach came rattling
down the lane in the direction of the road to Paris. It was
drawn by twelve black horses, and needed every one of
them, for the coach was made entirely of iron, and its
narrow windows were barred. The padlocks on each of
its iron doors made a din like rolling thunder as it passed,
and six mounted soldiers rode before and six behind, and
four more rode upon the coach itself, all armed with muskets.

"No," Meriel whispered in despair.

The Abbé de Condé lifted her to her feet. "You must
be strong, my child," he said.

It was long past midnight. Meriel knelt before the statue
of the Virgin in the village church, a borrowed rosary
between her fingers. She was numb with the prayers she
had said, but sleep was impossible. All she could think of

was that Louis—her Louis—was in the hands of his enemies.

Because of me. Always because of me. . . .

The Abbé had roused the town and made inquiries.
The drover Louis had spoken to was nowhere to be found,
though the man's cattle were still in the barn of a local
farmer. No one had seen sixteen soldiers and an iron
coach enter the village—but there were other routes to
the chateau.

Louis was gone. The Abbé was in his study, writing
letters that might help his young cousin but more likely
would not. And Meriel was kneeling here, beseeching the
Blessed Virgin, for a miracle. Not even a great miracle.
She would understand, she told the Mother of God, if she
could not set Louis free. But that he should die alone—
that Meriel should live without him—she could not bear.

"Only let me know where he is, Holy Mother. Only let
me go to him."

But there was no answer.

People came and went that day—some to pray for
young Louis, whom all had known and liked even when
they had thought him merely a young nephew of the *curé;*
some to pray for themselves, for if it became known that
their village had sheltered the Lost King, the Emperor in
his wrath might raze the place to the ground. Meriel remained, resisting all attempts of Mme. Carmaux to put
her to bed, until at last, in the late afternoon, the *curé*
himself came for her.

The Abbé de Condé had aged twenty years in a night.
His eyes were sunken in his head, and his skin was papery
and grey. Looking at his face, Meriel could see the *memento
mori,* the skull beneath the skin.

"Meriel?" he said. "Child, you must rest. You cannot
go on like this; it does not help him."

"Then my prayers are useless?" Meriel asked scornfully.

"But it is said that Our Lord loves sinners' prayers best—
and I have betrayed so many in my life that surely He
will listen to me now—"

"Do not talk so," the Abbé said sternly. "You are overwrought and grieving; you do not know what you are
saying. But do not mock God, child."

"I do not mock God, Father," Meriel said. "But I do
not think He is listening."

In the middle of the night, Meriel awoke abruptly, sitting
bolt upright in the bed, her heart hammering as if someone had shouted her name. The windows had been carefully closed and shuttered against the dangers of night air,
and the room was stiflingly close; Meriel slipped out of
bed and went to the window. Shoving up the sash and
throwing back the shutters, she looked out over the
garden.

Everything was calm and quiet. The only light was the
faint spark of vigil candles in the church. From within the
house, there was no sound—and there was no one in the
garden.

Louis. . . .

For a moment grief welled up inside her, shaking Meriel as a terrier shakes a rat. Roughly, she pushed the emotion aside. Now that she was awake, the determination
that she had taken to bed with her returned. There was
something she must do.

By moonlight, she dressed quickly in the *cotton de Nimes*
dress she had brought with her, and picked up a borrowed
shawl and clogs. Carrying the heavy shoes bundled in the
shawl, Meriel tiptoed from her room and through the silent house.

In the kitchen, she unbolted the door and stepped out
into the garden. Meriel was not certain what time it was,

but the hour was somewhere in the deep trough of country night, long after all the folk are abed and hours before the rooster crows to wake the dawn. She closed the door slowly, wishing she had some way to lock it once more, and went on her way.

No dogs barked as Meriel took to the road and began walking toward the village. She passed by the wall of the church; though she hesitated, Meriel did not stop. She had begged God for help and He had not answered. Now she would go elsewhere.

Every village in France had such a place: a well, a tree, a stone sacred to the Oldest People, where offerings could be left and boons begged. Good Christians were sternly forbidden to have aught to do with such, for (so the priests said) all Power came from the Most Holy God, and to worship His mere creations rather than God Himself was a grievous sin. But simple countryfolk knew a deeper truth: Christ's Holy Mother could not always aid them if it went against the wishes of her Son, who was less understanding than His Holy Mother, and God Himself was impartial, and just, and could not be bribed.

But the Fair Folk could.

Meriel had heard that their kind did not care for silver, but what she had brought with her was gold: coins and jewels she had sewn into her petticoat on the eve of her flight from England. Nothing that she could buy on earth mattered to her now: she would give them all as an offering, and hope that the Fair Folk would hear.

Louis had pointed out the place to her a few days before: a cluster of stones at the edge of two fields. She'd been afraid that day; when he'd dared her to step inside them, she'd run away instead.

Now she was coming back.

It did not seem like so fearsome a thing: three pale grey blocks of stone arranged in a rough triangle. They were not very large—the tallest of the three barely came to Meriel's chin—and looked like half-worked mileposts. Between them the grass grew lush and green (even, so Louis had said, in the deepest summer's heat), but that could mean nothing more supernatural than a buried spring.

But as Meriel approached the stones in the still summer's night, her heart beat fast with holy dread, and she was filled with superstitious fear.

It is for Louis, she told herself fiercely. Fear and anger at what might be happening to him even now drove weakness from her heart, and she stepped boldly into the center of the triad of stones. It was cold between them, though the summer air had been hot only a moment before.

This was her last hope. If this did not work Louis would be taken to Madame Guillotine. The soldiers would be back, looking for her as well, and if she too disappeared there would be no one else who knew where Sarah had gone.

Determined none of these things would happen, Meriel rucked up her skirts and with clumsy chilled hands ripped at the secret seam of her petticoat. Coins and jewelry spilled out into the grass. Meriel carefully collected gold and gems together, piling her offering in a heap upon her handkerchief. She stared at the small treasure—

—and then, standing within the fairy ring, Lady Meriel began to weep, for she suddenly realized there was truly no hope left. Not even for her Louis's life could she summon up the Fair Folk—she did not know how. She sank slowly to her knees, clasping her hands tightly together. She would have prayed, but in this place it seemed blasphemous, and she did not know who she could pray to. If Louis died—if her prayers were not answered—she would have no more faith in God, and she feared that nearly as much as she feared losing Louis.

Her eyes filled with heavy tears, and she clenched her

teeth to keep anyone from hearing her weep. And so, in her turn, she did not hear what approached.

"Who summons me?" a sweet musical voice asked.

Meriel gasped and looked up. Her astonishment at what she saw was so great that her tears dried immediately.

A woman stood between the stones. She was a tiny thing—the top of her head was level with the top of the tallest stone—and her gown was of a silk so fine and sheer that it shifted like layers of river mist.

"I—I—I do," Meriel stammered. "I need—"

"The King is gone from the land," the fairy woman observed, "and the Hills are gone with him. I came from far away to answer your call, Daughter of Earth, but your cry was loud."

"He is not dead," Meriel gasped, heeding nothing of the woman's message but that. "Tell me that Louis is not dead—I beg you, Madame!"

"The Young King lives, but he is dead to us, for he will never pledge to us in the old way." The woman's voice was cool and remote, as though she did not belong in the world and suffered none of its concerns.

"He lives!" Meriel clutched her joy to herself for a moment before remembering that she had come to ask for help. "Help me, Madame—and I will give you all of this," Meriel said, indicating the bundle at her feet. "And—"

And anything else you ask for, she had been about to say, when memories of her old nurse's teachings stopped her. Old Janet had been a Scotswoman, and traffic with the Oldest People was still common enough in the land beyond the Wall for Janet to have warned her infant charge sternly against such dealings. Most of all, she had warned little Meriel against the dangers of making vague and open-ended promises.

"—and I will honor you so long as I live," Meriel finished carefully.

The fairy woman smiled her cool lunar smile and knelt down, poking through the clutter of gold and jewels.

"It is not enough," she said at last.

"But it is all I have!" Meriel protested, fresh tears in her eyes.

"No," the fairy woman said reprovingly, and Meriel remembered the necklace and earrings she still wore.

Slowly Meriel worked her coral earbobs free and dropped them into the pile. The fairy woman seized them immediately, and held them up, admiring them.

More slowly, Meriel unclasped the chain around her throat. It held a gold locket; a cross picked out in diamonds adorned one side, and the engraved Ripon arms the other; inside was a miniature of her long-dead mother. The locket was Meriel's dearest possession.

She only wants to see if I will give it up, Meriel thought rebelliously, but knew her qualms were foolish. She was risking her immortal soul merely by being here and lives were at stake. This was no time to quibble over trifles. Meriel dropped the gold locket among the other jewels.

"It is sufficient," the fairy woman said. "What would you ask of me, Daughter of Earth?"

Meriel hesitated. Old Janet had told her that the Fair Folk would make a bad bargain if they could. What should she ask for? That the woman free Louis? That could mean anything. Send a rescue? The same thing applied.

"I wish you to supply me with the means to rescue Louis, and to send me to his side," Meriel said at last. The moment the words were out of her mouth she wished she could call them back, seeing a thousand traps set before her.

"That is two things. Which of them shall I grant you?" the woman asked playfully.

Meriel opened her mouth to speak again, but the form before her had begun to flow and change, melting like the river mist it so resembled until Meriel had to blink and look away.

When Meriel looked back, the fairy woman was gone and a grey pony stood in her place. When it turned its head to look at her, the pony's eyes flashed red as a ferret's. Meriel looked down. The gold, her handkerchief, and her mother's locket had vanished.

Determinedly, Meriel got to her feet and warily advanced upon the grey pony. She had ridden from earliest girlhood, but the uncanny animal was neither saddled nor bridled.

She could not allow that to matter.

The pony did not retreat as she advanced upon it. When she was within range, Meriel grasped its mane firmly in both hands and threw herself over the pony's back. Before she had quite settled herself it began to move, first walking, then trotting, then stretching itself at a run. Without reins, Meriel could not control it. All that was left for her to do was cling to the *phouka*'s mane and pray.

18

Pawn Takes Rook (July 19, 1805)

It was exceedingly boring to be imprisoned, Sarah decided. She had been Monsieur Talleyrand's guest these past four days, and found the entertainment decidedly flat.

If she had truly been the woman Talleyrand thought her—the gently-bred English aristocrat—Sarah might very well have been undone by her harsh treatment: locked in a cold bare room, her only food a single bowl of gruel each day.

But Sarah had been taught in a much harsher school, and had slept rougher on scantier provision than this. She had combed out her hair as best she could with her fingers, braided it into two plaits, and tied them up with strips of rag torn from her petticoats. She had lost muff, bonnet, and pelisse before she had arrived at Chateau Roissy, so she made herself a cape from the blanket upon the bed, and occupied her time pacing her little cell to keep her muscles supple and her body warm. She had abandoned her corset immediately, hiding the undergarment beneath the wool mattress in order to keep it with her, and without its constriction, she could move freely. It was true that her dress had been cut with fashionably narrow shoulders, but now that she had surrendered her corset the gown was laced only loosely.

Sarah would far rather have had a pair of trousers, such as she had used to wear when she went hunting, but she supposed she must make do, as her jailers did not seem to be the kind of whom one could make such odd requests. Except for the serving girl who came twice a day, Sarah saw no one at all, which was, she supposed, a thing to be grateful for: Geoffrey Highclere had struck her upon their brief acquaintance as the sort of pushing fellow who might be inclined to gloat and take other unpleasant liberties if he thought he might be able to get away with it.

However, Mr. Highclere had blessedly played least in sight, and so Sarah paced her cell, ate all that was offered to her, and planned her escape.

For escape she must . . . and soon.

She did not know if Wessex meant to ransom her— though she rather thought his chilly pride would make it inevitable—but she did know she must not depend upon his help to escape, for Talleyrand had admitted that he did not know where the Duke was to be found. If a nest of French spies could not discover his whereabouts, it was unlikely that Sarah Cunningham could, even if she did not happen to be a prisoner. So she must banish Wessex from her hopes.

And she did have hopes, for both Geoffrey Highclere and Monsieur Talleyrand had dismissed her as a mere female pawn. They had not even bothered to search her, but Sarah, when she had been taken, had been dressed in the first style of elegance, from coif to boots. The tube-shaped buckram corset that Fashion prescribed was stiffened with supple wire and whalebone stays, and she

retained the silver hairpins that had secured her long
brown hair in the upswept fashionable mode. With these
two items, she could pick the lock of her prison. The
moon had been just past full when she had arrived at the
chateau; once it waned sufficiently for night's darkness to
conceal her, Sarah would make her move.

Her circumspection was equally dictated by the fact
that the longer she played the cowed and spiritless prisoner, the less her jailers would look for any resistance from
her. But she did have to admit that the long days empty
of companionship or occupation were very hard to bear.
Only the discipline she had learned among the People in
her American homeland kept her from exhausting herself
by fretting over things she could not affect, from Wessex's
whereabouts to Lady Meriel's fate. Meriel was not blessed
with Sarah's own resources, and Sarah tried to make herself accept that she might never know what had happened
to her friend.

Sarah was lost in her melancholy thoughts, her feet automatically pacing out the dimensions of her cell, when
suddenly she came alert. She did not know what had
roused her, but as she stood poised, listening, she heard a
scrabbling at the lock of her door. Instantly Sarah fled to
the bed and sat on its edge with head bowed, doing her
best to impersonate a spiritless captive.

When the door opened, Sarah looked up. Several *chasseurs* in red-and-green uniforms were grouped in the hallway, holding before them a young blond man dressed in
a grimy smock and breeches. The young man's hands
were tied behind his back, and his face was bruised and
bloody, but despite his disadvantages, he continued to
struggle with his captors until they flung him into the
room, swinging the door shut behind him and locking it
once more.

Sarah ran over to him, but he was already trying to get

to his feet. The cords about his wrists were tied so tightly that his hands were dark with congested blood. Vainly Sarah plucked at the knots, realizing that they were too tight to untie.

"Wait here," she said. "I'll have to cut you loose."

She'd spoken in English; French had been among the accomplishments that her mother had taught to the young ladies of Baltimore, but Sarah had been an indifferent student at best and remembered none of her French lessons now. It appeared, however, that the stranger knew English, for he stopped struggling and knelt on the hard stone floor, watching her intently.

At the beginning of her captivity Sarah had stolen the spoon that came with her gruel. The utensil was tin (ever since that theft her porridge had come with a wooden spoon) and she had quickly realized that it would not be of great use to her as either weapon or tool. But she had sharpened the edge of the bowl to a knife edge anyway, partly for lack of any other activity to relieve the crushing boredom of her plight. Now she carefully worked the sharpened spoon free of its hiding place in her mattress and returned to kneel beside the young prisoner.

"So you are English, then?" he said in that language. Only the faintest of accents betrayed the fact that to him this was a foreign tongue.

"American," Sarah said automatically, before recollecting that in this bizarre otherwhere the word had no meaning.

"From the New World!" the stranger's face lit up, as though for a moment he had entirely forgotten his captivity. "You must tell me all about the place, mam'selle."

"Gladly," Sarah said, inspecting his bonds for the likeliest place to cut. "But I think we had better free your hands, first—if the circulation is not restored I think it will go badly with you."

"Those cowardly swine," the captive said without heat. "As terrified as old wives of one lone man—what can I do to harm them, who have been an exile in my own country since I was but a child? Ah, well. There is no uncertainty about my fate—if I could only be sure that *ma petite* is safe. She followed me to the rendezvous where I was captured; I should have known that she would."

"And so you should," Sarah said absently. She'd chosen her spot and begun sawing at the cord. The tin was sharp, but it was also soft, and she dared not press too hard for fear of breaking her feeble weapon.

"Perhaps you have heard something of another prisoner?" the young man went on. "Her name is Meriel— she is English, though she could pass as one of my own countrywomen—"

"Meriel!" Sarah stopped sawing at the cords and stared at him. "Do you know where she is? Is she safe?"

"Do you know her?" the young man said, puzzled. "But you must forgive me, mam'selle. I have been remiss in making myself known to you. My name is Louis. Perhaps it is best not to say more, given the singular nature of our means of introduction."

"My name is Sarah," Sarah answered.

Oddly enough, the simple introduction made Louis laugh, then groan as his bruised muscles protested. "You must, then, be my Meriel's Sarah—it is good to see that Monsieur Geoffrey did not make away with you entirely."

Their stories were quickly told—though Sarah sensed that Louis was holding something back—and by the time they had finished, Sarah had sawn through the cord. Carefully, she unwound the bonds from Louis's wrists, then massaged his swollen hands until circulation returned to them.

The dishes from her morning's meal were still on the table, and there was still some water in the pitcher. Sarah

tore a square from her petticoat and dampened the cloth
before using it to wipe the blood from Louis's face. When
she was done, he took the pitcher and drank thirstily,
draining it dry. Afterward, she helped him to his feet and
began to walk with him, helping him ease muscles that
were cramped from too-long confinement.

"So they mean to execute you?" Sarah asked, resuming
their conversation. She knew that Talleyrand meant to kill
her as well, but somehow her own plight seemed less immediate than Louis's.

"They must take me to Paris for that," Louis said. "It
is not enough that I die—I must die before the eyes of
the world. But before that time comes, the Black Priest
means to discover what I know, so that he may turn it to
his own advantage."

"Ah, a man of some importance, I see," Sarah teased
gently, hoping to keep his mind from his troubles. For all
his laborer's garb, Louis seemed an educated young man,
though she knew no more of him than that he had been
resident in a small village near where Meriel had escaped
from the coach.

"Only in the demented fancies of the Emperor Napoleon and his jackals," Louis answered wearily. "Perhaps
we must hope that your husband will rescue us, Duchess,
for I do not see any other way for us to be saved."

"That remains to be seen," said Sarah.

Sarah did not divulge her plans for escape to Louis both
from native caution and out of a desire not to upset the
young man. A few hours later, the serving girl brought
another pitcher of water and a bowl of broth, and Sarah
bullied Louis into eating and drinking. Afterward, she
made him lie down on the bed to rest. Though escape
would be much harder if she had to take Louis with her,

Sarah did not consider for a moment the possibility of leaving the young man behind. His arrival gave her a goal for her flight—they would return to his village, and there she could find Meriel again. Meriel spoke excellent French, and Sarah was certain that between them they could either bribe one of the smugglers to take them back to England, or at least to take a message there.

But to do all these things, Sarah and Louis first had to escape, and Louis was battered and weary with two days on the road. Though he protested gallantly, he was asleep and breathing deeply at almost the moment his head touched the thin pillow.

Sarah retreated into a far corner of the room and squatted down to wait. Her captors did not provide lamp or candles to light her prison, and her body had readjusted itself to rising and sleeping with the sun. Tonight she would not have that luxury; even if their jailers were willing to leave Louis alone tonight, tomorrow they would surely come for him and do their best to force him to give up his secrets. They must flee tonight.

Sarah set herself to awaken at midnight and fell into a light doze.

She came awake several hours later, instantly alert in the darkness. The open window was visible as a paler square against the darkness, but there was no light to see by. The only sound was Louis's quiet breathing.

Sarah did not need light. She had spent five days memorizing this room so that she could move about it without eyes. Pulling her improvised tools from the pocket of her dress and slipping off her shoes, she stalked cat-footed to the door.

A faint light shone inward through the lock; as she had determined beforehand, a lantern was left burning in the hallway all night somewhere near this room. She did not think a sentry was set outside the door, but she put her ear to the lock and listened intently for several minutes, all the same. If there were anyone in the hallway outside the door, he was as silent as one of the People, for she heard no sound.

At last she set to work. A corset-stay served as a probe and a bent hairpin as a lever; the lock was old, and consequently the iron pins were large and heavy—but someone had oiled this lock well, and the pins would move if she could only approach them properly.

Time and again she nearly had her picks in position, only to have the recalcitrant pin slip out from between them, but she dared not hurry, no matter how frustrated she became. After what seemed like a small eternity—but could not have been much more than half an hour—the pins finally slid back. The lock clicked open with the sharp furious sound of a cocking pistol.

Louis stirred in his sleep and then froze, coming awake to his grim surroundings. Sarah hesitated, agonizing over whether to go to him and keep him from crying out, or stay where she was and keep the unlocked door from drifting open.

Louis solved the dilemma by sitting up—she could tell by the sound—and swinging his legs over the edge of the bed. In her mind's eye Sarah could see him, peering out into the darkness, trying to see her.

"Mam'selle *la Duchesse?*" he whispered.

"Hush!" Sarah hissed in an urgent whisper.

Louis made no more sound, and Sarah slowly eased the door open. A thread of light appeared in the opening, dazzling illumination compared to the previous darkness, and slowly, breathlessly, Sarah swung the door open.

The corridor was empty.

Louis appeared at her side—moving rather quietly for

a city-bred man—and looked at her questioningly. Sarah held up her hand, motioning Louis to remain where he was, and eased herself out into the corridor.

Still nothing. A few feet past the door, a candle in a glass chimney rested on a battered table. Sarah crept down the corridor in the direction she had gone for her meeting with Talleyrand—moving warily for fear of creaking boards—and finally achieved the head of the stairs. They were dark and silent; if there were anyone on the floor below, she could not see them. Sarah retreated as silently as she had come to where Louis waited, motioning him to follow. Though his face was alight with curiosity, blessedly he had enough common sense not to ask any questions. He followed her as silently as he could.

Sarah suffered a thousand silent deaths as she and Louis descended the stairs, for they were both clumsy in the darkness and each tiny sound was magnified a thousand-fold in Sarah's hearing. When they reached the first floor at last, she was nearly too exhausted to go on.

Which way? The room in which she had had her interview with Tallyrand was on the floor below, though at the opposite end from the older stone section of the chateau in which she had been held prisoner. The chateau was built on uneven ground and she thought they could get out through the windows on that side; she had seen no sign of the water lily-filled moat seen from her prison window. Surely the *chasseurs* could not guard *every* window?

No matter, for they must try that route. It was now not long until sunrise, and they must be miles away from here by daybreak.

There were two staircases on this floor, at opposite ends of the wing, both leading up. Across the open expanse of inlaid marble was the stair to the ground floor, as wide as both the other staircases put together, with gilded and scrolled banisters that were still lovely despite the damage that had been visited upon the rest of the house.

Sarah took Louis's hand, feeling as though they were children tiptoeing through some dark forest, and led him toward the stairs. His hand was cold, and she could feel him trembling. For herself, she could barely breathe for the fierce desire for freedom that she felt. To be out of here—away—to be her own person once more. . . .

They reached the bottom of the stairs. Sarah stopped, orienting herself in the darkness.

"Wait," Louis breathed, pulling back against her hand.

But Sarah had already heard the sound. The scuff of a boot-sole against the stone floor. The rasping sound as a shuttered lantern was opened.

Sarah lifted her hand to shield her eyes from sudden brightness.

"Why, my dear Duchess. How positively intoxicating to see you again," Geoffrey Highclere said fulsomely. He set the lantern down and stepped into its light.

Mr. Highclere was wearing an unfamiliar but very ornate uniform of black embellished with silver lace and red flashes. A saber hung from his swordbelt, and his blond hair gleamed in the lantern light. There was a pistol in his hand.

"And your Royal Majesty. An unexpected bonus."

"I have never cared for the company of traitors," Louis remarked conversationally.

Sarah stared at Louis. France's Revolution had been an inevitable subject of conversation during the time she had spent in England, and so she had heard that Louis XVI had been executed; his son long presumed dead. Was Mr. Highclere saying . . . ?

"But my very dear Majesty, you will certainly not be forced to suffer such company for long," Mr. Highclere said cordially. "When Talleyrand returns from Paris, you go to your execution. And I'm very much afraid that the Duchess will be leaving us . . . now."

Illya Koscuisko and the Duke of Wessex had left Amiens that same day, heading westward to the coast. Wessex had refused to allow the Bishop of Amiens to pass a message to England for a ship to pick them up; in fact, the Duke seemed to be in such a towering inexplicable passion that even his partner trod warily. It had been foolish to leave the city that evening; their rooms were already paid for the night and their traveling papers, still damp from the forger, would not stand up to close inspection should suspicion fall upon them.

What was still more foolish was that Wessex did not seem willing even to keep to the road. Instead, he made side-trips through hedges, took them along narrow country lanes, and even backtrailed once or twice.

He seemed to be looking for something.

At last Koscuisko could stand it no longer.

"Look here," he said to his friend. "I don't mean to exhibit a vulgar curiosity, but where are we going and what are we doing? Princess Stephanie isn't here, and—"

"I don't," said Wessex pleasantly, "give a damn about Princess Stephanie."

Koscuisko waited.

"I want my wife back," Wessex said, as if the words hurt him. "And I've even been told where to look for her: *over stone and water, but not far from here.* So I must follow the setting sun until I come to the ancient regime."

"And are we to think this information reliable?" Koscuisko asked cautiously. "I should only wish to point out that the sun has already set, making it somewhat difficult to follow."

"I think it's all a bag of moonshine," His Grace said roundly. "Some Gipsy nonsense; I can't imagine why I ever listened to it," he added, his voice troubled.

Koscuisko shrugged. "Across stone and water, not far from Amiens. That could mean across the city and the river, of course, but where is one to encounter the *ancien regime* these days?"

"The prophecy improves," Wessex added. "I am told that the Duchess of Wessex is guarded by Time itself, and is about to take France into her charge, wherefore I must rescue her at once."

"Easier said than done," Koscuisko agreed. "So she has France? What did she do, pinch one of Boney's eagles? That's all the France I know of."

"Not," said Wessex in a peculiar voice, "if the Young King *is* alive, as everyone seems to think. If he is, King Louis the Seventeenth is France Itself."

"Well then, that much is made clear," Koscuisko said derisively. "Geoffrey Highclere is not in the pay of Napoleon, but of King Louis, to whom he has conveyed the Duchess. Now all we need to do is find Time and the *Ancien Regime*."

Wessex stood in his stirrups, stretching, and gazed around himself speculatively, as if he were hoping that his landmark would spontaneously appear.

"Koscuisko," Wessex said, a considering tone in his voice, "who do you suppose is truly Geoffrey's paymaster—and where do you suppose he is?"

The grey *phouka* that Meriel rode traveled faster than any mortal animal, swift as an arrow in flight. In moments the little town of Trois Vierges had been left behind as the fairy pony vaulted ditch and wall and hedge with equal facility. The sound of its hoofbeats were like a martial drumroll, too swift to impute any rhythm to.

Lady Meriel clung to the creature's back for dear life. There was no time now to wonder which half of her petition the fay had granted—discovery or rescue—or even to ponder what her destination might be. She buried her face in the animal's neck, feeling her tightly pinned braids dragged free by the wind until her hair streamed half-undone down her back. She lost her clogs the first time the pony jumped, and the wind quickly stole her shawl as well, leaving Meriel only her cotton dress and petticoats for protection against the summer's night.

But the *phouka* must be taking her to Louis. That was the only thing that mattered now. The landscape swept by faster than a bird could fly, so that a church steeple would loom into view and vanish behind them in scant minutes. Meriel looked for the waning moon in the sky; she could not see it, yet the landscape all around was as bright as if a full hunter's moon shone upon it. She dared not even pray, lest calling upon the Holy Names cause the fairy horse to vanish like morning mist.

The Emperor's bright new kilometer-posts flashed by like the white-painted pickets of a giant's fence, and Meriel's fingers and toes ached with unnatural cold. But she was determined not to give up, or to beg the animal to stop. She must rescue Louis. There was no one else to do it if she did not.

She did not know how long the pony had run tirelessly onward when finally its speed began to slacken. She blinked wind-caused tears from her eyes and looked around.

The brilliant blue moonlight had faded with the pony's slowing speed, and now the world around her was merely dark. Perhaps a mile distant loomed the ruined towers of some vast crumbling castle. Meriel could hear dogs barking in the distance, and the village clock striking the half-hour. Now the horizon was a faint dirty oyster color, harbinger of dawn, and her fey mount had slowed to a walk, though its coat was still as cool and dry as if it had not run tirelessly for leagues like some automaton.

"Where have you brought me?" Meriel asked unsteadily. The *phouka* had been supposed to bring her to Louis. That was the bargain she had struck . . . wasn't it? "Where is Louis?"

The pony tossed its head, as though shrugging off her questions, and began trotting once more. But this time the world did not make its strange shift into brilliant blue light, and Meriel found herself more conscious of her own foolishness with each passing second.

What could have possessed her to endanger her immortal soul in this fashion? And her sudden disappearance would be certain to grieve the Abbé de Condé, who would have no way to know what had become of her. As dawn brightened, the pact Meriel had made came to seem more and more outlandish—and futile, besides. Even if Louis were being held prisoner near here—perhaps even within that nearby chateau—how could she reach him?

I am no better off than I was before!

For the last several minutes, the *phouka* had been traveling along the highway; now Meriel became aware that two horsemen were approaching from the other direction. She dragged at the pony's mane, trying to turn it from the road, for she knew what a freakish sight she must represent, barefoot and with her hair tumbling down her back, and had no desire to be made sport of by early travelers.

But the pony did not respond to her tugging. In fact, her fingers passed through the wiry mane as though it were so much sea-mist, and the compact, muscular body between her knees melted away like sugar in hot tea. Meriel tumbled to the road almost at the feet of the approaching horsemen.

The two men had ridden through the night, with Wessex wracking his brain to provide some clue to the sorceress's riddle. The identity of Geoffrey's paymaster was simple enough: the Black Priest ran the network of agents confidential and provocateur who worked clandestinely for Imperial France. If Geoffrey Highclere were in French pay, it was Talleyrand who was paying him, and to Talleyrand that Highclere had taken Sarah.

But where was Talleyrand? Sarah was not in Paris—Saint-Lazarre would have mentioned that fact. Sarah had saved his life while he had been her guest at Mooncoign, and Saint-Lazarre would welcome the chance to even the score.

Suppose, however, that Talleyrand had not only the Duchess of Wessex but the King of France—or thought he did, at any rate. The spymaster was not above intriguing against his Imperial master, but even Talleyrand was not so bold as to plot against the Corsican in the City of Light itself. The spymaster would seek some out-of-the-way retreat where he could assess the worth of his prize at leisure.

For some time the White Tower Group had known that Talleyrand had a particular bolt-hole here in the countryside. Centuries before, Chateau Roissy had been a castle, and that ancient heritage remained in tower and moat. Later the castle had become more home than fortress, and later still an abattoir to the family and its servants who had lived here. After that revolutionary bloodbath, Chateau Roissy had fallen into disuse until the Black Priest had found a use for it. What pleasures Tallyrand indulged within the chateau's blood-soaked walls was something unknown to Baron Misbourne's busy agents, but one might as well assume the worst.

That Sarah had been taken to Chateau Roissy was, at best, a guess—and one built upon the most tenuous chain of inferences. If Highclere was a French agent—If Talleyrand was his paymaster—If Highclere had brought Sarah to Talleyrand—If Talleyrand was keeping her at the chateau—

If, and if, and if. But Wessex knew there was no other choice for him, for he only had time to act upon one guess. Let it be this one. He must break into the Chateau Roissy and search the ancient place.

He had not told Koscuisko of this plan, for the volatile Pole would only dislike it, and Wessex had no time for argument. By now Koscuisko knew all that Wessex had learned since the Duke had arrived in Copenhagen, and Wessex meant for his partner to cross the Channel with that report and deliver the information to Misbourne with all due dispatch.

So they rode on through the summer's night. When they reached the place where Wessex was to turn off for Roissy, the Duke reined in.

"This is where we part, my friend. You're no more than two days from the coast; the Bishop of Calais should be able to get you across, and then—"

"And then I can have the ineluctable joy of explaining to the White Man that you're wandering around France in solitary splendor? No thank you, Your Grace, I had rather face a line of French artillery."

"English artillery would be more likely to hit you," Wessex pointed out mildly. "But see here, Koscuisko—"

"Don't you 'see here' me, Your Grace," his partner objected. "You've figured out that Gipsy's riddle, haven't you? Well don't think you're going to cut me out of the fun—and as for your report, the Bishop of Amiens can forward it as well as I, so that excuse won't fadge," Koscuisko added gaily.

"I'm breaking into Roissy Castle," Wessex explained patiently. "I expect that M'sieur *le Pape Noir* will have something to say to the matter."

"Then we shall answer him as we always have," Koscuisko responded. "It sounds like grand fun—and surely you don't think you have the least chance of success without me?"

"You never did know how to follow orders," Wessex grumbled, but surrendered to the inevitable and spurred his horse into motion once more.

It was near dawn by the time they reached the neighborhood of the château, and both men were wary. Wessex knew he could not enter the château unobserved—success or failure depended upon whether Talleyrand was present at Roissy. For if he were not, then the shift they had employed at Verdun might work twice and allow them to enter the château in the guise of messengers from Paris.

But if Talleyrand were there at the château . . .

On a memorable occasion in the not-too-distant past, Wessex and the Black Priest had encountered one another face-to-face; Tallyrand would be certain to recognize the Duke of Wessex behind the thin disguise of Citizen Orczy. Koscuisko, uniformed as one of the Garde Polonnaise, might baffle Talleyrand a while longer, but not by much. And then they, too, could be executed, along with whatever poor fool Talleyrand had found to impersonate the Young King. . . .

Firmly, Wessex turned his thoughts aside from that path. What would be, would be. All he could do was to make the best of what came.

As they approached Roissy, Wessex began to wonder if

it might not be possible to sneak inside after all. The great house was dark, even though at this hour servants should be rising to begin their daily tasks. No guards patrolled the road or the grounds; there were not even dogs to bark and raise the alarm. Perhaps Talleyrand was, in fact, elsewhere.

Then the two men heard the sound of hoofbeats upon the road.

The noise came from the west, along the high road; as Wessex looked in that direction he saw a faint lunar glow, like a will-o'-the-wisp, moving toward him. Almost in the moment Wessex became aware of it the creature had closed half the distance between them and Wessex could see it clearly. A moon-grey pony, faintly glowing in the pale dawn light.

Wessex heard Koscuisko mutter an oath and sketch the sign of the Cross in the air between himself and the apparition.

And in that instant the spectral equine vanished, as if it were in fact the marsh-mist it had reminded Wessex of. The sound of hoofbeats stopped, but in the same instant there was a prosaic thud and a soft female outcry. In place of the horse, a black shape remained upon the road.

Wessex urged his horse forward. Behind him, he heard Koscuisko mutter something in disgust before doing likewise, but while Wessex believed in devils, in his experience all of them had worn human flesh. A man in his profession must accept the inexplicable, but he did not fear it any more than he feared a man with a loaded pistol. There was no irrational world in the Duke of Wessex's cosmos, only a world imperfectly understood.

In this case, the ghost-steed resolved itself into a grubby female person in a shabby cotton dress, her hair a tangled black mass of elf-locks. As she pushed her hair from her face and stared at him in fear, Wessex realized with a pang of amazement that this was someone he knew.

"Lady Meriel," Wessex said in disbelief.

"Oh, Blessed Virgin, it is you!" Meriel ran to him, clutching at his booted leg for support. "Your Grace, you must help me! I know not how you come to be here, but your wife and—and Louis are in terrible danger. Mr. Highclere spies for France, and—"

"Where did he take her?" Wessex demanded, cutting through her babbled explanations.

Meriel drew back with a cry of fear at the sight of Koscuisko in his fantastic costume. Wessex leaned forward, seizing her hands to keep her from fleeing.

"Where did he take her?" Wessex demanded again.

"I don't know—I don't know—" Meriel was nearly frantic. "She—the Lady in the Circle—she told me she would send me to him but I do not know where I am—"

"You are near the Chateau Roissy, mademoiselle," Koscuisko said. He removed his coat with the towering wings and dismounted from Spangle, hanging his shako on the saddle as well. Well trained, Spangle stood patiently as Koscuisko walked toward Meriel, holding out his pelisse. "If mademoiselle will forgive me for observing, she seems chilled to the bone—and to go out without one's footwear cannot be considered a prudent act, even in summer weather."

As he continued his nonsensical prattle, Koscuisko reached the girl and slipped his wolfskin-lined pelisse over her shoulders.

"Really, Wessex, that face of yours would be enough to frighten a gargoyle," he said chidingly. "I am certain that Lady Meriel means to be entirely forthcoming with us at the earliest opportunity."

Once more the Polish Hussar's easy charm produced the desired result. Lady Meriel lost much of her wild-eyed look and, encouraged by Koscuisko—and refreshed with strong brandy from his pocket flask—told them everything, from her arrival in Trois Vierges to Louis's kidnapping by the men in the iron coach as he tried to discover from the Royalist Underground the fate of Her Grace of Wessex.

"And I did not know what to do, but I went to the circle, and the White Lady came—I gave her my locket, and she said she would send me to Louis—or save him. I do not know which, Lord Koscuisko, and now the *phouka* is gone, and what am I to do? Why should everyone I love suffer because of me?"

"Be quiet," Wessex said sharply. "The bad bargain you made with the fairy woman hardly matters. We are going into the chateau—a matter in which you can be of some aid. As for your Louis, rest assured, Lady Meriel, that if he is there I will rescue him. Pretender or King, I would leave no man to the Black Priest's mercies."

Sarah stared into the barrel of the gun, transfixed with horror. Geoffrey Highclere smiled.

Louis stepped in front of her.

"I have spent all my life learning what it is to be a valuable pawn, M'sieur Highclere. I do not think that M'sieur Talleyrand will thank you for shooting me. Run, Sarah."

The last words were uttered in such a conversational tone that both his listeners nearly missed them. Of the two, Sarah reacted first. She turned and ran.

Every fiber of her being rebelled against deserting Louis, but to do so was the only weapon Sarah had. Louis had been right—Mr. Highclere dare not kill him. And so long as Sarah lived, and was free, there would be another chance for her to rescue him.

Behind her she could hear Mr. Highclere roaring for help. The corridor she ran down was unfamiliar, leading her away from the staircase to the first floor. She heard shouts as the house was roused; she had only seconds to find a haven.

She jerked open a door and found a narrow staircase leading both up and down. The servants' stair. When she closed the door behind her even the dim glimmers of light from the hall were gone. Sarah hesitated only a moment before stepping into the darkness of the downward steps.

But when she reached the next landing, the doorway was bricked over; she could feel the new rough patch of brick, colder than the old plaster that surrounded it. There was no escape from the stairs into the ground floor.

And from above she saw a gleam of light shining upon the wall. Someone had opened the door to the hallway.

Noiselessly, Sarah fled further into the dark.

Illya Koscuisko saluted gaily and turned the grey aside. The sky was light enough that the animal seemed to glow, though not as supernaturally as the *phouka* had done.

"Where is he going?" Meriel asked. She was still bundled in the Hussar's pelisse, and Wessex had taken her up before him on his horse.

"To make a diversion, to find another way in, to secure our exit," Wessex said dismissively. "Or to be shot, if our friend Talleyrand's notion of order extends to posting any sort of guard."

"I am sorry for all the trouble I have caused you," Meriel said diffidently.

"You may be sorry for it later with my good will, assuming we both live through the next few hours. I have no intention of leaving my wife in Talleyrand's hands."

"Do you care for her, then?" Meriel asked. "Because she did not think that you did—and when Geoffrey said he would hold her hostage for your behavior, she did not think it would answer."

"Women," Wessex groaned eloquently. "Listen here, my little adventuress: I am about to present myself at Chateau Roissy in the guise of one of the Red Jacks who has just come from tidying up the business in Trois Vierges— which is to say, you. In all likelihood, you and I shall be shot at once. If we are not, perhaps we can do something in the way of rescuing the prisoners. All of this is of quite enormous concern to me—a concern so great that some- how I cannot summon up the energy to discuss my mar- riage. Do you quite take my meaning?"

Meriel turned her back to him as best she could in her awkward position, her back poker-straight.

The stairs curved sharply around as they descended, the narrow staircase becoming narrower still until Sarah's shoulders brushed against the wall on both sides. She had left both plaster and brick behind—here the walls were of close-fitting stone, beaded with icy moisture from beneath the ground. Even the steps were wet and slimy, so that if she had not been barefoot, she would have slipped and fallen a dozen times.

She stopped in the darkness, listening. Whoever had come to the stairs to look for her had not bothered to come all the way to the bottom. She waited a few more minutes, then crept slowly through the darkness back up to the first-floor door. A thin line of light shone from be- neath it, making Sarah hesitate. If she opened that door, she might be walking directly into an ambush. Cautiously, she drew back, continuing on up the stairs.

No light shone beneath the door on the second floor. Slowly Sarah eased the door open. Darkness, and an unfamiliar hallway. For the moment she'd eluded her pursuers.

She crossed to a window and pulled back the curtain. It was just dawn; the light was grey and the grass was silver with morning dew. There was no escape in this direction: the window gave onto a two-storey drop onto flagstones, and there was no way for her to climb down.

Someone was riding up the drive. She looked—then stared.

It was the Duke of Wessex. And Meriel was riding with him.

She *must* attract his attention! Sarah tapped at the window, then realized Wessex could not hear the faint sound. After an instant's thought, she balled her fist up in a fold of her dress and struck the glass with all her might. Tinkling fragments showered out into the cold morning air.

Wessex looked up. Sarah pressed her face to one of the unbroken panes, hoping he would see her.

He stopped—and then swung himself and Meriel down from the horse's back, disappearing into the ornamental shrubbery near the chateau. He had seen.

What to do now? Sarah stared around wildly. She must find some way to get Wessex inside—but the lower floors of the chateau were filled with armed soldiers.

Then I must go up.

A few minutes' search found the stairs that led to the higher floors, and once on a higher level, Sarah squirmed out through a window and stepped onto the roof.

The slates beneath her feet were cold and wet; as smooth as glass. Her stockinged toes curled around the wet slates, seeking purchase, as she clutched at a chimney top for support. The countryside stretched out far below her, as tiny and unreal as a toy. Where was Wessex?

There was someone else on the roof with her; Sarah could hear scrabbling as someone clambered over the slippery slates. Sarah temporarily abandoned her search for Wessex and went in search of the intruder.

He was clean shaven and dressed in an unfamiliar green military uniform, his hair dyed an unnatural yellow. At the flutter of her dress in the morning breeze, he glanced up.

"Ah . . . the Duchess of Wessex, I presume?" Illya Koscuisko said.

A few moments later all of them were standing in the small room that Sarah had originally used as her egress onto the roof. She'd hugged Meriel, and assured the girl that Louis was indeed here, alive, and well—though Geoffrey Highclere's prisoner at the moment.

"Though I do not think Mr. Highclere will shoot him. He is waiting for Talleyrand to return from Paris—after that, I do not know what will happen."

"And before that, we will be gone," Wessex announced. "Sarah, you and Meriel go with Koscuisko, and—"

"No." Sarah's refusal was flat and unequivocal. "I'm not going to be whisked out of sight and out of trouble and leave you here to die. It will take all of us to save Louis. And there is something I must tell you, Your Grace—but not right now."

"I am relieved to hear it," Wessex said dourly. He looked at Koscuisko and shrugged. "As you wish, Duchess. We shall confound the enemy together. Places, then, ladies—and gentleman. The show is about to begin."

* * *

"I hope you will find your new accommodations . . . suitable, Your Majesty," Geoffrey Highclere sneered. He swung the barred door closed and thrust the iron bar through the slots.

He hadn't dared risk a shot at the Duchess with Louis blocking the way: his life wouldn't be worth a lead sovereign if the Black Priest returned to discover that Geoffrey had executed the King of France. His shouts had brought reinforcements, however, and he'd sent the *chausseurs* off after the damnable Duchess, with orders to turn the chateau inside out until they found her. Geoffrey wasn't sure how she'd escaped, but he had no intention of allowing Louis to duplicate the Duchess's trick.

He had brought Louis down to the lowest level of the ancient part of the castle. In medieval times, the Duc whose castle this had been had kept prisoners here; his descendants had found better use for the space as a wine cellar. But this section of the old dungeons was too damp for the convenient storage of casks and the wooden racks upon which bottles of fine vintage might repose. So this archaic dungeon had been left very much alone, much to its current owner's delight. Upon occasion, Talleyrand had cause to make use of this most unhealthy place, and in his absence, Geoffrey Highclere had felt it would be just the thing to cow—and secure—an unruly captive.

"I will find my accommodations familiar, at any rate," Louis retorted. "Take care that I do not take a chill upon the lungs and expire before you can make use of me." Louis retreated to the far corner of the cell, and kicked disgustedly at the moldy straw that lay in stinking, slimy piles upon the damp stone floor. "I console myself with the knowledge that whatever my fate, the Duchess has won her freedom."

"Not for long," Geoffrey snarled. "And once I have her

back, I shall see which of these antiques can be rendered serviceable once more."

It was a fine line to exit upon, but Geoffrey had taken Louis's words to heart also, and so he spent a further few minutes lighting the cressets in the iron baskets upon the walls, and lighting the coals in the braziers.

Louis stood at the back of his cell until he heard Highclere's footsteps fade from hearing, then came forward to examine the door. The bottom half of the barrier was iron-sheathed wood, with a slot in it for a tray. The top half was open, secured by iron bars as thick as a strong man's thumb. Leaning against the bars, Louis gazed out at an identical row of cells opposite him. The air stank of damp, burning coals, and rotting straw. With gallows humor, Louis wondered whether he *could* manage to sicken and die before Bonaparte's First Minister returned to question him.

He hoped the Duchess had gained her freedom.

There was a sound, but not from the stairs that Highclere had so lately ascended.

Ah, Mon Dieu, *let there not be rats.* . . .

It had been a stroke of luck to overhear Mr. Highclere explaining where he had put Louis, for Sarah had a very good idea that the curving stairs she had tried before must be a back way into the dungeon. She had tried to lead Wessex and Meriel along them, but soon the stairs had narrowed so much that Wessex could not pass. He had told them to go on while he sought for another way and returned up the stairs, leaving Sarah and Meriel the candle to light their way.

Soon the passageway narrowed even further, so that the

two women had to inch along it sideways, and Sarah began to fear that the stone walls would narrow to the point that she and Meriel were trapped. The candleflame danced wildly in the cold draft blowing up from below, and Sarah reluctantly passed the taper back to Meriel for safekeeping, for if it blew out they had no way to relight it.

The passage was so narrow that Sarah could not reach across herself to pass the candle back; instead she stretched both hands up over her head and Meriel did the same, passing the burning taper over their heads. She felt Meriel's fingers glide over hers and seize the candle firmly. Sarah released it and lowered her arms.

And a sudden gust of air snuffed the flickering taper before Meriel could lower it to safety.

"Pray pay it no mind," Sarah said, as soothingly as she could manage in the sudden darkness. "It is not as if we are likely to lose our way."

Meriel produced a shaky giggle, though Sarah could feel the girl trembling with both cold and fear. "This will teach me, I suppose, to make pacts with the Fair Ones," Meriel said aloud.

"Well, at least you are here," Sarah offered, though she could think of no good reason that anyone in their right mind would *wish* to be here. The darkness was so impenetrable it seemed to glow with unreal colors, and Sarah had to fight off a sudden surge of claustrophobia. It was as if she was trapped in a cave deep beneath the earth, where she might rest forever, with no one to ever know her fate. . . .

"Sarah," Meriel breathed. "I see a light."

To Louis's astonishment, the source of the scrabbling noise was revealed as the Duchess of Wessex, and with

the Duchess was Lady Meriel. The moment she saw
Louis, Meriel ran to his side, oblivious to what dangers
might lurk here, and clutched at his hands through the
bars.

"Oh, Louis—I thought I had lost you!" Meriel said,
beginning to weep.

Sarah closed her ears to the rest of their conversation—
they had switched to French, at any rate, a language that
Sarah did not know—and struggled with the iron bar. Mr.
Highclere might be an indifferent hunter, but his quarry
had multiplied to the point that even he could not fail to
draw some covert or other. They must get Louis out of
here—but even to save the young man's life, Sarah did
not think she could get him out along the servant's stairway.

Sarah only hoped that Wessex had done something per-
manent about Geoffrey Highclere.

Geoffrey had entered the grand salon to pour himself a
drink. His saber jingled at his side as he walked, symbol
of a rank and status that would vanish like morning mist
if he failed to retain possession of both Louis and the
Duchess.

It was no longer much of a salon, its furnishing con-
sisting of a table, a sideboard, and a chair, but there was
a bottle of brandy there with which Geoffrey had an appointment. The day was advanced enough for him not to
need a candle; the cold grey light of dawn gave the space
a sickroom clarity, but Geoffrey was intent upon the
brandy, and the castle was not heated well even at the
best of times. It therefore took him some seconds to reg-
ister that one of the windows had been opened to the chill
morning air.

"I have come to kill you, Mr. Highclere," the Duke of

Wessex said pleasantly. "Please be so good as to draw your sword."

A dozen feet away stood His Grace of Wessex, King Henry's noble executioner, dressed like a French clerk and holding a dueling sword that glittered like a barber's razor.

"Are you challenging me to a duel?" Geoffrey asked, playing desperately for time. If Wessex were here he must know everything. He must have come for the Young King. It would be a feather in Geoffrey's cap if he could deliver Wessex—alive or dead.

And then the inconvenient Duchess would be his to do with as he pleased. . . .

"Actually, no," Wessex said apologetically. "I've come to kill you, and a pistol would draw inconvenient attention."

And I have a pistol, Your Interfering Grace—and you do not.

Geoffrey did not dare to draw attention to his hole-card, but he could feel its weight dragging at his tunic pocket. Slowly he drew his sword with his left hand. Most right-handed fencers were hindered against a left-handed swordsman, and so Geoffrey had taught himself long ago to wield a blade with either hand. He held his saber point downward, edge out, in the German style.

Wessex, he saw, favored the Italian school. His grace came *en garde* and advanced quickly, the knuckles of his free hand pressed against his waist.

The swords clashed with a high rasping sound. Both men were excellent swordsmen; each had killed. But Wessex was fighting for the lives of others, and Geoffrey was fighting for his own skin. He pushed the Duke back again and again, until they had traversed the length of the salon. The stamp of their boots rang loud in the silence of the morning, but not as loud as a pistol-shot would have. Geoffrey slashed wildly, his entire aim to keep from being cut, and to free his pistol. Though it took only seconds for him to achieve this aim, both men were already sweating when he succeeded.

"And now, Wessex, it is time to resign the match."

"Must it be this way, Highclere? There will be a scandal, I expect, but at least your family might know that you died as a gentleman."

"You're mad, Your Grace. Who are *you* to talk of gentlemen and honor? But I digress. The victory goes to me, I think. Throw down your sword."

Wessex did, and Geoffrey kicked the weapon away as he closed in.

Then His Grace drew his pocketwatch and opened it, apparently oblivious to the pistol in Geoffrey's hand.

"It is just rising six, I think," His Grace observed, and shot Geoffrey Highclere through the throat.

The recoil caused the pocketwatch to fly out of the Duke's hand, smashing itself against the wall behind his head. The sound of the shot echoed loudly, and Wessex wrung his bruised hand—the hide-out pistol was a fearsome weapon, but at a price.

Quickly Wessex retrieved his sword and the smashed remains of the watch; it would not do to allow the White Tower's secrets to fall into enemy hands.

The door flew open.

"The *Anglais* has been shot!" Wessex shouted into the faces of the surprised *chausseurs*. "The assassin has escaped through the window! After him—quickly! Quickly!"

The upper storeys of the old chateau were largely uninhabited, Illya Koscuisko had found, forcing a window that let into one of the attics, but hardly empty. Wessex had told him to create a diversion, and so he would. The chateau had burned once: why not again?

Koscuisko spent a few minutes gathering straw ticks and ramshackle furniture together into one of the deserted attics. The best way to start a fire was never from the top down, but he was forced to work with the materials at hand. Having amassed a fine pile of potential tinder, Koscuisko crossed from that attic to the servant's quarters, and then to the attic on the far side, where he found an object that surprised him greatly—a wicker basket nearly as high as a man, ringed with sandbags.

"Interesting," he murmured to himself.

Even more interesting was the fact that the rest of the mechanism was also present, carefully packed in wooden crates. Koscuisko went over to the window and looked out. The roof canted steeply, and the walls were a sheer drop to the moat below, but to his left, the roof flattened out where it met the top of the old stone tower that formed the oldest section of the chateau.

Now the next question was, could he transport the contraption from here to there?

Whistling softly to himself, Koscuisko set to work.

The underground complex was a maze. Once they got as far as the wine cellar, where the sounds of chaos were audible: screaming servants and swearing soldiers, all shouting at each other. There would be no escape through the kitchen. And so Meriel, Sarah, and Louis turned back, trying to find the route that Geoffrey had taken to bring Louis down into the cellar, but only succeeded in retiring to the dungeon cells again.

"It is no good," Louis groaned. "There is no escape that is not guarded by Talleyrand's jackals. You must return the way you came, and leave me behind."

"No!" Meriel cried.

"I think there is another way," Sarah said. "Give me

your candle, Meriel—and you, Louis, bring me some of that damp straw."

Before Sarah Cunningham had ever become entangled in the affairs of alien nations, she had been taught to survive with little more than her bare hands to aid her. The other two watched uncomprehendingly as the thin thread of smoke from the tiny fire spiraled upward toward the roof.

"Forgive me, Madame *la Duchesse*," Louis said, "but what good can this do? A fire will not help us."

"A fire will show us the way out," Sarah corrected. And true to her word, the top of the smoke-thread streamed sideways, in the direction of the exit.

Three times Sarah stopped and kindled a tiny fire from the relit candle and a few wisps of dank straw. Each time the smoke followed the direction of the circulating air, pointing their way to freedom. She had safely explored caves near her home with this method, which could nearly always point the way to some exit from beneath the earth.

And once again—in an artificial labyrinth far from home—the trick worked its simple magic. They reached a door that none of them had seen before. The panel stood at the top of a long, free-standing stone staircase, and light shone beneath the door.

"Another dead end," Meriel said somberly. "Locked . . . or guarded."

"We don't know that," Louis said hopefully. He looked to Sarah.

"I don't think it is," she said slowly. She'd been doing her best to keep a map of the chateau in her head, and it seemed to her that they were at the opposite end of the great building from the narrow staircase along which she and Meriel had descended into the dungeons in the first place. That *ought* to put them beneath the old tower in which Sarah and Louis had been held captive.

"I don't believe there's anyone here," Sarah amplified. "I think every one is looking for us at the other end of the cellars—not here."

"And even if they are closer, we are rapidly running out of choices, are we not?" Louis said. He put an arm around Meriel's shoulders. "We cannot stay down here forever."

"No," Sarah agreed. She took a deep breath and started up the stairs.

The door will be locked, she told herself hopefully. If it were, she would at least not have to choose whether or not it was safe to open. There was a small grille set into the door; through its lattice, Sarah saw that the light came from a narrow arrow-slit in the left-hand wall of the tower. The sun had risen; it was morning.

She pulled on the handle. The door didn't move. But it rattled, and Sarah saw that it was secured by a tiny latch on *this* side of the door, not the other. Carefully she eased back the small bolt. Now all that was left was to open the door and see what lay beyond. Mustering all her reserves of courage, Sarah opened the door.

The half-circle room that lay beyond the doorway was empty. She pushed the door open and beckoned to the others.

"This way. Hurry!"

The Duke of Wessex was a busy man this morning. His ruse had worked about as long as he'd thought it would— three minutes—but that gave him a three-minute lead, and His Grace used the time to good advantage. With Talleyrand absent, and the over-busy Mr. Highclere now among the angels, the soldiers and servants had no one to give them orders—leading to an amount of confusion that could only work to England's benefit.

That confusion did not mean, however, that Wessex would not be shot on sight.

He managed to deprive one soldier of rifle and ammunition bag, and thus armed, held off his pursuers while allowing them to drive him backward through the chateau. He'd wanted to make for the dungeons, but was balked in this—however, from Sarah's information and his own early reconnaissance, Wessex had a good idea of where he wanted to go, and what he meant to do when he got there.

Wessex gained the top of a staircase and flung himself into cover. The cartridge-bag hit the floor beside him with a dull thud, and he swung the weapon down into position.

A well-drilled infantryman could deliver three shots a minute under field conditions. Wessex lacked that peak of training, but he could manage two. The first shot exploded the wall in a shower of splinters and plaster, filling the stairway with a thick veil of acrid white smoke. He reloaded and fired again, and then, while his pursuers waited, expecting another shot, Wessex ran.

As he'd hoped, the tower was separated from the newer building by thick, inward-opening doors. He slammed the door behind him, jamming a piece of a broken chair through the iron staples meant to hold the wooden bar. The barrier would not keep his pursuers at bay forever— he would have to find something stronger.

And then he heard movement on the stairs below him, and realized that perhaps his plan would not serve after all.

"Who's there?" Meriel called out nervously, before Sarah could shush her. Desperately, Sarah wished for a weapon—any weapon, even a knife.

There was a clatter of boots upon the stair.

"Sarah?" Wessex demanded.

His face was blackened with gunpowder, and Sarah's heart gave a treacherous leap of joy to see him alive and whole. And then she grabbed for the weapon he held. Relief washed over her as she took the familiar weight in her hands—whatever else had altered when she had been wrenched from her own world, the light single-barreled gun she had used all her life remained unchanged. She slung the ammo-bag over her shoulder and rummaged in it, then automatically swabbed the barrel clean and began to load the weapon.

Wessex regarded her with a nonplussed expression.

"Sarah?" he said again.

Sarah glanced up from her loading, and in that moment realized what a freakishly un-English picture she must represent. There was nothing she could do but smile apologetically.

"I got Louis out of the dungeon," she offered hopefully. She rammed down the charge and slid the ramrod back beneath the barrel of the musket.

"So I see." Wessex was struggling not to smile back, she could see—even though the situation was as black as it could possibly be.

"What do we do now?" Louis asked.

Sarah saw Wessex's face change as he looked at the young man; saw the pang of unwilling recognition that told her that the wild story was true: that somehow, this bedraggled young man whom she'd rescued was the true King of France, saved from his executioners a dozen years before by Wessex's father.

"Come on," Wessex said shortly, leading them back up the stairs.

*   *   *

His plan was to escape across the roofs—or at least to see if such escape were possible—but when Wessex reached the tower room he was met by a grinning Illya Koscuisko.

The Polish Hussar was stripped to his shirtsleeves, his dyed-blond hair hanging in his eyes. But he looked far too pleased with himself to be bearing news of anything but success.

"Your chariot awaits," Koscuisko said, bowing and flourishing in the direction of the open trapdoor in the ceiling.

"What . . . *is* that thing?" Sarah demanded in astonishment when all five of them were on the roof. The day was fully advanced—blue, bright, and cloudless—and the stones of the roof were already warm beneath her feet. The air smelled of smoke.

"It is a hot-air balloon, I think," Louis said. "One was demonstrated in Paris a few years ago. They allow a man to fly."

Meriel crossed herself, looking as appalled as Sarah did.

"It is unnatural," Meriel said.

They were staring at a wicker basket the size of a pony-trap, secured by stout ropes to an enormous bag of bright-colored silk that was attached to an iron ring suspended over the basket by iron rods. A brazier filled with burning coals hung beneath the ring, and the air above the coals shimmered with hot air that was slowly inflating the balloon.

"This is your idea of an escape plan?" Wessex demanded of his partner.

"It has the virtue of originality," Koscuisko explained. "I set fire to the West Wing about an hour ago—they ought to be discovering the blaze soon—and I have hopes that it will distract them, as well as conceal our retreat."

"In that," Wessex said without inflection, regarding the hot-air balloon skeptically. He crossed the roof and looked out over the edge. "The fire seems to be working well, at least." .

Another gust of smoke sailed past the tower as the wind shifted, and Sarah fancied she could hear the distant crackling of flames.

"Well," Koscuisko said modestly, "between that and the gunpowder—"

There was an earsplitting roar, and the tower shook. Meriel screamed.

"Ah," said Koscuisko with satisfaction. "I hadn't been entirely certain of the timing of the slow match. Still, I think it works out well."

"You're mad," Wessex said comprehensively.

Koscuisko shrugged meekly. "I think we ought to get into the basket. I wasn't able to tie it down particularly well, and we'd best be aboard when it decides to fly free."

"Well," said Sarah, almost at a loss for words. "Well. If it does not work, it shall almost certainly kill us, which I suppose is all to the good."

Once the five of them clambered aboard, Koscuisko untied the ropes with which he had bound the balloon to the battlements. He piled more coal into the brazier from the sack at his feet, and the swelling sides of the balloon began to lose their softness and take on the taut aspect of a windjammer's sails.

"Can this possibly work?" Sarah wondered, clutching at the barrel of her musket. Now that she was armed at last, she had no intention of leaving her weapon behind.

"A question that is on everyone's lips," Wessex murmured.

Meriel simply clung to Louis, more terrified of the airship than she had been of the White Lady, the dungeon, and all of Talleyrand's soldiery combined.

It seemed like an eternity, but it could not have been more than a quarter of an hour before the basket began to bob gently as the upward force of the heated air began to lift it from the roof. They were playing a dangerous waiting game—could the balloon whisk them away before the soldiers discovered where they were and broke through the trapdoor to the rooftop?

The balloon inched upward, pulled by the wind. It slid the length of the tower and stopped, held in place by the crenelations.

"The sandbags," Koscuisko said. "It is time to lose them, I think."

"Look!" Meriel—who had been staring back at the trapdoor as though it offered her only hope of eternal salvation—shrieked and pointed.

A *chausseur* had climbed up through the trapdoor and seen them. Only the man's upper body was visible, but he would reach the roof in a moment, and it would be a matter of only a few saber-cuts to detach the balloon from the basket, stranding them here.

Wessex reached for his own sword, as Louis and Koscuisko frantically untied filled bags of sand from the basket.

"Get them out of here, Koscuisko," Wessex said, preparing to climb out of the basket. "I'll join you later."

"You will not," Sarah said, lowering the musket and taking aim. "I've chased you all over France, Your Grace—and I'm tired of it." She squeezed the trigger. There was a flash as the powder in the pan ignited, and the *beau sabreur* fell backward into the room below with a cry of surprise.

Sarah calmly began to reload. As the last of the sandbags fell free, the balloon surged upward with a bound, sailing westward on the wings of the morning.

19

The Road Not Taken

The five of them arrived at Trois Vierges in the dead of the night, but Sarah would not allow anyone to approach the Abbé's house. Instead, she settled her little band into the shelter of a hedgerow to watch the house until dawn.

If not for Sarah's woods-cunning, they would never have made it this far. With only one horse among them—Koscuisko's Spangle, who had followed the balloon until the contraption had settled to earth several hours later—there was no possibility of outrunning their pursuers.

They had hidden from them instead. Shabby as tinkers, traveling by night and hiding by day, living on what they could catch or steal, they had taken three days to traverse the distance that Meriel and the *phouka* had covered in a single night. Sarah's greatest worry had been to keep the grey Andalusian hidden, for the only way such a motley crew as they currently appeared could have come across such a fine animal would have been to steal it. But Koscuisko refused to abandon his horse, and Wessex had agreed with him: if they were surprised, at least one of them might be able to reach safety on horseback.

There was no certainty that they could find sanctuary in Trois Vierges, but neither Louis nor Meriel had been willing to abandon the Abbé de Condé, and Wessex himself suspected that the old priest would be a useful ally . . . if, of course, the Abbé was not dead.

Lying pressed against the cold damp earth of France, Wessex regarded his Duchess.

Her face was smeared with earth and animal fat, her hair skinned back into a greasy braid. The traveling dress that once must have been grey twilled Gros de Naples was now mud-colored, its shoulder seam ripped to expose an equally dirty chemise. Her feet were bare, her lisle stockings now swaddling the precious musket against damp and dust. She was as impassive and unmoving as the carven figurehead of a sailing ship.

Wessex realized that he did not know her at all. Here at last was the woman he'd thought he'd met at Mooncoign: the savage, efficient warrior, fellow soldier in a private war. But that woman had vanished when King Henry had forced their marriage. All that had been left was the reputation of a flighty, heartless, fashionable hostess, a woman of the sort who held no interest for the Duke.

They must talk. She knew what he was now; he owed her the chance of an honorable release from the wedded state. But the business of survival had taken up every waking hour since their escape from Roissy, and now was no time to strike up a conversation: voices, even whispers, carried too damnably well in the absence of all other sound. Instead, he watched as she did, and with as much suspicion. Louis had been taken from this place. It was not unreasonable that Talleyrand would again be looking for him here.

Louis. The long-lost King of France, returned to the political chessboard, to the consternation of friend and foe. His reappearance among the living would redraw alliances all over the map of Europe. Royal blood and rightful kingship was a powerful lure.

But young Louis did not wish to rule. He had told Wessex what he wanted—to emigrate to Louisiana, there to live out his life as an ordinary man . . . with his wife.

Lady Meriel even now had not agreed to marry Louis—something which did much to repair her reputation in Wessex's mind—but only a fool wouldn't know that it was Midsummer Moon with the chit. And even though Mr. Highclere was dead, Lord Ripon remained, and would have to be dealt with. So something must be arranged for the girl.

Something must be arranged for Wessex, as well. It would be months before the White Tower knew whether Wessex's true identity was known to the French, months in which he could not go abroad with any degree of safety. If the Danish Princess had been recovered, there would be work enough for him in London.

If he still had a Duchess.

Lying beneath a hedge in the middle of the night, watching the serene intent face of his wife (who flatly refused to surrender the rifle for any reason whatever), Wessex discovered that he very much hoped that he did.

The sun had risen. The Abbé had said early Mass, and returned to the little house across the garden. A few hours before, just as the sky was turning light, Sarah had moved the fugitive band from their perch beneath the hedgerow to a new hiding-place at the bottom of the garden. Now it was time to make their move.

"Louis?" she said, as politely as if they were all in her London townhouse. "Would you care to go to the kitchen door and see if your uncle will receive us?"

"No!" Meriel instantly protested, clutching at Louis's arm.

"It must be, *ma petite*," Louis said. "Madame Carmaux will let me in, but she does not know Monsieur *le Duc* nor Madame *la Duchesse*, nor yet the excellent Koscuisko. And I am afraid we are such as to make any prudent housewife recoil in alarm."

"What if the Red Jacks are there?" Meriel persisted. No matter how long they had watched, the fear remained.

"Then Madame *la Duchesse* will shoot them with her large gun," Louis said. "But I do not think they are there."

With that, Louis wriggled out of his concealment and got to his feet, walking across the garden as if nothing in the world were the matter. He reached the kitchen door, opened it, and disappeared inside.

Silence.

"It isn't that I'm in any way apprehensive," Illya Koscuisko said apologetically. "It's simply that I'd like to know how long we are to wait here."

Meriel began crawling out of her hiding-place next to the wall.

The door opened. Louis stood in the doorway, beckoning them on.

By the time luncheon was placed upon the Abbé's gleaming white linen tablecloth by a much-less-than-mollified Madame Carmaux, the five refugees had been restored to some vestige of tidiness. The Abbé de Condé assured Wessex that he could arrange transportation to the coast, where the Duke could signal a patrolling English warship and arrange for the party to be picked up.

Talleyrand had not come to the village—possibly he thought that his captives were all dead in the fire that had engulfed the chateau, though Wessex did not believe the spymaster was quite that simpleminded. At any rate, they would be gone from here in a few hours, for to stay longer was to place the villagers in more peril than the Duke cared to.

The only question was, who would go . . . and who would remain here?

"I should very much like to encourage Your Majesty to come with us to England," Wessex said, when the dishes had been cleared away and the servants had departed, leaving them alone. "Naturally I cannot compel you—"

Here Illya Koscuisko coughed, and Wessex's mouth twitched.

"Say rather I shall not compel you, then, Your Majesty, though it must be known—in certain circles—that you survive. Surely you understand that?"

"And what of Lady Meriel?" Louis asked. There was an undertone of anger in his own voice, but he was too much a man—and a King—to let it show.

"She shall be under my personal protection," Wessex promised. "There is nothing more she need fear from the Earl of Ripon or his plots."

"So. You dispose of us all very neatly, Monsieur *le Duc*. But I do not wish to be so disposed of, either to France or to England. And I do not wish to be King."

"My son—" the Abbé said, but Louis raised his hand for silence.

"I am sorry, *mon oncle*—I know how very much you have sacrificed to this dream, and how many good men have died to keep me safe. But it is not my dream. Let me renounce it, here and now."

Stricken, the Abbé stared at his royal charge.

"It is better so, *papa*," Louis said. "Let it be so."

"Has Your Majesty fully considered what your renunciation of the Crown will mean?" Wessex asked. "You are the last of the True Line—if you are not King, who will there be to make the Great Marriage with the soul of the land?"

"No one," Louis said briefly. "Let me be, Monsieur *le Duc*."

"Is that what you will choose for France?" Wessex persisted. "That the magic will be gone from *la Belle France*, and she will become a mortal kingdom at last?"

Louis shrugged, looking Wessex in the eye. "That happened upon the day my father was murdered, Your Grace. I was far too young to be taught any of the Old Rule, and all those who might know the Covenants and Pacts are surely dead. The Corsican Tyrant has broken the power of the Hollow Kingdoms—he has boasted of it—and whether there is ever again a King in France or no, he will not have the power of the Old Rule to call upon."

"But Your Majesty—" Wessex began to protest, and Louis held up a hand, stopping him.

"Do not call me that; what do I know of being a king? No." Louis shook his head. "If I *were* mad enough to claim the throne, I would be no more than a puppet dancing upon gilded strings." Louis's voice held a quiet dignity; his words a finality that admitted no argument. "Let me go, Your Grace. France's fate and mine do not lie together, and . . . and I would start a new life with the woman I love, far away from crowns and thrones."

Louis looked toward Meriel. She smiled at him, and

then looked back at Wessex. All her arts of dissembling could not disguise the hope in her eyes.

"Very well," Wessex said, hesitating only a moment. "It will be as you wish. Come with me to England, and I will see you and your bride safely boarded on a ship bound for the American colonies—but I hope I may call upon you, Your Majesty, should there be need?"

"For anything save to rule France," Louis promised, breathless and laughing with relief. "And now my lords— and Madame *la Duchesse*—may I invite you to attend upon my wedding?"

"I must speak to you," Sarah said to Wessex.

The Duke turned to face her. The others had already left the church, returning to the priory for a small cele- bration, but Wessex lingered in the doorway, and Sarah had turned back to find him.

"I had thought that you would," he said quietly. "I assure you, once we have returned to England I will place no obstacle in your way, but you might consider whether it would suit your purposes better simply to live apart. Mine is a dangerous life, and it is quite possible that you will soon be a widow. It is a less scandalous end to a marriage than dissolution."

"What are you talking about?" Sarah said blankly. "I have come to tell you who I really am."

And she did, with brisk efficiency. The strange tale was soon told—of all of it, the part that Wessex found hardest to believe was that the Americas would revolt against their King—or that Englishmen would not always have Stuarts to govern them.

"But the ring you wore—the one that was your fa- ther's—what of that?" Wessex asked. Did the Boscobel League exist in both worlds? And if it did, how had England's rightful king in Sarah's world ended his days a hunted outcast?

"I never knew the ring's story," Sarah said, "and now I never shall. But what am I to do, Wessex? For I cannot go home."

"Not unless Grandanne has another string to her bow," Wessex agreed, "though I shouldn't discount that, my little Colonial. But you were brought to this world a-purpose—do you think you have discharged your task?"

"I don't know," Sarah said honestly. "What work could the Marchioness of Roxbury have left undone that was so important that she needed to call *me* from another world to finish it? I do know that that creature—that Jack-in-the-Green—said that I must become one with *this* land: and I have not figured out what he meant, much less how to do it."

"As to that," Wessex said, "I think I may have some notion."

He drew her gently to him—she did not resist—and carefully sealed her mouth with his own.

The Lioness of England

✽ The heavily-laden haywain rambled down the road to the coast in the fading afternoon light. It was months too early for the new hay harvest to be ready, and thus, highly unlikely that such a waggon would be making this journey, but the cavalry units that patrolled this coast had very few farmers among them, and Wessex and the Abbé both thought the deception would pass.

Sarah, Louis, and Meriel were hidden in the false bottom of the waggon, while Wessex and Koscuisko, in suitable rustic disguise, rode upon the box. Koscuisko had finally been persuaded to abandon his mount; Spangle remained behind in the Abbé's stables until the animal could be sent for—the gelding was far too valuable to abandon if there were any hope of rescuing it later.

The pickets on station in the Channel would know to look for them, thanks to the Bishop of Amiens. They were within sight of the sea; at the farmhouse the Abbé had marked out for them they could leave the haywain. Then all they needed to do was walk a mile or so to the coast, wait until dark, and signal with the dark-lantern and mirror that the Abbé de Conde had provided.

It seemed, on the face of it, a simple matter, and Wessex had been in and out of France more times than he could count in the years since the Revolution. But there was always something that could go wrong, even when the situation at hand verged on . . . boredom.

Case in point: what should have been a simple drive in the country.

A dispatch rider had passed them an hour before, heading eastward. They had seen nothing since, nor had they expected to; it was the wrong time of day for traffic along this offshoot of the Paris–Calais road.

But there was a sound of hoofbeats in the distance. Koscuisko pointed in the direction of the rising dust cloud and shrugged inquiringly at his partner.

If it was a French patrol, in all likelihood it was searching for them. The only question was, would a patrol recognize them when it found them? They could bluff, or they could fight: Wessex would prefer to bluff, if the choice were offered. He shook his head at Koscuisko and made a clicking sound at the horses, encouraging them to pick up their pace.

The mounted troop appeared—six French *chausseurs*, light cavalry whose primary use in war was scouting and skirmishing. They were also used to patrol disputed areas, such as the coast near Calais, and it looked as if one of their sweeps had borne fruit, for they had a prisoner, riding, hands bound before him, at the center of the troop. Wessex recognized the mustard-colored uniform of the *Kongelige Livgarde* amidst the black French *chausseur* uniforms.

"A Dane," Wessex said quietly. "One of the *Queen Christina*'s complement. He might have news of the Princess." The *Livgarde* had not tendered his parole—if he had, he would still possess his saber and pistols—and so would be likely to fight if the chance of rescue loomed.

"It is our duty," Koscuisko said piously, reaching for his sword and pistol. "Denmark is an ally of England, or ought to be."

*   *   *

The waggon was prudently pulled off to the side of the road, leaving the highway clear for the soldiers. The unexpected shots rang out when the troop was a few yards from the haywain.

The Captain and his Lieutenant fell, and Koscuisko ran out to seize the lead horse's bridle and drag the wounded rider from the saddle. In an instant Koscuisko was mounted, turning the skittish animal and galloping back upon the others.

Wessex emptied both pistols—a provident gift from Abbé de Conde—and then ran forward with his saber. A man on foot was at a great disadvantage when facing a man on horseback, but there was no time now to count the cost.

A shot whistled past his ear; Sarah had slithered from her hiding-place and had added her expert marksmanship to the fight.

The *Livgarde* at the center of the melee had not been slow to seize this opportunity for freedom. When the first shots rang out, he had flung himself at the nearest *chausseur*, throwing both of them to the ground, where he was giving a good account of himself even with his hands bound before him.

It was over very quickly.

The *Livgarde* got to his feet. He'd freed his hands with the aid of a bayonet, and stood surveying the carnage surrounding him, a cocky grin on his face.

"A most provident rescue, m'sieur," the *Livgarde* said in French as Wessex approached him. Sarah and the others were standing beside the waggon now—confused, perhaps, but blessedly unhurt.

The Dane's voice was light and husky, and from the look of him he hardly needed to shave yet—the bushy mustaches and sideburns favored by the *Kongelige Livgarde* were conspicuously absent.

"To a certain extent it was motivated by self-interest," Wessex said as Koscuisko joined him. "You were on the *Queen Christina*, were you not?"

"I think so," Koscuisko commented, and reached out swiftly to knock the *Livgarde*'s shako from his head.

"Damn," the *Livgarde* said ruefully as his—*her*—blond hair tumbled down over her shoulders.

"I'd had you fooled, didn't I?" Princess Stephanie of Denmark said.

Princess Stephanie told her story to Wessex and the others as she helped them collect the members of her former escort. There was no need to execute them all; bound and gagged and concealed beneath the hay in the waggon, the survivors would live to fight another day while giving the five—now six—fugitives the headstart to reach England that they needed.

And the French had kindly donated mounts enough for the party to quickly reach the shore, as well.

"I must say, Your Highness, that such a masquerade shows a great deal of personal resourcefulness," Koscuisko said respectfully, as the party rode westward.

"Oh, pho!" the Princess said. "No one ever looks at a soldier—they expected to see a Princess in a crown and a gown, and looked no farther than that. And my lads wouldn't give me away—they are my grandfather's regiment, but it is I who wear their uniform and drill with them. But you are *Anglais*, and will think my wearing men's dress very shocking, *hein?*" she added, grinning at Koscuisko.

"Polish," Koscuisko corrected. "The disapproving gentleman on your left with the terrible hat is English. May

I present to Your Highness the Duke of Wessex, one of Your Highness's great admirers?"

Princess Stephanie threw back her head and laughed. "What a company we are—Dukes and Duchesses, Princes and Princesses! What trouble we could make for the French, if only we stayed!"

"Alas," Wessex said. "I do not need to remind Your Highness that her duty is elsewhere?"

The Princess heaved a deep sigh and gazed at Wessex saucily. "What a bore that I must marry this tiresome Prince! We could have had many adventures."

Wessex and Koscuisko glanced at each other.

"I do not think, Your Highness, that you will find Prince James lacking in a sense of adventure," Koscuisko said soberly.

The Princess made a rude noise.

"And somehow I doubt the Prince will be disappointed in his future bride," Wessex observed in English.

TOR
BOOKS The Best in Fantasy

ELVENBANE • Andre Norton and Mercedes Lackey
"A richly detailed, complex fantasy collaboration."—Marion Zimmer Bradley

SUMMER KING, WINTER FOOL • Lisa Goldstein
"Possesses all of Goldstein's virtues to the highest degree."—*Chicago Sun-Times*

JACK OF KINROWAN • Charles de Lint
Jack the Giant Killer and *Drink Down the Moon* reprinted in one volume.

THE MAGIC ENGINEER • L.E. Modesitt, Jr.
The tale of Dorrin the blacksmith in the enormously popular continuing saga of Recluce.

SISTER LIGHT, SISTER DARK • Jane Yolen
"The Hans Christian Andersen of America."—*Newsweek*

THE GIRL WHO HEARD DRAGONS • Anne McCaffrey
"A treat for McCaffrey fans."—*Locus*

GEIS OF THE GARGOYLE • Piers Anthony
Join Gary Gar, a guileless young gargoyle disguised as a human, on a perilous pilgrimage in pursuit of a philter to rescue the magical land of Xanth from an ancient evil.

TOR
BOOKS The Best in Science Fiction

LIEGE-KILLER • Christopher Hinz

"*Liege-Killer* is a genuine page-turner, beautifully written and exciting from start to finish....Don't miss it."—*Locus*

HARVEST OF STARS • Poul Anderson

"A true masterpiece. An important work—not just of science fiction but of contemporary literature. Visionary and beautifully written, elegaic and transcendent, *Harvest of Stars* is the brightest star in Poul Anderson's constellation."
—Keith Ferrell, editor, *Omni*

FIREDANCE • Steven Barnes

SF adventure in 21st century California—by the co-author of *Beowulf's Children*.

ASH OCK • Christopher Hinz

"A well-handled science fiction thriller."—*Kirkus Reviews*

CALDÉ OF THE LONG SUN • Gene Wolfe

The third volume in the critically-acclaimed Book of the Long Sun. "Dazzling."—*The New York Times*

OF TANGIBLE GHOSTS • L.E. Modesitt, Jr.

Ingenious alternate universe SF from the author of the *Recluce* fantasy series.

THE SHATTERED SPHERE • Roger MacBride Allen

The second book of the Hunted Earth continues the thrilling story that began in *The Ring of Charon*, a daringly original hard science fiction novel.

THE PRICE OF THE STARS • Debra Doyle and James D. Macdonald

Book One of the Mageworlds—the breakneck SF epic of the most brawling family in the human galaxy!